Having Sex (3 Bc

1)

Humorous + Fantasy + Lesbian (Porn)

Pamela Vance

Explicit Erotic Sex Stories

THE TALKING WAS DONE THROUGH HER EYES (HUMOROUS)

A special 25-year-old lady, the guy she falls in love with, and more

Pamela Vance

—— At Work — Wednesday ——

"So Danny child, you going to make it to my party Friday evening?" Azariah leaned against the short cubicle wall. I'm sure there will be several girls who are delighted to see you!"

Daniel admired her self-assurance and cheerfulness, as well as her tall, toned, well-equipped figure. He thought her name was appropriate because she had natural Azariah hair and eyes. He valued her relationship so much that he didn't want to jeopardize it by dating her since this had ruined certain female friendships in the past.

"Sure!" he exclaimed, "Do you need me to carry anything?" He was looking forward to this party since he had never been to Azariah's house, and she didn't seem to have many, if any, parties in his mind.

"No, we've already bought everything." "Just carry your hunky self with the huge grin sometime after 6:30 p.m., and look sharp for the ladies!" Azariah answered. You have two days to get up. "Goodbye!"

Azariah's flirty compliments and invaluable insider information were often fantastic for his ego. For example, Azariah had recently disclosed to him that his office girl nickname was "Horse." Daniel had always believed his appearances were fine, but he realized that that might have been why, when he was out with a group from college, the office girls had hovered around him.

He was a little naive because he had never had a sister to learn about girls from, and his mother was not the one to guide on such matters.

Daniel has a sibling named Billy, who died years earlier after hearing issues that prevented him from noticing an oncoming vehicle while pursuing an errant basketball.

He hadn't had an official girlfriend in three years at the age of 27. He did have a few mates for booty calls, in whom he could exercise his hormones, and they named him rather than they called him. Some of them were also successful female companions for specific occasions. But he was getting tired of seeing just these friends and one-night stands.

So he resolved that this Friday at Azariah's would be a new beginning; he needed to find different people or try a different path to dating.

Azariah's Party is on Friday. ———

When Daniel arrived at Azariah's house, he locked his Soul Red Mazda 6, double-checked his clothing, and proceeded to the front door. Martha from accounting opened the door as he rang the doorbell. The bleach-blond was dressed in a gold lame gown with such an open plunging neckline that he assumed more of her well-enhanced breasts were uncovered than concealed.

"Hello, Danny!" Martha said with a big grin on her lips. "Aren't you looking delicious tonight?" she growled after the grin. Please come in. And spare me a slow dance because my girls will love to see you." "Certainly, Martha," Daniel said, clearing his throat. "The 'wives' have always seemed to be very accommodating!" She laughed out loud and childishly.

Martha had risen from almost translucent breasts to those he guessed were at least 38D's in a little over a year, all during a two-week break. Since then, she'd strutted around the office in low-cut or tight tops (or tops with both features), swooshing the mass of her bought boobs in front of every single, straight guy in the business, and some of the married ones as well, if they drooled appreciatively.

She still used to pretend to be innocent as she brushed her firm breasts against men in the large hallways at work, ostensibly squeezing past them. Martha enabled everyone curious to have a close look at her new riches (well, except for that gal in shipping who had done a hands-on check of their size the first time she and Martha were in the restroom together). Daniel had never tried to date her since his kitten act was too hard-handed for his tastes.

Daniel glanced around as Martha jiggled back into the crowd, realizing the room was crowded with people, several of whom he recognized from work.

A smattering of pretty girls may be seen. The most amusing to see was a big, dyed redhead he didn't recognize who was dancing very energetically. She was dressed in red short shorts and a white tube top over her large breasts, with both arms swaying over her shoulders. Her protruding nipples swung back and forth under her skimpy top, ready to explode at any moment. Her height and big, muscular frame reminded him of Azariah, and he imagined Azariah clad in the dyed-skimpy redhead's clothes.

Daniel then found a slew of residual feminine looks his way, with a handful of girls exchanging glances for clear eye contact and big smiles. He returned a grin and a nod to the latter two, none of whom he knew from the workplace.

Azariah's huge living space had been stripped of much of its furniture, and the hardwood floor served as the dance floor. The family room was next to the living room in the open-plan house, and several people were sitting or standing in there, as well as in the adjacent kitchen.

Daniel had noticed the music from outside, but it wasn't until now that he knew how well-insulated this house could be because the music was even clearer inside, with a heavy bass pumping out.

As his gaze wandered, he found a girl standing at the end of the stub wall separating the dining room and family room. Standing was a little misleading when she was swaying to the sound of the song. Her long hair was strawberry blond with big wavy curls. Her features were well-balanced and very warm, but she wore a thin, contented smile on her well-balanced and very warm features. Her breasts were modest yet full and moved gently in time with her motions.

He guessed she was 5'5" without her platform sandals. She wore a simple satiny wrap dress with spaghetti straps and a low-cut front. The dress seemed to be a darker blue with big orchids painted on it, but he wasn't positive because of his distance and the lighting.

Since her eyes were down, he was able to keep observing her without being seen. If the other performers were wiggling, shaking, and twirling, this strawberry blond was just swaying, but her soul was in her movements.

Her expressions were beautiful and fluid, and they were reflected in her hair and clothes. Her hands gently grasped the hem of her almost knee-length dress on either foot, and they swept the dress fore and aft, contributing to the rhythm of her swaying.

He was lost in his reflections of the swaying girl when Azariah bumped his arm and shouted harshly over the song.

"Hello, Danny. We're glad you made it! Drinks are available in the kitchen as well as on the patio off the family room. I've also fielded some inquiries about who the stud who just arrived is, so you've been heard. "Would you like me to make some introductions for you?"

"Uh, no thanks," he said, "but might you tell me who the girl in the blue dress over there is, swaying to the music?"

Azariah's smile shifted from that of the bubbly host to one of contentment and happiness. "My name is Kaitlyn." She's my friend, and I bet you'd find her fascinating." Azariah smirked as she rested her hand on his forearm. Daniel observed Azariah's tall, goddess-like figure as she went off to meet everyone and wondered what her emphatic "VERY" might indicate.

Daniel took another glance around the venue, taking in all the scantily dressed girls mixed in with guys in tees or polos, many in shorts. He looked a little overdressed in a newly tailored short sleeve sweater, Docker slacks, and loafers. He was about to get a beer when a waving Martha captured his attention and pointed to the dance floor. He hadn't known it was a slow tune, but he felt obligated to keep his earlier promise to dance, so he went to the dance floor.

Martha followed him there and planted her chest against his, her nipples hardening as she rubbed against him. "You know, if you invite me out any day, you might get to know me a LOT more!" she said, still growling. She pressed into his groin to emphasize the term 'LOT.'

"I'll hold that in mind," he said, trying to sound convincing without appearing eager. They got next to Kaitlyn as they slowly danced across the stage, and when he glanced at her, she was staring straight into his eyes. Her warm eyes were the same shade of lake blue as her shirt. Her gaze matched his until he was drawn away by his dancing. He immediately switched Martha, who was cooing contentedly, so he could return his gaze to Kaitlyn, who was still pursuing his gaze but now seemed to be laughing at him. He replied to her with a big smile, which she returned.

The song finished abruptly, and Danial led Martha across the floor to where she had been standing before their party. "Oh, just one dance?" she inquired.

"Maybe another today," he suggested. He stepped off to the left while the dance floor filled up, returning a few female smiles. He chose a spot to stand, but it was across the room from Kaitlyn, and his vision of her was obstructed by the big redhead, who was currently pulling up her tube top.

When Kaitlyn came into focus, Daniel noticed she was already swaying and gazing about. When her eyes spotted him, their wandering came to a halt, her grin returned, and her gaze remained fixed on him. His vision of her was intermittently obscured due to the ebb and flow of the performers, but every time she returned into view, she was staring at him with the same sparkling expression.

Daniel was uneasy with her intense focus on him, but he also wanted to keep staring at her sweet eyes, and she had his imagination running over time.
He felt it was time to appease his appetite and maybe have a drink after both the latest and following songs had finished. When the audience began to leave the dance floor, he made his way over to Kaitlyn.
As he approached, he saw her eyes twinkle, and she stretched her arm out, level with her hip, and with her hand free, palm up.
He gently placed her hand in his.

She ushered him into the dance floor, her eyes twinkling up at him. Before he could say something, another dance music with a heavy rhythm began to play, and Kaitlyn began to dance.

Her emotions were more intense than when she was standing, with more hip activity and her hands occasionally weaving over her shoulders. Yet, the simple movement was the same swaying, only exaggerated.

Her gaze was fixed on him for the majority of the album. When they weren't on him, that was because she had turned her back on him to dance in front of him.

He saw her lovely rear swaying in front of him. He noticed her hair had grown to around the bottom of her shoulder blades, and the lovely reddish-blond color suited the middle of the orchids painted on her dress precisely.

As the song ended, he knelt to present himself to her neck about six inches below his.

She drew back a little from him and delicately put her index finger over his mouth before he could say something.

As he stopped, perplexed, the music resumed, this time with a slow love tune.

She was thoughtful, as though she was trying to hear something. Her grin broadened, and she wrapped her palms around his neck and began to rock softly.

Daniel was not going to refuse this invitation, and he laid his palms on her waist, feeling her slender figure through the thin material of the outfit. He began to move in time with the beat.

To imitate his motions, she adjusted the tempo of her swaying.

When he glanced down and found her staring back at him, he realized how profoundly blue her eyes were. When she blinked steadily, he realized these were the sexiest eyes he'd ever seen.

She closed her eyes and danced with him, pressing her cheek against his stomach.

He savored the sound of her face against his and inhaled the soft floral scent of her hair.

Her hands left his neck and drifted down inside his arms before wrapping around his back and cupping his shoulder blades.

He bent forward to lay his head on hers, her scent much better this close to her.

Kaitlyn splayed her fingertips over his shoulder.

When the song finished, he was enjoying the sensation of her body against his.

Her swaying started well though he had stopped driving.

Daniel was about to ask Kaitlyn if she had something to drink.

She grabbed his hand and began to drag him through the crowd until he could. Azariah saw them when she exited the kitchen, and she grinned and winked at Kaitlyn, who then skipped for a few moves.

Kaitlyn looked back at Daniel with the twinkle in her eyes as she cleared the crowd, about the edge of the kitchen entry, and began to guide him down a corridor. They moved through many partners, the first two conversings and the third of whom were locked in an embrace. Her gaze shifted to the last pair for a brief moment before returning to Daniel with a playful twinkle in her smile.

When they approached the end of the corridor, where there was a door with a paper sign attached to it that said "OFF LIMITS," he reasoned that she would like some protection for a kiss.

She pushed open the gates.

His mind was sharp enough to recall that she resided here; this had to be her home.

She drew him about five feet into the bed, then let go of his hand and walked around behind him. When he turned to face her, her soft eyes fixed on his.

She reached behind her back and searched about until she located the doorknob. She took her time backing up, shutting the door as she went. There was a rusty sound as she turned the lock in the middle of the door handle after the door had closed.

She bent down and took off her sandals.

His perplexed expression must have shown as she swayed steadily up to him, hands still behind her back and softly chewing her lower lip.

His mind was caught in opposing views, uncertain whether what he believed was happening was true or not, although it was difficult to accept. He had promised himself that he would stop making one-night stands, but this girl was so peculiar that he had to see how this night would play out.

Kaitlyn's arms wrapped around his waist as she stood standing in front of him. She rose on her tiptoes, closed her eyes slowly, and put a soft kiss on his mouth.

Daniel was astounded by her delicacy of contact. "If ever a kiss could be claimed to be whispered, that was it," he thought.

His manhood was rapidly growing in anticipation of what was about to happen.

Daniel's thoughts were racing with questions: how could he react to all of this; how did she want him to be? He glanced down at the wonderful eyes and the ever-present grin.

He remembered the authors who wrote of being trapped in the bottomless pools of a woman's eyes. He had always assumed it was just a writer's license, but he knew it was completely valid when he looked into Kaitlyn's eyes.

He gently wrapped one arm around her back and focused on her eyes to absorb her reactions.

She gave a little tilt of her head, and her eyes closed for a few seconds before reopening with an even softer expression than before.

His other hand reached out and softly stroked her face.

She closed her eyes and tipped her head back, revealing some of her jaws.

Daniel accepted the bid and rubbed his hand down the side of her body, then behind her neck.

He lowered his head and kissed her softly on the lips.

With her eagerness, she replied to his kiss.

He was taken aback at how tender those lips were. He'd never felt anything like them before. He had never seen something remotely comparable to this whole evening, but he was excited for the moment. He drew his mouth away from hers gradually.

She opened her eyes sluggishly.

He could see a grin on their faces. He eventually concluded that she would want a sensual, gentle seduction with no words.

Her hands moved away from his neck, and her arms drew in between his sides. Her side discovered his top shirt button. She made her way down the row of keys, never breaking her gaze away from his.

He pulled his loafers off.

She began to loosen his belt buckle. Her grin widened as she removed his zipper, her action brushing against his stiffness.

He got out of his trousers, which had dropped to the floor.

He stared into her bright eyes and wondered if he could react to hers with all the respects her eyes talked to him. He decided to learn a foreign language.

He stood there in his boxers, taking in the fire in her eyes. The face was a wonderful blend of pleasure, contentment, and peace, with traces of desire and knowledge.

When he stared at her, a bright grin spread over his face.

Her eyes widened with mischievousness, then lowered when she grasped for the bound bow of the sash that kept her wrap dress closed.

Daniel's hand shot out and snatched hers.

She raised her head, a subtle query and worried on her lips.

He grinned, his hand resting on top of her bow.

Kaitlyn grinned as her hand slipped free. Her mischievous expression returned, and her gaze watched him as he moved around behind her.

He pressed his palms on her hips.

She sashayed her sassy bottom over his boxers and their sealed manhood, pushing her hips back a bit.

Daniel raised his hands and began to tug on the ends of the sash's bound bow.

Kaitlyn lowered her gaze to see his hands at work. She remained motionless as the bow unraveled and the ends of the sash fell free.

She reached out to her side, still with her back to him, and grabbed the loose edge of the outfit. She then swung the front panel of her dress to the right side and came to a complete halt, putting her hand on her right arm.

On his right side, he reached over her back and pulled the dress from her grasp.

She drew her arms down to her sides.

Daniel brushed the spaghetti straps from each of her wrists, hanging tight to the left strap, while he began to ease the dress down her back gently. He cradled her beautiful shoulders. He confirmed she had not to wear a bra when he lowered the dress further.

She slid her arms out when the dress passed her shoulders, and he drank in her sleek back and softly tapered waist. He simply yanked the dress down, put it aside, and reveled in the fact that she had no panties at all.

She stayed in place as he stepped in behind her, slipping his arms under her arms and then wrapping his arms around her, under her breasts. His firmness brushed against the lining of his boxers and lay between her buttocks' upper halves.

He saw her draw a deep breath, keep it for a second, and then exhale contentedly.

Her head cocked around to face his. Her arms rose to her sides, allowing her to place her hands in his hair.
He drew his hands down to her arms, then lifted them to cover her breasts.
Her back arched slightly as she lay back into him.
Daniel fondled her breasts slowly, discovering them to be unlike everything he has ever seen. Her breasts were like two tiny down pillows; they were so cute.

He reached for her nipples while her fingertips worked with his hair and felt her hips begin to rock towards him. He discovered another fluffy, tiny mound in the middle of each soft downy breast during his hunt. He felt a heavy button in the middle of one of these smaller mounds, but it barely protruded outward. He thought she had puffy breasts, even though he had never had them before.

He rubbed his hands down her smooth chest, framing her vulva with his fingertips, as his thumbs touched her neatly cut and baby soft pubic hair.

Her hands slipped from his hair, her back straightened, and her legs started to tremble.

Daniel stroked her throat and ran his fingers through her hair.

Kaitlyn sunk slightly into his lap, her legs quivering.

Daniel returned his hands to her hips and used the strength to push her around to face him.

Her gaze met his, and he saw so much joy in those blue eyes.

He encircled her and clasped her petite, firm ass before bending down to embrace her.

Her lips rushed to reach his halfway, and they engaged in a far firmer embrace, the tips of their tongues scraping across each other's lips.

She slipped her hands behind them and under the waistband of his boxers as they kissed. Her soft fingertips curled over the top of his dick, reaching for his girth. She refused to make contact with her opposite fingertips.

He exclaimed in her lips.

She ended the embrace and glanced up to find his contented expression staring back at her.

She slid her hand down his heavy shaft and bit her lower lip.

She swept her hand down a third time, touching the base of his long shaft, and her brows raised in the center, anxiously.

She let him go, then yanked his boxer's waistband out so it was free of his erection. She noticed his hands slip off her ass and up her back as she knelt to slide his boxers to the floor.

She took a step back, and Daniel saw her rosy, puffy breasts, strawberry blond patch, all on a wonderfully proportioned body for the first time. And he remembered the sparse freckles that his subconscious had always overlooked.

He looked for and turned off the overhead light switch.

Her hand grabbed his shoulder, which was still on the light switch, and her breasts rubbed against him.

He took the cue and returned the light to its original place. Then he bent down and pulled his wallet from his pockets on the concrete.

Her grin vanished as he unfolded his wallet and searched for the money inside.

From behind the bills, he drew a rolled condom.

Her eyes brightened even more as she saw what he was holding. She snatched it from his grasp and crammed it back into his unfolded pocket. Then she closed the wallet by wrapping her palms around his.

He gave them a wide smile before picking up their clothes and placing them on a chair. He put his wallet and watch on her desk.

Kaitlyn jumped onto her bed and folded the bedspread and sheets down to the footboard. She sat on the other left, holding out her hand for Daniel to join her.

He sat down next to her lovely frame, savoring the sensations of her warmth, soft lips, and gleaming eyes.

As she looked at him, he began to run his hand down her arms, hips, and almost to her knees until reaching the limits of his arm's length.

She replied by arching, turning, and lifting her legs, allowing him to explore farther down her legs.

As he kissed her, his hand moved down to her foot, then up and over her neck, ribs, then over those ever soft breasts.

She trembled at his fingertips, sinking into his kisses.

He softly grasped one breast and lowered his head to kiss it, as well as run his tongue across it.

Her back curved.

He realized he'd never had so much fun touching anyone before, for almost every new contact he put on her skin was met with wiggles, quivers, or twitches, as well as those liquid blue eyes.

He gave the other breast the same amount of focus, pausing to draw lines across the freckles in between.

Her breathing became more rapid, and her hips started to move often.

After this period, like other girls he'd been with, a girl may have fallen to her knees to demonstrate how good they could inhale his dick. But here he was with Kaitlyn, needing this touching to last forever while seeing her beautifully warm face lose concentration as the pleasures he provided stole away her energy.

He took his time, kissing her cheek, tracing his tongue along her earlobe, over those freckles, and even kissing her closed eyes.

Daniel propped himself up on one arm and locked his gaze on hers. Then he slipped his hand down her stomach painfully.

Her body arched under his palm, the bow from her following his hand downward. He saw her eyes enlarging and her upper chest and neck becoming crimson. He was losing himself in those lake blue eyes as they steadily closed in reaction to his hand reaching for her baby-soft pubic hair.

She slid back onto the bed and opened her legs in greeting.

His palm pressed against her vulva, and a digit slid between the bottom of her inner lips. He traced one finger over her slickness and pulled it back across her clit.

Her grin had faded, and her mouth was open. Her fingertips jiggled erratically above her breasts; her expression tensed; her whole body jolted sharply and then shuddered...multiple times.

He was taken aback. He'd just kissed her once, but she seemed to have an orgasm. He observed the lovely feelings that crossed her face as she transitioned from tension to bliss.

She slowly blinked up her eyes. Her gaze drifted about, almost unfocused until she came across his face. Then her eyes glowed with delight, and a satisfied grin stretched over her lips.

Daniel stared at her, admiring her apparent contentment but also curious whether she had orgasmed.

She happily nodded, noticing the query on his lips.

His grin broadened. He realized what he wanted to do that night: he wanted to see how many occasions he might induce ecstasy in this incredible creature.

He leaned into her, watching her body tremble with slight aftershocks. He used the opportunity to prepare his strategy.

He stood up and coaxed her to turn onto her stomach in response to her curious gaze. He then made Kaitlyn extend her arms from her sides to shift her beautiful, wavy hair to one side.

He placed one finger on the top of her spine. Then he drew his finger down her back, steadily and softly, to her tailbone.

As his finger ran down her, her face dug into the cushion, her fingertips clenched to grab the covers, and her hips rolled upward.

He leaned over her and wrapped his hands and thumbs across the tops of her ribs, his nails scraping across her squashed breasts. He then ran his hands down her arms, past her hips, and to her ankles.

Her legs were slightly stretched, her shoulders were tensed, and her hips rotated the whole time.

He moved his palms along the inside of her thighs, just brushing across her labia.

Her fingertips squeezed and unwound. Her hips rolled high, and her legs opened, revealing her gleaming cunt.

His hands caressed her buttocks and slid up her back.

Her hips shifted side to side as she melted down into the mattress.

He continued to move his hands across her body for at least another five minutes. He kneaded her muscles at times, then rubbed his whole open hands over her, frequently accentuating his contact with feathery brushing of his fingertips or the backs of his fingers.

Her body was constantly squirming, expanding, and tensing. Her breaths were larger and more rapid.

Daniel enjoyed what he was doing to her, and he became more creative with each new idea he tried. He was still aroused, but he had no immediate need to touch her or achieve his orgasm. He believed he might continue to contact her for hours.

He coaxed her to turn onto her back but had to wait for her to remember his order and her languid reaction.

Kaitlyn sighed deeply as she cautiously spread her legs out and pulled them apart.

He saw her eyes twinkle with desire and enjoyment. He dropped his hands to lick her on the back corners of her jaw. He offered his tongue, which he then traced along the inside of her lips.

Her chest heaved, and her tongue rubbed against him, inviting it to explore.

As he arose from her, he let his hands slip down her freckled neck, across her breasts and chest, and then brush her pubic hair before reaching her bottom.

Her back arched, her hips grew sharply at the brush of her pubic hair, and she sunk sluggishly when his hands moved closer to her bottom.

Daniel began kissing the soles of her feet and massaging her heels.

Kaitlyn's knees twitched and twisted, forcing him over marginally, and her legs stretched a little wider.

His hands slid up to her inner thighs, encircled her outer labia, and he began massaging them up and down.

Her abdominal muscles rolled, her breathing stopped and restarted, and her fingertips gripped the sheets tightly before releasing them to begin their erratic dance in the breeze.

His thumbs pulled across her moisture, up her, inside her labia, and across her clit. He massaged it softly between his fingers, anticipating just what was going to happen next. For the next 30 seconds or so, he focused his attention on her face.
Her chest and neck red brightened; she pursed her lips tightly; her pulse came to a halt when her neck arched and her shoulders raised. Her eyes widened as her body stopped for a brief second. Then her legs began to tremble. When her mouth opened, she felt some strong jolts. Her body finally sank back into the bunk, and she began to breathe quickly.
He stroked her body gently, sensing the outward quivers subside. As she lifted her head, he saw her eyes focus on his. As the fire of her desire illuminated the blue of her eyes, he was reminded of fire on flame.
He took a step closer to her and began kissing her heaving breasts. Then he began kissing her stomach, which was already warm and rolling at his fingertips. He ran his tongue through her pubic hair and was about to slide his tongue down her middle when he felt her tight grip his dick.

When she saw Daniel looking at her, she sent him an excited, desiring look as she stretched her legs eagled. She reached out her free arm, palm out, and placed it over Cunt, beckoning him between her thighs.

He stepped gently over her when Kaitlyn stood up slightly, but he didn't let go of his dick. As he was eventually able to put himself between her thighs, he sat down on his knees and hands.

She wrapped her palms around his shaft and rolled her hips up to cover his broad crown with her wetness. She then placed him at her opening and softly drew him down into her vagina.

Daniel noticed her worried face, closed eyes, and how tightly she bit her lower lip while keeping her breath. He took a hiatus to ensure she had all of him inside her.

Kaitlyn raised her eyes after a lengthy pause and began breathing in quick huffs.

After a few seconds, he saw her expression relax, her eyes sparkle, and she rolled her hips back some further, driving him in another inch. Her eyes momentarily closed, and a soft wince passed over her forehead.

She removed her hands from his shaft and reached up to stretch her thick hair behind her head before returning her head to the pillow.

He put forward another inch after she nodded and smiled at him. When her fingertips went to his waist and gently pushed him closer, he inserted the fourth inch.

When he pulled back out of her, her mouth shaped an "Oh." As she lowered her hips back to the mattress, she used her fingertips to signal him to please reenter her.

Daniel glanced down to see almost half of his shaft covered with her wetness, and he began to smell her lovely perfume as well. He melted further inside her than ever.

When she saw him stretch her, her back arched.

As he started to sink into her, he kept his gaze fixed on her lips. Her palms grasped his sides and pressed for him to stop when he had less than an inch to go before thoroughly exploring her waters.

She bit her lip again, locked her gaze on his, and steadily rolled up her hips. She winced at the strain he'd placed on her. She moved steadily, moving her shoulders until her body paved the path for his whole duration. Her hold on his waist relaxed, and her hands dropped down.

As he felt her absorb his whole length and her grasp loosen, he began with deep, steady strokes. He'd never felt a female with such a silky smooth inside. He could also detect ripples inside a female for the first time as he stroked her.

Her eyes wanted to hold on to his, glistening with delight. Her gaze, though, kept roaming as the emotions he produced drifted through her.

He'd just had a dozen or so strokes down before he saw her fingertips dancing and her crimson flush returning. He could feel her stomach churning against his. He could see her knees rising to lean against his sides. He slowed his strokes even further, then lengthened them by completely slipping out of her, then pressing back into her crack, and finishing pushed tight against her.

Her hips started to move in time with his strokes; her head began to roll side to side; her fingertips danced quicker across them as if attempting to touch him but unable to gain even the sliver of leverage.

He lost himself in her and stayed there as he felt a slight jolt. Big jolts ensued, and he struggled at first to remain inside her while she bucked, arched, and squirmed. And he felt something incredible. Her pussy was so tightly wrapped around his change that he couldn't abandon her even though he tried. He watched, held there for a long time, while all her tremors and twitches faded.

She slowly opened her eyes, struggled to concentrate, and then saw his profile. She took a few quick breaths, then placed a firm kiss on his mouth as her fingertips threaded around and clenched his scalp.

He'd never had a more intimate embrace. He sunk into her fervor, rubbing his whole body against hers and hearing her heaving breast.

Her hands slowly let go of his clothes, and she gently pulled him up, causing his shoulders to rise off of her.

Daniel looked down and noticed the most devilish twinkle in those beautiful locks, as well as the most mischievous grin he has ever seen. He could feel her internal hold loosening on him.

He took her release as a signal to restart his long, intense strokes of her.

Her back arched slightly as her heart came to a halt.

Before she shot her ace in the pit, he played a few lovely, smooth strokes.

She continued her breathing, lowered her back, and winked at him.

He could feel her tightening around his shaft. Not as firmly as before, but always a stronghold. He realized his dreams were doomed at this moment because he wasn't going to last long with what her taut, silky tunnel was doing to him.

She saw his focus slipping away, his eyes closing more and more each time. She gave a sly grin.

He stroked into her a few more times, more slowly, as he struggled to retain enough control to pull her with him, to be reunited at the moment.

She kept her hold, but her other muscles were taking on a life of their own. Her breathing huffed, and she let out tiny "whooshes" from her full lips, which had lost their grin. Her back was arched off the mattress as the vibrations from each moment he sunk into her depths rushed into her.

He could see her back sink and then bring her knees up to his hips. He saw the crimson stain creeping over her, as well as her neck muscles and shoulders tensing and her hips twitching. He felt her grasp on his shaft loosen, and he realized he was running out of time.

He increased the tempo of his strokes, banging into her repeatedly.

Her breathing stopped; her eyes froze wide, wild, and unfocused; she couldn't regulate her hold on him or every other muscle in her body any longer.

He hoped this was it for her when he just had a moment to drink in the crazy expression on her lips, the sound of her trembling legs, and those humming fingertips. The time flew by when he felt his face contort, the energy in his crotch, and then his powerful bursts exit through her while tightly pressing himself into her hips.

His final swelling, his depth inside her, and the additional warmth he sent through her delivered feelings beyond Kaitlyn's ability. Her mouth opened wide, and her legs encircled him, squeezing him tightly against her. She shook violently, her palms tightly grasping his back and her whole body attempting to curl up around him.

Daniel fought to remain deep inside her writhing, trembling body while still trying to hold his pulse and establish eye contact with this beautiful being. Her pulsing, rhythmic clamping on his shaft was palpable.

It took some time for them both to adjust to their routine, although fast, breathing patterns. Their happy eyes were shut the whole time, and they both smiled like fools.

Finally, his softened shaft oozed out of her, and he saw her saw face twitch with a teasing pout. He let out a long "WOW!" exclamation.

She bent her upper body under him, reached into the nightstand drawer, and pulled out a notepad and ink. She drew something rapidly with her left hand and then handed the tablet to him.

He laughed when he saw five massive exclamation marks, each with a heart in place of the mark at the bottom. He smiled widely, thinking it was a delightful display of wit and enthusiasm on her part to have drawn that portrait. And how tempting it had been for her to remain quiet all this time, even when experiencing numerous orgasms...

His mind abruptly came to a stop "...Is there silence?

...Are you writing?

No way!

...It's not possible...

Is it possible?"

Kaitlyn's grin vanished when she saw his expression change from confusion to desperation.

Daniel's mind raced back through time, recalling how he had spoken to his younger brother, Billy.

When he stood up, Daniel stared at her worried expression. "Are you deaf?" he said, cautiously raising his palms.

"Yes, and silent," she responded. Her face lit up with anticipation, and she studied his shocked expression with bated breath, hoping that the next moment meant everything.

Kaitlyn noticed a look of clarity on his features, as well as the beginnings of a grin.

"W-O-W," he signed in individual lines, but he was inexperienced with sign language, and his vocabulary had never been that extensive.

Her smile softened nervously. "All right?" she signed.

Daniel grinned contentedly, gazed into her lake blue eyes, and swept her hair away from both sides of her head. He bent forward and softly kissed one of his ears. The kiss was then replicated on her other ear. He then placed his hand behind her neck and applied pressure to her jaw with his thumb, causing her to tip her head back. His next kiss was lightly planted on her freckled throat. He lowered her head and delicately kissed her mouth.

She saw his lips slip away, and the greatest grin she'd ever seen spread over her face as she saw Daniel grow up and clumsily sign, "Really O-K."

Kaitlyn grasped his neck, drew herself up to him, and lavishly kissed him.

He relished the lengthy, playful embrace as a slew of doubts and emotions raced through his head. He slowly drew back, glanced down at those gleaming, blue eyes, and realized he wanted to be trapped in them forever.

She instantly signed, "I can read lips pretty well," with a bright grin on her face.

"Slower, yes," he signed back, puzzled.

She laughed silently and echoed what she had said more slowly.

"Good," he said. "I'd like to chat with you for a long time, but it's getting late. Can I spend the night with you?"

"Y-I-P-P-E-E-E-E-E-E-E-E-E-E-E-E-E-E-E-E-E-E- She signed "W-E-T" and pointed down between them. Then she hurried out from under him, seeing him fall onto his foot. She went to her room's desk and pulled a few sections of paper towels from a roll in a cabinet. She returned and washed the bed as thoroughly as she could, as well as him and herself. She switched off the lamp, made her way to the bunk, crawled in, and then wrapped herself around him tightly.

Daniel's last memory of her was him stroking her wavy hair along the side of her face and feeling her react by snuggling her face against the side of his chest.

—— Saturday Morning, After Azariah's Group ——

Daniel awakened to the sound of soft knocks on the threshold. His focus was drawn to the silence after last night's party before he could even react. Since this was not his place, he waited for Kaitlyn to answer before realizing his mistake.

"Please come in," he added.

Azariah's expression could be seen across the small distance as the door slid open gently. Her face lit up with a grin. "Does anybody like breakfast?"

"Sounds amazing to me," Daniel replied with a grin.

Kaitlyn crawled out from under the covers, his chest reverberating from the conversation.

Azariah's grin widened when she saw a messy mass of strawberry blond hair appear from under the covers, just below Daniel's jaw.

Kaitlyn brushed her hair away from her ears. She glanced at Daniel's face and noticed his mouth "Azariah" as he grinned at Kaitlyn behind her. She turned over easily, the sheets slipping off her bare upper half. She smiled at Azariah and wrote, "Thank you!"

"You're welcome," Azariah cheerfully said. "How about we get breakfast in 20 minutes unless you two have any unresolved business?"

Kaitlyn turned to look at Daniel and saw him wink. She returned her attention to Azariah and nodded sharply. Kaitlyn's wavy hair had fallen over her ears.

"Twenty minutes," Daniel grinned as he brushed Kaitlyn's hair away from her ears. When he saw the door closing, he stepped back to allow Kaitlyn to fall onto her back. "Good morning, gorgeous," he murmured as he leaned over to embrace her, gently closing those lovely eyes. He brushed his lips to hers, then rubbed one hand across her breast and down her chest.

Her hand gripped his wrist, bringing him to a halt. She touched his nose twice with her free finger while his face drew back, then signed "Breakfast...you puppy!" with a sparkle in her eyes. She replaced her hand on his and raised it away from her navel. She stood up, twisted, and sat down on the concrete. She noticed his hand dragging down her back and grabbing her buttocks as she stood. Kaitlyn swatted his hand aside amusingly.

——— At Breakfast ——————————————————————————-

They entered the breakfast nook, Daniel, in his somewhat wrinkled clothes from the night before, and Kaitlyn in a tangerine-colored, silk kimono robe, loosely wrapped in front. Azariah seemed to be very well-dressed, with washed hair and dressed in a jogging suit.

Daniel and Kaitlyn glanced about, finding glassware on the kitchen counter and two wide-open garbage bags in one section, mainly crumpled cocktail napkins, paper plates, and smashed beer cans. Surprisingly, the remainder of the building was spotless.

"How come you didn't get some sleep in this place?" As Azariah finished plating breakfast, Daniel inquired.

"A few hours," Azariah answered with a smile. "But, tired heads, it's almost 10:30."

Daniel glanced at his naked wrist, then at the clock on the wall, startled. "Good argument," he said. He noticed a touch on the nose and glanced down to see Kaitlyn's eyes sparkling and her sign, "Not too late for..." as she pushed her kimono back to reveal her breast. As he pulled her kimono closed and Azariah took the plates of food to the table, he sighed and signed back, "Dog."

Kaitlyn pranced over to her chair between them and sat back. She began eating her fried eggs, bacon, and sourdough bread. Her gaze shifted from Azariah to Daniel and back again before Daniel spoke.

"Do you suppose you have anything to do with this, Azariah?"

"MMMmmm...," Azariah muttered as she bit through her bread.

"Wasn't that moment in the office when you signed to be a test when you heard about my deaf brother?"

"Uh-huh," Azariah hummed as she chewed, nodding and closing her lips.

Daniel glanced at Kaitlyn, who smiled then soon returned her gaze to her meal. Daniel mouthed "WOW" to Azariah and bowed to Kaitlyn as her head was down.

Azariah winked and grinned knowingly. "I want to go on a run as well as do some errands, but you two have the house to yourself until at least 2 p.m.," Azariah said, seeing Kaitlyn's eyes light up.

Daniel saw Kaitlyn's eyes transform to him with a mischievous sparkle as he smiled at her. "Thank you," he said quietly, "I hope we'll make reasonable use of the time."

They finished their meal quickly, and he took their plates and brought them into the kitchen. "Thank you for the rice," he said as he waited for Azariah to make room in the sink for the dirty dishes. "Mind if I stick around here...often?" he asked Azariah, who was almost as tall as him as Kaitlyn stood behind them.

She placed the plates in the sink and said, a little shyly, "It will be nice for all of us."

That response took Daniel off balance, but Kaitlyn tapped him on the shoulder before he could react.

"What?" she said, signing her name.

Azariah and Daniel all turned back.

"What exactly did you say?" Kaitlyn repeated herself with hand motions.

"I just said 'I liked the crowd,'" he smiled.

Kaitlyn animatedly set her palms on her shoulders and angled her head with a curious frown.

Azariah and Daniel exchanged glances, and by chance, both glanced at Kaitlyn and shrugged at the same time.

Kaitlyn shifted her gaze from one to the other, smiled broadly, and then jumped up, across them, and embraced them both.

Dan kissed Kaitlyn on the cheek.

Azariah left on her run and errands shortly after turning on the dishwasher.

He noticed Kaitlyn's eyes focus on his and see her biting her lip as her hands fiddled with the knot in the sash that kept her kimono closed.

Daniel approached her and saw the robe fall apart. He stared her up and down, toes to forehead, taking in the details of her anatomy. "Have you always been...this way?" he demanded, looking into her mind.

Her wavy hair shifted up and down as she nodded steadily.

"I would like to see you a lot more frequently," he said after that inquiry. "Not all of it like this," he said as he brushed his hands across her breasts.

Her eyes melted, and she prepared to smile.

"I'm hoping you like that as well?" he inquired.

Kaitlyn's head bobbed up and down, her hair shifting all over and partly covering one eye. The grin erupted.

He took her over to the sofa in the living room, remembering it hadn't been there the night before. He also recalled that the house was on a cul-de-sac because it was doubtful that any neighbors might glance in the windows to see a naked Kaitlyn. He sat down and put Kaitlyn on his lap.

"How much did Azariah reveal to you about me?" he inquired.

Her gaze shifted to the stars for a brief moment before returning to him with a wry grin. She began to sign, then realized she was too close to him, so she simply signed "Wait."

She stepped back off his lap and sat on the sofa, her head on an arm pillow and her knees on his lap. When she saw him looking down at her bush, she spread her legs wide, then clasped them back together while she chuckled, which came out as little huffs. Her kimono was draped at her sides.

She decided to keep her words plain and slow, as his capacity to interpret sign language seemed to be minimal. "Azariah tells me several little pieces," she smiled, "like this rumor." She drew her foot back from his stomach and rubbed his groin with her heel. "Better than the rumor," she said, her mischievous expression returning.

He blushed shyly at the last comment and hated having to pull his gaze away from hers so he could hear her hands speak. He put his palm on her thigh and softly petted it.

She discovered that the loose kimono sleeves were interfering with her signing and slid out of them, leaving her nude on top of the cloth.

She continued, "Azariah defined your appearance to me as follows: "Better in person." She said you were courteous and kind... As he seemed confused, she spelled P-O-L-I-T-E...funny and cheerful. All seems to be right. She said you were fantastic at your role and that you and she had been coworkers for three years. She even advised me about your brother's deafness and death."
"But you knew I knew sign language before the party?"
"Yes," she said, averting her gaze for a moment. "I wanted to see you, but just K-A-I-T-L-Y-N me...not deaf and stupid me."
"I understand," he admitted, "but that was an unusual way for you to present yourself!"

"It was not my idea," she signed, a little shyly. I knew the small talk wouldn't succeed because it would reveal that I was deafeningly deafeningly deafeningly deafeningly deafeningly. I didn't want you to believe I was a slut...S-L-U-T..., but when I watched you, looking into your eyes, and later danced to that slow tune, I realized there was no point in waiting. "I was looking for you." "I'm happy I did, and I know I'll want you a lot more," she said with a wide smile.

He grinned and bowed, saying, "I am very happy you did...and that you want to see me again." I'm assuming you're familiar with my surname, Taylor (which he pronounced carefully). So, what's your first name...last name?"

"R-A-I-V-I-N, C-Y-N-T-H-I-A," she signed, "K-A-I-T-L-Y-N, C-Y-N-T-H-I-A." Azariah refers to me as "S-I-N-F-U-L." Her lustful features twinkled.

"Kaitlyn Sinful Raivin," he said softly, returning her lustful gaze.

"What is your real name?" she inquired.

"Daniel Ev..." he began before changing his sign to "E-V-E-R-E-T-T."

"Good," she said, "can I name you D-A-N to make it easier to talk?"

"Certainly," he said, raising his hand to rub her stomach.

"That's cool as well!" she said.

Their dialog persisted, with brief stops for Kaitlyn to catch her breath as his hand touched her more vulnerable areas.

She discovered a lot of new concepts. He stayed in a house near the old Hamilton Field airbase in Novato (California), some 10 minutes south of Azariah's home in the initial section of Novato. Dan's parents lived south of Sacramento, about a one-and-a-half-hour drive to the east, and he no longer had any brothers or sisters.

Dan discovered that her parents stayed in Oregon. She had two sisters, one older and one younger, and no one else in the family had her limits. She was an artist, but she didn't make a living off it. She had a family trust that offered a respectable income, but selling art made some splurging on wants rather than needs. She volunteered twice a week at a deaf school in San Francisco. And, as he had expected, she was a big fan of sex.

He started running his thumb over her mons after she officially announced the last thing.

Her hands stopped talking, and she began to wiggle under his fingertips.

Dan abruptly moved his hand to her knees when the garage door opened.

Azariah entered the room, holding grocery bags, and stared at Kaitlyn, who was nude on the couch across Daniel's lap. "Are you two done yet?" she smirked.

Dan immediately replied, "We spent the time getting to know each other better."

"I see where you did your studies," Azariah mocked.

Dan's face flushed.

Azariah burst out laughing. "Don't be concerned, Daniel. She spends more time nude in the house than clothed!"

"Hello!" "That makes me sound like a whore!" Kaitlyn immediately signed.

Dan saw Kaitlyn blushing profusely.

"Sorry, Dan," Azariah laughed, "but she does spend a lot of time naked, but not on her back with guys!" You can see her with color all over her body. On the other hand, you'd love cleaning her up."

Dan smiled as he noticed Kaitlyn's flush disappear.

Azariah chuckled as she walked down the hall carrying her packages.

"So, are you my whore now?" Dan said quietly to Kaitlyn.

Kaitlyn seemed to be surprised, then bit her lip and nodded shyly. She turned around and did not see Azariah; she stretched her legs for a long moment before closing them.

He caught the incoming sunshine bouncing off her gleaming folds until she closed her legs.

"Think I sprang a leak...L-E-A-K...think you can repair it?" she signed.

He nodded and grinned.

She rose to her feet, draped her kimono across her back, and extended her hand to him.

He snickered, stood up, took her hand in his, and pursued her lovely bottom, like he had done the night before, except this time the butt was naked.

"S-T-R-I-P-!" she signed as she shut the door to her bed.

When he undressed, he kept his gaze fixed on her ferocious-looking pupils. When he was nude, he searched for her breasts.

She caught his hands, moved him back to the bed, and he flopped on it. She sat down, tossed her hair on one side, and knelt. She licked up and around his semi-flaccid member in her lap. She continued doing this, sometimes popping his crown in her lips until she had his undivided attention.

Dan lay there blissfully, feeling the rising urgency in his hips that she was making. He sensed her come to a halt, and then he grabbed and lifted his thighs, which were stretched across the edge of the bunk. She positioned them on the mattress's end, aligning him with its length.

He saw her climb onto the bunk, and he scarcely had time to raise his head and look until she was straddling him and pushing her way in.

She grimaced mildly, closed her eyes, and bit her lip as she came to a halt with him just inside her. When she opened her mind, she locked on his, like she had done so many times before.

As she lowered herself into him, he focused his gaze on her eyes. He saw glimpses of worry in her eyes, but they were soon replaced with resolve. He noticed the shock on her face when she immediately lifted back up after she had slipped down him the last two centimeters. Her determination returned, and she began rocking her hips forward and back.

As she rocked, she eased down the last inch onto him, ensuring that her cervix would enable him to move. She flung her head back in relaxation and satisfaction and took a long break until she rested her entire weight on him.

Dan was enthralled by his breadth inside her, as well as the sweat that was streaming down his balls. As she bent over him, her gorgeous hair touching his chest, he felt her gently begin to ride him in long strokes. He massaged her sensitive breasts, savoring the same feelings as the night before: her unbelievably silky tunnel and the ripples of the tissues inside her that he moved with each stroke.

She stood up and began to bounce on his legs.

Dan saw the red rising rapidly in her upper chest and throat, the intermittent bite of her tongue, and the on-off clenching of her fingertips against his chest. He realized he wouldn't be able to handle these wondrous feelings for long. He noticed the obnoxious wet noises and remembered that she had never heard them with a tinge of regret.

It didn't take long for her to convulse and shake. She then hesitated while she struggled to take control of her body, ready to do it all over again. She did this twice. She read his expression as similar after the third orgasm. She used every ounce of leverage she had to hold her gaze fixed on his as she clamped him on her upstroke and released him on her downstroke.

She was on the verge of falling over when she saw Dan's mouth spread wide. Under her hands, she could sense his grunts. When she felt the new warmth wash through her, she let go, throwing her whole weight onto him and convulsing so violently that she almost fell over.

Her hair fell over his forehead as her head dropped to his lap. She clamped down on him firmly and repeatedly. He groaned over his last pulses, holding her up while her body lost strength.

They remained in that place, both experiencing the return of aftershocks that had overtaken her. Her body eventually landed on top of him.

After a few minutes, she was slowly able to lift herself and her hair away from him. She could see their sweat clinging to them. "Yes, your whore," she signed as she realized she couldn't hold herself stable without her weapons. I'm going to need a lot more of this!"

She heard him chuckle and felt it from her hips.

——-——-

After a fortnight, - On Sunday ———

Dan and Kaitlyn arrived at Azariah's house mid-morning on Sunday and were greeted by Azariah, who said, "Hello, strangers. It felt strange not getting you two around for a few days after having you both here every night after the party!

"I need clean clothing," Kaitlyn said.

Azariah laughed. "How do you like Dan's place?"

Kaitlyn's pupils glowed. "Dan's spot has a California king bed." And a massive tub." She grinned up at Dan, then returned her gaze to Azariah and signed, "With endless hot water and plenty of soap!"

Dan's face flushed.

"I can tell her goals haven't shifted!" grinned Azariah.

Dan and Kaitlyn all blushed.

"Yeah: I figured I would have to drop her off for a few days so that I can get some rest!" Dan smirked atAzariah.

Kaitlyn stabbed him in the shoulder and smiled.

"So, are you two hanging around today?" Azariah questioned, chuckling.

Kaitlyn was the first to react, saying, "He's bringing me to a beach on the coast that he thinks I'll enjoy." Yes, yes, yes, yes, yes, yes, yes, yes, yes, yes, yes, yes, yes, yes "I need warm clothing."

"Sounds amazing," Azariah responded. You're welcome to return, but I may have a WB buddy here this evening."

Kaitlyn bounced and clapped.

"We possibly won't be back before 7 or 8," Dan said. So let's get this party underway."

Kaitlyn nodded and entered her bedroom.

With just Azariah's present, Dan shouted, "Thank you, Azariah. I'm falling in love with her at a breakneck rate. She's unlike anybody else I've ever known. She is aware of everything about her and...well, you know...such a sensual being."

"Well, I do," Azariah said, a wicked grin on her face.

Dan was drawn in by her smile. "Do you mean..." he began nervously.

"Yup, many occasions," Azariah said with a grin. "But don't worry, she's not Bi, only interested, and she didn't have many dates...so..." she reached out and grabbed Dan's forearm.

"I think I shouldn't be shocked, but I hadn't thought about it."

"She's a package of surprises; don't ever presume you're through with them," Azariah smiled.

Kaitlyn left, clad in a jogging suit with a zippered top and shoes, as he contemplated the proposal. She was carrying another heavier jacket, a small travel bag, and two beach towels. She lifted her eyebrows and put the towels out in front of Azariah as though to ask a challenge.

"Of course," Azariah said, "you can borrow them."

Kaitlyn grinned, took Dan's arm, and guided him to the entrance, waving goodbye to Azariah over her head.

As Dan and Kaitlyn approached his vehicle, he opened the trunk and attached Kaitlyn's supplies to those already in the trunk of his Mazda 6. She walked back to the passenger door, one finger trailing up over the roofline, as she had done before. "Still a lovely car, such a great red paint," she signed while she was seated.

He rubbed her thigh with a smile.

"How long?" she inquired.

"Nearly two hours," Dan said as he pulled north.

Kaitlyn reached over and switched on the radio, scrolling through the automated information before she came upon an 80's rock channel on Sirius XM. She tested the radio to make sure it was still tuned to full BASS. She switched on the music and began to move with her hair.

Dan stroked her thigh and inserted his finger into his ear.

Kaitlyn turned down the music and stroked his leg. Dan took his driving seriously, but she had always learned not to be too playful in the car. She'd simply reserve her carnal desires for a less "distracting" moment.

He glanced over to see her already squirming as she bounced in her seat and drank in the sights as they drove across the rolling valleys on their way to the coast highway, with the ancient oak trees and dried-grass colored hills.

He stroked her arm and saw her shift her gaze to him. The sunshine streaming through the window illuminated the color of her eyes in a way he had never seen before and will never forget. After each glance at the lane, he returned to her eyes.

Kaitlyn noticed the adoring looks he was sending her. He shifted his hand from her back to her bra-less breast as she unzipped the top of her dress.

He took one more look at those molten blue eyes before returning his attention to the road. His grin remained, as did his hand on her breast. He slid his hand away after a few seconds, sensing her puffy nipple had grown. He felt her snatch his hand and place it back over her breast until it completely left her skin.

His grin broadened, he squeezed her breasts, and he returned his hand to the steering wheel. After a brief look at her, he burst out laughing at the ridiculous pout on her face as she pulled her top open, revealing each of those beautiful breasts.

Kaitlyn held her chest bare for around ten minutes as they drove across the rural countryside, except while entering oncoming vehicles. She zipped back up as they reached the turn for the coastal Highway 1 and the tiny town that existed at the intersection.

Dan turned to Azariah and asked, "What does Azariah's WB boyfriend mean?" as he waited for a break in the flow, which was backed up for about half a mile behind a sluggish motorhome.

"With B-E-N-E-F-I-T-S," she replied, thinking his sign language vocabulary had not yet advanced significantly.

"Ooohhh," he said, realizing that the description should have been clear to him.

"You have any WB mates besides Azariah?" he asked casually as he waited for the last few sluggish cars to leave.

"She told you about her and me?" Kaitlyn hesitated, becoming a bit flustered.

He turned and pulled into the parking lot of a grocery store/gas station because he didn't want to be crawling at the end of this line of vehicles. He turned off the antenna.

"It seemed to come up," he said, "but no specifics." "Once she told me, I knew the thought might have occurred to me."

"So you're cool with the fact that I've been with a woman? It's just happened three times with Azariah, "She inquired nervously.

"I guess I can't blame you," he joked, "I've been looking at Azariah's body for years with some of those emotions."

"The mood is M-U-T-U-A-L," Kaitlyn signed, smiling.

"What are you talking about? You and I have only...OOoh...Are you talking about Azariah with me?"

Kaitlyn grinned cheerfully, her hair swirling in the wind and a wide smile on her lips.

"Well, that one certainly got by me," he admitted.

"She's wanted you in her bed for a while, but she felt it was more necessary that we meet...

Don't tell her I told you!"

"Of course: And she's such a nice friend? That is incredible! "He said.

"We grow up as neighbors," she said. "She is three years older than me and has watched out for me." Her house belonged to her parents, and my relatives lived next door. My parents relocated to Oregon after my sisters and I left home, and I moved in with her."

"Really," he said, taking in this fresh outlook.

"To spare you the trouble of counting, I am 25 years old. "And, Mr. S-N-O-O-P, no WB mates," she said. So, how are you, stud...S-T-U-D?"

Dan chuckled, particularly when she spelled'stud.' "Yes," he admitted, "but they no longer pique my curiosity." "They cannot keep a torch to you, by any measure," he said solemnly, looking at her.

Kaitlyn seemed taken aback, and her hands rose, but she said nothing. Her grin had faded, and a single tear streamed down her face.

"I can't keep you out of my head," Dan explained softly, "I don't even have thoughts about doing things that don't include you."

Tears were now streaming down both of her cheeks. When her hands thawed, they fumbled out, "Me, too."

He brushed her tears away before leaning in and kissing her long and softly.

She was blinking at the sight of fresh tears.

He said with a smile, "Let's go to the shore. We still have almost an hour until we get there."

He turned north on a now-vacant highway and adjusted the speed control to 58 mph. They passed the motor home that had slowed traffic in a couple of miles. It was parked on the shoulder, steam streaming from the front, and flanked by two motorcycles.

For that hour, she had a small, contented grin on her face as he smiled at her, and her eyes danced between him and the beauty of the Pacific Ocean, which she could see out the window and through his side of the vehicle. Her palm remained on his thigh the whole time, with her thumb sweeping back and forth. She turned off the radio.

—— A Day at the Beach —— Sunday —-

When they arrived at the location Dan had chosen, he pulled into the narrow parking lot. There were no other vehicles in the parking lot of this less well-known establishment. They unpacked the trunk, hoping not to be swept backward by the gentle incoming sea breezes. Kaitlyn put on a baseball cap and try to keep her flying locks in check, and she put on her heavier jacket to allow her hands to hold other things.

Dan even placed on a baseball cap, which required the band to be tightened to prevent it from blowing off. He threw on his windbreaker over his bulky t-shirt and tucked a few little things into the pockets of his worn-out jeans.

They passed the state's single-stall toilet outhouse on their way to the stairs Dan had indicated. The steep stairs curved down the cliff face to the beach, which was only 30 feet below. Kaitlyn was in the lead.

The farther down they went, the further Kaitlyn returned Dan's gaze, her grin becoming larger with each passing moment. When they got to the beach, Dan led her to a cliff with a tiny cavern that wasn't noticeable from the lane. It provided almost total insulation from the storm, but its form also intensified the dramatic noises.

A steep rock point just outside the cavern had been worn ideally to make thunderous crashes as the waves reached them every few seconds. A small sea spray drifted down on them now and then.

Dan was about to unravel the beach blanket when he saw Kaitlyn doing something. When he saw her, he got up and soaked in her sheer delight.

Kaitlyn was standing in the sand some 50 feet from the cavern. Her shoes were already off, and she was staring out at the rolling waves. Dan saw the sun making her hair shimmer as she removed her baseball cap and threw it back in his face.

As the waters rumbled overhead, she grinned gleefully. She opened her arms to embrace the deep, powerful noises that were affecting her body.

She took off her heavier coat after a few minutes. After another minute, she turned to Dan and winked before unzipping and removing her jogging jacket. She put her arms around her bare chest and bounced on her toes as the ocean produced the next major boom from the rocks.

Then she came to a halt, lowered her arms, and looked reflective. She turned to face the cavern a split second after the next boom of surf, her hair still whipped all over her face.

Dan enthusiastically saw her do this many times, knowing she would be able to hear the cavern's short echo. She seemed to be laughing at him. Then he saw her come to a halt, grin at him briefly, and then start running towards him, breasts swiveling. He hardly had time to prepare himself before she jumped into his lap, her arms around his neck and her legs wrapping around his waist.

Dan chuckled warmly but held his eyes and mouth shut as she slapped short, wet kisses all over his face, knocking his cap off. His hands feel the chill of the water spray and soft sea breezes on her skin. And he sensed the embrace of a powerful kiss planted on his laps, which he returned after a long time.

He persuaded her to get off him and stand. "Let us finish setting up so that I can display you something," he said, lightly palming both her breasts.

She pressed her breasts into his hands ever more firmly; her twinkling, wide-open eyes fixed on his.

"Really?" he said, smiling.

Her brief nods threw her hair over his shoulders.

Before withdrawing his hands, he used his fingers to press on her chest above her breasts, allowing him to push her back into a relaxed stance. "Work first, play later," he said with a grin.

She shrugged cheerfully and dashed off to get her cap, jeans, and two coats. She returned to the cavern, re-applied her jogging jacket, and pushed her hair through the gap in the back of the baseball cap, leaving her with a broad ponytail.

He picked up a beach towel and draped it over his back after she had done assisting in the placement of the rug, pillows, and snacks. "You'll need the other jacket because we're going to get muddy, and you'll need your shoes for the rocks."

She did as he asked and took his hand in his, and he guided her out into the rocks and waves. She came to a halt, raised one finger, and rushed back to the bag she had packed. She took out her phone, tucked it into her purse, and zipped it shut. She dashed back to him.

"Do you have a mobile phone?" he inquired, "And who do you call?"

She cocked her head and stared at him, hoping for his insanity to wear off. "D-U-H," she said. He took his time with this one, so she signed, "Facetime, paws, get it?"

"Sorry, I don't know why I am so rusty on picking on those topics with you," he blushed, smiling at her eyes, which danced in the sunshine. This is not my normal demeanor. So, perhaps I do remember... I'm far so caught up with your gaze."

Kaitlyn smiled and nodded her head, then gently swatted the back of his head and pushed him to move. She retook his hand, led him into a crevice, and then cautiously guided his movements across the muddy rocks as he crawled up about 10 feet.

Dan pointed to the roaring tide as she appeared on top of the nearby cliffs.

She stood there for a second and saw water shot up from a break in the rocks. She'd never seen a blowhole before, and it was making her hot. Dan escorted her a little farther forward, where she gleefully gazed up at the towering spray of water. When a thick spray fell on them, she ducked.

Dan felt her warm embrace as she wrapped her arms around his middle and jumped on her toes. He snatched the beach towel off his back, unfolded it, and draped it around their shoulders, covering much of her hair. He saw her pull out her phone and take a few pictures of the scenery before changing camera settings to take a selfie of the two of them.

They stayed there for another half dozen waves, looking like those YouTube party kitten posts, tilting their heads up to watch the rocketing water, then ducking their heads as the water crashed beneath gravity's touch.

Kaitlyn raised her head to Dan, washed the saltwater from her eyes, and nodded her order to leave.

Dan observed as she removed her wet scarf, sneakers, and ball cap as they returned to the cavern. He stripped off his windbreaker to get out of the wind in the cavern, and then he opted to take off his shoes as well. They relaxed on the blanket and ate the cookies he had packed, as well as the bottled sodas (liquor was not allowed on the beach).

She signed, "Will you email me your mobile phone number?" as their consumption of nuts and chips slowed to sporadic nibbles. And then searched for her phone in the pocket of her bulky coat.

Dan took out his phone, displayed his phone number on the screen, and showed it to her. When she was done, she sent him her phone number. "You may have said you had a mobile phone," he said after entering it.

Her eyes opened, and she made a funny smile. "Rather than when you're at college, when in the last week was I further apart than the other side of the bed?" she signed.

"Taken," he chuckled.

"I have one bar, how about you?" she scooted up next to him and signed.

"Two" means "two people."

"Try calling me," she instructed.

As he reached for the Call button, he saw her stuffing her phone down the front of her jogging pants.

He pressed the call button, her phone buzzed, and she began giggling quietly.

He began to chuckle and then obliged as she motioned, "Again." When her knees clenched together and she dropped backward, laughing in those tiny huffs, he fell on his ass, laughing.

When the laughter died down, he inquired, "Did you place the phone in your pants?"

She undressed to her knees in her jogging pants and signed, "What panties?!"

He glanced at her bush, then up to her eyes, and they told him just what she desired.

He began cautiously unzipping her jogging jacket.

Kaitlyn then kicked her jeans off. Then she slid out of her top, got up, and raised her foot to straddle him. Her hair spilled over her ears as she bowed at her neck. Then she undid his belt buckle and popped his jeans' waist button.

"I want you nude," she wrote, almost in front of his nose, her eyes through her hair. She came to a halt, frowned, and then added, "N-A-K-E-D when I get back!"

"Back from where?!?" he shouted.

She didn't react, instead of turning and fleeing the cavern.

Concerned that it was a public beach, but one with no one else around, he removed his tee-shirt and then saw her nude body sprint until she was knee-deep in the water. He was about to take his jeans off when he saw her switch her back to a huge wave, and then she vanished.

When it dropped her to her feet, the cold shock blew all over and over her. She staggered to her feet and began to sprint backward, but the outflowing water slowed her. She gave Dan a mockingly surprised expression that became more genuine when another cold wave struck her at the thighs, causing her to stumble once more. She swam across the next wave and began to swim but then hopped for a few steps when she unwound a bit of kelp from her hobbled ankle.

As he saw she was well, he finished removing his jeans and socks before she returned to him.

She approached him, still wet, her hair already even deeper from the sea, and raised his boxer's waistband to clear his still firm erection before yanking his boxers down his thighs. She jumped above him and dropped herself into him. She didn't hesitate this time and let him all in with the first slide, though not without grimacing and straining her neck muscles.

Dan noticed her huffing a couple of times and her eyes widening. "All right?" he inquired.

"In a second," she said, still feeling a little nervous about her daring assault on him.

"You see, this is a public beach," he laughed.

"Then I'd best hurry," she signed, smiling. Her eyes twinkled under her dripping hair as she wrapped her fingers around his shaft. She suddenly began bouncing against his legs, quick and strong. Water sprayed from her body. The red was blooming on her upper chest within a few bounces.

When she beat him, he sensed the sand move under his blanket. "You had best be fast, you beautiful lady, because I won't last long with you are clamping on me all the time," his mind exclaimed. She abruptly came to a halt, just when he felt she was about to finish him off.

She stopped, leaning on his hips, and gazed around the cavern, her face puzzled.

Dan saw a smile of appreciation on her lips, and then she smiled at him with a love he hadn't noticed before in those great eyes.

She pushed herself away from him, almost allowing him to abandon her. And, without colliding with him, he sunk into his hips in one firm stroke. She stopped for a couple of seconds before repeating the step several times.

It was a fresh sensation for him, and it became much more unique when he learned her downstrokes were paced to balance the thunder of the waves. As he realized this, he applied an upstroke of his hips during the thunder in the cavern.

He saw her crimson flush intensifying and spreading to her throat. Small shudders echoed through her, and he saw her eyes unable to focus. When her legs clamped to his hands, her eyes closed, and the arms rubbing against his chest buckled, he realized she was there.

"Cum, my love, come strong," pleaded his voice. He felt a brief pause until many painful jolts went through her. He was almost there, but he waited before her breathing returned to normal. When it did, he began moving his hips in strokes that reached up into her. He saw her straighten up, her eyes widen, and her mouth shapes an "Oh."

He shifted his pace to drive as quickly as he could, their hips slapping twice or more every second. He only waited a few seconds before tensing, grimacing, and growling with each aching heartbeat.

She fell on top of him; her only coordinated response was to brush her damp hair away from his ears. The sea air's coolness on her skin became evident. She steadily rose on her forearms, then sunk to embrace him, wishing it would never stop.

His mind was torn as he relished the embrace, one portion remembering he had said "love" to himself. "I have never said I loved a lady, not even to myself," he reflected. "Is this truly the one?" He was ecstatic when his mind said "Yes" without hesitation.

He realized he had to be the rational one and proposed they dress. With his sweet "nudist," he chuckled to himself at the thought that getting naked was never a fashionable option.

—— After the Beach at Azariah's - On Sunday ———

It was almost 9 p.m. when they arrived at Azariah's place, and they were still exhausted, plus the pizza they had stopped for on the way back was contributing to their drowsiness. They entered the house after unloading Kaitlyn's belongings.
They didn't see Azariah, but they wanted to take a shower together and get rid of the saltwater and then relax for the rest of the day. They undressed in Kaitlyn's bed, and Dan borrowed a terry cloth robe from her, even though it was too short for long-term modesty. They entered, and she used the bathroom while Dan opened the softly textured glass door to the spacious shower and changed the water temperature.
Dan was already reaching in, waiting for the temperature to increase, when Kaitlyn's hand wrapped around his shaft. As she stroked him to attention, he started to climb as well. When the temperature was just right, Dan told Kaitlyn to go in first because he knew he wanted to drape a towel over the top of the shower window. He changed as he walked into the room to retrieve a towel.

The bathroom door slammed open. Azariah rushed in, nude. She got about three moves before the shock hit her face. She stared at Dan's surprised expression, then down at his completely erect organ, and then placed a hand over her vulva, as well as crossed one arm over her breasts, squashing their ample height.

"I...I...I...I...I...I...I...I...I...I...I...I...I...I... Azariah shouted, then dashed past Dan to the restroom, tightly scraping up against him due to the small space.

Dan climbed into the bathroom and turned his back to the glass, which faced the toilet, as soon as he regained consciousness.

Kaitlyn was taken aback and asked what Dan was up to.

Above the rhythm of the rushing stream, Azariah exclaimed, "I'm sorry...

My date was using my bathroom, and I couldn't stop myself. I didn't care about you being in here, Dan, because I was in a hurry. I'll be gone in a flash!"

Kaitlyn signed, "What is wrong?" as she glanced at Dan's flushed face, stiff, strange stance, and now-flaccid dick.

"Azariah...on the toilet...nude...now!" Dan said, perplexed by her expression.

Kaitlyn's eyes sparkled with joy, and a wry smile stretched over her lips. Kaitlyn walked halfway out of the tub so she could see Azariah. Kaitlyn motioned Azariah into the bathroom.

Azariah's face went into shock once more, but she was able to say, "Certainly not!

...er...

My date is in the restroom. I needed to pee badly. I'll be there in a moment."

Kaitlyn shrugged and signed, "Your loss."

Azariah gave Dan a little smile and pointed. "OMG," she exclaimed, then put her hands apart, wide apart, as though telling a fisherman's tall story.

Kaitlyn nodded happily and formed a large circle with her hands. Azariah's eyes widened as she listened as Azariah flushed the toilet and walked away. Kaitlyn waved goodbye to Azariah before closing the shower door.

"Is she gone?" Dan inquired.

Kaitlyn grinned, a wide grin on her face. "Did you like what you saw?" she asked.

"Well," he said, pausing before proceeding, "I'm a man." She has a lovely body, massive boobs with large nipples, and a lovely, shaved cunt. Will you trust me if I told you, "NO, she is not beautiful"?"

She signed, "I do trust you when you claim she is stunning because she is," as she stared down at his once-again solid erection.

Kaitlyn then made a pouty smile, cupped and bounced her far smaller breasts, and combed her fingertips over her pubic hair. Then she waited for Dan to begin the back-peddling, trying not to laugh.

"NO...NO...NO...!" On cue, Dan began, "Do not shave it! Your breasts are also stunning! Don't alter a thing...I adore you just as you are!"

Kaitlyn's face went numb. She was not going to budge until she understood Dan had remembered what he had just written.

Dan stopped for a second, worried. And he glanced down at those worried, incredibly addictive eyes. "I...L-O-V-E...Y-O-U," he signed, sighing, relieved that it was now out in the open.

He saw her and saw those eyes, surrounded by wet, straight hair, begin to break into tears, which were soon washed away by the shower water.

Her hands raised tentatively and shook. She tried her utmost to sign simply, "Since that slow dance at the wedding, I've been in love with you. I tried to convince myself that love, at first sight, isn't real...that it was just lust...L-U-S-T..., and that maybe I'd fall in love with you later. Now I realize I was mistaken; it has always been love...and I don't want it to end."

He grinned and tapped her on the nose, which made her grin back. "I don't either."

As she forced him back against the shower wall, he assumed she was about to kiss him. Instead, she pressed both of her palms against his stomach, her head lowered. He stood there watching, waiting, and counting the drops of water that trailed from her hair.

She finally lifted her head, tears streaming down her now-sad face. She took a step back and stared him between the eyes. "There's something I have to tell you, then...right now."

He was now looking at her with concern.

Kaitlyn lifted her hands then stopped to attempt to calm herself down. After a brief pause, she signed, "I...cannot...have...children."

"Cannot, or do not want to?" he questioned quietly, looking at her downcast expression.

"Both," she signed, "because I'm split in that sense." And I don't want to raise children who are deafeningly deafeningly deafeningly deafeningly deafeningly deafen I have triumphed... I've C-O-N-Q-U-E-R-E-D...many things in my life. Still, I've also seen what my shortcomings will do to the feelings of others. Enough for me is to assist deaf children."

Dan straightened her back by keeping her shoulders. "I...DO...NOT...CARE," he declared, "If we get to that stage, we will make a decision then." No baby, or even adopting an infant, even a deaf child: I'm fine with any choice. I want you, and I have no aspirations other than having you in my life."

Kaitlyn flung herself against him and wrapped her arms around him closely.

He rocked her body for a few minutes before he felt the hot water dwindling. He touched her on the shoulder, and she raised her head. "The hot water has drained out. We'd best clean up fast and get out of here."

She gave a smile.

They all easily cleaned themselves and each other before turning off the water. They dried off, changed into their robes, and went to her bed. They undressed and got into bed without saying anything.

Kaitlyn had snuggled up to him softly. Dan reached into her nightstand drawer and pulled out a notepad and notebook. He wrote "I LOVE YOU!" with her heart sign at the bottom of the floating exclamation mark. He positioned the portrait in front of her, and she grinned broadly.

He saw her gazing up at him with a big twinkle in her eyes, and when he saw her remove the pen from his grip. She drew a horizontal arrow with an arrowhead at both ends underneath what he had said. She then put a notepad between them.

He chuckled and grinned before replacing the notepad and pen in the drawer and turning off the tiny light on the nightstand, leaving them in the dark. He reached her face and gently kissed her before closing his eyes and settling in for what he hoped would be the greatest night's sleep he'd ever have, with her snuggled closely to his side.

He was about to fall asleep when he began to hear noisy exclamations flowing through the wall. Azariah's space seemed to be next to the wall where their headboard was located. The female exclamations he encountered appeared to fit into the ranges of "Yes, Yes," "My God," and "Fuck!" He laughed when he heard a rhythmic thumping against the building.

Kaitlyn flipped onto her back and switched on the light when she heard him laugh. "What's funny?" she said.

Dan grinned as he grabbed one of her arms by the elbow, lifted it, and set her hand against the wall.

Kaitlyn hesitated, smiled, then retracted her hand before signing, "She wanted that!" Kaitlyn switches off the light, only to switch it back on again. "It's your turn in the morning!" she said as she switched off the switch. She could hear him hum happily.

—— Monday Morning After the Beach ———

Dan and Kaitlyn were dressing comfortably when they entered the kitchen at 8:30 a.m. the next morning. It should have been sooner if Kaitlyn hadn't kept her promise. Azariah sat at the table, her Apple tablet in hand.

"Are you not going to work today?" Dan inquired.

Azariah blushed when she glanced up and saw his profile. "We're lucky to get flex time. I simply informed them that I would be arriving later. So, how are you?"

"Same," he replied.

"Did you have breakfast?" Kaitlyn inquired of Azariah.

"No, my date went out late last night, and I've just been up for about 20 minutes."

"Ok, then, I'm making breakfast," Kaitlyn signed, "oatmeal and English muffins, okay?"

Azariah replied, "Yes," and Dan agreed, but he wasn't sure what food Kaitlyn had signed for.

Kaitlyn entered the kitchen, and appropriate cooking sounds could be heard.

Dan stood at the table next to Azariah.

"She makes such a racket in there, doesn't she?" Dan remarked.

"Yes, it does. "It makes a lot of clatters," Azariah answered, "and often I have to switch to another place."

Azariah kept tapping and swiping her finger around the screen of her phone. "Sorry for barging in last night," she said without looking around.

"I was a little ashamed because it threw me off balance at the moment," he laughed. "But what man in his right mind would object to seeing you naked?" As he nudged her forearm, Dan said.

Her head remained down, and she worked hard to prevent her grin from being too broad. "And I discovered that the workplace gossip around you don't do you right, Horse!" she exclaimed, looking up at him.

"TMI on that one!" Dan blushed now.

Azariah laughed and then continued, "You all seem to be the proverbial cat that ate the canary this morning. Have a nice night?"

"More than that," he responded, "I've fallen in love with her."

"Wonderful, but I'm not shocked," Azariah chirped.

Dan smirked and said, "After the tub, we had a peaceful night and fell asleep to the music from your bed. It had a perfect 'beat' to it!" He nudged Azariah's elbow once more.
"Oh my God, the music in my...?" Azariah nearly squealed in delight. She blushed a lot and covering her lips. After a brief pause, she murmured, "I had been used to little miss Sinful not hearing anything that I had forgotten about myself. I'll have to get things under control the next time...if there is a next time. And, just so you know, I don't notice you two doing...well, Kaitlyn has told me a few things, so I know you're not monks in there.
Dan smiled.
Azariah smiled.

They remained silent for a few moments, but their eyes both sensed the delicious, toasty aroma of perfectly fork-split English muffins.

Kaitlyn served them the dinner, which featured a wide serving bowl of steel-cut oatmeal, a tray of 8 deeply buttered, crunchy muffin pieces, as well as white sugar, brown sugar, butter, and maple syrup. Kaitlyn stood next to Azariah, just across from Dan.

They pushed the oatmeal bowl around and fed themselves. Kaitlyn and Dan then each searched for and grabbed the bag of brown sugar.

Kaitlyn placed on a jovial expression of resolve and fierceness.

Dan stifled a laugh when he saw those luscious blue eyes and warm features attempting to appear strong.

Azariah abandoned politeness and waited, reaching over their warring palms, which remained clamped on the brown sugar bag, and snatched up the maple syrup of her choice. "No war, kids!" Azariah chastised.

Dan smiled at Azariah and let go of the brown sugar.

Kaitlyn had ignored Azariah's reprimand because she had been focused on Dan. As Kaitlyn saw Dan's gaze on Azariah, she signed "W-H-A-T" with her free hand.

Azariah smirked and signed, "No war, children!" with her mouthful.

Kaitlyn stuck out her tongue and ate her hard-earned brown sugar. When she was done, she smiled triumphantly at Dan and placed the bag on his side of the table.

"I should add 'Brat' to the long list of qualities I admire about her," Dan reflected.

Two muffin halves were remaining when the meal came to an end, and Azariah slid their serving plate in front of Kaitlyn, who shook her head. "All yours, Danny child," Azariah said as she slid the muffins over to Dan.

He smiled and took each of them. Until biting into one, he told Kaitlyn, "My parents own a Lake Tahoe condo. They will not be there the next weekend. If you want to head up there next weekend, leaving on Friday evening?"

Kaitlyn's face lit up, she gave a huge smile, and then she looked at Azariah. "However, Azariah's birthday is on Saturday. She'll be... 2...9..."

Azariah was swatting at Kaitlyn's hands, attempting to silence her.

"Are you having a dance, or is anyone planning one for you?" Dan inquired, giggling at Azariah and Kaitlyn's swatting session.

"There's nothing important," Azariah said.

"Then you come, and you can also carry a date if you like. Three bedrooms are available, "Daniel told Azariah.

"Well, I will just be..." Azariah began. Kaitlyn was waving her arm and laughing brightly as she came to a halt.

"I suppose Kaitlyn just replied for you!" With a smile, Dan said.

"All right," Azariah said. "Why don't we put in any extra hours over the next few days and quit after lunch on Friday? We will take my VW Atlas, which has plenty of room."

"Excellent," Dan said. "I think that's okay?" Kaitlyn inquires.

She enthusiastically nodded.

"Can you then be ready when Azariah and I return from work on Friday, and should you pack any perishable foods that we may like to consume in a cooler? Nothing new is held there."

Kaitlyn sent him her approval with two thumbs up.

"You all, as well as your date Azariah, would require strong windbreakers, comfortable clothing for dinner out, and proper walking shoes for that dinner," Dan said.

He saw two sets of puzzled brows lifted. Azariah also said, "I doubt I'll have a 'date' since most of my friends have tickets and parties scheduled for this weekend's Giants-Dodgers game at Oracle Stadium. I'm not a lover of baseball."

Dan mumbled to Azariah as he bit into one of the two remaining English muffins, "Maybe you'll run into someone up there. The walls of the bedroom do not adjoin!"

"You were feeding, and I didn't hear what you just said," Kaitlyn said when he saw Azariah knock him under the table.

Dan just grinned and smirked. He saw Kaitlyn's face get agitated, and she turned to look at Azariah for a response. Azariah snickered with her ears down.

—— Friday, Lake Tahoe ——

The three of them were almost to Tahoe City after leaving at 12:30 PM, escaping rush hour traffic and traveling north of San Pablo Bay to meet Interstate 80. Azariah had completed the whole three and a half hours of driving. They were on State Highway 89, which runs across the beautiful Truckee River.

Azariah turned to Kaitlyn as Tahoe City approached, touched her shoulder, and said, "I haven't been here in a long time. So, how are you?"

Dan unbuckled his seatbelt and moved forward from the back seat to see Kaitlyn's answer.

Kaitlyn signed, "Never."

Dan said, "Take the exit for 89 South. As we reach the bridge, we can see the lake behind the tiny dam as we turn."

Kaitlyn signed as they crossed the small bridge, "Oh my goodness! What a lovely image. It's far larger than I thought. So what were all those people staring at below the bridge?"

"The lake is 25 miles long, 11 miles large, and big," he said, adding that "the bridge's nickname is Fanny Bridge since people hangover to look at the many massive trout down there, which are off-limits. To fishermen."

"Azariah, you'll turn left at the peak of this little rise in around a half-mile," Dan said.

Dan said to her as she turned around, "The Tahoe Tavern Properties have arrived. Continue straight and enter the first parking spot on the right."

As they arrived at the condo, they gathered armfuls of baggage, and Dan unlocked the front door and ushered them in.

"Wow," Azariah exclaimed, "look at the lake view!"

Kaitlyn's mouth remained full.

"So, how do you like it?" Dan laughed.

Kaitlyn nodded enthusiastically, her hair flowing about her ears once more.

"Hell, yes!" exclaimed Azariah.

"This way to the bedrooms," Dan said. He guided Azariah to the left and Kaitlyn to the right as he leads them upstairs. "Sorry, you have the parking lot view, and we are in the master, so we get the lake view," he explained to Azariah.

"I have no concerns," Azariah hummed happily.

They were both done unloading. Dan then declared, "Azariah's birthday will be celebrated a day early with a dinner out. You both ought to be up at 6 p.m., with the appropriate walking shoes and something to keep your hair from blowing about."

Kaitlyn and Azariah exchanged confused looks before looking at Dan and nodding in approval.

"I have an errand to do," Dan said, "so I'll be back in half an hour." Dan stepped out of the patio doors and onto the huge common area grass, into the lakefront condos.

As he returned, there was no one downstairs, so he went upstairs. Azariah was washing, so he thought the guest bathroom was locked. He entered the apartment, then the master bath, where he discovered Kaitlyn nude and applying lipstick.

She caught sight of him behind her, through the slight smudge she had cleared from the steamed-up mirror.

He approached her from behind, put his arm around her breasts, reached up with his fist, and traced a heart in the steamed mirror.

"Enough, your dog, I have to get up," Kaitlyn said as she nodded and wiggled her buttocks towards him. His reading capabilities were tested by the reflected, inverted picture of her signing in the mirror.

He nuzzled her neck, inhaling all of her newly cleaned scents before returning to the bedroom to shift.

They had assembled in the living room just before 6 p.m. Dan looked around at his "tourists." Azariah's just-over-the-shoulder length, straight hair was pulled back in a ponytail, emphasizing her long neck and sharp jawline. Dan's gaze was drawn to Kaitlyn's face when he saw her hair braided for the first time. It widened her eyes, offering her a lovely charm that he had not expected."

"Do you like it?" Kaitlyn signed and bowed somewhat.

"Hell, yes," Dan mumbled. As he gazed down at Kaitlyn's emerald green wrap dress printed with yellow roses, he lost his ability to talk. He was drawn to the mid-thigh length and deep neckline, which revealed her cleavage and above since it was cut to just below her breasts.

Kaitlyn moved about behind Azariah after seeing his eyes were transfixed and not showing their lust. Dan's eyes widened when he saw Azariah's tentative grin; even though Azariah was around a half-foot taller. His gaze returned to the ground, and he noticed how little she was wearing. She was dressed in a bright yellow romper with a neckline that dropped to her slender waist. She was wearing a long gold chain, the strands of which intertwined as they succumbed to the extent of the cleavage between those round breasts.

Azariah half-turned to show him that it had no back, just two thin straps that crisscrossed across her shoulder blades. And her pronounced nipples made him think of how much time she would put in at work to hide them. The romper's slender, short length made her athletic legs seem incredibly long.

He was about to shape a sentence in his head when he saw Kaitlyn peeking out from behind Azariah with a huge, lecherous grin, and she winked. "Shit Azariah, any living male, would not skip you this evening," he said, pausing to swallow.

Azariah smiled shyly and said, "Ok, but I'm not shopping. In any case, you look pretty tasty dressing up like that."

"Well...thanks...with those...necklines...you'll certainly want your windbreakers," he stated, coming to his senses. We ought to keep going." He took a tiny flashlight from the counter and stowed it in the pocket of his windbreaker. He let them out by opening the front gates. He found they were still wearing the sensible shoes he had recommended.

The girls began walking towards Azariah's parked SUV, but he led them to a tarmac walkway instead. They pursued him for about 300 feet before coming to a set of stairs. The party descended the stairs for around 20 feet before they hit the pier's shore end.

"Wow, that was a long sentence!" Azariah said.

Dan turned around to meet them. "Although the pier has been restored, it dates back to the 1920s, when steamships docked here." It's 1,000 feet tall, but the water at the T-shaped end is just around 15 feet deep.

"So, we're having dinner on a boat?" Azariah inquired, delighted.

"Happy last day of your 28th year," Dan replied, a pleased smile on his face.

Kaitlyn hopped on her toes and clapped.

As they were almost at the end of the tall pier, they moved down a few steps on one foot, giving them entry to a lower decking where a boat was moored. As the girls climbed into the ferry, Dan extended his hand to steady them.

"This is fantastic!" "What is it?" Kaitlyn signed.

Dan answered, "A 22-foot Cobalt 220 bowrider."

As Dan went to untie the moorings, Kaitlyn glanced at Azariah. Azariah spelled out what Dan had meant in separately signed documents.

Dan started the boat and then idled out of the restricted area into a quiet bay. "Better sit down now and put on those windbreakers." It's just about a ten-minute flight."

Azariah kissed Kaitlyn on the arm, her eyes twinkling as she soaked in all around them, then nodded to the seat and the windbreaker. Kaitlyn gave a smile. Azariah and Kaitlyn stood across from Dan in the side-facing chairs.

Dan took the Cobalt up into the air and set an easy cruise to the south at about 33 miles per hour. He indicated a few of the big, old estate homes along the route.

—— Saturday Lake Tahoe Dinner ———

When he began to slow down, he looked ahead and said, "Sunnyside Restaurant." He docked between two other vessels at the marina facilities of the restaurant and helped the girls out. "This evening has been delightful. "Would you like to leave your coats here?"

Both Kaitlyn and Azariah tossed their jackets back onto the boat. The trio noticed the restaurant was reasonably busy when they stepped up to the back door. They have found that they were getting a lot of coverage, with several people staring at Azariah. They requested to be seated outdoors, on the deck, and rewarded with a beautiful view of the bay. Dan sat in the seat between them.

They requested cocktails (Kaitlyn-Mojito, Azariah-Chivas Regal/rocks, Dan-Herradura Margarita/rocks & salt, those interested) and easily got their beverages. Dan proposed a toast in honor of Azariah's birthday. Following the toast, the three became very still, taking in the landscape and the dark, evening shadows thrown by the tall pines into the crystal clear sea. Dan, too, glanced at the ladies sitting next to him and enthusiastically clicked his fingertips on the table near the base of his drink bottle.

"This is fantastic, Dan; thank you very much!" Azariah said, reaching out and wrapping her hand around Dan's. Azariah cast a glare at Kaitlyn, who sent her a threatening look before breaking into a big grin, winking, and reaching for Dan's other side.

Azariah laughed and wrapped her hand around Dan's.

Dan looked away, contentedly holding each of these women's paws. Their enjoyment of watching the shadows creep over the lake towards the eastern shore was cut short by request for their food orders (ok, for the curious out there: Shared Starter/Crispy Monterey Bay Calamari; Kaitlyn, Apple & Candied Pistachio Salad with Sautéed Fresh Fish; Dan, Caesar Salad with Peppercorn Crusted Ribeye; Azariah, Caesar Salad with Maine Lobster Tails [which Dan had]; Dan, Caesar Salad

Dan was surprised when Azariah's palm, almost accidentally, settled on his thigh after they had ended their meals, which included a shared bottle of Chardonnay. Kaitlyn was squeezing his side now that he wasn't enjoying his meal. They all stared back at the darkening horizon, where the shadows had hit, and left, the mountains on the lake's eastern shore. Kaitlyn was the most enthralled, her head swiveling and her eyes occasionally smiling at Dan with a delightful sparkle.

Dan offered a round of Sambuca since everybody was too tired for dessert. Kaitlyn and Azariah had no idea what Sambuca was, but they were intrigued when identified as licorice (anise) flavored. Dan placed an order for three burning Sambucas while whispering something to their server.

Azariah and Kaitlyn were a little drunk and readily listened to Dan's option.

When the server returned, three snifters of Sambuca were placed in front of Azariah, along with a serving of Lava Cake with a candle in it and a tiny box that began playing "Happy Birthday to You..." The torch, as well as the three Sambuca snifters, were illuminated by the server. Azariah and Kaitlyn were amazed by the flickering flames of the drinks as they danced around the table in the dim evening light for the few seconds of the flames' brief lives.

Kaitlyn signed, "Make a wish and blow out the torch!" as she clapped. Azariah hesitated before bending to extinguish the lone flame. Dan drew in his breath when the top of her sweater relaxed and bent out, revealing one full breast.

"To Azariah's birthday wish; can she get everything she needs," Dan said as he lifted his beer.

Azariah stroked Dan's leg a few times before removing her lingering hand. "Amen," she said.

Dan definitely noted Azariah's stroking of his leg, and then he noticed Kaitlyn's eyes shining at Azariah, with a look he didn't recognize but was probably intrigued by.

They all stood for a moment, taking in the rest of the view and sipping their Sambuca (which Kaitlyn and Azariah thought was delicious) before dusk deprived them of the last of the glory. What little illumination was left was now given by the almost full moon.

When they weren't admiring the local lights reflecting in the mist, Dan and Kaitlyn exchanged lustful glances. Azariah had been distracted at this time by two older men who had just entered and were sitting a few tables apart. Both persons, who seemed to be inebriated, were seated facing Azariah. Neighboring tables were writhing and staring at the two boisterous guys.

Kaitlyn first observed the improvement on Azariah's face. Dan captured Kaitlyn's gaze and shifted to face Azariah. Her transformation was palpable. He compared her expression to that of restrained anger.

"Are you well, Azariah?"

"But they're not going to be!" She snarled. She swiveled her chair.

Dan snatched her arm. "What are you doing?!?"

"There are two...dick wads...over there presume Kat and I are a bunch of cheap whores who should be on our hands and knees crying for their cocks," Azariah spat out. And they believe you're too dumb to know what to do about our...pussies." Azariah's face twisted into a malicious smile, and she exclaimed to Dan, "I read lips, too! "You two wait here, and I'll be right out."

Azariah sprang out of the chair, snatching Dan's wrist. She then took a hiatus to arrange her face.

Dan began to turn his chair when he noticed Kaitlyn's strong grasp on his shoulder. He jerked his head up to look at her and saw her calmly sign, "Just wait." "She'll be perfect."

Azariah faked a sexy grin and walked over to the two men with her finest runway model move. "Hey babe, you comin' over for some real action?" exclaimed the bulkier of the two guys.

She knelt and placed her palms on the counter. Both men's gazes are drawn to her jiggling, almost bare chest.

"I read lips, you two fucking scumbags!" We're not whores, even even though we were, I wouldn't touch your pathetic Viagra-powered dicks for a million dollars. Given your wedding bands, I'm guessing you two have wives that would not want you two slime balls to access their bodies either. And if you assume I'd crawl and ask for some man's dick, think again...

"BITCH!" exclaimed the bulkier guy as he got up from his position.

Dan jerked around in his chair, but Kaitlyn's grasp tightened. He calmed down but remained stressed while he listened.

Azariah saw the bulkier man's shoulder and elbow drawback, accompanied by an open hand. "Thank you," she said to herself when she noticed the slap approaching from a mile out. She quickly stopped his arm before grabbing his hand and bending it down at his wrist. The guy yelped in confusion and discomfort before settling back into his seat.

"HEY!" shouted the other guy at the table, reaching for Azariah. She had already practiced for this by slamming her heel onto his foot. He screamed in agony, his arm retracting.

"I am the boss," a trembling voice beside her said. Is there an issue here?"

"Of course!" Azariah retorted. "These two testosterone clowns believe my friend and I are for rent and that we should be crying at their foot for the honor of...entertaining their manhood."

"Bitch, I'm going to..." yelled the bulkier guy, his face already red and contorted from Azariah's grasp on his hand.

"Another term and I'll charge you with the attack," Azariah snarled, "and another pass, and I'll crack this chicken wrist, you fucking misogynist!"

Azariah turned back to find the boss and some other employees gathered around the table.

"Sirs," the manager said, "you are no longer wanted at this restaurant, now or in the future." Your payment will be treated. I'll call the cops if you don't quit right away."

"

"Okay, okay, we're off," the two men agreed. Azariah relaxed her grip on his wrist.

The boss led Azariah back to her table while the workers accompanied the men out. "I'm so sorry, miss," he apologized amid cheers.
"It wasn't your fault, and you treated it very well," Azariah said. She sighed as she relaxed in the chair he had taken out for her.
"Of course, your dinner is on the house," the boss said.
"Oh, that sounds overly kind," she remarked, before adding conspiratorially, "No, I quite enjoyed myself!"

The boss smiled easily before regaining his calm. He motioned to the waitress, who approached, and the manager drew a circle around the bar. The server nodded and walked forward.

"How about lunch here tomorrow, my actual birthday?" Azariah asked Dan and Kaitlyn.

Kaitlyn enthusiastically nodded, and Dan nodded as well, releasing anxiety with a deep sigh.

"Deal?" Azariah inquired of the boss.

"More than fair," said the boss, "whatever you like, plus all liquor tonight is complimentary."

Kaitlyn tapped on the bar, and everybody turned to look at her. "Are bikinis permitted on the deck at lunch?" she signed. Azariah relayed the query to the director.

"They sure are, and you two will make a beautiful addition to the scenery," the boss said, winking.

The manager then excused himself just as the server returned with three more Sambucas, easily lit.

When the fires were extinguished, Kaitlyn tapped her glass and wrote, "To Azariah's bravery!" before raising her glass. Dan lifted his bottle in celebration. Azariah smiled at them as they sipped their drinks.

"You had me scared; you had me worried!" Dan said.

"I'm sorry," Azariah said shyly, "I forget you didn't know." She sipped her Sambuca after having waited the appropriate amount of time.

"Wait, what?"

"That my father was a former police officer and that I have a second-degree black belt."

"Wow, if I had realized that before you took off, it would have helped my adrenaline level!"

"Once again, I apologize," Azariah said, placing her hand on his face.

Dan was taken aback by Azariah's contact, particularly because Kaitlyn had placed her hand on his. Azariah retracted her hand, and they all sipped their Sambuca slowly.

He advised them to return as soon as possible since it was almost 9 p.m. and they would drive longer in the dark. He motioned for the server to deliver the bill, then resisted Azariah's requests to split the charge.

When he eventually persuaded Azariah that he was serious about covering the whole bill, she bent over. She embraced him, saying, "Thank you for one of the greatest evenings I have ever had."

Dan froze for a second, then stared at Kaitlyn, who seemed strange, as though she was attempting to hide a healthy smile on her face.

They marched to the boat after paying the bill. Dan helped them board, and they put on their windbreakers while Dan started the motor and untied the mooring ropes.

Dan pulled away from the docks, turned on the marker lights, and then idled away. "Can you bring the fenders in?" Dan inquired.

In the dusk, Kaitlyn couldn't see his lips clearly, but she noticed Azariah pull up the string on one of the fenders, so she pulled up the other one.

He took the Cobalt up to a deep plane at around 25 mph, at which stage the bow fell back down for improved visibility. There was plenty of moonlight, and he understood just how to get back.

Dan saw Kaitlyn standing by the windshield, her braided hair blown across her waist, smiling at him. Azariah's hands were on his shoulders, and he thought she was standing behind him on her feet. Dan saw Kaitlyn motioning to Azariah but couldn't see what she was doing enough in the dim sum. He couldn't see Azariah shake her head and say, "No!"

Whatever they were talking about, Dan couldn't drive and think simultaneously as they cruised through the darkness. Their boat was the only one they could hear and see on the glassy clear seas.

Dan saw Kaitlyn was quiet, and she pointed above his head. Azariah's breasts brushed against the back of his head when she bent forward to kiss his forehead as he glanced away. When he lowered his head, he saw Kaitlyn grin and wink at him, and he felt Azariah pat his shoulder twice.

He was perplexed as to why Azariah was giving him so much publicity. "Sure, it was her birthday dinner," he reasoned, "but it seems to be more than that, and Kaitlyn seems to be involved with whatever is going on."

Azariah bent down into Dan's ear shortly after the forehead kiss and exclaimed, "Uh oh, I see the look!"

Dan saw Kaitlyn removing her windbreaker as he glanced at her. She then untied her wrap dress and stuffed her belongings into a holding bag. Dan stood there watching her drive her nude body past the two access panels to the front. He saw her rise, lean down, hands on the bow fence, and watch her braided hair thrash in the still, cold breeze. He could see the joy in her smile.

He shook his head at the sight of her pleasure, completely oblivious to the fact that this action will brush against his mammary headrest. When he felt Azariah lean forward, he said to her, "That is the lady I have fallen in love with."

"And she loves you very much," Azariah responded to his ear. Remember that sometimes though she's...extremely...generous."

As they approached the Tahoe Tavern pier, Dan pondered the answer as well. Kaitlyn stepped back behind the windshield, laughing from ear to ear as the moon illuminated her lovely frame, and then she re-applied her dress and windbreaker.

They soon docked, and he assisted the ladies. "Give me a couple of minutes: I need to attach the boat to the buoy." He tethered the tender dinghy to the stern and cruised around to his buoy. He rowed the tender back to the port after securing the Cobalt.

He could tell Kaitlyn tried to say something as he approached the children in the dock's dim illumination.

"I am a bit intoxicated," Kaitlyn signed. "Can you just hold me up?"

He turned to Azariah, who replied, "Me too, please?"

Dan grinned and stepped between them, wrapping his arm around both of their necks.

Azariah wrapped her arm around Dan's neck, and Kaitlyn reached into Dan's back pocket and grabbed his butt. They walked the length of the pier before splitting up when they needed to go up the stairs, which they did by hanging on to each other.

—— Friday Night at Lake Tahoe at the Condo ——

As they returned to the condo, they put up their windbreakers, decided they were exhausted, and went to bed. Kaitlyn began to unbraid her hair. All went upstairs and into their respective bedrooms.

Kaitlyn whipped off her dress as soon as their bedroom door closed, signing, "I have had a wonderful evening so far."

"I'll see what I can do to keep your fun going," Dan said, a wide smile on his face.

"Why don't you begin right here?" she said as she stretched her legs eagle on the king-sized bed.

Dan immediately undressed and sank to his knees to run his tongue along her folds.

When her legs began to quake, she had to retract them to get her foot on the top of the mattress.

Dan proceeded, inducing two orgasms in her before entering her.

This night, she tried to be a tiger, so she clamped his shaft. Kaitlyn managed to concentrate long enough to see him cum. She narrowly made it because a few seconds after he finished, deep inside her, her own body stunned her in that peaceful moment, bursting out in shudders, and she hung on for the bliss that followed.

Kaitlyn glanced at the clock as they lay there, relaxing in pleasure, and noticed that it was 12:03 a.m. She stood up, soaked a washcloth in warm water, ringed it, and handed it to Dan to clean himself. She waited as he did before cleaning herself.

She shifted to the foot of the bed after putting the washcloth in the toilet. With a big twinkle in her smile, Kaitlyn signed, "I love you very much." Can you believe me when I claim my feelings for you can never change?"

"Uh...Yes...Of course," he replied, perplexed by the existence of the query and the time of night.

Kaitlyn unlocked the bedroom door and exited nude. She came back in a minute later, guiding Azariah, who was clad in a mid-thigh length nightshirt. Azariah's gaze was fixed downward.

Dan was taken aback as he saw Kaitlyn's bright smile.

"I decided to send Azariah her birthday gift now, if you accept," Kaitlyn signed.

"Well...uh...sure...but where is her present?" fumbled Dan.

Kaitlyn's smile widened, her eyes sparkled with envy, and she hopped on her toes. "It's you!" she signed.

Dan looked at Kaitlyn, perplexed: "There was no doubt, she was extreme." "So you want me to have sex with Azariah tonight?"

"Tonight, this morning...I want you to be hers for the whole day!" Kaitlyn agreed to sign.

Azariah's eyes were filled with expectation as she smiled up at Dan.

Dan scooped up onto the bunk. "Why don't you two come to sit on the bed with me and help me get my mind around this?"

As he had asked, Kaitlyn and Azariah sat on the edge of the bunk.

"Are you cool with this?" Dan asked Azariah.

"Danny child, I have had the hots for you for as long as I have known you...and before there were workplace stories regarding you," Azariah said, giggling at the last section.

"But I felt you and Kaitlyn were a perfect fit and that she always wanted you in her life," Azariah said. I like you a lot, but I've also lusted for you in my bed. But I had no hope of following through with that thought. I cherished our relationship and didn't want to jeopardize it."

"This is all because of Sinful, here: this beautiful, caring friend who needs me to get everything I've longed for, even though it's the guy she likes," Azariah continued. I warned you of her unexpected gifts and kindness."

Kaitlyn smiled broadly and bounced on the bunk, shifting her sparkling eyes to hear what Dan had to suggest.

"I...I am...well, very conflicted," Dan sighed, "seeing the woman I love, dearly, urging me to take another woman, her best friend, and show her all the affection I have for her...Sinful...if I understand correctly?"

Kaitlyn enthusiastically nodded, glanced at Azariah, and then back at Dan. Signed 'Sinful,' "No exceptions, whatever Azariah desires and whatever you believe would satisfy her. And I would never have single remorse until you put your whole self into satisfying her...even though it means ignoring me for the whole day."

"God, this sounds weird, he said, admitting to this. "But it's still very enticing now that I've permitted myself to consider it. I lusted after you as well, Azariah, but didn't want to jeopardize our healthy relationship. I believe that doing things this way would help us in any way."

"It's getting late, and it might seem strange just to hop into this," Azariah said, "but can I recommend that we get some sleep...all three of us...here...and, like they claim, 'get a fresh start on stuff' in the morning?"

"Just act like I'm not here," Kaitlyn signed.

"Doubt that would succeed!" Azariah grinned as she stared at Dan.

Dan agreed with a smile.

"Come on in, my lovelies," Dan welcomed them.

Dan slid under the blankets and lay flat on his stomach. Kaitlyn scooted in on his right, and Azariah was about to enter on his left when she saw Dan looking her over.

"Correct," Azariah said, squeezing her nightshirt over her head with a sexy wiggle. Kaitlyn's playful grin peered across Dan's chest.

Dan was shocked by Azariah's physique, her toned abs, and then watched her huge breasts scarcely move as she transitioned from reaching above her head to holding her hands at her feet.

She slid in next to him and took his hand in hers. "This would be a memorable birthday," she added.

Before Dan could react, he felt Kaitlyn, aka Sinful, knock on his back, causing him to roll into Azariah.

"Seems the manager, back here, is getting restless," Dan said softly as he rolled against Azariah's tall body and felt her hand release his.

"There aren't any complaints here," Azariah purred. Then she leaned up towards him and kissed him gently on the stomach.

Dan put his hand on her back and stroked it softly. He brushed his hand across her tight buttocks after a few strokes.

She reacted by draping her upper leg over him and pressing her stomach against him.

He traced his fingers up the leg that was covering him, around her thigh, then up her side, finishing with his palm on her breast.

Azariah lavishly hummed.

"Good night, gorgeous," Dan said as he shifted his hand to her waist. Dan could feel Kaitlyn relax behind them and then spoon up behind him, kissing his shoulder blade.

Azariah said, "Good night, to the 'three' of you," as she gently stroked her hand up the broad shaft rubbing against her mons, before coming to rest on his shoulder.

"Mmmmm," Dan muttered when he noticed Kaitlyn lick his back again.

Saturday Morning —— Lake Tahoe ——

Azariah awoke, spooning against Dan's back, her arm stretched around his hip, her fingertips scarcely sensing his pubic hair. She put her hand on his hip bone, using it as support to pull herself up. She saw the time was 8:32 a.m. but did not see Kaitlyn. Then she heard the sound of a shower going, but it was in her guest bathroom, not the master, and the bedroom door was shut.

"Morning Azariah, you sexy creature," Dan murmured.

She said, "Then you remembered it wasn't Sinful, just me?

"I'm sorry, my darling, but I don't wake up with globes pressing against me."

"They're true, too," she said quietly.

"Let me check," Dan said as he rolled over and massaged her breasts. He knelt and sucked on her breast.

Her air came in as a hissing hissing hissing hissing

"Damn if they aren't!" he exclaimed, "because these nipples are incredible." The nearest analogy I can think of is the caps on a bottle of lipstick balm. How do you keep them hidden at work?"

"I'm glad you like them. To let you know, they even have a way of turning me on. So take things slowly unless you want to spend the whole day in bed with me. I sometimes wear nipple covers to function. It's a nuisance, but seeing pokies like these keeps the men occupied."

"They'd be a distraction to me!" "And, just testing, but are you really on board with Sinful's plan?" he asked.

"I am overjoyed," Azariah said, "but I did have an idea to change it." Kaitlyn's damp head poked in after she noticed two taps on the handle. Azariah waved her in, saying, "Just on cue!"

Azariah winked at Dan and shifted her side, which was still under the covers, to Dan's groin. She began to move her hand up and down, causing the sheets to rise and fall quickly.

Kaitlyn's mouth opened for a split second before her pupils sparkled.

"Just trying to see if you were all on board with this idea!" Azariah said. Azariah had unintentionally left her hand lying over Dan's hardening dick, pinning it down.

Kaitlyn rolled her eyes before smiling and nodding.

"I'd like to change the schedule," Azariah said.

"All right, how?" Kaitlyn agreed to sign.

"Because we have a free lunch today, and I'd like to do some boating, and maybe even water skiing, if that's okay with Dan, I'd prefer we all enjoy today, then he's mine for the evening, night, and morning? After that, can we gather our belongings and return home?" Azariah volunteered to help.

Azariah turned to face Dan, who nodded.

Azariah glanced at Kaitlyn, who had her arms crossed and was attempting to be agitated.

Dan and Azariah began laughing madly at a naked, soggy Kaitlyn.

Kaitlyn agreed to sign, "Okay, we'll put it off until tomorrow. But then, you fuck Azariah senseless. Otherwise, you'll have to live with me!" Kaitlyn stormed into the master bathroom.

Dan and Azariah exchanged a playful smile of surprise. "I guess we've got our orders!" With a short joke, Dan said.

"We don't want her to be upset, do we?" Azariah concurred, smiling as well.

—— Lake Tahoe —— Afternoon ——

They stood up to return to the boat after finishing their delicious free lunch. Kaitlyn and Azariah's little bikinis drew much more attention than when they first visited. Kaitlyn wore a yellow thong bikini with three triangles of very thin cloth, just enough to cover her clipped strawberry bush and those rosy, puffy areolas.

Azariah's bikini was a little less revealing. It was a teal blue with a triangle in the back and sides, connected by cords tied in bows. The top was similar to Kaitlyn's, except with somewhat bigger triangles to shield the bottoms of her much larger breasts. The top, as the bottom, was bound around the neck and below the shoulder blades with bow-tied cords. Azariah had used a thicker terrycloth material to conceal her prominent nipples. Neither swimsuit was conducive to ogling.

Dan refueled the ships, and they set off south along the shoreline. Fortunately, it was another quiet day, and the journey was good. As she traveled in the bow seating section, the sunlight reflected off of Kaitlyn's fair face, making it seem much brighter. Behind her sunglasses, she grinned incessantly as she glanced about. Azariah sat behind Dan, her hand on his back at times, her fingertips in his hair at others, and sometimes sitting up and playing the part of his headrest.

He took them to Rubicon Bay after going through many bays. He had a lot of fun getting visitors here. He eased the boat to a leisurely pace. The bay's floor was made up of large swaths of white sand. It did, though, have massive black volcanic boulders scattered around it. The boulders were shocking when the boat quickly crossed each one, even though they were 20+ feet underwater, due to the clear water allowing visibility to a depth of 75'. Kaitlyn was startled sufficiently by the first one that she jumped aside.

Azariah climbed the stairs to the bow seating to search after herself. Both girls were wearing polarized lenses, which amplified the visual impact of the boulders. They were all smiling as they walked over more boulders. Dan then maneuvered the boat to a location where the lake floor abruptly fell, revealing sand on one side of the boat and just blue water on the other.

Kaitlyn turned to Dan and signed, "Wonderful!" before sprinting over to him and kissing him on the lips.

Dan noticed her eyes exactly mirrored the lake's hue when she removed her shades, and he looked into them.

Kaitlyn took a step back and then signed, "Enough of this, my love. Remember, Azariah is your love for today... I'm off to the pool!"

She had bounced to the back of the boat before he could alert her. Azariah saw Kaitlyn standing up on the stern. Azariah placed her hand over her mouth when she heard Dan say, "Wait," but she realized his speech was futile and recognized the reflexive action.

Kaitlyn executed a stunning plunge, slicing through the clear sea. She drew herself up on the hard landing about 4 seconds later, a shocked expression on her lips. "Shit, that's freezing!" screamed her lips.

Azariah and Dan burst out laughing as they watched Kaitlyn take her towel and tie it around her, concealing her now-translucent bikini.

"You didn't give me a chance to warn you that the lake is so deep that the majority of the surface temperature is in the low 50's, and lower, it's around 37," Dan said as he shifted the Cobalt back towards forwarding.

For the few minutes it took to get to Emerald Bay, Kaitlyn sat behind the windbreak of the windshield, with Azariah looking back at them in the bow seating. He slowed to the appropriate "No Wake" level and enabled them to look about. Kaitlyn followed Azariah in the front row and replenished her sunscreen lotion. He showed them Vikingsholm and Fannet Island, Lake Tahoe's only island.

Dan waved to Azariah as they exited Emerald Bay. As she returned, he wondered if she wanted to go water skiing. She did, and she just needed to use one ski. He showed her where they were kept, along with the ski ropes and belt, and apologized for the lack of a wetsuit. Azariah retrieved the objects and attached the ski string. About the fact that he had a rearview mirror, he told Kaitlyn how to spot for him.

When they returned to Rubicon Bay, the water was already somewhat quiet, so he brought the boat to a halt. Azariah donned a flotation vest and made her way to the stern platform.

When he had carefully tossed out the ski rope so that she could easily grab it, he said, "Ready?"

She grimaced as she sunk into the cold bath. "Oh crap, get this fuckin' boat going!" she screamed as he moved to the driver's seat.

He pushed the boat along easily but cautiously to tighten the ski rope. He increased the power after she waved. Azariah swayed twice before straightening up. They'd been on the road for around 6 minutes, with Azariah doing several crossings of the wake before Kaitlyn patted Dan on the back and said Azariah was able to drop off. Kaitlyn indicated to Azariah to ensure they were set, and he agreed.

Azariah let go, almost coming to a stop, before grimacing and sinking to her shoulders. Dan had already swung the boat around and was on his way back to her. Azariah climbed to the stern deck, and Kaitlyn drew in the rope because she had already promised Dan she would not bother skiing.

"Great lake to learn to ski on," Azariah said, "and you don't want to plunge into the icy water, SOB."

Azariah sat beside Kaitlyn, across from Dan, who got the boat back up to cruising level.

"Looks like your nipples felt it was freezing!" Dan grinned when he glanced down at them.

Azariah lowered her gaze and then drew her bikini back, exposing both breasts and their fat, wrinkled nipples. "I believe," she said.

Dan glared for as long as he could stand it before Kaitlyn bent forward to suck the closest nipple.

"Greedy," Azariah said.

Kaitlyn's eyes glowed with mischief, and she yanked off her bikini cover. She went to stand in the bow like she had done the night before. Her shades were protecting her eyes this time, and her hair was flailing about.

A moving vessel honked its whistle. Kaitlyn motioned for Azariah to follow her as she grinned at the ferry. Azariah was reapplying sunscreen as she went up front and stood next to Kaitlyn, hanging onto the railing. When the next boat passed, it began to toot its horn. Sinful yanked down on one side of Azariah's bikini bra. Azariah's dark red areola matched even more with her complexion than Kaitlyn's rosy pink did with her pale skin. The other boat blared its trumpet for a long time.

Azariah swatted at Kaitlyn's hand and, after it was removed, grinned back at Dan with amusement. Dan smiled and shrugged.

Azariah placed her hands on her bikini front as the next boat approached. Kaitlyn reached behind her and yanked on the thread, untying the lower knot. Azariah didn't care as she kept her gaze fixed on the approaching ferry. Azariah removed her hands and grinned while the next boat tooted happily.

Her bikini top blew up underneath her chin. She lowered her gaze and immediately protected her nipples. As the other boat happily tooted its whistle, it wasn't fast enough. When the boat passed by, Azariah saw two girls onboard, one driving and the other topless, and they waved cheerfully.

Kaitlyn reached up and began yanking Azariah's top off her ears. Azariah raised her hand to stop her, then withdrew to cover her breasts.

"Damn you, brat," Azariah retorted.

Kaitlyn protruded her tongue before stuffing Azariah's top under one of the cushions.

The next two vessels, which were racing together, were not usual of the sport boats on this lake. They had small, flat-bottomed hulls with uncovered engines that blared from unsubmerged exhausts. Both vessels had a driver and a customer, both of whom were well-tanned young men. As Kaitlyn waved, they tooted long blats of their air horns.

Azariah may hear their engines appear to fade away as they died but then rev up and become louder again. As she noticed the boats coming, she tapped Kaitlyn on the back and pointed back before rapidly retrieving her breast. The boats drew up alongside Dan, close but not too nearly, and shouted, "Show us your tits!" and hooted.

Kaitlyn smiled and raised both of her fingers at Azariah's breasts, turning her pointing fingers back and forth. The cries from the two warships were much more audible. Azariah dropped her hands, blushing and staring at Kaitlyn.

"OH, YEAH!" yelled one passenger over the din of the engines as he slid out of his seat. Azariah waved nervously, and the two vessels honked, their passengers waved, and the boats peeled off, turning south again.

Azariah covered her face behind her paws. As she looked up, she saw Dan give her a thumbs up. She poked him with her tongue, then looked at Kaitlyn's smiling smile. She was so preoccupied that she didn't see the next sail, a bigger cruiser. When a deeper horn rang long and hard, she turned around to find at least six people on board staring at her.

Azariah waved, almost cheerfully, despite her defeat. Kaitlyn jumped behind Azariah, put her arms around her, and danced her palms up and down under Azariah's huge tits. The whistles could be seen over the deep diesel thrum. Azariah swatted at Kaitlyn's hands before re-covering her lips.

Azariah swallowed her humiliation and kept her breasts bare for the remainder of the cruise back, even jiggling them playfully for a hooting boatload of what seemed to be adolescents.

When they got closer to the Tahoe Tavern dock, Kaitlyn returned Azariah's bikini top and placed her own back on.

As the clock approached 5 p.m., Dan wondered whether they could pick up a slice. They all decided, so Dan sailed past the Tavern's pier and docked at the city pier, aka the Safeway supermarket pier, a few minutes later. Dan tested the girls' topping preferences before returning around 10 minutes later with a take-and-bake type pie. He discovered multiple young men attempting to chat up the laughing Azariah and Kaitlyn.

Dan handed in the pizza, had Azariah start the engine, and then let go of the mooring ropes. He hopped in and took a seat.

Kaitlyn wiggled her almost naked butt at the young men and then climbed on Dan's lap.

Azariah stood behind Dan, blushing slightly, shaking her breasts, and then performing her headrest routine.

The young men on the dock were crying, patting their chests, and begging Kaitlyn and Azariah to return. Their excitement was also visible in their bulging swimsuits.

Azariah and Kaitlyn slumped on the bench seating and burst out laughing as the Cobalt idled by the moored ship, with Kaitlyn's huffs becoming the loudest Dan has ever heard from her.

Dan's amusement had subsided by the time he returned to the Tahoe Tavern dock, and he said he ought to moor on the buoy and cover the boat in case they didn't need it again until they departed.

Kaitlyn and Azariah agreed to carry the pizza back to the condo. Azariah even spoke about arm and shoulder aches from not having water skied in a long time. They took the keys to the condo that Dan had given them.

Dan saw them reaching the shoreline and ascending the stairs while he made final tests for oil volume, bilge water, and other items before covering the boat and rowing the tender dinghy back from the buoy.

Saturday Evening —— Lake Tahoe Condo ——

When Dan returned to the condo, he saw no one but noticed several groans from upstairs. He went upstairs with caution, attempting to stay discreet. As he reached the peak, he looked into the second guest room and saw Azariah sprawled out on the massage table, with a naked Kaitlyn massaging her shoulders. He reached out and gently kissed Kaitlyn on the back.

She turned and smiled at him as she continued to massage Azariah.

He placed a finger over his lips to prevent her from detecting his existence. He signed his name, "So you found the table and the gasoline, I see. It's about my father's sore back." Then he looked at Azariah's legs and then at Kaitlyn's.

Kaitlyn paused for a second before grinning ever wider and going down to rub Azariah's calves, which elicited even more groans.

Dan rubbed his hands down Kaitlyn's back, finishing with a butt squeeze, and felt her wiggle in response. Then he moved to the side of the massage table, away from Azariah's face, and applied massage oil to his palms. He then took a step forward and began massaging her hair.

"HELLO! oooooh..." "Didn't realize I had an octopus for a masseuse!" Azariah screamed, then purred.

Kaitlyn asked Dan a question because she couldn't see Azariah's lips, and she saw Dan smile back at her and tell, "She is content. I'll let you know if she mentions something important."

Dan was at the far end of the massage table, above Azariah's head. He then shifted his weight into his hands and ran down all sides of her spine until he hit her bikini bottoms; the top was nowhere to be found.

Azariah purred loudly, "MMMmmmmmmmmmmmmmmmmmmmmmmmmmmmmmmmmmmmmmmmmmmmmmmmmmmmmmmmmmmmmmmmmmmmmmmmmmmmmmmmmmmmmmmmmmmmmmmmmmmmmmmmmmmmmmmmmmmmmmmmmmmmmmmmmmmmmmmmmmmmm

He drew his hands back up along Azariah's sides, touching those flattened breasts, then out over her upper arms, which hung over the table's sides. He could see her body arching and then sagging. With Kaitlyn's help, he saw her legs shifting and rolling gently.

After a few minutes of working together, Kaitlyn began massaging Azariah's feet' soles. Azariah's body tensed, and she reached out and grasped Dan's waist as a reflex. Recognizing her chance, she reached down the front of his stomach, beneath his swim trunks, and gripped his thick shaft, which had been bumping against her head. She squeezed it firmly before beginning to massage him.

Kaitlyn had been laughing at Dan when she saw his face alter. She glanced down and found Azariah's hand gone, as well as the movements it was doing.

Dan saw Kaitlyn's eyes mischievously and then saw her untie the cords at the side of Azariah's bikini bottom before exposing Azariah's butt.

Kaitlyn swatted one buttock and watched Azariah's hip bounce.

Azariah said, "OUCH, Hey!" followed by a joke, which Dan overheard. Azariah's free hand then reached out and extended her middle finger at Kaitlyn.

Kaitlyn had foreseen what was about to happen and had even knelt. So, when Azariah flipped her off, Kaitlyn knelt, stuck her finger in her cheek, and pulled hard.

"Now this IS fascinating," Azariah exclaimed as she stroked Dan and Kaitlyn licked her finger.

Dan saw Kaitlyn's eyes looking up at him after a couple of minutes, and he motioned for them to turn. Dan then slowly loosened Azariah's grasp on his tight manhood.

"That's not fair. Please return my doll!" Azariah said with a pouty tone.

He saw Kaitlyn shrug and said to her, "She is horny...wants her toy back."

"Poor kid," Kaitlyn signed with her oily hands before grinning and returning to work on Azariah.

Dan rubbed some oil into his palms while he saw Kaitlyn dig her claws into Azariah's shoulders. Dan placed his hands on Azariah's ankles for a few moments before sliding his hands up the inside of her calves and then her thighs. He kissed her labia before spreading his palms and massaging her tight buns.

"Mmmmm...fair enough. Forget what I said and stay where you are, "Azariah uttered a coo.

Dan indicated Kaitlyn make Azariah change over after a little more pelvic treatment. Then they all helped Azariah, who was mildly panting, sit centered on the table and remove her sagging bikini bottoms.

"You realize we're entering hazardous territories here, don't you?" Azariah said this with her eyes closed but a wide grin on her face.

Dan separated her wings. "Yes, it seems to be risky. A guy might easily get disoriented in there."

Dan stared at Kaitlyn, who had the sly grin on her face as she wrote, "No mercy!" He agreed with a smile.

Azariah responded to Dan by saying, "Just let me know if you get stuck in there...assuming you want to get out. I will assist you...SHIT!" The last term came out when she saw Kaitlyn pinch both of her nipples and Dan's oiled hands slip tightly across her vulva.

Dan rubbed both thumbs into her wetness and then tightly up between her outer and inner labia as Kaitlyn ran her fingertips in soft circles across Azariah's tight nipples.

Azariah's back arched immediately, and she hissed, "Really, both of you!

...Oh, DAMN!"

Dan heard a beeping from downstairs and asked Kaitlyn, "Is the pizza in the oven?" after a minute or two of Azariah's arching and hissing out more four-letter terms.

Kaitlyn's expression flashed in surprise as she dashed out of the room and downstairs, holding her oily hands off the railing.

Dan swept his thumb over Azariah's clitoral area. He sank the middle finger of his free hand into her wetness when he felt her arch again and heard her scream. He replied with a second finger after hearing a louder gasp. He then curled his fingertips around until he discovered the texture of her g-spot.

Azariah was writhing on the table; her legs stretched with her knees dangling off the edges. Her paws were in a death lock on the table's arms. Her mouth hanging open after a repressed yell of "YEEeeeeeeeeeeeeeeeeeeeeeeeeeeeeeeeeeeeeeee

Dan stroked her insides and rubbed his thumb across her clitter.

Azariah exclaimed loudly, "GEEeeeeezz...And...FUCK YES!" Kaitlyn returned with three plates of pizza, which she put on the table.

With her mouth full but a smile on her face, she signed to Dan, "I'm glad I didn't skip the major end. I'm starving, so get her off."

Dan smiled and took off his circling thumb. He made up for it by placing his lips on her dancing clit while his fingers were occupied inside Azariah.

Azariah was still on the verge of orgasm, and Dan's wet tongue laps and twirls pushed her off the brink. "FU........." she screamed, and that was the extent of her vocabulary until she drew in a big breath, pressed her hips against Dan, and started to shiver. It began in her thighs and rapidly spread from there. Azariah was limited to heaving breaths and twitches after many long moments.

Azariah's vacant stare looked up as she opened her eyes, and she saw Kaitlyn smiling back.

"Great show...loved the closing," Kaitlyn said, adding, "Would you like some pizza?"

Azariah chuckled, her face contorted in a ridiculous smile "You precious knucklehead. I think I should get washed up first."

"I'll help," Dan said as he cleaned the soles of Azariah's foot. He then escorted her to the master bath and switched on the water. He stripped naked and rubbed his body against her oiled, toned body, giving her a leisurely, deep kiss. Azariah's strong body sank towards him.

He followed her into the bathroom and continued to soap away any remaining massage oil vigorously.

Azariah moved up to him, put her arms around his waist, and gently kissed him. After a brief pause, she drew back, kissed his nose, and said, "Thank you, this is the greatest birthday I've ever had."

Dan grinned. "Wow, that was Kaitlyn's birthday gift. You haven't received mine either."

"Oh my goodness! I suppose I can start cooking by consuming some pizza to hold my power up!" Azariah purred as she stepped out of the tub.

Dan shut off the shower and joined Azariah in toweling themselves and each other off.

When they were dry, they entered the master bedroom and were met by a still-naked Kaitlyn, who was happily munching on pizza. They stood and joined in when they saw she had put two more plates of pizza on the bunk.

"It was the first time I had pizza served by the sea. Not unpleasant at all, "Azariah muttered.

Kaitlyn went on to say, "I'm curious if the boys on the dock are still waiting for us to return. I'd guess they could keep Azariah and me entertained for a while based on the tents they had in their swimsuits!"

Azariah and Dan exchanged glances with Kaitlyn, uncertain how real those twinkling eyes were.

When she chewed, Kaitlyn winked and grinned.

"Incorrigible," Azariah licked her lips, "are you sure you want to hold this wildcat?"

"As long as she remains MY wildcat," Dan smirked, his last bite of pizza poised in front of his lips.

Kaitlyn placed her pizza plate on the floor, flopped onto her back, and spread-eagled her thighs, her foot narrowly missing Dan's head. She wrote, her hands now in the air here, "I am prepared! Bring it on! You can sell seats!"

Azariah leaned back to peek at Kaitlyn's ridiculous smile. "What are your thoughts, Dan? We should draw a large neon arrow over her. Get 50 dollars each...Easy money."

Dan returned Kaitlyn's gaze "Yeah, and Wednesdays are two-for-one. We could include a free shot in her navel on Fridays. We could retire early if she were still on her back. Do you think that's enough sex for her?"

"Probably not!" Azariah exclaimed, stifling her laughter.

Dan tossed his napkin over Kaitlyn's smiling face before grabbing her nearby foot and licking at her arch. He listened as Kaitlyn squirmed and kicked her free leg frantically. "It's a lot of fun tickling a deaf teen," Dan mused as he let go of her foot.

—— Saturday in Lake Tahoe — Azariah, happy birthday! ———

Kaitlyn slowly stood up, brushed her hair away from her ears, and gathered up the pizza crumbs that her flailing had scattered. She signed with a frown, "Now, eat up, you two. You don't want Aunt Sinful to get crazy when you're about to have some heavy sex, do you?"

"No way, ma'am!" Dan laughed.

"All right!" Kaitlyn agreed to sign, "Dan, this is how Azariah operates. The side of her body, just behind her head, is very sensual. Nipples are still very responsive, so work them hard if you don't have any teeth. Torturing her with foreplay causes her to cum quickly and violently. Kissing is a big turn-on..."

"It's sinful...STOP!" Azariah squealed, cradling her flushed face between her palms and shaking her head.

"I'll be in Azariah's place," Kaitlyn said, picking up the nearly empty pizza dishes. She came to a halt, set the plates down, and added, "My darling, I can't support you with what your big cock will do to her. Simply be inventive!"

"Let's go!" Azariah yelled as she pointed to the entrance.

Dan laughed as Kaitlyn shut the handle, "Didn't realize you come with an instruction manual!"

"You'd assume I'd be used to her embarrassing me by now," Azariah muttered, looking up at the ceiling.

"Let's see; Sinful said I could......" Until his lips rubbed against Azariah's throat, under her jaw, Dan whispered.

She shivered and jerked in response to the unexpected feeling. "That's not fair; I didn't get any instructions about what you like!" Azariah grumbled as she twisted her head to face Dan.

"At least send me a couple of tips," Azariah purred as she shifted Dan onto his back and rolled towards him, her firm breasts resting on his stomach.

"And I have to be fair?" he inquired.

"TIT for tat...whatever a 'tat' is," she chuckled.

"Well," he began, "first and foremost, I'd like to explore your body, as you are spectacular."

"High praise, good sir," she cooed, "but that doesn't tell me what YOU want or need." Azariah pressed her finger into his arm to emphasize her point.

"Let's see," Dan pondered. "One thing to keep in mind is that it may take me up to half an hour to recharge,' so you may want to plan your attentions accordingly."

"I bet I can get you back to 'absolute operational performance' in 15 minutes or less," she said, using a phrase from their mutual boss and rubbing her breasts over his chest to hint at her tactics.

"I think I'm going to risk the bet!" Dan went on, "Okay, I like oral attention, but I'm not a fan of messy, drooling throat stuff: seeing a woman do that isn't a turn-on for me. I, too, like being explored. Furthermore, I am not a 'backdoor' kind of person. I'm looking for a mutual, euphoric moment. Although I will desire to be in command, I have no desire to objectify or conquer you. Does it fit for you?"

"I knew I was right all these years lusting after you," Azariah sighed. "That sounds perfect, and let's bring it together with the way nature meant. I have first dibs on leaving!"

"I've got my instructions," he smiled, "and I'm yours to do with whatever you want."

"To begin, I'd like you to turn over," she said as she stepped off of him.

"What exactly do you have in mind?"

"What I have in mind is the 8 inch, or maybe even 9 inches, play toy that I had a grip of while on the massage table...and dreaming of it stuffed deep inside my damp depths...which is why I want you to change over and cover it for a little while," Azariah growled.

Dan snickered and turned over, feeling Azariah gradually lower her warm body, vulnerable, on top of him.

Azariah placed her mouth next to his ear and said in hushed tones, "To be clear, Mr. Daniel Taylor, I believe you are hot, hung, a delightful guy, and a friend; also a very good friend, now, and I care for you. But you're Kaitlyn's, and by the looks of it, you'll be for a long time. And, though I'm not IN love with you, I'd like to believe that I am for the night. Is that all right?"

To keep his face out of the cushion, Dan propped himself and her up on one shoulder. "I believe you expressed just how I felt. But for the fact that you are a hot, stunning, and unique woman to me, and I believe that playing in love is ideal. To be honest, if I hadn't fallen for Kaitlyn and seen what it's like to be in love with that rare and unique lady, I might have assumed I was in love with you. Is that a lot of information?"

Azariah waited for a long moment before kissing his ear gently, her tear wetting the back of his throat. "I think that is the best, most exquisite compliment you might offer me, Daniel, and no matter how nice a fuck you are, those terms would mean the most to me of our relationship moving forward."

She climbed back up, straddling him, and brushed away a few more tears. "I would be hurt by your comments if I didn't love Kaitlyn as my BFF and even girlfriend. But coming in second place to that delightful, lovely guy is such a bonus that I can only smile... Let's get back to it, stud because all this mushy stuff is getting my pussy hot, as you can see. So, return your gaze to the ground."

He nodded, feeling her hands gently glide along with his elbows, spine, and back. He let his muscles roll at her contact, as he'd remembered from feeling Kaitlyn in that way and enjoying her reactions. Yeah, he did feel her wetness on him.

After a minute, or maybe two or three, he felt a single fingernail begin at the base of his skull and eventually drag down to his tailbone, causing the nerves all over his back to light up and tingle. "AAaaaahh...Wow, that twitched my nerve endings."

"Before you inquire, indeed, our little Sinful told me you did that to her," Azariah smiled gently. She rolled off of him and off the bed, allowing her hands to brush along his legs and feet. She bent in and rubbed her breast against the luckily smooth sole of his foot, turning it about while her strong nipple firmed. She could see his foot arching and see his toes twitching.

"That was a memorable foot massage!" he shouted.

"OK, tiger, switch over," Azariah growled. She began rubbing her hands along his legs after he replied. After a few minutes, she bent forward and kissed his knees, at first lightly. She pushed the kisses up his legs steadily, reaching the play toy she had been fantasizing about for so long.

Dan's breathing was deepening and growing as he, too, realized, or hoped, that her kisses were going in the right direction. He also realized that his 'play toy' was standing tall, preventing most of her head's advance.

She didn't keep one of them waiting long before turning and running her tongue up the underside of his dick. She groaned, and he echoed her groan. "I have to keep my mind off this matter. Otherwise, there will be no more foreplay," Azariah grumbled aloud.

"Your night, your call," Dan chuckled.

She frowned sadly as she rose and moved on hands and knees over him, letting her lips rest on his. She let her tongue rove across his lips and the back of his teeth.

The curve of that 'play toy' had brought his crown to rest against her wetness at that stage. When she split the embrace, she let out a loud whine. Her hips swayed, mocking herself and grinding her wetness against him. Azariah stared Dan in the eyes and revealed the desire she was suppressing.

"I lack in self-control," she whined, adding with a growl, "I need you NOW!" She was about to push his palms against her breasts and pinch her nipples when she felt his hands cover her breasts and squeeze her nipples.

"OOOOOOOH!" She screamed and involuntarily collapsed her hips onto her feet, pulling him deep inside her. "Fuck, too high!" she grumbled, tensing her body.

Dan saw the combination of anguish and joy on her lips. He inquired gently, "Are you all right, my lovely? That wasn't the reaction I was hoping for."

She responded in a rather forced tone, "It wasn't quite what I had in mind, either, to say hello to this big boy in one shot. You certainly piqued my interest!" She began to slip on him, thoroughly coating him softly, and the pressure on her face dissipated.

"But now that he's in there, it's delectable...

Ye, I adore you! "She growled ferociously, "You know I'm referring to your penis, right?" she asked, smiling.

"Wow, just having fun tonight," he said as he drew her down for a kiss.

"Mmmmmmmmmmmmmmmmmmmmmmmmmmmmmmmmmmmmmmm mmmmmmmmmmmmmmmmmmmmm Then she saw him meet her moving movements with his colliding thrusts and exclaimed, "MMMMMMM!!" "Stop, wait!" she begged after breaking the embrace, "I haven't yet found enough space in there for you to bottom out...yet."

"That's easier," she said as he held his strokes short of balls deep. "And that's Much cooler," Azariah purred between short breaths as he returned his focus to her breasts. "Fuck," she said as she swayed back and forth on her hands.

Dan noticed her pulse quickening, which corresponded to the intensity at which her throat and upper chest flushed. For each brush, his mind became hazy with the pleasure of sinking into her oceans.

"Fuck, FUCK...this is going to be good...don't make me fall, lover!" she struggled to get out of deep breaths, "Fuck, FUCK...this is going to be good...don't let me; fall over!"

"Will you handle all of me now?" he demanded, feeling the rising intensity in his groin.

She nodded immediately, her face contorted with sexual excitement.

"Are you ready?" he questioned quietly.

"Yes, Fuck YES, do it!" she exclaimed.

He sped up his strokes and pounded into her with each one, hearing a brief "huff" leave her tightening face with each hit.

"GOD...FUCK...Oh, Fuck...Yes, YES," Azariah yelled between hits, her head sunk to his chest and her fingertips moved to grab at his sides.

"I can't put it off any longer!" Dan sighed.

"YES, CUM," she yelled into his face, slamming her hips forward, pinning him to the bed, deep inside her, and tightening herself around her current favorite "play toy."

When his pulses raced through her violently shivering flesh, he felt great satisfaction.

"Yes, warmth, so deep...oh yes," Azariah cooed, shivering. She resisted her trembling limbs so she could stand up and kiss him, which she did softly, and for a long time, it took her body to relinquish power to her brain.

When she did shift, she straightened her legs out, remaining on top of him and keeping his softening shaft inside her. With each deep breath, the stack of their bodies rose and dropped. Her head hung over his shoulder, right next to his. "Okay, now I'm officially envious of Sinful," she sighed, next to his ear, "your 'toy' set off nerve endings I didn't even realize I had...my god!"

"Hey, I had instructions from Sinful," Dan explained between deep breaths, "but I don't think that counted as senseless.'" If you think so?"

"Ecstasy, bliss, heat...sure, but pointless?" She purred loudly. "No, it does not... We'll just have to work harder, so we don't disappoint. Sinfully, you know?"

"Speaking of which," he chuckled, "aren't you on the 15-minute clock for our bet?"

"Oh, right...

I had no idea I'd transform into a puddle of jelly afterward. Okay, well, a bet is a bet. "She said this as she lifted herself off of him and made her way to the restroom.

Dan was in the shower when he heard her scream, "Is there anything else you're going to shoot? I swear I've got a gallon of you pouring out of my cunt...but it's a really happy pussy!"

"That's for me to figure out and you to find out," he teased back. When he noticed the starving expression in her eyes as she slithered back to the bunk, he almost gasped.

"So, how much money do I have left on our wager? Doesn't eight minutes sound reasonable?" She smirked, her cheek resting on his groin. She didn't wait for his answer.

"All right, eigh...DAMN Woman!" "Now I realize why your workplace nickname is 'Hoover,'" Dan exclaimed.

She tipped her head up, slowly removing her lips from his. "So, can I have a nickname?" "Well, this 'Hoover' thinks you taste very nice, particularly with me still coating you!" she said, licking her lips.
Dan could only groan in response as she sucked him in, all of him, through her tight mouth. When his growing member began to rub at her neck, he realized he'd gladly risk the bet.

Still, in her mouth, she pulled back sufficiently to brush her tongue over and through him. Azariah was also aware that she had triumphed. Then, with a deliberate "Pop," she let her lips free him. "So, what do I win?" she slyly inquired.

"Lay down on your back, and I'll show you," he said quietly.

Azariah complied quickly and glanced up at him, curious to see what he might do next.

Dan rolled off the bunk, placed himself at the foot of the bed, and looked at her. "Unbelievable," he grumbled.

She quietly inquired, "What?" when she noticed a change in the tone of their playful talk.

"You, my friend," Dan said hungrily, "look like somebody from most men's wet dreams in these lights."

She blushed when she noticed his apparent profound sincerity, and no words appeared fitting in response.

He made the first touch with his prone Aphrodite, softly dragging one of each hand along the outer sides of her legs with his index and middle fingers. After a short pause, he shifted to the bed to straddle her and resumed his fingers' journey up the sides of her legs, through the curves of her waist, then up the sides of her ribs, halting next to her breasts. He rubbed his thumbs across her wide breasts, stretching his thumbs inward. He noticed a slight shudder inside her, her nipples crinkling, a small whimper, and her licking her lips.

Dan's thumbs retracted, and the initial fingertips of this quest slid up to her elbows and down the outside of her arms to her upturned hands.

Azariah's fingertips easily encircled the two explorers in each hand, and she hummed, "HMMmmmmmm..." and rolled her hips up slightly. After a brief moment, she relaxed her hips and casually let go of his fingers.

He took advantage of her delay to slide up and over her, placing her favorite play toy on top of her stomach, just below her navel.

With an open palm, her left hand went to protect the touch. Her hand slid up to his tip, then she jammed a finger into her gut, causing a depression. "I want you up here when you cum," she closed her eyes and said quietly.

"Noticed," Dan said softly, "but patience for the time being." He began his journey, this time up the insides of her arms, over her shoulders, and up the sides of her body, ending behind her ears. He heard her inhale deeply, felt her move under his hips, and then saw those lovely breasts gently descend back into the bed as she exhaled a long sigh.

Her hands shifted to sit on his thighs.

He gently massaged her forehead and then her temples with his absolute, open hands. When he was working there, he saw her eyes slowly open, look into his eyes, and then shut again.

Now his palms rubbed down the sides of her nose and out to her cheeks, pausing to run his fingertips over her open mouth. Before draping his palms down her long throat, he traced her lips and teased the tip of her tongue as it slipped out.

She let out a happy, loud purr, hoping he could sense it in his hands on her throat. "This is fantastic," Azariah said with a languid coo. "I very like..." She abruptly came to a halt, her lips pursed and her eyes closed.

"We're just playing tonight, right?" he inquired nervously after a brief delay. He saw her steadily nodding. "I think I should go back to lust," he added. He saw another nod.

As her chest raised into his hands and her moist eyes widened with a desirous stare, he traced his palms across and then across her breasts and got the response he desired. He dropped down lower on her, enjoying the way her nails dragged down his thighs as they slipped out of control.

When her play toy was pulled over her mons, her hips instinctively rotated. Her legs struggled to stretch before realizing they were suffocated by him straddling her.

He lowered his lips over her left nipple and swished his lips across her fat nipple, tickling the big tip with his tongue, now in the place he desired. He could see her anxiety rise, and he could hear small tears that came from her mouth but never left her face.

He didn't want her to ramp up so much, so he merely shielded her right nipple with his hand before his mouth moved to that side and began in with the same attention.

Azariah's screams were louder and more desperate.

He wanted to reserve the erogenous appeal of her nipples for later, no matter how enticing those beautiful breasts were, topped with the most sensual nipples he had ever tasted.

He arose from her slightly panting body and moved his hands to divide her thighs.

"Yes!" she exclaimed joyfully.

He knelt between Azariah's long legs, raising her thighs higher, then sat upon his knees. His next goal was the bottom of her sternum, which he gently kissed before sliding his tongue down to her navel. His tongue circled her navel, chasing it a little while her firm abs began to move in reaction.

"Enough with the teasing!" Azariah begged softly.

"Not quite enough," Dan grumbled, remembering...senseless.

"Sinful, you're a jerk." "I just want to be fucked too badly right now," Azariah moaned sadly, "but we have to do it her way!"

"Maybe I should take a little pity on your 'problem,'" Dan snickered, before kissing his way down to one hip bone, over her mons, then to the other hip bone. When her hips writhed underneath him, it became more difficult to locate certain goals.

"If you don't hurry up...and bring the big boy in me...I'm going to cum...just out of anger!" In deep breaths, she declared in a mildly agonized accent. She reinforced her claim by raising her legs higher and wider.

"Just what I was looking for," he growled before placing the tip of his tongue on her exposed clit with no movement.

"Really?" she hissed, her legs softly trembling.

Dan lowered himself gently and braced her legs with his hands to keep her upright. To the accompaniment of her more strained curses, he gently licked the exterior of her labia, then replicated on the other foot.

As he looked up at her, he was faced with fiery, begging pupils. Dan grinned and continued his attentions, this time kissing between her inner and outer labia and circling her moist entry. The legs he was keeping were now trembling violently.

"Dan!" she pled, "I'm going to cum!!"

He replied by gently sucking in her clit and stroking her anus with his finger.

The pain, as well as the torment she craved from her clit, went beyond her expectations, and she yelped, "SHIT," right as her body tried to curl into a feral clench.

Dan couldn't keep put because her unexpected curl and determination were too much for him, so he stepped back and grinned as he studied her. He stroked her thighs gently to convince her that he was there.

Azariah descended into shivering, interspersed with intermittent bursts of heavy trembling, as her fetal curl gave way. "That's never happened before!" she exclaimed as the commotion subsided.

"I suppose Sinful's instructions came in handy, my beauty," he smirked.

"OH MY GOD...that was AMAZING!" Azariah drawled, shivers coursing through her limbs.

Dan's response was to lower his head and run his tongue down the whole length of her slit.

"Shit," she yelled, "I still haven't recovered from my last...explosion!"

"Exactly," he hummed, digging his tongue deep into her still-wet vagina.

"I'm not going to live long if you keep doing that!" she begged.

He stretched his forefinger just below his nose and began to circle her clit as his tongue resumed its exploration of her wet, sensitive inner tissues.

"Oh no!"... "Oh yes!"... "YES!"

He picked what he felt was the best moment to shift his mouth to her clit, and the finger moved to slip inside her while listening to her escalating expletives.

"That's it...there...don't stop...I'm so near," she said.

Dan opened his mouth to kiss her rolling stomach, and the finger eased out of her and up her slit.

"Oh...no...no...no...no...no...no...no...

...I was on my way...PLEASE! "She moaned quietly.

He walked up to her and pressed his lips to hers.

Azariah's tongue flew between his legs, emphasizing all of her latest vocabularies and tasting herself in his mouth with her greedy lips.

He moved a hand over one breast and slowly squeezed the hard nipple that jutted against his thumb, sensing her withdrawal from the precipice.

"Oh, indeed! I may also come this way...HMMMmmm "As she split the embrace, she tendered.

He continued the embrace, his weight pressing against her. He shifted his other hand to the impatient, previously neglected nipple. He applied a light pinch to both nipples.

"mmmmeeeeeeeeeeeeeeeeeeeeeeeeeeeeee She squealed into his lips, and her hands desperately looked for a space between them to grasp the hardened cock she felt pressing against her stomach. She was not effective.

When he rubbed her breasts between his fingertips and watched her hips move strongly, his tongue danced with hers. Sensing her urgency, he stepped down rapidly to position his lips on as much of her breast as he could and used his tongue to lap over the areola and nipple he had surrounded.

"Yes, please...there...functioning, it's I'm moving close!" she hissed, her mouth no longer entangled with his. She searched for her play toy while she spoke, but it had shifted out of her control. IIer vanquished hands drifted around Dan's back to dance.

He shifted his focus to the other breast, leaving fingertips behind to rub the thick, wet nipple that his tongue had previously stimulated. When he began to suckle his new prize, he saw the shaking of her legs kick into high gear.

He backed off, his fingertips slipping away from the first nipple, his lips freeing the other now-wet nipple. He grew gently on his knees, releasing the pressure on her body.

"What happened to you?...No...not again...come on back! Allow me to die in bliss! "Her hungered, pleading cries of desperation were uttered through heaving breaths.

Dan planted a wild series of small kisses over her strong upper arms, breasts, and broad stomach. He kept doing this until there was a little more space between him and a possible orgasm.

"Oh beautiful," she exclaimed as she took deep breaths, "but you know what I like!"

He slid upwards while remaining aligned with his hips between her thighs.

She stared at him with fierce eyes when she felt his length approaching the opening of her tunnel "Daniel Taylor, don't you dare to stop short of emptying everything you've got into my waiting for pussy. This is just what I've been looking for!"

"Did you say 'Long?'" he asked, his tip brushing against her wetness.

"So long, so big, SOOOO..." When he slipped across her door, she came to a halt with a hiss. "So Correct!" she exclaimed, arching her back against him.

"It's too wet," he said. He wasn't going to let her get this moment, but he waited, only his crown inside her.

Azariah begged, "Plunge it deep; I want it all."

"You'll have it all," he said with a grin.

He moved in at a snail's rate but never stopped.

"That's not it!

...My birthday was not meant to be punishment, inch by inch. "In mock-contempt, she cried.

"Torture?" he grinned, "I'm just halfway there." Isn't it true that I should still stop?"

"Don't you fucking dare stop," she yelled. Then, in a gentler accent, "I've never felt anything like this before! Your fat cock crawling past human nerve endings... Only reassure me we're not going to end this route, either."

"Remember, you have to be stupid, but I'll do whatever it takes," he smirked.

"If Sinful could understand me, I'd yell at her for this...yes, exquisite...torture!" Azariah muttered, her teeth clenched.

"I'm almost all in," he declared. "Can you handle me completely?" he inquired quietly.

"I don't care what you get through; please send me all of you right now!" she pleaded.

"Are you happy now?" he inquired, now buried into her.

"Oh yeah," she sighed, smiling, "but I'll be even happier if you do that about twice a SECOND!"

"Like this?" he asked, grinning as he stroked her with two quick, long strokes.

Azariah pulled her legs up and down, her head lolling back and pushing into the pillow. "Oh, fuck, yeah," she hummed as she drew her head back and pressed into the pillow.

Daniel began with long, sluggish strokes and was met by lurid, damp noises emanating from behind them.

"So, fucking, wet for you," she purred, her legs quivering.

He accelerated his strokes somewhat and finished each with a slap against her hips.

"Yes...so goddamn Correct!" she exclaimed, taking quick breaths.

Dan found himself sweating rapidly, and he saw her occasionally clamping around him, as well as her legs trembling violently.

"Starting to get to me...you sound so fucking wonderful," he moaned to her.

Azariah continued in brief bursts, "I won't be able to live much longer...do me...

Simply put, DO ME HARD!"

Dan placed his palms on her thighs near her knees and pressed her trembling thighs further back as he raised to his foot.

Azariah cheerfully cooperated by rolling her hips higher, accompanied by torrid slurps from her vagina. "Fuck, FUCK...FUCKING NOW!" she yelled.

Dan pounced on her, pounding down and watching the color of her eyes roll beneath her eyelids.

"It's over!" Dan barked and pushed her hips into the mattress with all his weight.

"Right there!" she exclaimed softly when she felt his warm pulses reach her.

"OOHHhhhhrrrrrrrrrrrrrrrrrrrrrrrrrrrrrrrrrrrrrrr

"I...I...SHIT!" says the narrator. Azariah yelled as her powerful body bolted backward, knocking him off her.

Dan, his mind already foggy and likely depleted of oxygen, stared at Azariah, her quivering body arched up, held only by her feet and shoulders.

Her throat let out an unintelligible squeak shortly before collapsing onto the mattress.

"Azariah?" he questioned nervously, looking down to see her dead pupils.

He immediately got up and went to locate Kaitlyn, hoping to clear his muddled mind. When he walked in, her eyes were wide open, and he motioned for her to obey. As she ripped off the blankets, he noticed her nude body and led her to Azariah.

Azariah's gaze moved from side to side when Kaitlyn glanced down, and she had already spotted Azariah's leaking cunt.

In the dim sun, Kaitlyn suggested, "Talk to her."

"Azariah...dear...do you happen to be there? Hellooooooooohh, "He inquired.

"What the hell did you do to me?" she muttered as her eyes rolled towards the echo.

"You had me concerned," he laughed, "Happy birthday!"

Azariah mouthed, "Oh My God!" as her eyes rolled to the other side to see Kaitlyn.

"Just chill for a bit," Kaitlyn signed.

"A Blob...body won't react yet," Azariah said softly.

Dan stared at Kaitlyn as she took a step back, and he saw her looking at him, though not at his eyes, as he slid off the mattress.

"You might use a cleaning," she said as she approached him.

He exclaimed, "My, god," as she knelt, pulling him all into her mouth and sucking hard as she removed.

"Azariah on you, Y-U-M-M-Y-!" she signed, her tongue flicking over a couple of missing spots.

"Oh my God, I adore you!" Dan said this when he saw a big grin on Kaitlyn's face.

Kaitlyn, who was also laughing, signed, "Azariah, too, needs washing. Can you clear up the mess you made?"

Dan's eyes widened slightly when he realized what she was doing. "I never have..."

"So, chicken out and use a washcloth," she winked.

Dan was well-versed in taunting, even in sign language. He figured there would be more moments like this in his life with her, so he may as well start now. He grinned and shifted his place between Azariah's thighs.

Azariah's eyes immediately focused, and she gasped, "What!" and looked down. "Oh, SHIT," she squirmed, "I'm always sensitive, don't get fancy down there!" "Dear God, what a night," she said as she lay her head back down on the pillow.

Dan stood up again, a huge smile on his face, and saw Kaitlyn come up for a kiss.

Kaitlyn turned her lips towards Dan before licking his chin. "There was a piece of her on your chin," she signed, her smile mischievous.

And those shining eyes glanced down and realized that his body wasn't done for the night. "I'd suggest you succeeded in getting her senseless," she said, studying his strict manhood, "Would you like to go for two in one night?"

"Azariah's place," he said as he motioned towards the entrance.

Kaitlyn took a step back and shook her head. She shifted to drop down next to Azariah with a wide grin before pulling her knees up almost to her feet.

Dan cast an awkward look at Azariah.

Azariah grinned, "Remember who you love, and offer her what she desires. When would you claim you had two hot chicks in the same room, side-by-side, lover...or have you?"

Dan blushed and shook his head.

Azariah let out a sigh. "I am absolving you of your birthday responsibilities. So fuck your sweetheart before Aunt Azariah gets crazy!" She finished with a smile.

He returned his gaze to a beaming Kaitlyn.

"Wet and prepared. There's no need for foreplay, so please pound me senseless!" Kaitlyn eagerly signed.

"What have I gotten myself into?" Dan chuckled as he shook his head.

"If you don't rush, it'll be my vagina!" Kaitlyn signed with a playful glare.

He crept in beneath her, then returned his gaze to Azariah, his face flushed once more.

"Is this the first time in front of an audience?" Azariah inquired quietly.

Dan gave a smile.

"You'll forget I'm here really fast," she said, reaching forward, grabbing his dick, and pointing it at Kaitlyn's wet entrance. "Now row, row, row your......fucking fine dick," Azariah finished. "She is so eager; give her the slow start you gave me," she said as she sat up next to his ear.

The bit of dialogue moved him beyond his humiliation, and he did as Azariah had said, gently falling towards Kaitlyn.

Kaitlyn's mouth formed a shocked "No!" as she glanced down to see how much of him remained in her. Then she closed her eyes, leaned back, and concentrated solely on the sensations.

As he bottomed out in her, he noticed that, for the first time, he didn't need to stop to allow her body to make space for him. He also found she had a faint rose hue on her upper chest and was sucking in larger breaths.

He began with slow strokes, feeling her body squirm.

As he increased his pace somewhat, he saw her hips rise to meet him. He also noticed her remove her hands off her legs, but her thighs remained almost as far back as before.

He saw her hungry eyes open over the red that reached her neck and latches into his.

"Torture," Azariah murmured, hoping Kaitlyn couldn't see her lips.

As he saw Kaitlyn's leg shivering, he took Azariah's advice and slowed down.

Kaitlyn's hungry eyes raised their brows slightly.
Dan lowered himself to give her a long kiss while continuing to brush her with slow strokes, and she returned his kiss with the same hunger her eyes had shown. Dan applied spontaneous kisses to her breasts now that her knees had stopped quivering while still watching for her breathing to pause and the red to leave her neck.
When he saw the slowed reactions he was expecting, he switched to a relatively quick stroking style and loved the shocked look in her eyes. And he saw the eyes drift away from the sensations he was inflicting.

He noticed the red return to her neck and felt the quivering return to her legs after a few minutes or so. He was about to attempt something he'd been doing in the bathroom mirror. He managed to put on his best expression of animalistic lust for his eyes as

Kaitlyn's eyes refocused sufficiently to look at him and noticed a very surprised look on Kaitlyn's face.

He was on his toes again until the expression left her lips, pounding her into her from above at full tilt. Dan observed as her head sank into the cushion, her mouth agape.

Just when her knees began to quake, he saw the brilliant crimson of her upper chest and bare neck. Then her fingertips began to move in unison.

He was there, then he pulled her onto the mattress, much as he had Azariah, and unleashed on Kaitlyn.

He could only explain what he saw in her face as a scream with no echo. As he noticed her legs fall flat to the bed, he reached out and took Azariah's shoulder. As her body arched toward him, Kaitlyn's other hand caught hold of the covers. As he pinned her hips to the mattress, her jerking began; rapid, repetitive jolts across her body.

It all came to a halt for her, save for her panting, and her glazed eyes searched about but noticed nothing specific. She slowly wrapped her legs around his thighs to hold him close.

Azariah's hand fell away from her, releasing the crumpled papers. With his face next to hers, she slowly signed, "WOW! "Where did you get that?"

Dan smiled, his panting escaping between his jaws.

Kaitlyn then glanced at Azariah, her forehead furrowed.

"Not me," she smiled, "but it seems your lover is getting imaginative."

Kaitlyn smiled as she stared at Dan, her breathing already deep.

"Isn't it senseless?" Dan inquired.

"Close enough," Kaitlyn said quickly.

Dan glanced down and grinned to himself when he saw two women below him, all with tense expressions.

"Do you think you should let me go so we can get some sleep?" he asked, and Kaitlyn pouted as she lifted her legs off of him.

The two women pushed aside to make space for Dan in the center. Azariah spoke up before he relaxed, saying, "Sorry, major Dan, but can you bring us some heated washcloths first?"

"That's a good point," Dan said.

When they had both washed up, he sat in the center, and the three of them cuddled loosely. They were both fast asleep in less than five minutes.

——— Lake Tahoe ———————————————————- —————-

Dan volunteered to drive the car on the way back to Novato, and Azariah agreed. Azariah stood behind Dan this time, with Kaitlyn to her right in the back seat. Azariah relayed much of Kaitlyn's comments to Dan, as driving and interpreting sign language in the inverted vision of the rearview mirror were still beyond his abilities.

The talk had been all about the stunning views, beautiful (and cold) bay, boating, and the condo, with occasional remarks, primarily by Kaitlyn, about having Azariah go topless in the cabin. The topic then began to veer through generalized and gently phrased thoughts on the evenings, as well as compliments on each other's attributes. As the girls' compliments regarding Dan became more precise, he became quiet and asked Azariah to avoid interpreting Kaitlyn's positive remarks.

Azariah used sign language to communicate with Kaitlyn, and it provided her with more privacy from Dan. "His fuck this morning was awesome, and I'm still glowing," Azariah screamed, "but I'd already released him from his birthday commitment." He's going to be all yours now. "What was it?!?"

"Wow, I almost came just to watch him fuck you, and I'm already smiling from the way he made me cum as well," said Kaitlyn. "Maybe he is the blessing that keeps on giving?" she said, with a rye grin and a mischievous twinkle in her eyes, "wouldn't you want to 'borrow' him for an odd night or even share him? with me?"

"What do you mean?"

"Hell, yes!" Azariah erupted in phrases.

"You two whisperers alright back there," Dan said as he glanced in the rearview mirror.

Azariah blushed and snickered, "So perfect."

Kaitlyn smiled from ear to ear as she signed, "I hope he may be open to a 'continuing deal'!"

"But he's yours, and you two deserve each other," Azariah sighed anxiously, "How do I not mess with that?!"

Kaitlyn kissed Azariah's hand before pulling it back to the state, "I love you, and I am in love with him." And I don't think he's lost any affection because I'made' him fuck your hot cunt and 'torture' your beautiful body."

Azariah blushed slightly and just managed to utter, "But..." until Kaitlyn's hands prevented her from speaking.

"Seeing the two people I love...with me, and sometimes in bed with me, is great," Kaitlyn continued. It makes me happy that those two people will share things in this way. Who knows, maybe you and I should put on a show for Dan once in a while...or Dan can attend our show?"

"Do you think he's up for that?" Azariah asked, smirking.

"One way to find out," Kaitlyn said, "and if he isn't, I doubt he'd be insulted by the deal or our show!'!" "And Dan's shower is much better than yours, with the limitless hot water," she punched Azariah in the arm.

"A tiny girl-on-girl in his bathroom to get his engine running...HMMmmmmmmmmmmmmmmmmmmmmmmmmmmmmmmmmmmmmmmmmmmmmmmmmmmmmmmmmmmmmmmmmmmmmmmmmmmmmmmmmmmmmmmmmmmmmmmmmmmmmmmmm

"But," Kaitlyn said solemnly, "none of this can get in the way of you seeing the right guy for you...there are no responsibilities with Dan and me, only pleasures."

"And," Kaitlyn continued, her smile and twinkle back, "if you do find your man, you don't have to share him with me!"

And I'm not sure what Dan will think about the second guy in bed!!"

Azariah let out a loud chuckle. She saw Dan staring in his rearview mirror. "Not talking about you...well, not too often!" she responded to his amused expression. She also found that they had exited the mountains and were now in the valley, with largely straight paths.

"Do you have some paper and a pen?" Kaitlyn inquired of Azariah.

Azariah nudged Dan to raise his elbow off the center front armrest/storage and then took out a notepad and pencil, which she handed to Kaitlyn.

"A junk mail charity notepad...did you keep this?" Kaitlyn inquired, intrigued.

"Hey, it fits in the console," Azariah shrugged.

"Will you appreciate it if Azariah got a couple of 'birthdays' this year?" Kaitlyn wrote on the pad. She adjusted the dot in the question mark to a core, as she had done on their first night together. Azariah returned a tentative smile when she gave her the note.

Kaitlyn tapped Dan on the shoulder and handed him the note.

He took the notice, switched off the radio, and checked to ensure there was no traffic in the parallel lanes next to him. As he read it, he waited for a longer period than he wanted, only to make sure he understood what she was asking.

"Stay in your path, sweetheart!" Azariah gave a soft order.

Dan raised his eyebrows, adjusted his lane spot, and glanced up in the rearview mirror, where he saw Azariah's beaming smile and Kaitlyn's smiling grin.

"With all those birthdays, you're going to get a lot colder in a rush," Dan chuckled.

Azariah replied a little shyly, "Funnyman...now what is your answer?" Azariah paused to pass his out-of-her-sight words to Kaitlyn.

"Was that 'Hell, Yes' I heard as your response?" Dan inquired.

Azariah followed a similar pause: "It was," which she said softly when blushing again.

Kaitlyn saw Dan's eyes questioningly looking at her in the rearview mirror. She replied with one of those short nods that sent her hair all over her face.

"Then 'Hell, Yes!' for me, too!" Dan grinned. A second later, he heard seat belt latches click behind him and felt Kaitlyn's right arm wrap around him. Azariah's arms encircled his neck and the headrest after she eventually let go, and her lips kissed his right ear.

"We'll leave the 'L-word' we were 'playing' at last night off the table and just make it about the fantastic sex...okay?" Azariah said into his ear. Dan's head nodded in agreement. "Good," she said, "it would be the greatest birthday gift." And don't suppose I'm second fiddle to 'Miss Sinful' here. We both enjoy her so much to be jealous, right?" Dan nodded once more.

"And, when you marry this evil woman next to me," she said, "will you always find a little time to render me senseless?" There was a brief moment until she saw him nod multiple times. "That's Danny," I say. She kissed his ear once again.

Kaitlyn grinned as she signed, "Getting started, already?" after Azariah had sat back and reattached her seat belt.
"We're just going through the ground rules," Azariah said.
"Like, like what?" Kaitlyn inquired.
"Dan and I have to have a couple of our mysteries, don't we?" Azariah smiled contentedly as she spoke.

Kaitlyn gave her a puzzled look before grinning and signing, "Of course, as much as you like."

"I love you, sis; always will," Azariah said slowly to Kaitlyn.

"I would not have met him if it hadn't been for you, and he wouldn't be mine if it hadn't been for your commitment to Dan being in my world, rather than yours," Kaitlyn said with a tear in her eye.

"But, I am not in love with..." was the extent of Azariah's rambling when Kaitlyn cut her off.

"I love you, too, sis," Kaitlyn signed, tears streaming down her cheeks, "and I know you... know you...and you'd be in love with him even though I didn't exist, right?"

"All right..." Azariah replied painfully, now with tears in her eyes.

"Correct," Kaitlyn signed, "but just remember that I know and that I can never overlook what you did for me." "The least I can do is share him with you for as long as you want."

Dan saw two teary eyes in the mirror and replied, "Are you two...back there in 'women' land...planning how to use this beautiful body of mine to fulfill your carnal lust?"

"Oh, shut up...(sniff)....you great guy," Azariah retorted.

Kaitlyn grinned and took Azariah's hand in hers.

Dan grinned, sensing that those were healthy cries, and he didn't need to hear any more.

Explicit Erotic Sex Stories

Understated Joblessness (Fantasy)

A young space colonist faces a difficult task.

* * *

Racheal went to work as usual the day after she lost her virginity. She shook off her raincoat and mud boots with the same fast and untouched motions that had first attracted Dr.Brian's attention to her hands. She felt almost fine, except for a nagging ache in her vagina (anterior, as expected). She nodded sharply to Dr. Brian, a hidden grin on her thin face, and went to get her lab coat. "Good morning, Chonn."

"Racheal! Racheal!" Brian's grin was unmistakable. That was never the case. "Did you get laid last night? How did you find it?"

Slight shoulders shrugged twice: once into the lab coat and once in response to the surgeon. "That's fine. There are no problems."

"Are there any problems?" Brian burst out laughing. "That's a joke. Racheal, I need in-depth analysis." With a sick vicarious glow in her mind, she hiked herself off the bench. Brian was fascinated with stories of other people having sex. That was the majority of the reason she became this kind of doctor, she often said. "By the way, it's going to sound great."

Racheal examined her legs and hips as she took her seat: mild soreness. Nothing that outlandish. Perhaps some light chafing on the inner thighs, but Roni had been involved. Very active. Brian held a close eye on Racheal while she thought, thoughtfully fondling a chess knight she kept by her bed. "Really?" The doctor clapped her hands together while her concealed grin twitched once in genuine laughter. "I liked it."

"She liked it," Brian sneered. She sighed and rolled her eyes. "Racheal, I've seen your cunt. There is plenty of room. Of course, you liked it, dipshit, with no malformations and a prominent clitoris." She looked over at the younger woman. "Do you, on the other hand, sound any different?"

Racheal sighed as she considered it. She was conscious that some of the girls had become emotional since their first time: Leonor, who was just two years Racheal's senior, had sobbed for a week. Elon and Rina were both trying to work out how long the months could be here after an Earth week. But did she feel any better? She was tense as a result of the inquiry. "How am I going to feel any better?"

"You're going to be energized. I'm still here. Completed." Brian rested his chin on the doorjamb. "It's magical. I'm still giddy the next day after a night of sex."

"I'm never ecstatic."

"You're not," replied Brian. "However, you are aware. So ecstatic as you can be." She gave a smile. "You need to feel like a lady."

Racheal shook her head. This was still bothering her; she had work to do. "If that's what you mean, I orgasmed. Currently, twice."

"Of course you did," snorted Brian. "Roni was the one. He's well aware of what he's doing." She examined Racheal closely, concluding that she'd been mistaken in expecting some of the typical signs of post-coital derangement syndrome and that PCDS wasn't something that occurred to Racheal's kind of individuals. "Did he aim it at your face? That is what he enjoys doing."

"No," Racheal said flatly. "That wasn't the point at all. He arrived in my van. Every time. May I go to work, Chonn? This is starting to grow rusty, and I didn't get much sleep last night."

"Of course you didn't," cackled Brian. With a sigh, she returned to her bench after determining that the girl was well. "Please notify me if you experience any fatigue, bleeding, leaking, or pain. I'll put you in your place." She cocked her head, but the twinkle in her eye said it all: she was amused. "On your thighs, you'll need a salve. Roni, please..." She grinned, a feminine earthy laugh. "He's always the same."

"Thank you." Racheal has already turned on the microscope. "I made my concoction. Any of the yellow berries that we discovered last year? Those we ran through the spectroscope?" Her gaze slid sideways as she examined the condition of her inner thighs. She gave a smile. "The chemist said they'd be good for chafing, so I combined them with some gum paste and went to work." She shook her head. "It seems to be functioning."

Brian cracked a grin. "Good kid," she said with a smile. "You're an astute observer, but I've known that for years."

"If it works, you should ask Elon to make it for the other women," Racheal smirked. "However," she reflected, fiddling with the coarse emphasis, "I think Roni will profit from just shaving his damn legs." It's the hair that's to blame." She made a shaky motion of her head. "He's a fucking beast."

"Most of us like the fact that he's a fucking animal," Brian said absently as she returned to her autopsy. Brian was curious about how Erno's dog had taken in one of the nearby marsupials overnight. She was still searching for mesmerizing; early detection of lesmeric species was critical to the colony's importance, and she could write it up for the papers. "Did he sound... delighted with your performance?" she asked, laughing.

Racheal smirked. It was in her character to take even the most insignificant questions seriously, and this was no exception. As her scope warmed up, she thought on the night before: the interesting flutter in her stomach when he came up to say hello at dinner, then the intensity and concentration of his gaze into her eyes; Racheal had known Roni for years, and she understood just how sex operated, much like any frontier colonist. If she was completely truthful, she was shocked that he had taken so long. She'd turned eighteen almost nine days ago. "I wanted to wish you a happy birthday, Racheal," he'd said quietly, those wide purple eyes warm and welcoming, and the flutter had started. He was well aware of what he was doing.

Roni already had five babies from three separate colonists in the village, and he'd gotten Jitsuko up the stick a couple of months before. Real. He was well aware of what he was doing.

"Thank you, Mr. Pfeiffer," she said softly as she sat back in the plastic chair, her arms folded under her little breasts. She looked up at him, waiting, still solemn. That was how she preferred to introduce herself to this modern country.

"Would you please?" He took a step back, his hands up. "You are now a resident. A mature person. You're no longer a Domestic." He winked, and she found herself drifting into his orbit despite herself. "Please refer to me as Roni. Someone else is doing it."

"Then, Roni, thank you." Despite the gnawing in her stomach, she wasn't going to play the naive waif. Even lower down. Of course, she was aware of everything; she was a professional apprentice surgeon. Dr.Brian's strong hand had made gross anatomy second nature to her when she was fourteen. She was conscious that the faint dampness she felt sluicing over her labia minora was exacerbated by the excitation of Skene's gland on her anterior vagina, that the fluid was just there because she wanted Roni to fuck her and that he'd be able to tell based on her pheromones.

But she didn't have to make things comfortable for him. She cocked her head. "Did there happen to be someone else?"

Roni gave a soft smile. Racheal was the fourth of the Domestics to reach eighteen and enter the final colonial pecking order. Most of them went through a time of confusion, even humiliation until they felt like true people. Racheal didn't seem to have the issue. "So there you have it. There was, in truth, such a thing." He grinned brightly as he drew out the next chair over, standing only a little too near. "Can I take a seat?"

Of course, after the two of them moved to the Cottage, he did a lot more than that. He'd appeared shocked she was still a virgin, despite the reality that it was part of her deal, but she'd noticed with pleasure that he became much tougher when he came to that realization. She'd also remembered how much she loved seeing him hard, thinking his cock was for her. His name is Ronit Pfeiffer, and he is the most famous human male in the world. Come to it, in the whole scheme.

And late at night, when he slept with his drool streaming over her left breast, she'd given herself a brief sigh of relief as she remembered she'd outlasted him. There was nothing remarkable about him fucking her first, she realized. He was the colony's dominant sexual entity, and everybody knew it. So, of course, the other men had waited until he had decided on a time and place. But he'd crammed before she did the second time, and Racheal was still woman enough to realize that he'd appreciate that.

She frowned, returning her attention to Dr. Brian's query. "I'd claim he was really happy." Racheal's accent was smug, but neither woman was conscious of it. She paused, then agreed. "True. Satisfied. Twice."

"He's a very reliable ejaculator," Brian agreed absently as he moved the viscera aside. "Hey, if you have a chance, come over for a couple of minutes. I'd like to hear your thoughts on this duodenum."

"Just a second." RachealFourbee's mind was not the type to wonder at the absurdity of digging through anonymous gut loads the morning after she'd given up her virginity.

But if she had, she would have just shaken her head and gone on her day.

* * * *

The call came in after lunch, and it was about an issue with one of the indents at the Plant. "There's goddamn blood everywhere," Vivian said over the vox box, her accent as tight as it had always been. "It's spreading around the drafting station. It's a serious issue." Her mind acted in this manner; she meant the station, not the injury.

Dr. Brian frowned, already dripping wet from the tub and wrapped in a fuzzy towel. She and Racheal shared looks. "What portion of your leg, Vivy?" It had been a long night for her, with endless phone calls from the crèche about Rina's new baby. She'd ended up just passing out in the hospital. She yawned into the microphone. "What comes first, the top or the bottom?"

"What is the best? Halfway above the knee, for example." They could hear distant yells in the background. "There's a lot of blood here. They're already dragging him back." She had been unable to include the man's identity. Vivian was not the kind of woman who might note the indents. "That's great. The cleaning robots are now at work." She sounded at ease.

"Just a minute." She raised her head to look at her apprentice. "Racheal will appear and greet you on the way. She'll be able to control it and get him to the hospital, hmm?" Vivian had already left when the vox box clicked. Racheal swallowed and cleared her mouth.

"I'll take the lead until I have him here as well," she said flatly as she stepped into her boots. "You're completely drained. You might help."

"Is that true? Wow. Thank you." The sarcasm was thick. "Considering I'm a fucking specialist and you're a fucking apprentice." She let out a yawn. "Nonetheless. You can do it in your sleep if it's only a simple femoral tear." Racheal got her arteries sutured until the teenager reached fifteen. "If I'm not around when you come in, it's because I'm going to the bathroom."

"Does that refer to the clinical term?" Racheal's grin widened slightly; it was an old story between them, Brian's frequent checking while she was a Domestic, constant study of the medical vocab. "I'll see you later."

"Don't miss the saw," Brian said as she loosened her towel and made her way to the restroom. "In case you need to break it off."

"Of course, Doctor Brian," Racheal replied sarcastically. "Chonn, this isn't my first day." She tossed the rucksack over her back and dashed out into the forest, her grey eyes already looking past the Dorm, scanning for the Plant's group; they'd be coming right through the woods. She wished they'd have the foresight to do the tourniquet themselves. Otherwise, the fucking indent will most likely be dead by now. That wasn't exactly lethal, but it was almost. There you have it. Roni and an indent called Juukko were leading him cautiously on a pallet. Racheal hopped nimbly across the puddles, her voice rising. "Who exactly is it?"

"It's Morrison!" says the narrator. Juukko cast a sideways gaze. "I believe he's gone, or nearly so."

"Thank goodness you're a goddamn dentist and not a doctor." She liked Juukko, but the indents needed to be moved. Even though, like Juukko, they were nearing the end of their term. "Hello, Roni." She was detaching herself, feeling the calmness come over her, ready to be shocked by whatever came her way.

"Racheal," she says. Juukko was curiously observing the two of them as they both gathered at the edge of the forest. It was clear that they'd fucked, and the indents were generally curious regarding sex among the citizens. "The printer head of type three. It almost severed his leg."

"I see what you mean." She knelt by the pallet, making a rapid calculation and swiping at the blood with her hand. "Juuk, stand over me," she said. "Please keep the rain at bay."

"Certainly, Ms.Fourbee." The woman took a step closer and bent over the pallet. She cast a downward glance past Racheal's shoulder. "Do you see what I mean? I believe he is no longer alive."

"No way." This wasn't a problem; Morrisen had only lost about three and a half liters, based on his whiteness. That was concerning but not as horrific as it might have been. Janicka had lost about four pounds from the arm thing just a few months before. She drew his eyelid open and examined the pupil. "He's well. What a jerk! "She yelled into the man's ear, watching for iris flexion. "Hello there! What a jerk! Are you alive?" She'd treated him for... whatever it was. What was it like two years ago?

Racheal grinned as her eye twitched. "That's nice." She returned to the knee, staring intently and dismissing the odor. "Roni?" she said, not looking up. "Would you mind doing me a favor?"

"How are you?"

"Return to the Plant. Mikhail is in command over there before Rina recovers, correct?"

"Mm-hmm," he says.

She pressed her thumb against the cut. The skin tear was very important, which was a positive thing. Access will not be an issue. "Oh, I see. There we have it, "She whispered, the artery resembling a used condom next to the splintered femur. A two-centimeter laceration is most likely. She'd like to hold his legs spread because he's medial. She frowned as she plucked at the vessel. "Yes, indeed. Return to the plant. Tell Mikhail to abandon everything he's doing and update his citizens on tourniquets. Just now." She raised her head. "By Dr. Brian's order; she'd knock your asses if she saw this shit." She scoffed at the tourniquet with a sarcastic finger. "Juukko and I will pick him up. Tell

Mikhail that this will be five days of wasted time." She brushed away even more blood and saw that the laceration had nicked the adductor as well as the sartorius. "Oh, no. It was my fault. It has been six days. Is he scheduled for the hatchery examination next month? What's up with Plastic?"

"How do I possibly know?" Roni's sparkling grin shone brightly. "I'll inform Mikka. Racheal, I'll see you later."

"Mm-hmm," he says. She had already moved on to the next issue; he was no longer in her mind. She gave a smile. "That's all right, Juuk. Let's get him moved." No, no! That's what there is to it. She'd handled Chirk with a coccyx cyst. He had the strangely asymmetric anus, she remembered. The two women had the pallet going again, even though its batteries were low on charge; she'd need to make Brian talk with Mikhail about it as well. The Plant's first-aid condition seemed to be abysmal. That was Rina's dilemma, after all. She paused. "You're short, Juuk, aren't you?"

"Two more months," Juukko confidently responded. Many citizens could not survive a colonial indenture lasting seven years. Before they took her here, she had been on a permanent colony. She gave a smile. "I'll become a citizen once more, just like your happy butt. However, I am still employed at the Plant. But just for monetary gain."

"Yeah, yeah." Racheal was also getting accustomed to getting compensated, to the idea of money quietly piling up in her account. "You can even render anything you want up there."

Juuko burst out laughing. "Even sex dolls."

Racheal laughed. "Do you have any other plans?" They came around the corner, close to the sickhouse entrance. "Are you going to sit here?" The terraformers had left about 20,000 square kilometers of backcountry primed for settlement, and there were still the hinterlands beyond that for any settler who felt like rolling their own. She entered the door code.

"Who can say? First and foremost, I'll make you rip out my meter." They all burst out laughing. "It's time to have a child or two. That is to say, fucking. Not like you don't realize how that feels, Ms.Fourbee. I recall turning eighteen." She let out a breath. "The first time is a doozy." When they placed the pallet on the track, the batteries began to recharge automatically.

"At least, that's what they mean." Racheal gave a smile. "You're free to go now, Juuk." She wiggled her toes as she got out of the pants. "He'll be just right." On the pallet, ChirkMorrisen was sheet-pale. She stroked his throat with her fingertips. She had a pulse meter in her rucksack but hadn't used it because it was an unusual pulse that RachealFourbee couldn't identify. She counted in her mind as she marched cautiously alongside the pallet as the track pulled it through the vestibule and into the exam space. She faintly heard Brian calling from the restroom.

"Do you need my assistance?"

"No," I say. Bradycardic at 40-42 beats per minute; it was horrible, but not terrible; the pacemaker will remedy it. Morrisen's blood volume was more concerning, but there was a computer for that as well. "I'm not going to mess with the operating room. I will take care of him in the exam room." If she had to estimate, he was possibly just 56 or 57 systolic, with a diastolic pressure closer to 25; she was excellent at assessing this stuff, so it didn't matter. The condition was unmistakable, and the medical choices were limited; the numbers didn't matter. Only the protocols and whether or not she could complete them quickly. If she couldn't, the statistics wouldn't matter in the end. "One thing's for certain," she said to the latrine curtain, "the garden should be fucking fantastic fast." He almost passed out near the flowerbeds." Ironic. It wasn't present in sufficient quantities in the local soil.

"That's great." The blood-spattered haphazardly across the floor under the pallet. "It'd be cool if there were more flowers around." Racheal was restraining Morrisen. He wasn't awake, but pain stimulation had a habit of having people twitch. The disinfector buzzed above, sometimes interrupted by the portable pacemaker.

"Mm-hmm," he says. Racheal shrugged her hair back and waded in, the Collins needle on her fingertip. She'd been slipping for several minutes when she remembered she'd missed everything. "Oh, I see. Chonn, you are right. I need your assistance."

"In a moment. I'm rubbing my brow." Racheal nodded to herself, putting the fix to the test, the Collins still to the side. As Brian finished up, the composting stir rattled the wall, and the curtain slipped open. "How does the prognosis look?"

"Oh, he'll be great," I say. The fix was flawless, as intended. "Would you like to double-check?"

"No way. I tutored you myself." Brian was buttoning her pants; her head cocked at the indent on the counter. "Blood is needed. Is he alive?"

"Nearly. Don't be concerned." Racheal kissed her nose, wiping out some of her patient's blood. "Could you please do me a favor? For the clutter, I neglected to look up his skin aspect. Could you please search for me?"

"Of course." Brian cocked his brow. "Is he a dentist? Do you work in the plant?"

"ChirkMorrisen," says the narrator. Racheal grabbed the bone stimulant. He was in a bad way. A few months after they'd arrived, he'd already lost a finger in that damn Plant. You must be sloppy. His whole body shuddered as the stimulant entered, and Racheal began undressing him as the bone began to recover. His face was whiter than his protruding, jagged femur, and his tunic and trousers were rigid with smeared grease beneath the blood. He was well-built, maybe twenty-four years old? Maybe a little older. Nice, heavy arms, with an old surgical scar three centimeters dorsal to the emergence of the epigastric vein. Hair growth in adolescence is normal.
"The factor is eleven-four." Brian had returned to the archives closet. "Do you need anything else?"

"No, thank you." She introduced the element into the blood dump. "All I have to do now is wait for profusion."

"Goddamn stone-age medicine," Brian sighed as he re-entered the bed. She cast a look over at her assistant. "You'll never realize what it's like to handle patients in a true operating room." She took a close look at the needle. "Racheal, you're a master of the Collins. I can't think what you'd be able to achieve if you had the right equipment." She smacked the younger woman on the buttocks. "Excellent job."

"He's pinking up," Racheal said quickly. She despised being praised. She slipped her finger up to Morrisen's ankle and felt the distal heartbeat. "Come on over. I'll end here."

"Do you just want to wake him up?" Brian had a look outside. "That is the most enjoyable aspect. The expression on their faces."

"No way." Racheal wiped her hands. "That aspect doesn't do anything for me. The weaving is appealing to me."

Brian let out a short, barking laugh. "All right." She bowed low and took the patient's hand in both of hers. "Can you tell me again what his name is?"

"Chirk," he says.

"He's adorable." He was starting to sweat, his body increasingly reactivating and becoming functional. "Nice huge balls as well."

Racheal scowled and sarcastically talked into the auto-log. "Natural and well-formed tests."

"Wake up!" Brian was gently but insistently stroking his fingertips, her mouth near to his ear. "Wake up, Chirk," she said quietly, motherly, her gaze fixed on him. "It's all right. You are welcome to contact us again." Racheal watched impassively as his pupils darted beneath his lids, fluttering wide, thus fusing his leg closed. "There you go," Brian murmured, never taking her hands off his. All pretended they couldn't smell the cautery. "Hello, buddy," she said softly.

His eyes opened, flapped in surprise, and then concentrated. "Wait, what the fuck?" His voice was hoarse and flat. "What exactly..."

"You're all right." Racheal shook her head. "Chirk, you had a bad dream. Keep an eye out for certain type three printer heads. They will mess with you."

Morrisen sighed, scanning his body for pain, and his eyes widened as he began to recall. "No," I say.

"Of course." Racheal removed her hand from his ankle, did the Furman test on the wound, and shook her head. "You were almost manure."

Brian glanced at Racheal sidelong, like a guy looking at a pair of boots he needs to purchase. "I've spoken to you about your bedside attitude before, Racheal." She cracked a grin. "Caring impartiality. Put any effort into it."

Racheal stopped, considered, glanced back at her panting patient and her flawless operation, and smiled at the surgeon. "I'm not interested."

The older woman's forehead furrowed. "Excuse me?"

Racheal shook her head. "I'm proud of my bedside manner." Brian had been working for years to get Racheal to be only a little bit more sympathetic, and that had always irritated her. "Look at this shit, Chonn," she encouraged, slapping her patient's healed leg while dismissing his flinch. "Thank you, but I'd rather work on my clinical skills."

Brian was frowning now, an unusual occurrence that deserved to be recorded in the commandant's chart. "We can chat about it another day," she said, looking down at the sweaty guy.

"No," Racheal insisted, "I disagree, Doctor Brian." This galaxy's only medical doctors are you and me. I'll be a professionally trained physician in two years." She nodded, acknowledging Brian's instruction. "In reality, I'll outlive you." She gave a quick blink. "I'm not positive my bedside manner would be much of an issue until that occurs."

"Well, Racheal, we're fourteen years away from the Second Wave pioneers," Brian sighed. They'll bring doctors, true doctors, like me. There are a lot of them. You'll be 33 years old and a colony-trained journeyman surgeon." She paused, letting the words sink in. "You should start dreaming about how you'll compete after the entrepreneur process is finished. That's everything I have to offer, Racheal."

The patient was amusedly observing them, like a guy at a sports match. Racheal looked him in the eyes. "I just saved your life, sir," she said solemnly. "When is your indent about to expire?"

The guy wiggled his fingers. He licked his lips once more. "Two years more, Ms.Fourbee." He was powerful and a constructor. He'd never be short of jobs.

Racheal gave a smile. "That's great. And, after another twelve years, you'll be a stable citizen?" She didn't bother waiting for a response. "You'll accept me into your home and provide about me. You should be my backup plan." She nodded quickly and shifted her gaze to Brian. "There you have it. The issue has been resolved." Dr. Brian was only shaking her eyes, but her grin returned, as it often did.

She made a shaky motion of her head. "You're one-of-a-kind, Racheal," she quietly sighed. "For the most part."

* * * *

Reille, on the other hand, had lied to Dr. Brian, and she believed Brian was aware of it.

It wasn't about the weaving, not at all. Racheal had always felt euphoric, sometimes triumphant, during a good operation. When she forced her face to its normal controlled smirk, the ecstasy manifested itself in flushed cheeks, dilated eyes, heightened nasal congestion, and a mild tremor in her legs; these were signs she'd cataloged for herself, brutally frank and relentlessly observant, since the beginning of her apprenticeship.

Yet there was something else when she washed her hands after rescuing Morrisen.

She stared at herself in the digital mirror as she struggled to sort it out: a soft, tight abdominal warmth she hadn't felt before, and as she looked internally and tried to describe it with her clinical mind, an accompanying thought brought her the diagnosis at once.

She was in a good mood.

The thought that accompanied it was of Roni above her, thrusting into her body, the moment halfway into their night together when Racheal realized how much she loved sex.

Before she risked another inner examination of the feeling, she compelled herself to cool, choppy deliberation, the disinfectant, the blower, and the change of clothing. It was simpler now than it had been before: the euphoria she'd once feel at a job well performed had morphed into a punishing desire to be fucked.

Racheal leaned on the counter, looking at herself in the mirror, then seeing the distribution of the vasocongestion; steadily up out of the neckline of her clean new shirt, a pinkness so faint at first that it was almost indistinguishable. She let out a breath. "What do you mean, Chonn?"

"Are you sure?" She sounded as though she was already in the examination area.

"You're fine with Chirk, right? I need some new air and maybe a nap."

"Of course." Brian's head appeared down the small corridor. "He's completely stable, but you knew that."

"Yes," Racheal replied apologetically. She looked in the mirror and grinned, curious who might be in the Hall at this time of day. I was wondering whether she could get Roni out of the Plant in a decent manner. Brian had seen her good, swift fingers on the voyage out, searching for an apprentice, and she wondered whether they might work as well on her clitoris as they did on other people's wounds.

No, it does not. What do you mean, masturbation? How should she do it now that she'd tried the real thing?

She quickly put on the shawl; even though she hadn't seen the rain pounding on the roof, it was likely that it would be a rainy day. It just seemed more natural to wear the shawl all the time. With neophan woven into it, this one was good, the colony's first neophan; April 78-F had created the shawl for Dr.Brian after her boy's birth, the very difficult one. Clones were notorious for having difficult first pregnancies, but this one had exhausted Brian and her young apprentice over three nights. April was overwhelmed with gratitude.

Nobody had been surprised when the child developed purple pupils.

But since Brian liked caps, April had gotten to see little Racheal parade around the colony in the fine waterproof shawl, which was much too large for her at the time. Racheal crawled into the Hall from the side door, shedding the sluicing fog. She took a light step out of the boots, tossed the shawl over the hooks, and swept her hair back into its normal loose ponytail.

Marianne Fuentes sat on a dusty tabulate in the northeast corner of the vast room, reading one of her agronomy books. They exchanged friendly glances, but Racheal hadn't gotten along with Marianne while she was a Domestic, and the agronomist hadn't spoken to her much since she'd been a resident. But she was healing from a traumatic birth, which had softened her. Racheal stopped for a moment to reflect; the majority of the colony was comfortably bisexual, and Racheal assumed Marianne was attractive enough, but she'd never had much attraction to the guy.

There had to be another alternative, ideally one that included a penis.

The rest of the room was an echoing emptiness, disturbed only by a faint rattle from the kitchen, as she'd predicted. Racheal's flush had hit her face by this stage, and Morrisen had a supplementary exam in forty minutes. She took a deep breath and made her way back to the kitchen.

"The hell!" snarled Racheal as she emerged in the doorway. Via the steam flowing from the clave, Bar squinted. "Do you need anything? I'm preoccupied."

Real. The chef is Niall Bar-Shaughnessy. He'd do it.

Racheal wasn't sure what to say for a moment. Still, then she realized it didn't matter: she was a planetary citizen, eighteen and fetching, almost a qualified surgeon, and he was merely a freeloader from the ship that had brought them all from the Heart, a freeloader who'd decided on the spur of a five-year-gone moment to leave a promising career reheating meals on space vessels a He couldn't care less if she was speaking Dutch.

"Hi," Racheal said, her speech bright enough to drown out the clatter of Bar's pans. When she reached the kitchen, she pulled herself up, her optimism propelling her into a strut. "Have a few minutes? Let's take a rest together."

He grinned confidently and took a stim-stick from his mouth. There were stories about the stay-backs, but no decent citizen would ever confess to fucking them, so they'd have to stay rumors. Racheal, on the other hand, served in the sickhouse and encountered more than mere gossip. "I'm taking a break." He moved his eyes up and down her torso. "I'm not able to mate, Ms.Fourbee," he said unequivocally.

"How kind of you to say so," Racheal chuckled. "I'm not obligated to, Bar." The steam was already disappearing as she walked into the kitchen. "I'm so... bored," she says. Her body was shouting at her to untie the stays on her tunic. "To be frank, I'm at a crossroads." The tunic slid down onto the tiles. "Of course." She grinned, her naked little boobs bouncing over her pounding core. Her brain detected mild tachycardia. There is little therapeutic meaning. She rested her arm on the sink. "Can you spare a couple of moments?"

Bar's eyes twinkled. "I'm poaching trout," he clarified calmly as he drew his damp shirt over his head. She remembered absently that he had pale, muscled skin and a medium build; he was a healthy guy. Scarification, as seen on long-distance space sailors with little else to do than brand themselves. "The shellfish they discovered in the upper lake? If you cook it long enough, the chemicals are removed."

"That's comforting." Racheal's jaw tightened, and her smirk turned wild as she pulled off her underwear. "I'm not a fan of poisons."

"Nobody does." He looked out into the Hall as he undid his waist string. "Ms. Fourbee, you may like to pull the curtain."

"Your laws, your kitchen." She whirled around and sauntered back into the doorway, swinging her butt, with little real consideration of what she was doing, on the brink of fucking a dirty stay-back cook over a kitchen sink. Yet, she realized that she would have become much more aroused if she had been dreaming of it. She was also aware that the air surrounding the clave was dense with pheromones. "Like I mentioned, just a few minutes, Bar."

"Yeah, we'll see," he said, tall and lofty, nude amid his hot pans. "Are you going to report me if I name you 'Racheal?'" he said, looking at her nipples.

She smiled, thinking it was too noisy but not worrying a bit. It was pointless to remain silent. Marianne would be aware, which suggested that everybody else would be as well. Her faith as she strode toward him, eyeing the cock heavy in his grasp, astounded her. Her whole being trembled inside, as though she'd been wired into a drive module, as bored kids used to do to get high back in the Heart. Oh my God! She sensed a weight between her thighs and reached forward, scooping out a big, sloppy fingerful of her vaginal muck. Her fucking glands were still running overtime, she informed herself distantly. She was aware that her airway would be constricted, and she had to clear her throat twice before she felt confident enough to talk. "How shall we proceed, Bar?"

"As a wise young woman recently found out, Racheal," he hoarsely explained, "my kitchen, my law." He rubbed his brow with the palm of his hairy wrist. "Climb over the counter. When I fuck my girl, I like to see their buttocks shake." In response, she heard herself chuckle again, and all was laughter and passion, as well as the red cloud of her desire firing out of her limbic system.

She had no idea where it had all come from; something about taking Roni's dick had done it to her, but it wasn't her style to doubt those stuff. Emotional stuff. She briefly considered whether she might offer to suck the thick cock jutting from the man's brownish bush of dense, wiry pubic hair. "I'm in a rush, Bar," she murmured, closing the gap. She had no idea what to do with a dick in her mouth, so what could be so difficult? Nonetheless, that wasn't why she'd gone in there. She observed as his gaze lingered over her naked body.

"I won't be here for long." He was standing loose and primed, exuding a pride Racheal suspected she shared. "It has been a bit."

"Mmm," I say. Many of the stays back, and freeloaders remained alone on the outskirts of the village. With the people fucking each other as though the colony's wellbeing relied on it, Bar Shaughnessy certainly spent most of his time with his side. That's just what happened. Racheal turned to face the sink, her calm, sharp little fingers grasping the hard stone sides. She saw remnants of Chirk Morrison's blood sticking under the nails; she must have been in a rush. "Then have a good time."

"Oh, I'll do it." With her mind on fire, she bent her head down toward the sink as Bar walked up behind her, the heat of his body reminding her of what was to come. She felt his big, scarred fingertips gripping her a$$ as she'd seen him do with breadfruit to measure its ripeness. "I forgot to compliment you on your citizenship, Racheal." She loved how he mockingly said her name; it was filthy. He licked his other hand and rubbed it over her cunt, then grumbled. "Fuck you. You don't need my assistance, "He snarled. "Slut, slut, slut. Spread the foot a bit wider."

"How is this?" She pulled her sandals off and walked outside, feeling his fingertips close on her cheek once more. She'd look later for contusions, five of them scattered around half her ass; his thumb was near to her anus, which surprised Racheal. "Come on, Bar," she insisted. "Insert it."

"Oh, I'll do it." She shuddered as he painted her labia with the blunt head of his penis before stepping inside her. "Nice and close," he groaned hungrily as he separated her, his cock slowly inching inside with patient practice. "Are you sure you're not a virgin?"

"No," I say. She arched her spine and strained her hamstrings, recognizing he was too big for her and that it would help her open up more fully. "I'm afraid you're number two." Her voice caught the gasping enthusiasm there; this seemed much more wickedly passionate than it had with Roni. She shook her buttocks from side to side. "Come on, let's go. Don't be soft."

He laughed. "Of course." There was no further pomp, his dick completely plugged into her, the weight pushing her thighs into the stone basin. He seemed to be driving a cannon barrel into there. She exclaimed. "You begged for it," he hissed, grinding his claws through her skin. She wondered whether he'd spank her, and then she wondered if she'd like it if he did. She frantically eased her pelvic muscles, attempting to find space, and then it felt great; he still filled her as tightly as he had before, but the fullness was now fun rather than painful. He was aware of that as well. "That's what there is to it. I'll have the pulse."

Racheal closed her eyes for a second, then smirked as she glanced over her back, flexing and relaxing, flexing and relaxing, flexing and relaxing. Her mind wandered to the gross anatomy of her cunt, the muscles; she flexed what looked like the levator ani. She soon acquired strength, triggering fluttering spasms on both sides of her vagina and learning how they rippled. When she noticed the look on his face when she saw what she was doing to him, her whole body glowed with pleasure. "How is that?"

"I adore it." He eventually let go of her skin, putting both of his hands comfortably, proprietorially, on the sides of her hips. "A man could become accustomed to this."

She laughed. "He couldn't do it." She was just looking to scratch an itch. It was best that he knew that as soon as possible. She abruptly came to a halt, slackening her pelvic floor and watching him notice it. "Don't take this lightly, motherfucker."

"Understood, Racheal," he murmured. He pushed softly on her, pushing her down into the sink as he backed away, the sensation intensely rewarding. Roni, she remembered, had been hammering into her like a motor.

This appealed to her more.

He was grimacing, his beady eyes darting between her face and her vagina, feeling himself pull out of her. He let out a sigh. "There's nothing like watching your cock coming out of a new young pussy," he reverently said. "None at all."

Racheal twisted about in mock astonishment; every muscle etched on her skin in the steamy glow of the kitchen. "Yes, Bar! So obnoxious." When he thrust back into her, his body jarred hers hard, resulting in a grunted squeak. "There's more."

"It's yours." He was heaving effortlessly now, not quickly but powerfully, each thrust beginning with his butt being pulled far, way back. Their legs collided with a series of swift, harsh slaps. "You seem to be in high spirits." She meant to react, her mind searching for the right expression, but all of a sudden, she felt liquid heat pooling down at her clit, intensifying rapidly each time the cook rubbed his shaft over it, so she groaned into the sink, biting her lip for Marianne Fuentes in the next bed. She wished dully that the clave was drowning them out, then stopped hoping for something.

It had felt fantastic for Roni, but she'd been so focused on soaking it all in that she'd missed something crucial in the process. Still, she hadn't known that before now when the orgasm was killing her senses. "Wow," she saw Bar hiss through a fog of anesthesia, his pure expression satisfaction. "Cum, babe." She was trembling with enthusiasm as she bent over for this guy, the wickedness, the humiliation. His fists tightened again, holding her brutally hard while his pace broke down, the dick stabbing into her spastic vagina, and then she heard a strangled scream from behind her, and his weight was a concrete wall pinning her to the sink.

His cock was in now, impossibly deep, twitching like a snagged eel. She understood what was going on inside there on several levels: the dynamics were obvious from Dr.Brian's lessons and diagrams, and Roni had been much like this in the tangles of her experimental complexity, but this was different. She'd brought it on herself by her aching desire, and she crumbled against the wet, heaped pans as Bar Shaughnessy poured himself inside her body. "Yes," he exclaimed, his expression ecstatic. "You're so sexy."

"Give me all of it," she heard herself say, stunned at her desperate whine; she wasn't surprised when the nails dug deeper into her hips, the dick twitching in reaction. When she put her underwear back on, she realized she'd be flooded. As though it was relevant now.

He took his time disengaging, almost apologetically removing his hands and genitals from her flushed young body. Racheal continued to seek the terms, knowing that it was her responsibility to finish this like she had begun it, yet as shaking arms pushed her upright once more, there seemed to be too little to tell. As all of them panted, she stumbled back to face him, her buttocks poised on the edge of the sink. The bar was a sweaty mess, his dick already mostly engorged (clinically, it was straighter than Roni's) and wet from all of their discharges. "Wow," she breathed, her breath escaping her lungs. "Thank you so much, Bar."

"The fun was entirely mine." He was looking down in awe when his sperm seeped into her slit and landed on her tip. "I hope... I mean, I doubt I got you pregnant..."

"Stop it," she exclaimed sharply. "It's not a problem." The metering implants were among the most closely guarded objects in the colony, with only she, Dr. Brian, and the indents having them. She relaxed, knowing the smirk had returned. "Please get me a towel. I have to return." The rain was pounding on the windows behind him, and she was still wondering what she'd see on Morrisen's leg by now.

After she swept the curtain back, her boots cut rapidly through the tiles, and she considered putting her head down and hiding Marianne's eyes. Instead, something about her caused her to stop, straight and tall, and look at the other lady. "Good afternoon, Marianne!" she called into space, and Fuentes couldn't help but smile back.

"Racheal," she managed, and then the shawl was back around her unkempt hair, and the doorway beckoned.

* * * *

After almost six years, the colony was finally able to deliver a healthy meal.

That was the news the next day, as Racheal sat down for the first time to a well-balanced, entirely indigenous meal that tasted fine. "This is a huge moment," Leonor insisted, directing her food over her bloated stomach. That morning, the baby had just started to kick. She'd arrived as a Domestic as well, two years older than Racheal, and now she had her little holding, along with a greenhouse. Racheal hadn't decided on hers yet, even though there was a whole world for them both to spread out on. "This doesn't taste shite."

"You make an excellent argument." Mikhail was tapping away at his tabulate at the other end of the table. "It was a huge breakthrough to figure out the sauce." Racheal looked at Leonor, then at Chonn; the baby Leonor was carrying around belonged to Mikhail, and only the two surgeons understood. Mikka and Leonor, on the other hand, had never gotten along, and speculating about how they'd hooked up took up a good part of Dr.Brian's everyday life. Nonetheless. Racheal realized it didn't even matter; the infant was alive and well.

Janicka, the youngest Domestic, was only two years out from turning eighteen, and now she and Sergey were the only ones left to cope with the workload they'd all shared once. Even the eldest babies were just five years old, barely mature enough to work in the Plant. Janickahurried through the Hall, down from the commandant's seat, her eyes big like the field elk they'd seen in the woods recently, and crawled up to their table.

"Good day, Racheal." Like anyone else in the colony, the girl was slim, but her bones had a faint heaviness about them as adolescence spread them. "I have a message for you."

Racheal sat back and grinned in the Domestic's direction, her eyes roving over the faces at the table, her current status coming naturally to her. They'd shared the same living room only a week before, but now eighteen years separated them. "Call me Ms.Fourbee, Janicka," she chastised, loud enough for all to notice. "You should know better."

"Certainly, Ms.Fourbee." The girl said it as if she were spitting khat milk. "Sorry about that. I have a letter for you, "She said it again. "Commander wants you to see him after lunch."

"No way." Racheal made a shaky motion of her head. "Tell him I'll be there at four o'clock. After lunch, I have a crèche inspection. Rina's child needs medical attention." Janicka frowned, unable to fathom a reality in which her old colleague Domestic could speak too confidently about ignoring a summons from the Commandant. Racheal marginally lifted her voice. "I'll be there as soon as my responsibilities permit. Please accept the post, Janicka."

Racheal felt the eyes on her, measuring, assessing, as the girl slipped backward. When she switched to Dr.Brian, the old Domestic Racheal must have said something like, "Why would the Commandant want to see me, Doctor?" Instead, she just stood there staring at Brian before the older woman posed the issue. "What's up?" she said, her tone strained. "Do you have any suggestions?"

Racheal had already prepared a fast and lethal response. "He just wants to fuck me," she shrugged, and while the laughter started slowly, it quickly spread around the table, and Racheal realized she'd made the right decision.

Racheal strode down the route toward the commandant's office in the side of the Hall, her hands already stinking of disinfectant from her inspection of Angerina's little child. They were now building their concrete, and this route was the first to be capped; it was a pleasant shift from the constant red dirt. She hadn't been there in months because she'd come to deliver a letter about the commandant's boy, and she hadn't talked with Elon in a fortnight since he'd released her planetary citizenship papers after the major community dinner.

He'd held her a little too closely, she recalled.

Racheal slapped the door summons with her sharp-fingered palm. A faint chime from inside accompanied Elon's deep voice. "Please come in!"

His office was, at least technically, the planet's oldest living human structure, the first structure they'd erected upon landing, and Elon had promised not to leave it before the Permanent Commandant came. This was bad since the east wall was already collapsing. She poked her head through the doorway. "Did you like me?"

"Good day, Racheal." He was sitting back in the chair he'd carried from Earth, his feet on the bench, a large stone slab left behind by the terraformers. "Please take a rest."

He wasn't beaming as brightly as he always was.

"Thank you." She sat straight-backed on his desk like they'd trained her as a Domestic; she did so now out of tradition and because she felt it was the proper way to sit. Hands-on calves, knees together, gown smoothed Just the way you like it. She stood quietly, her gaze fixed on his with her typical stillness.

He laced his hands behind his back, still not laughing, and decided to plunge straight in; this was not Elon Weathers' usual approach. Also, with the indents and Domestics, he wanted to be a cajoler. "So I haven't had a chance to speak to you after the ceremony," he started, "and although I normally only leave it to the other citizens to kind of carry along with the fresh ones, there are moments when I feel the need to... well, there's something I'd like to make plain to you, Racheal."

She stood there and waited. She realized what was going on and determined not to delay any longer. "Elon, I'm not a breeder." His eyes widened as he stepped in sharply. He wasn't ready for her to speak yet, and she noticed his eyes darting sideways as he tried to think about what to suggest. But she'd already discovered everything. "As a person," she continued, stressing the term, "I can now make my own choices." And, as a physician, I am not obliged to have children."

Elon purposefully raised his foot off the desk, the chair squeaking. "No, you aren't," he agreed. "But how does it relate to anything?" He was trying to force her to justify, and Racheal saw no excuse why she shouldn't. Brian had selected her at the age of thirteen for two reasons: she had deft hands and made swift choices, something Elondiscovered.

"I'm positive you summoned me because I fucked Niall Bar Shaughnessy last week." She stood tall and confident, being as calm and straightforward as she'd been told. "I was worried, as I'm sure you are, that we were doing that in a food-prep environment, and I supervised when Bar Shaughnessy disinfected it afterward. " This was no exaggeration; Racheal took food sanitation quite seriously. "Dr. Brian and I are thoroughly trained to deal with any medical issues that might arise. Elon is a fictional character." She grinned, anticipating his annoyance.

He certainly was.

He frowned, his fingertips occupied with some paperclips in one of the little clay bowls the Domestics had created for them when they'd all arrived. The quiet was multiple seconds longer than it should have been. "All right," he finally replied. "We'll all jump straight through it. Every day, Racheal, my main priority is morale. I have complete control over any member of this colony—unquestionable life-and-death authority for all non-citizens of the globe. And I have the authority to expel everyone, even civilians. That's a lot of force, Racheal, and I'd rather not have to use all of it." He gave a quick blink. "Are you sure?"

Racheal sat with her head down. He wasn't intimidating her with exile; instead, he was working up to something. The paperclips in their bowl shook.

"And I'm better if the colony representatives are pleased." I don't need confidence issues like the ones that occur when people fuck stay backs indiscriminately." She hesitated, then nodded; she was about to correct him on his usage of indiscriminately politely, but she had to accept he was correct.

"In the future, Elon," she said softly, "I'll make a distinction."

"That's not the point." The commandant was warmed up to his topic. "Here's the issue, Racheal, and I'm sure you're aware of it. Citizens in the pioneer wave are chosen such that as the permanents arrive, they can have indigenous breeding stock. Biodiversity is needed in that stock. So everybody fucks everyone else, we all have a lot of kids, and the colony, in principle, gets off to a good start."

"You're right, Elon." Racheal pushed her hair back behind her neck. "I'm aware of this. "You people raised me."

"So I'm not sure you understand how it applies to your choice of fuck-partners," he retorted. Elon didn't like being humiliated, and his luck had run out. "You and Chonn are exempt from getting children. As a result, you have more freedom and less pressure in your decisions."

Racheal nodded, the conclusion solidifying. It was similar to diagnosing a pulmonary disease in that you heard, paid attention, and the response came. "Marianne Fuentes is enraged that she is unable to screw Niall Bar Shaughnessy." She nodded solemnly as Elon's mouth steadily opened. "She came in and complained about it. You first attributed that to postpartum hormone imbalances. So you reconsidered, and now I'm being criticized for her envy." She shook her head. "Elon, she'll never see or hear me get laid." I guarantee it. "Is there anything else?"

Elon stared across at her, and she realized at that moment that he'd never forgive her for making him feel stupid. Her mind raced; she didn't care for his forgiveness, but she had fifteen more years before he'd go. "I apologize, Elon. She cocked her chin sideways. "Please accept my apologies."

He was steadily smiling. "I can see why Chonn adores you," he whispered. He'd given up on molesting the paperclips. "She chose an excellent apprentice." "Will you please do me a favor, Racheal?"

"Maybe, Elon," says the narrator.

"Can you promise not to remind the majority of the colony how clever you are?" He sighed and sat back again. "For a variety of causes, people aren't going to appreciate you. But you'll be a physician soon, and they'll have to put their faith in you. That's your dilemma, but I can tell you it's going to become mine."

She couldn't help herself from tutting, which irritated her. "I'm Elon. You're mistaken. "I'm liked by people."

"You're using the past tense, Racheal." They preferred you because you were a gentle little Domestic who helped people with hernias and fractured toes. "Right now?" He gave a lopsided grin. "You have the same privileges and standing as they do." So you're now a rival." He took a hiatus to let it soak in. "There is, nevertheless, a distinction. You're a one-of-a-kind, but you can tend to be less cautious. And you're stunning."

"Thank you," she said with a dry wink. "I have no idea you noticed."

"Do you see?" He helplessly extended his palms. "Because of you, there would be envy and bad blood." Do me a favor and strive to remain more discreet for a couple of years." He let out a sigh. "Wasn't you old enough to know the trouble when Scott turned eighteen?"

She gave a smile. It had been three years, maybe a bit longer. Scott Fifteenay had become the first of the Domestics to reach adulthood, and he'd sliced a swath into the Wad's women since the night he'd received his documents. That had been the two-year-old colony's first major confrontation, an ugly moment before he'd calmed down. April 78-F was now pregnant with his son, and there were rumors of a bastard having an affair with one of the stays back. "Boys will be boys," she quietly said.

"Unless they're kids." Elon was becoming more at ease now, more certain of his role with her. "Keep an eye on yourself. Please, sir. For the good of my sake."

"Cross my heart and pray to death," Racheal said with a smile. "And if I make a mistake, you should fuck me in the a$$."

He gave a quick blink. Elon arched an eyebrow after a lengthy, heavy pause. "Are you serious?"

Racheal grinned calmly. "I'm not going to screw up."

"It's just that you should be cautious about what you mean." Some of us haven't seen each other in... yeah, it's been a while. Since we've got a newcomer, that applies to both people and non-citizens." He gave a nervous chuckle. "I mean, isn't that the joke?" Why should men apply for pioneering expeditions?" She held her frozen grin on her lips, showing him nothing. "Do you go on holidays like this, or you can go on trips like this?" "Have you ever seen the one?"

She sat back and relaxed. The interview had been completed; he just wanted to reach the same point. She asked if she should be smug, thinking he'd be rough under the desk. "I'll go now, Elon." Thank you for your advice and assistance."

He shifted his weight absentmindedly. "What is it?" Oh, I see." He let out a sigh. "Indeed. Thank you so much, Racheal. Hopefully, this would not be needed again."

* * * *

She hopped over a puddle on her way out of Elon's room, checking the Wad for someone else that could be out this early in the evening. The sight of Aron 471-G both shocked and delighted her. "Hey!" she exclaimed. "It's been a long time, stranger!" She'd rebuilt his MCL the previous year, one of the few occasions Brian had let her operate alone on a big joint. "How's your knee?"

"All right, thanks." She drank in his toothy smile as she approached him and extended her side, well conscious that Elon's office window was directly behind her. "I haven't seen you since you received your driver's license, Racheal. "Thank you so much!"

"Thank you," she said with a smile, turning her head to welcome a short kiss on the face. The beard tickling her was one of Aron's practices. "But because we're so close to Elon's workplace, you can address me as Ms.Fourbee." Or he'll expel you."

Aron smiled, the intense chuckle that everybody found contagious as he came into the community on special occasions. She backed away from him, her dark brown eyes in that rare whiskered face staring up at him. "Remove me." He made a shaky motion of his head. "I've always been exiled." "I designed my own house and all!" His eyes glowed. "I'm here to report the location with the commandant and maybe persuade him to grant me citizenship." He cocked his chin. "That way, I can f*CK as many women as I want."

"But if you've already made a house on the Fringe, why would you ever need to come back and meet us in the Wad?" she grumbled.

"Are you? "I'd come back to see about you," Aron responded. He took a dab at his mouth.

"I've got my eyes up here." Racheal burst out laughing, which was unusual for her. There was no way to justify the old clone's allure. She placed her hand on his shoulder. "You know," she winked, "if you ever manage to persuade him, Dr. Brian and I may need to conduct a genetic motility study as part of the procedure." You'd come over and masturbate for us."

"Why should I wait?" He clung to his genitals. "That's what I should do right now."

Racheal went up on tiptoes on the fresh asphalt, aware she was in clear reach of the commandant's glass, to send him a kiss on the lips on the spur of the moment. She'd never done something slightly similar before, and she didn't want to; all was new now. She kept the kiss for longer than necessary, having her pussy settle gently on the back of his neck, not being sure what she was doing; when she finally backed off, she was laughing. "Hold it for me," she said quietly. "I'll pay you a call and admire your lovely native architecture."

"There's a phone message!" Aron burst out laughing. "Thank you. I'll notify you." He examined her from head to toe as though she were a meal. "Of course, I'll let you know. "I'd better get in here before it starts raining." He grinned and turned toward the entrance, and when Racheal looked past him, she saw Elon peering through the glass. She shrugged and dissolved into the mud, making sure he saw.

* * * *

Racheal was kneeling, holding Mikhail's balls in her hand a couple of days back. She carefully palpated. "There's an irregularity here," she pondered. Brian reached forward for a closer look at the scanner.

"Isolate the correct testicle," she said solemnly. "The vas deferens is getting in the way." "I can't seem to get a decent picture."

Racheal sighed as her fingertips probed softly, locating the coiled duct and nudging it anteriorly. Above, Mikhail frowned. "Relax," she yelled at him. "It isn't all that awful." Brian scowled alongside her but said nothing as she brought the scanner closer.

"I'm not confident," Mikhail said ponderously, "that I can express to two females the basic pain involved in watching your fingers do that."

Racheal grinned, but a sidelong look revealed that Brian was not in the mood. "Here, Mikka, we aim to have first-rate medical care," the doctor whispered primly. "Now, please quit running." Racheal could sense him grinding his teeth. "We're almost there."

"You're in safe shape. "We're the best care center in the galaxy," Racheal said, her fingertips frozen in place. The scanner served as a replacement before Rina could repair the original. Her brow furrowed. "You'll return for a second interview, Mikhail, and when you do? It sure you thoroughly wash your hands."

"Everyone is a skeptic." The tone of the speech was acidic. "As though the majority of them aren't working like chickens." Racheal smiled up at him under his hairy chest and squeezed the testicle between her fingertips lightly, almost imperceptibly. 'Faughh.' He seemed to be trying to vomit.
"That's plenty." Brian straightened up and turned off the scanner. "That's all right. Mikka, please take your pants back up." She gave a blank stare to the readout before smiling at their patient. "Do you mind if Racheal learns about the diagnosis? If you like, I will take her away." Racheal recognized it as a negative omen. On the way back, Brian and Mikhail had become near.

"It's all right." Racheal took a short step forward, releasing his scrotum, and bowed to him.

"Come take a peek at this, Racheal," Brian said softly, angling the readout so she could see it: the false-color picture displayed the magnetic field.

"Mm-hmm," he says. Racheal gave a smile. "That's exactly when I thought it. That's right next to my thumb." She fixed her grey eyes on Mikhail, trying hard not to show any emotion. He was a decent breeder, with two children by Rina and then Vivy's twins on the way, not to mention the one he'd implanted in Leonor.

"Sit back, Mikka," Brian instructed gently. "There's positive stuff, but there's still negative news." She sat alongside him on the exam table, taking his hand in hers and interlacing the fingers. "Your development has returned, hon."

"Of course." He grinned, almost unsurprised. "I knew something was wrong when I saw the urine turn pink."

"That's right." She drew his hand into her lap and leaned in tight. "We'll take your stem cells from the seminiferous tubules and position them in a prosthetic testis, so you can always cum as before." She took a hiatus. "Pretty similar."

"Your left one, on the other hand, would be untouched." Brian cast an alert glance Racheal's way. "At least for the time being."

"However, you'll have to amputate my right ball." Mikhail cast a mournful glance at Brian, who rolled her eyes.

"That's putting it mildly," she chuckled. "It's an easy outpatient treatment." Brian cast a glare at her assistant. "Racheal has amazing paws." She kept her eyes fixed on him, obviously anticipating his answer.

"I'll do my utmost, Mikhail," she assured him nervously.

Brian gave a smile. "The most difficult thing would be making the prosthetic." She pressed her hand against his. "Don't be concerned. There is everything we should do."

Mikhail let out a sigh. "It would finally destroy me," he observed, and Brian nodded.

"Yes, we are aware of this now. But that's not the case today." She had gleaming eyes as she craned her neck to see his profile. "Hello there. And what happens after the surgery is over and it's time to evaluate the surgical outcome? See how good you are at fucking?" She gave a soft smile. "I'll take care of that, Mikka." She slyly winked. "After all, it's always my job to double-check my apprentice's work."

"That's perfect." They exchanged smiles, Racheal feeling acutely unneeded even though she was the one standing there with the specimen bag. She was eager to get started because they required a semen sample to correct the baseline. Still, under the conditions...

"Dr. Brian," she said softly as she held out the jar. "I know it's normally my task, but Mikhail would prefer it if you collected the sample?" Feeling phony, she spread her smirk into what she figured was a warm grin. Brian took the bag after Mikhail nodded. "So I'll abandon you."

The echo of them fucking carried well into the night through the thin walls separating her quarters from Dr.Brian's. Racheal considered returning to her old Dorm room to sleep. But it was raining, and she was tired, so she just laid there and listened.

* * * *

"All right." Elon leaned back, his fingertips steepled under his chin, pensive. "That stinks."

"It narrows our choices," Rina agreed. She was here as vice-commandant and as the person in charge of the relief effort. If the colony did need to request a cloning chamber, she'd be the one in charge of the logistics until she left. Racheal realized she was getting better: her color had returned, and the test the day before had cleared her to search for another child.

Rina has a difficult life ahead of her. She'd take the relief flight out of here and take Elon's work on another new colony, where she'd put in her twenty years before becoming the founding mother of a third colony as a Permanent Commandant. Maybe it would carry her back into the nearby galaxy, but they were trying to stop that. And two in the way? Perhaps three more children? Racheal didn't believe she was capable of anything more.

"It's all right." Brian leaned back, sipping some of the nearby tea. "This is why we have redundancy. Guys, I believe discussion of a cloning chamber is premature."

"But that's just the point, Chonn. Which reduces our redundancies." Elon made a shaky motion of his head. "How can we decide the other two Domestics would be any good for mating?"

"They'll be just right." The others turned to face Racheal, who had only checked the genetic tests a month before. She grinned as she stirred, still seated upright on the bench. "In four months, he'll be eighteen. And then there's Janicka, nineteen months later; all of my research shows they'll both be dependable."

"Yes, and Sia performed admirably. What about Leonor?" Elon lifted his brows at Brian, who responded with a nod. "Her pregnancy is still on track." He let out a sigh. "Maybe you're correct, and we shouldn't talk about cloning just yet."

"If we do," Rina said softly, "I'd like to apply the form over the next three months." Time to prepare. That was the problem. Customizing the chamber, redistributing the payload, and including a better booster in the flight queue all took time. But Elon's career would be doomed by Rina's form, as they all knew; a temporary commandant who couldn't handle the colony's breeding program to plan for the permanent commandant may as well be collecting garbage on one of Perola's moons.

"Okay, then. It has been three months." Elon licked his lips and glanced around the bed. "We're both aware of the real problem." He listened before someone else spoke up; the reactions of Chonn and Rina suggested that this was something he'd tried to mention previously. Racheal paused for a couple of seconds before deciding to proceed.

"No, I don't think so. What exactly is the problem, Elon?" The other two women glanced over, relieved, but Racheal just stared at the commandant. He cocked his head.

"Racheal, why are we dipping into our redundancies?" He returned her stare with his own, and her mind went into the normal sorting shuffle before it came to her.

Racheal gave her typical precise nod while opening her mouth into a soundless O. "True. Without a doubt. Taconic, Erno"

"Taconic Erno." Elon returned the nod. "He isn't reproducing."

"Not with a lack of trying," Rina said, sighing. "He and I would have fucked at least fifty or sixty times? Early on, after the birth of my first child. We attempted for several weeks.

There is nothing. Not a single one." She shook her head. "Then, a few weeks back, Mikka and I got together, and I was pregnant in only three nights."

"There's nothing wrong with his sperm," Brian maintained as he leaned in closer. Racheal had the feeling she'd had this conversation previously. "Elon, you've done the tests. He has a lot of virility. Nice, powerful bursts."

Elon gave a thoughtful nod. "Who the hell is he fucking these days?" All was looking away. "Wait, what?"

"I don't think either of us wants to bother attempting to work with him any longer," Rina said defensively. "He becomes irritated, and then he becomes... distant? What does it all mean?" She cocked her head and considered it. "gloomy. That's what there is to it."

"Hello." Bexley sat back on the throne, her palms outstretched. "You are not required to inform me. Per fifth, I'm the one who has to go through genetic therapy with him. Elon is fully demoralized." Of necessity, he was the only male resident who had failed to complete the task.

"It isn't his main issue." Rina was warming up to her subject. "The only issue is that he's a nerd."

"There's no such thing as shit!" Elon cocked his brow. "Like, the flowy gowns?" Bexley simply shook her head, perplexed. "Are you from the desert?"

"You're not a sheik, dumbass," Bexley yelled. "A nerd. As if I were a geek."

"I'm a nerd." Elon gnawed on his lower lip thoughtfully. "I'm not familiar with that word."

"Well, you were born on the moon."

"I've been in space for a long time," he said defensively.

"There's no reason," Bexley scowled. "It's a word from the Old Earth. Geeks are smart and may be cool, but they seem to be too focused on one or two major interests. It's usually an uncommon or extraordinary love." She paused. "For example, suppose a guy is interested in nano-boost technology and decides to become a self-taught expert in it."

"Or, tell, a fascination with sleight-of-hand," Racheal added sweetly. Elon was notorious for his fondness for card tricks, and he stared at her until she was certain he'd grasped the point. She sent him a friendly smile.

"Erno's into a variety of strange things," Rina remarked. "He enjoys Old Earth music as well as spacecraft architecture. The past." She chuckled to herself. "Once upon a time, he became agitated when discussing tubas."

Brian slurped her tea and bit after a brief break, the rain pockmarking the roof. "What exactly are tubas?"

"They are an antique musical instrument. Similar to a promo phone." Elon was relieved that he understood everything Brian didn't. "Doctor, you grew up on a goddamn moon?" Chonn responded with her middle finger. "I believe they were built of aluminum. Very likely, zinc."
"Brass," you say. Rina shook her head. "Believe me. He told me everything." She paused and seemed to decide she had to mention it. "Some of us have a hard time fucking him.

He's seen us all too many times that it's almost as though he's lost interest? And if he's... yeah, it's not just that fun. He's all right."

Elon looked down at his desk, then stirred and looked back at Racheal. "Are you doing Mikka's surgery?"

She gracefully nodded. "This afternoon, I finished forming the prosthetic. All that remains is to implant the stem cells, allow them time to ensure their viability, and then remove the moralistic testis and replace it with the fresh one." She shook her head. "It's easy."

Elon smirked. "Have you ever had testicular surgery?"

"Of course not," Racheal replied with a grin. "But how difficult will it be?" She debated if she should make the pun and then realized that someone else was considering it. "If he's flaccid, it'll be a smoother process," she tittered.

"It's not funny." Rina was staring at Racheal from her plastic chair, and Racheal reminded herself that she had given birth to two of Mikhail's twins. Racheal sent her a wink.

"Of course, you are welcome to be there to watch the process," she said softly. "Just to be certain that it is handled correctly. After all, I am just a student."

Elon made a snide remark to Brian. "Why don't you go ahead and do it, Chonn?"

"Because I want Racheal to do it," Brian said right away. "She has stronger hands than me."

"I hope," Racheal said softly, "that I should try to solve our other issue as well." She'd been worrying about it ever since Rina mentioned it. I'm a geek. It was an interesting idea, and she enjoyed spacecraft architecture as well. "It seems like an opportunity I'd like to see what I can take on."

"What in the world are you on about?" Elon snarled.

Yet Rina was aware. Her mouth dropped. "Just wait." She gave a quick blink. "Would you like to fuck Erno Taconic?"

Racheal shook her head. "I've previously investigated him. Nothing is wrong with him. I had no idea he was having such a challenge."

Elon cast a look at Brian. "I'm shocked Chonn didn't mention Erno's issues to you."

"No, I'm not." Racheal maintained eye contact with the guy. Yeah, he was in command, but only before the Second Wave arrived. She was conscious that he was threatening some of the colonists. "Why does she do that? I was a Domestic a month before." She shook her head. "Unless necessary, master surgeons do not exchange patient details with their apprentices. And Erno Taconic's semen meant little to me a month earlier." She took a firm step forward. "If I'm truthful, it still doesn't, but as I said," she grinned, "I like a challenge."

Rina assumed command. "How many men have you messed up to this point?"

"I know, it's only been a month," Racheal reasoned; she hadn't kept track. Last week, Roni, Niall, and Mikhail got together "to build a baseline." Lance, the Plant's indent, like a compact penis. Niall, once more. Twice, once. Scott Fifteenay that she felt obligated; they'd grown up together and agreed it was better to keep the sex out of the way. Then there's Merner from the computer shop... "Six, I believe." Females didn't count, but she'd had a surprisingly fun evening with Jitsuko.

Elon made a mildly disgusted noise, but Racheal had long ago opted to disregard him. She suspected she'd end up in his bed sooner or later; he was drawn to her. She had the choice of waiting. Rina pondered the number "six." "That's a fairly decent month, in my opinion. Can you like fucking?" Racheal remained calm, wondering what the vice-commandant was talking to. Rina agreed with a smile. "I like fucking. Nothing is wrong about it."

Racheal was aware that Brian and Elon were looking at her. She arched an eyebrow and cocked her head, her movements as precise as ever. "I've discovered that I'm pretty decent at it," she admitted. "At least, that's what I believe."

Rina kept her eyes for a couple more seconds before shrugging. "The problem is that we need him to reproduce. Racheal, your contract does not compel you to give birth, but you are always free to do so if you so like." Racheal's slender hips caught the older woman's attention as she trailed her gaze down her frame. "To be honest, I doubt you'd like it. I'd give it a few more years."

"Waiting won't fix Elon's mating dilemma," Racheal pointed out peacefully. She took a hiatus. She reminded them of the term "redundancy."

Elon let out a sigh. "That is right." He took a hiatus before nodding to the two surgeons. "So, girls, here's what I'd like to do. Rina is planning to create a cloning chamber just in case.

Meanwhile, you have two months to find a genetically compatible guy who can mate with one of our women. So, how is that, stay back? What among hermits? If you didn't locate someone else, even indents would suffice. Go through the genetics and propose someone, and I'll write a temporary sexual dispensation for them. If they're willing, I know a number of them don't want anything to do with us, which is perfectly well as well."

Brian shook his head. "It's not like I would go about snooping on these individuals. Are you able to bring all of them into the Wad? Elon, I'm an active lady."

"Look, it's not perfect," he said calmly. But here's the crux of the matter. Erno isn't much of a pioneer citizen if he can't knock anyone up. And ordering a cloning chamber is an indication that our people have suffered in every way. Too much is riding on the next few months, and we must all share. What if Erno is unable to participate in this way?" He shook his head. "I'll find some place for him to help, most likely not here in the Wad. That is what he wants to consider."

Brian nodded uncomfortably. "I comprehend."

"That's great." Elon sighed convulsively and turned to face Racheal. "You offered to help, so go get it. I need Erno Taconic's zygote in your body as soon as possible."

"Are you sure you want to do this?" Rina was aggressively facing over, her hands on her feet. "Are you certain?"

Racheal shook her head. "What's the harm? It might be entertaining."

"None of that nonsense," Elon snarled. "This is so. Are you certain, or are you unsure?"

"I'm positive, Captain Weathers," Racheal said quietly, hoping he picked up on the mockery. She could make exceptions because he did have a tough career, but he could be a total jerk at times. "Let me do it. Dr. Brian will inform you that I don't make mistakes too much, and I don't want to do so this time either. Within two months, Erno fertilized a zygote that was headed through my uterus. I've got it."

"I hope so," Elon sniffed, "or else he'll be out to the Fringes to plant plants." That is if Chonncan locates another breeder." He frowned as he shuddered at the prospect of a cloning chamber. "It's incredible that my profession has come to depend on the sexual skills of stay back and domestics. That's not right."

The walk back to the sickhouse was tense, owing to Brian's knowledge that Racheal was lying. "You're not going to get pregnant," she charged as soon as they were out of Elon's office. "You're having a lot of fun."

"I predicted that a zygote would move into my uterus. I never said that it had to remain there." She shook her head. "I'll just take it out and insert it." She continued walking for a couple more steps until realizing Brian had come to a halt. "Wait, what?"

"Place it there." Slowly, the doctor shook her head. "If I might inquire, into what? In case you hadn't heard, we're running low on human wombs."

"They've conceived human copies in all kinds of ways," Racheal objected. "Pigs, ducks, vats, camels, and bags are all examples of farm animals. It's not that difficult. We have everything we need right now."

"What are you on about, Vats?" Bexley made a shaky motion of her head. "That's heinous." She resumed her stroll, kicking a puddle.

"Nothing more disgusting than throwing Erno out of the Wad simply because his penis isn't working." She shook her head. "Particularly because both you and I know it's a perfectly good penis."

"How come he hasn't fertilized anything?"

"I'm not sure." Racheal shook her head. "He masturbates, as do all adults. Perhaps he simply overdoes it."

"It's possible." The raindrops scattered as Brian shook her head.

"Perhaps he raised his masturbation levels because he knew he was losing sexually and therefore lost confidence."

Brian let out a sigh. "Does it make a difference?"

"Did you fuck him, Chonn?"

Brian gave a smile. "On the way back, a handful of times. Space is tedious." She smirked. "As you know, I don't take advantage of the locals. It seems to me that it jeopardizes my success as a medical professional." She said it. "It's difficult to keep a professional distance from a guy you're always fucking. This results in prejudice. That's a large part of why we're not allowed to get pregnant."

"Chonn, you remember who I am. I'll be fine."

"Yes, I'm starting to think you might. But it's not about you that I'm concerned for." She slammed the sickhouse door open. "How are you going to pull that off?"

Racheal took a shift out of her sneakers. "I figure I'll just turn up naked in his bed. We'll take it from there. I used to work with Scott." She hesitated as the older woman stared at her, then smiled. "No, it does not. I'll come up with something more discreet. But not by much; I don't have much time, and I have my ovulation to think about."

"Racheal," Brian continued softly. She waited until the younger woman turned around and hanged up her shawl. "If you're serious about this, what are your plans? What is implanting?"

"Yes, I am."

"Fuck you." She let out a breath. "I suppose we'd best go find a cow."

* * * *

Racheal sat down at her computer, rubbing her eyes as she closed the tabulate. Her gaze was drawn to her chess warrior, silhouetted by the glass in the gray morning light. She'd been looking into pheromones, but their resources were small. She'd submitted a letter to the library on Kysten, forty light-years away; alas, the book would take days to arrive, and Racheal was in a hurry.
She decided to achieve something that no other woman on the earth has ever done.

Her strategy was concise, if not simplistic. She had to keep an eye on Erno to make sure he wasn't masturbating. Meanwhile, she needed to make him want her; she planned on using pheromones, accompanied by a chance encounter or two, resulting in witty dialogue and subsequent sexual intercourse. It's that simple. So she summoned him to the sickhouse the next morning, shortly after seeing Bexley remove her metering implant.

Erno was a tall guy with wide shoulders as a result of years of his beloved hobby. He'd graduated as an agronomist, although no one could tell if he'd chosen his profession because he loved farming or whether he enjoyed farming because he'd chosen it as a career. In any case, it was fun to be around someone who enjoyed what he did, and Erno had a way of having people happy. Before they wanted to take a kid from him, that is.

He didn't come to the sickhouse too much because he looked uneasy there. Racheal raised her head from her seat as his figure filled her doorway. She smirked, as was her wouldn't. "Oh, Erno! Thank you for visiting."

"Congratulations on being a resident, Racheal." He spoke in a quiet, tentative sound, with overtones of isolation. She cocked her head.

"That's what you said, Erno. Twice during the last month. Ok, a month or so, depending on how long they are today." She sat back and propped her feet up on the desk. "You were there when I received my letters. Can you recall? You embraced me?"

"Oh, no." He shook his head.

"I'm glad I made such an impact," she chuckled. Still, she thought the chuckle sounds hollow, but she hoped Erno was too much of a nerd to note. "Women like understanding that men don't remember kissing them."

She'd put on a fresh, clean dress for the occasion, with the neck ties fastened looser than normal. There is no bra of default, bare feet. She considered arching her spine, but she didn't have much tit; it wasn't going to improve, and she might do it later while he was standing. Delicately. "Please take a rest. I'll get to the topic quickly." She observed him as he stood, his motions deliberate and self-conscious. "So there you have it. You've probably learned by now that Dr. Brian and I have discovered borreliosis in Mikhail McWong's scrotum once more."

It wasn't a concern at all. The Wad wasn't big, and a borreliosis diagnosis still spread quickly. As he nodded solemnly, Erno's eyes widened behind his old-fashioned lenses.

"Morlio may be infectious in certain cases, although this is unlikely to be the case this time. However, we're also not sure what exacerbated Mikka's illness. There are several hypotheses, but they are only important insofar as they can help us reduce the likelihood of subsequent cases." She made a demonstration of piling several data cards on her desk, the charade being second nature to her.

Of course, the ethics committee at a real sickhousein a real-world will certainly have plenty to say regarding an eighteen-year-old apprentice surgeon subjecting men to excessive testicular groping merely to screw one of them, but whatever. Racheal convinced herself it was all undertaken to save Erno from being exiled and improve biodiversity in the community. As a result, there is no legal issue. "Dr. Brian and I are developing scrotal baselines for both of the men in the Wad in order to understand further the risk factors involved. Do you agree to this?"

"What are scrotal baselines?" He gave a quick blink. "What the fuck? You still have more information concerning my scrotum than you can handle." He averted his gaze, licking his mouth, as Racheal sat silently. "I don't like being fussed with," he grumbled.

"Hello." She swept her feet away from the desk and bent in toward him, her gaze locked on his. Maximum gravitational pull. Should she work on her bedside manner? No, thank you. "Stop worrying, Erno. This is special. That's borreliosis prevention; it has little to do with the motility." She placed her hand on his knee. "Believe me. Erno, I'm not the one who's concerned with your sperm."

He swallowed and attempted a grin. "It's only been five years, and I don't have any children. Chonn has sent enough samples to fill a bathtub."

"Oh, I see. That explains why she doesn't use a moisturizer on her face." Racheal paused until the meager joke landed, a faint grin spreading over Erno's face. "Erno, calm down. It's just a testicular exam and a sample or two. Chonn's bathtub, not mine." She enabled herself to laugh once more. "In all seriousness. I'm not going to count the semen. It may be what Elon wants from you, but I'm not sure. You are my patient for this." She sat back some more. "Do you believe me?"

He shook his head. "I don't care." She frowned when she saw the strain in his jaw and shoulders; his failure to hit on either of many females and the criticism that came with it had done a number on his morale.

Not hers, though. She couldn't wait to get started. "That's very. Go get up and take your trousers off." She stepped back to calibrate the scanner, operating the calipers while she saw his pants slip. She'd seen his penis several times before, but she'd never evaluated it to bring it inside her. She'd discovered that becoming sexually engaged changed her perspective on men. Since she was thirteen, all the men in the Wad had been a claustrophobic force in her life, hauling stone through the mud of their new planet; now that they were deserving sexual partners, she found herself thinking of them as artifacts rather than humans. "Please accept my apologies in advance if my hands are cold," she noted absently.

"It's all right." Racheal swiveled her chair back to study him as he stood there with his collar tugged up under his armpits. He had the usual Wad frame, the result of so much walking and not enough rich foods; the muscles on his chest were pronounced, as were his hipbones. The penis in between was natural and stable, and his balls gave off a friendly heat when she reached for them.

She could see him tense up a little as she touched him. "Try to relax," she murmured as she bent in, her soft fingertips encircling his hairy scrotum. She reminded herself to be subtle; she planted seeds today, and she made sure to hold her back arched tightly as she leaned toward his frame. He'd glance down, and any cleavage she had would glare up at him with her unblinking grey eyes. She held her fingertips steady, just a soft grip against his flesh. His balls were huge, resembling a meaty handful. "I'll be right there, Erno."

She realized his gaze was on her as she bent in and focused on nothing, on where the base of his cock appeared from its brushy coils of thick brown pubic hair, and she saw the hair stir slightly in the warm breath from her nose. "Take it easy." One minute turned into two, and Racheal did little but breathe on his crotch while watching the hair move. She noticed goosebumps on his tummy. She sent him a few sidelong looks through her short lashes, meeting his eyes before averting her gaze.

He'd recall her smiling up at him with his balls nestled in her lap, and he'd remember what that felt like.

And with that, her job was over. She was stepping back, his vaginal moisture thick on her fingers, the last of her breath on his cock. "You should get ready now, Erno," she said softly. "Exactly what I wanted."

"All right." As he tied himself up, she swiveled sideways and pretended to take notes.

"All right, then." She returned her gaze to him, her ponytail fluttering over her shoulder. "Now comes the difficult part. Are you prepared?" He cocked his head. "I did a lot of research about this, and Dr. Brian agrees. Okay, no masturbation for two days."

He gave a quick blink. "Wait, what?"

"Only so you can return to have a taste." She shrugged, jumping into the lie with ease. "The morliosis test involves a certain degree of special richness. That's it, Erno; forty-eight hours, so you can go back to whacking it if my examination comes back normal." She grinned to let him know she was concerned, though not overly so. "All right?"

"All right." He remained awkwardly still, allowing Racheal to set the agenda. She smiled and waived.

"Now go and stop sinning. Please send in the next guy." She witnessed Erno leave with closed eyes, only to be replaced at her door by a tall, gangly figure. "Merner, oh Merner. Hello there." She sighed and resumed her output. "So there you have it. You've already read that Dr. Brian and I have discovered morliosis in Mikhail McWong's testicles once more."

* * * *

As Racheal and Brian strolled along the pond shore, both moons had set, and the night was near and quiet. "It was a rough one."

"Mm-hmm," he says. Brian frowned, her natural glee dulled by fatigue. "They can be like that at times." She threw a stone into the sea. "Regardless of how much we grow as a community, how many clones we create, or how many strides we make? Gestational diabetes is always a pain."

"Tikva is incredibly strong." Racheal caught a glimpse of the Creche's lights when they passed by. "You remember, do you?"

"No, it does not. No, you don't."

"But she'll be perfect. The path is well-known, and the prognosis is favorable. It's just that we discovered it too late."

"Mm-hmm," he says. Brian shook her head as though to switch channels in her mind. "Oh, no! In that vein, I obtained Elon's permission to begin implantation tests on your embryo." She cast a look down at Racheal's flabby tummy. "Well, the future embryo."

"There's no such thing as shit!" That's great stuff. "What kind of animal?"

Brian smirked. "A bisch is the obvious alternative. They're big and heavy, but I'll have to do comparative anatomy from the ground up to find out whether they have a viable womb. And it all depends on how quickly you work..."
Racheal gives a conscious smile. "Go ahead."

"So the other way is to catch a look from the herd on the other side of the hill. They're tiny, but they're promising, and I believe four legs can have more support than six. Also, the terraformers have provided me with womb experiments. This should fit." She shook her head. "Once I get started, it'll be pretty easy."

"And you're going to use the vacavalls as a control?" They'd taken a herd from Terra with them. "That is if Elon allows you to destroy one."

"I don't believe they'll perish." Brian paused. "Well, obviously, a few of the bisches would. But, according to April 78-F, her research shows that there are abundant species all over the world, and they're taking advantage of the terraforming. Then there you have it." She shook her head.

"Meat, on the other hand, sucks," Racheal remarked gently.

"True. However, the milk produces excellent clabber." Brian's lips were licked. "I believe it's the greatest indigenous food we have."

"That's your point of view," Racheal scoffed. "All I need is a plate of smoked purgeon, and I'm in paradise." She climbed the hill to the sickhouse. "Immediate orgasm."

As they walked out of the rain, Brian smiled. "If smoked fish makes you cum, Racheal, you're doing it wrong."

* * * *

The next day, she sat at her desk with the Antares Journal of Medicine (Special Podiatry Version!), blinking away her drowsiness and preparing to carry out the next step of her scheme.

Delicately.

But staying subtle with the new flames, scarcely banked in her cunt, was proving difficult. She'd never thought, after that first uncomfortable half-hour or so with Roni, to learn to love sex so easily. It had been a week since she'd been laid, and she was tossing and turning in her bunk at night, worrying which of the colony's men were dreaming about her cunt.

According to the loose timetable she had in her head, Erno was already at least a week out. She intended to taunt him so much that he'd give as much semen as his penis could throw. But that meant six more days without a penis, which was becoming painfully terrifying.

She'd attempted twice before, trembling into Jitsuko's thin bunk shortly after local midnight. It was their second liaison, and they'd resumed where they'd left off the first time. "Racheal! Racheal!" Jitsuko had been pitifully happy to see her, her slender dusky body not yet too ruined by Roni's fetus in her womb. She'd grinned as she propped herself up on one elbow. "What has brought you to my door?"

"Oh, you're aware." She'd slammed the flimsy door shut behind her. Sex in the dorm was frowned upon, but no one ever ratted anybody out. "I'm just passing the moment." She'd grinned and stepped quietly through the light-filled space to the bunk. "I was thinking you would be involved in sharing it along with me."

The older woman was lying on her pillow with a textbook open; she was in charge of much of the colony's education. Via her heavy, blue-black eyes, she grinned. "Maybe." Racheal was nude, and space smelled pleasantly of plants and books, as well as a slight whiff of body odor, which she found mildly arousing. She backed up against the building. "Do you need a spot to stay tonight, Racheal?"

She was still 90% moving out of her old space in the Domestic portion here at the Dorm, but back at the sickhouse, Brian was letting Mikka fuck her again, which Racheal was finding difficult in her current state of horniness. "As if you'd mind, Jit."

"Not that I can," Jitsuko sighed, thumping her book to the dusty surface. "I slept very well the last night you came."

"As a medical practitioner," Racheal said loftily, "I'm glad I was able to assist." Her dress whispered to the board, and her body slid into the sheets with the usual fluid ease, Jitsuko's moist mouth finding hers before she could relax. Last time, the schoolteacher had surprised everybody by being an incredibly good kisser, and she didn't fail this time either; her lips were warm and full, the right combination of soft and hard, and not nearly as challenging as most of the men was.

Of necessity, demanding men may be exciting as well.

Racheal's knee slipped up onto Jitsuko's hip in a dry slither of flesh, but something was strange, the women knowing naturally when and how to contact each other. Jitsuko's tongue slipped into her mouth just as Racheal slid her arm between their bodies, her fingertips curling upward into her slit. She sensed Jitsuko's wet thighs and the soothing heat of the crease at the superior end of the adductor.

The older woman breathed into Racheal's lips, soft and inviting. At the same time, her nimble surgeon's fingertips reached the edges of Jitsuko's labia, softly stroking off the midline, scattering the fluid she already felt there among her sparse dark hair. Jitsuko lay back, saliva falling to the pillow. "Yeah," she simply muttered, her eyes widening, and Racheal let the hormones rage through her bloodstream as her partner yielded.

Racheal attacked Jitsuko strongly, licking at the spicy meat with her own back arched in the air and her palms gripping hard on her partner's rear. The first time she had been shocked at how much she loved eating Jitsuko out, hearing the other woman react in real-time as her tongue and lips explored.

"Fuck you." Racheal subdued Jitsuko by licking her mouth and pawing at her boobs, her eyelids fluttering. "You're assassinating me, Racheal."

Racheal stepped back, Jitsuko's juices staining half her lip, looking evenly up at the other lady, through the subtly rounded abdomen and between the pregnancy-engorged breasts, and waiting for Jitsuko's dark eyes to find hers. "I know that Jit," she half-smiled, waiting for the woman's mouth to unlock, for the revelation to hit her fevered brain: no way could a competent woman with a Ph.D. and nearly thirty years of age, with a trail of achievements and two safe kids, plus another on the way, encourage an eighteen-year-old apprentice to play her so easily.

Racheal bent her head back down, her teeth bared for Jitsuko's clit, and coaxed a jagged, screechy orgasm out of her body, the sheets and pillows tossed aside while Racheal steadfastly neglected her achy lip, a price she was able to pay to make Jitsuko yowl.

And, gradually, return the favor; late at night, both of them were tingling and jittery, finally slipping off to sleep in each other's arms, and Racheal's latest fuzzy thinking was how thankful she was to have asked Jitsuko, so hesitantly, to carry her to bed.

Jitsuko, on the other hand, lacked a cock. And a penis was just what RachealFourbee was dreaming of as she propped her feet up on her desk and tried to concentrate on the podiatric story. As footsteps jarred the board, the little chess knight she held by the window trembled. A throat cleared behind her, and she turned her ears back, dulling the music in her aural implants. "Are you sure?"

"I'm done, Ms.Fourbee."

Oh, I see—the charade. "Thank you, Niall," she said casually, her gaze returning to her report as she flapped her hand out. "Sure, I'll take it." The asterisk of sperm was warm and unusually strong. "We'll monitor it and let you know if there's a chance of morliosis." She said it loudly, and she didn't realize anyone was listening in the waiting room. "I apologize for the discomfort."

"There's no issue." The cook fidgeted for a second longer, but Racheal was in surgeon mode and didn't have time to reminisce over old times. In the kitchen, for example, a few weeks back.

"You can dispatch the next man, Dr.Brian!" She yelled toward the front of the sickhouse; her voice pitched to the loving neutrality Brian was often mentioning. "Thank you once more." She waited until the curtain swished closed again before peering nervously into the bag as the big man shuffled out. His sperm, like all of them, was smooth and dense, and she marveled for a moment that this had been inside her. The morliosis screening in a radio spectrograph took forty minutes, but as it was just for Erno Taconic's advantage, she only threw the cumbag into the wastebasket under her seat. Just like everybody else.

"Who's up next?" The irony of Brian's accent was obvious to her. At some stage today, Erno will arrive at Brian's station in the front room, presumably to produce his semen sample for the morlio examination. Bar-Shaughnessy was one of the two men who had arrived thus far. The survey was voluntary, but Erno was a nerd, so he'd come. And a variety of forms. Meanwhile, the two surgeons needed to catch up with their reading. "Yes, indeed. There is no one here. Racheal, just go ahead and sleep out home. That's just what I'm going to do."

Racheal chuckled and sat back in her chair, the starchy scent of the sperm coming from the wastebasket. The daylight streaming in through the full glass window cut through her office like a razor, tickling her bare feet as it rolled off the edge of the desk; Racheal flexed her toes in the bright yellow glow, studying the tendons. She'd been fascinated with the human body since she was a kid, scratching at the vessels on the back of her hand or turning her kneecap around, asking what all the pieces were supposed to do.

She'd leaped at the opportunity to become a surgeon when Dr.Brian proposed it early in the voyage. The Domestics had all been passing the time in Jitsuko Swope's schools, asking which of the people would take them on and give them apprenticeships or whether they'd all continue on their own.

The preparation had started immediately: gross anatomy, microscopy, and countless chemistry lectures. Prosthetics are artificial limbs—orthodontic care. Microstructures are small holes in the ground. RachealFourbee, who was fifteen at the time, was also a trained corpsman, doing superior incisions than Dr.Brian. And now she was reviewing foot experiments while keeping a cumbersome wastebasket close to her leg.

"Hello!" Chonn, speaking loudly from the waiting area. "We've been waiting for you! And have a rest." Racheal was alerted by the gush in her accent, the swooping vowels: this was Erno. "Please allow me a moment to ensure that the space is safe." She noticed the doctor's jerky movements, the swish of the curtain in the supply section, and soon she was peering in at her apprentice with a smile. "He's here, Racheal!" she said quietly.

"Yeah, that's what I thought." Racheal didn't have to fake the cool, even languid demeanor or the nonchalant raise of one eyebrow. "I'd say you give Janicka or Sergey around to the rest of the men, canceling their tests until he begins. I don't need any additional sperm sacks."

Brian gave a smile. "This is going to end poorly," she predicted, but she smiled, her eyes gleaming with delight. "But that's not the case today. Best wishes, Racheal."

"Thank you." Soon, Racheal heard Brian and Erno rushing about the small supply room, Brian's optimistic tones: "We don't believe this is something urgent." We just need you to shoot well, Ern, straight into the asterisk. No, the chances of developing testicular borreliosis are very slim. What are you talking about? No, additional research should not be needed. The rustle of the disposable cloth, the squirt of the sanitizer, and the soft flapping of Erno's bare feet punctuated the silence. Oh my God. It's not that I haven't seen it before, so just get naked.

Racheal sighed and set down her book. Podiatry wasn't very fascinating in and of itself, but in a world where almost everyone moved almost everywhere, she realized she wanted to brush up. The itch between her legs and the proximity of her mark, though, became too much of a diversion. She closed her eyes against the yellow glare, letting the exhaustion from the previous night go away.

She knew he'd be fine now. Three men had come in that week to do their fake frictive job, and she had learned by seeing the recordings that they seemed to get down to business fast. The average time for them to get hard was three minutes and fourteen seconds, and no one had seen any justification to believe Erno was an outlier, even though he'd previously shown a longer plateau cycle. Three minutes... it wasn't worth worrying about until they'd done it.

But, in any event, he'd be almost there in a couple of minutes. Racheal calculated the time and set her alarm, wondering if she should strip down to her tanktop; the outer robe was perfect, but she wished it obscured her butt. He hadn't seen her nude, of course, but still. She realized she looked best in the snug leggings, but she left the robe pooled at her feet when the timer went off. Later, he'd ask if she'd taken it off but let him have it.

After a couple of days, it wouldn't matter. By then, he'd have impregnated her.

She quickly gathered herself, back straight, shoulders wide, exuding the gentle confidence she'd been taught during her apprenticeship. Grace, poise, competence: she strode effortlessly toward the curtain that divided her from Erno, emptying her mind, ready to be stunned at what she found in the surgeon's way. She swept the curtain back, missing the wet-flesh sound inside, the rapid rhythmic snick-snick noise she knew she'd hear when she walked in.

"Please excuse me! Arriving too!" The ruse demanded that she come in and get a handful of clotters from the high shelves against the outside wall, reaching high to take out the bin. She walked right in on a nude Erno Taconic, masturbating wildly, his teeth clenched and his eyes dull on the tabulate he'd hooked up to the armrest, where some porn flickered on the phone. "Oh, no! And accept my apologies." She respectfully grinned, claiming not to note his cock's size. "I'll only be a moment. Please disregard my presence."

In the corner of her eye, she saw a man looking blankly at her, tentatively, his hand Schlup-schlepping toward a stop; he didn't know if he could proceed. So Racheal went on her business as though he wasn't even there, her mind urging him to keep driving, barreling toward the teeth-gritted climax he'd been on before she joined. The sound of his slipping flesh slowed, but she was glad that it didn't completely disappear. His gaze was almost tactile, darting down her bare shoulders, down her back where the tanktop revealed her protruding ribs, and down her butt and thighs.

So, what do you think? She stood back and let him see.

She planted her feet slightly apart and craned her neck toward the clutter bin, her calves straining; he'd be able to see every muscle, defined sharply against her top and leggings. She kept the position for a beat, waiting, hoping for the sounds to come louder, to recover their rhythm, and after a few tentative seconds, she was relieved that they did.

His breathing was fast, as was his hand. Racheal reached deeper, picturing the sperm in his body, the internal muscles tensing to force it to his urethra, and the pudendal nerve eagerly waiting to give the warning. He was getting ready to cum, looking firmly at her ass, and he wouldn't forget. She was rummaging through the bin now, and she realized she'd already succeeded; he was getting ready to cum, staring squarely at her butt, and he wouldn't forget.

But she drew a pair of clotters and relaxed, about to go but unsure if to say something more. He was back up to pace, and it didn't seem like he'd be long now. So Racheal slowly turned her head toward him, keeping strong eye contact with his big, red-rimmed eyes, making sure he saw her staring at his face before she stared at his dick. Erno swayed, his whole face vibrating with the immediacy of his impending climax, and she sent him a coy half-smile as she looked at his cock, purpled and straining, his left hand cupping at his huge balls.

It's now your turn to talk.

"Watch your target, Erno," she said quietly, her face shining for him, and she motioned to the sterisack lying on the chair's arm. "Waste not, desire not," the adage goes. She was already walking at that point; the parting shot a soft warning that she knew he was on his way, that she'd be right in the next room when it happened. So she walked out with little of the aloofness she'd approached with, and as the curtain closed behind her, she made sure there was a space to one foot. As Erno saw the difference, it reminded him that she was, on the other hand, listening as his cock exploded.

And she was; when her chair creaked under her weight, she detected the guttural grunting sigh of a man in ecstasy inside the storeroom. Racheal closed her eyes as Erno slashed his semen through the sterisack, the light already hiding behind a mist. "Fuck," he said softly. She imagined it idly, the milky whiteness pouring into the bag, the deep contractions of the man's cock, and the porn pushed aside by the memory of her bare shoulders and spread thighs.

Racheal's body shivered.

She swept the journal back up, informing herself of all the forms the medial plantar nerve might go wrong, and no longer had she begun furrowing her brow at the diagrams than the curtain slipped aside, hesitantly, like a rat detecting a pit. She forced an internal grin away and directed her gaze to the journal; she'd let him make the first step.

"So there you have it. I'm sorry, but I'm finished."

Racheal lifted her chin, her short lashes swept up as if men gave her spermbags every day. "I hope you liked it," she said softly, pausing for a moment before reaching out her hand. She cocked her head. "Seems like it, Erno."

"All right." He blushed, his shyness returning, and took a step toward her. "I know, having an audience is still, um, fascinating."

Fuck you. He also flirted clumsily. Racheal's slender lips curled into a grin. "Any assistance I might provide was entirely unintentional," she lied, noticing the weight of the bag as he turned it over. "I apologize for the inconvenience. I completely forget you were there."

"Oh, it's perfect," he said quickly, his gaze flickering toward the exit. Rain was spotting it again.

"We'll monitor it and let you know if there's a chance of morliosis." She kept her eyes fixed on him. "I apologize for the discomfort."

"Of course." He was unsure. "Are you sure I'm done?"

Racheal understood what he intended and considered winking, then realized she'd be overdoing it. Instead, she gave a quick nod. "You should go back to masturbating whenever you want, Erno." She leaned down, only to realize she hadn't put her robe back on. As though it was relevant now. "Thank you once more."

"I'll see you later." He walked back toward the front entrance; his whispered farewell was drowned out by Brian's. Come back and see us whenever you like! The doctor returned to see Racheal and grimaced at what she found.

"I'm not sure what you're looking to achieve," she muttered as she pursed her lips. "It'll all taste like the sterisack." Racheal had just taken a semen-glazed digit and brought it to her mouth.
"Now come on, Chonn." This time, she did grin. "You said that taste is an integral aspect of diagnosis." She inserted her finger into her mouth and tasted the smooth starchy richness of the sperm. She nodded after letting it rest on her tongue. "Seems to be rid of morliosis," she declared with a slap of her mouth. She shot up a short smile at Brian and inserted her finger for another sample.

Mmmmm. Is it possible to go six days without a dick? No means, no how. She considered the Cottage and prepared a letter to deliver.

* * * *

"I had no idea people slept too long," Racheal confessed that night, overwhelmed by her sweat and Roni's semen. "It's crazy how much you get laid."

Roni shook his head on the pillow, still trying to catch his breath. "Oh, just stop talking. You should know better." In the starlight trickling through the tall windows of the Cottage, he saw her petite, nude form. "We're trailblazers. We've come to fuck, live, and fuck some more. Spawn a few children, then fuck. And get to work. Go screw and go to work." He grinned, causing his whole chest to vibrate against her face. "Wait a couple of years if you think this is impressive." He let out a yawn. "When the permanent colonies arrive? Oh, no."

"Pussy for days," she remarked, gently stroking his oily dick.

"No, for weeks," he answered absently. Roni considered it. "I'll be 43," he pondered. "Weeks," she says.

Racheal pressed her ear to his chest, listening to his lungs. "There's always tons of testosterone."

"Only if you think so." He didn't seem to mind. "Most of our children would be able to fuck by then. You are aware of the series. The explorers are here because of native breeding stock. Both first-generation mutations have been comfortably sealed in for the newcomers." He deliberated. "Racheal, have you ever considered getting a child? I realize you're excluded, but I'm sure you have those badass genes."

She considered telling him about Erno but concluded it was not a smart idea. "We'll just have to wait and see," she said evasively, still worrying about the spermicide she'd be taking in the morning to combat what Roni had injected into her bloodstream. She was a little bloated from the marathon evening. She'd made him rough three times. She considered telling him to spit it on her boobs, but she realized that would elicit questions from him. She let out a breath. "You're obtuse," she said, drawingling. "There's more to it than fucking and spawning. You, too, are doing valuable work."

He cracked a grin. "Of course." He was messing with her hair; she'd learned from the other women that this was something he enjoyed doing. "It's strange," he admitted. "I believe we're both perplexed."

"Are you perplexed?"

He shrugged once more. "I work as an architect. Engineers, scientists, and zoologists are among the others. Climatologists study the weather. But we've all been taught. Other people from another world conditioned me. What are you doing here?" He looked about at the Cottage's very Terran design; it had been one of the first buildings constructed, and it was still showing signs of wear. "This location is poorly designed. It's fine for life back home, just not for life here in the Wad. We're all trying to adjust our teaching to meet the demands of this setting." He yawned again, this time more profoundly. "It may be perplexing."

"Yes, indeed. We don't have to be concerned with the nonsense." Everywhere I went for surgery, it was the same. "However, the nearby wildlife is causing us problems."

"I overheard. Chonn brings it up sometimes." There were normal trials with prosthetics and implantation. "Is there nothing suitable?"

"Well, I wouldn't claim 'nothing,'" she says. She reflected on the looks and bisches. "There are several options. But, before we can write, Chonn and I prefer to remain silent."

"Of course." Roni's fingertips were spasming again, which was incredible. "I'm aware of how it is." She noticed the burr in his accent, felt him warm beside her cheek, and hoped a fourth time wouldn't hurt.

* * * *

"Does this sound right, Miss Fourbee?" The child was adorable, one of the Tikva/Roni crosses, and with genes like that, the cuteness was a foregone conclusion. She looked down at the child as she held up her first-aid bag. "Did I pack it correctly?"

The secret, as any colonist kid was taught from an early age, was to carry a first-aid kit with you everywhere you go, which meant it had to be tiny so so people wouldn't purposefully miss it, which meant it had to be packaged a certain way: sterilizers, chemical tourniquets, downer syrettes, bandages, glue, all crammed into the little sacks they created for export up at the Plant. Racheal gave a smile.

"You did an excellent job, baby! A big thumbs up!" She didn't like kids in general, but she didn't want the kids to realize it. "You're trying to take over my work shortly." The little kid, who had no idea what a career was, just smiled. "All right!" Racheal became agitated and lifted her voice. "Make a decision. Let us discuss lacerations!"

Racheal has been teaching practical first aid to the colony's seven school-age children for years. Meron, the indent who ran the crèche, stood in the back of the office, about six months out from filing for citizenship and chomping at the bit. Jitsuko stood next to her, kicking one of Marianne's boys back to attention. "Focus!" she yelled, much as she'd yelled at Racheal and the other Domestics on the bus. Racheal made eye contact with the girl, Beck, a sullen little fucker. She indicated with her finger.

"You're the one. Come on up here. I want a demonstrator." He awoke warily, no question anticipating what was to come; he was the first human born on this earth, doomed to go down in history, and he knew it. It had all turned him into a jerk. Racheal grinned as he shuffled to the front of the bed. "Excellent." She arched an eyebrow at Jitsuko's beautiful little girl. "What about a Kiwi? What do we do for a centimeter-deep laceration, for example? The term "transverse" refers to the direction in which Thigh, upper." The youngster was standing with his head cocked.

"Well," Kiwi sighed; such a lisp! "First you avoid the blood, then you cau-cau-causterize?"

"Caution is advised. There is no S." Racheal gave a smile. "And you do that on the beam with the Number Three head? Is that correct? To reduce scarring?" Racheal took out her dagger, bent forward, and sliced sharply through Beck's left calf, the wound cruel and gaping and still pumping blood into the boy's sandals. He uttered a choked grunt and remained motionless. "Go for it, young man! He's entirely yours."

Kiwi skipped up to the front and shoved Beck to the deck, the stunned teen collapsing like a felled oak. He was as white as a mask already. "You begin with the sterilizers," Racheal explained to the other kids as Kiwi's little fingers swabbed and burrowed. She was going fine, exactly like she had been taught the day before. "Notice how the vessels have already been revealed..."

Meron, in the rear, was still pursing her lips in response to the volume of blood. She'd have to cover the carpet, and Racheal realized she'd gone a bit too far. She piqued the interest of Lena, the other indent in the crèche. "Go to the hospital and get some blood." She cast a judging glance down at the waxy Beck. "How about two units?" The indent bolted, and Racheal smiled at the class. "What about the kids? Do you want to hear more about transfusions?"

Later, as they concentrated on their creations, Racheal and Meron leaned against the wall, wondering how long she'd be able to sleep this afternoon. A child was staring at her, with the recognizable look of trepidation and resolve that said she had a concern. "Are you sure?"

"Why do we name this spot a Wad, Miss Fourbee?"

"The Wad," she corrected herself. She exchanged a hidden look with Jitsuko, only enough to know the instructor wasn't giving the kids the entire tale. Not a challenge. She'd go along with it. "As a result, a wad is a collection. An amalgamation of various parts that come together to form a single large mass." She knelt down to look into the child's dessert-plate eyes. "Do you see what I mean? Coming together and functioning as a squad, much like all of us."

"Wow!" says the speaker.

"Isn't that right? All of the coordination is wonderful. Collaboration." Beck, who was also pale close, looked over. He strongly disagreed. "We're a huge, sweet wad."

"Liar," Meron said quietly as she rose to her feet. "You should know better." Racheal returned the nod. Well, she knew better, but this wasn't a children's tale of how the very first crew of terraformers had called this sodden spot "Wadlwengula," after the term in their language that represented the offense that had gotten them convicted here. Captain Weathers had tried to persuade them to amend the name to New Promise, and when that failed, he tried to persuade them to change it to Wengula, but The Wad had held. It provided countless punning options for people of all ages, whether they talked about gum or semen. "What does it all say again? What is a Wadlwengula?"

Reille bent in and returned the whisper. "Anal has raped."

"Oh, I see. That's right." They shut their mouths when they saw Jitsuko Swope offer them a stern look; she'd been their instructor as well, and old traditions die hard: stern looks from old teachers bore a strong feeling of shame. And after you'd eaten them to climax, as Racheal discovered.

* * *

She noticed, with some pleasure, that Erno was beginning to look at her inadvertently during meals and when strolling about outside. Racheal picked at her food one evening a few days after seeing him masturbate and listened as he brooded over his plate of cevapi. She sat patiently, putting up with Mikhail's inane commentary as they hunted the last cube of pekmezli around on the tray, biding her time until she was certain he was studying her. She then gave the rest of the food to Mikka, contenting herself with a glistening dab of grape molasses on the tip of her middle finger.

Her hand slid daintily to her mouth, and she was certain Erno was already looking as she sucked her glossy finger between her lips, keeping it there long enough for him to see what she felt like with hollowed cheeks.

Enough now.

"Night, Mikka," she said rapidly to her morbid friend as she rose to her feet. She had another impromptu idea, and it allowed her to arrive at the Dorm before Erno. "Sleep well."

"Racheal," he grinned back, and she saw the flicker of his gaze over her body as she grew in a detached manner. "I'll see you in the morning."

"That's correct." Her sandals slapped gently against the flagstones as she walked away from the chaos. A quick look through to the open kitchen reminded her of the solid sensation of Niall Bar-penis Shaughnessy's twisting inside her body, and as always, she felt the quick tickling rush as her pussy woke up; the time with the cook had been a powerful orgasm.

That's great. The more liquid there are, the better.

Erno stayed in the west corridor off the lobby, directly across from Captain Weathers. She pushed swiftly, catlike, past the mail slots and the commandant's coding table, coming to a halt at Erno's entrance.

For a brief moment, the idea was simple: slip inside and glide through Erno's suite, leaving her clothes as she went, before her returning quarry returned from dinner, cards, a movie, reading about spacecraft construction, or whatever he did, and pursued her sartorial trail to find Racheal nude and willing in his room. He'd feel uncomfortable, anxious, and possibly humiliated because she'd have to take more of a lead than she felt comfortable taking tonight.

No, it does not. The long game, with Erno marinating in his love for her, was stronger in the beginning. She drew her dress up and rapidly reached down into her bra, dipping her specific finger up into herself. There was the normal pulse, the jab of need as she reached herself, but she ignored the desire for deeper contact and focused: this was a work. She carved her finger through her slit twice, three times, four times, deep and fast, and when she gently removed her hand from between her thighs, it wasn't molasses that glossed her fingernail.

She smeared her pussy juice over the palm reader with a decisive swipe, knowing he'd position his hand there. He'd ask why he was smelling pussy any time he went to scratch his nose after that.

The cameras would capture what she'd accomplished, as well as her rapid escape back into the lobby, but only the commandant would see the video. And he was already aware of what she was up to.

* * * *

"You have it!" Brian sounded positive, but that wasn't surprising: she was an expressive lady. On the other hand, Racheal understood what this was about based on the course of her latest study. She leaned back from her microscope, turning off the music in her and implants.

"Doctor, do you agree?" Stretching her jaw, she said softly, almost mockingly. "Did you discover our enzymes?"

"I certainly did." Brian was staring back at her glasses, her fingertips pressed on the tabulate beside her. "Just one more pass to validate..." Racheal frowned and bent over herself to switch on the repeater as she squinted, fully concentrating. The picture flashed to life on the ceiling display, ChonnBrian's field of view scrolling as her lens sorted out the twisted chemical links, the electrons color-coded through the image, and there it was. "That, my poor Ms.Fourbee, is mesmerizing," Brian cackled.

And there it was, as plain as a rainless day in the crowded, bumping haematocytes in the lumpy drop of bisch blood. "Are you certain it's not a mutation?" Racheal muttered something.

"No, but it doesn't really matter," Brian shrugged. As mutant or not, the animal from this study is likely to survive a human embryo transplant." She smiled and nodded. "There's transplantability where there's mesmerize," she shrugged. "It's that simple. But there you have it. I'll dispatch Janicka to collect samples from the rest of the herd this afternoon. Now that I know what stain to use, what do I do? I'll find out if those jerks are mesmeric right now." She laughed. "Do you see what I mean? You can be happy. When you do have Erno Taconic to conceive you, you won't have to transport your embryo." She took a look outside. "How is it going?"

"Fine," Racheal responded. "Perfectly," she said, adding that she wanted two items more: an opportunity for him to see her nude and dirty, and about a half-hour alone with him, hopefully with two to three days in between to allow his mind enough of time to function. "Do you know if the travel to Plastic Harbor is still on for next week?"

"As far as I'm aware." Brian was entering the code that would summon Janicka Netanya. "Ahhh," she said, nodding. "I see your strategy."

"Erno works as an agronomist. He is still accompanying me to inspect the algae." Racheal rubbed the front of her dress with her nails. "I mean, it's a smart thing to have a medical professional around. That is if it is conceivable."

"Mmm," Brian said, smiling. "I believe I will spare you for such a journey."

"That's nice." Naked, filthy. Racheal grinned and took up the vox box to contact Juukko at the Plant. There were preparations to be made.

"Of course." Weathers swept crumbs from his tunic's neck. "That leaves one more thing, I believe. The review of the incubator."

The people groaned; except for those who spent every day in the slight claustrophobia of the Wad, the annual checks of the incubators at Plastic Harbor were not in high demand. Erno Taconic or Marianne Fwentes had to go, since the agronomy facets of the algae farms out there, as well as April 78-F's zoology inventories, were the entire point of the visit; apart from them, there was still sharp rivalry to find something else to do on the day.

"I know it stinks out there," Weathers continued patiently. And after four years of hard work, the conditions at Plastic were downright brutal. "However, there are turbines to run and sensors to manage. What is that?" He grinned and looked over at Reille. "We're running low on Domestics now that Ms.Fourbee is a resident." They'd still made up the most of these inspections because they couldn't say no. Racheal had made her last journey out there when she was seventeen, and she had vowed never to return.

But that was back then. This was the time.

"April and Erno will be there, as will Janicka and Sergey." Yes, really. The remainder of the Domestics. "However, we'll need someone to operate the shuttle out there, as well as another for odd work." He took a look outside. "May I give you more money?"

"How high is it?" Leonor, the apprentice programmer, had a mother back on Klarus III to love, and she could sail.

"No," I say. Chonn gave a sharp shake of her head. "Leonor, you've been six months. There's no chance you're off." She was carrying her first boy, which would most likely be the last one they'd get out of Mikka. The sort of genetic variation couldn't be taken for granted.

Racheal sees an ability to be noble when obtaining Erno's semen. "That's nonsense," she snarled. "I'll accompany her. She'll be perfect, and it'll just be a matter of days." Brian seemed to be about to protest but only lifted an eyebrow. "Plus, she will assist me in practicing flying the shuttle at the same time." Racheal had no inclination to learn to ride, which was a lie. So it couldn't hurt to try.

Weathers cocked his brow. "How about eighty shekels?" he asked. Leonor smirked.

"Seventy-five."

"Done." The commandant stabbed his fist into the air, scribbling letters and numbers into the visible ether. Two other names popped up. "Is there one more? Are there any takers?" He looked back.

"No, captain," Scott said with a shrug. He'd achieved plenty of these as a domestic as well. "Those are your terms, Leonor and Racheal."

"They'll be in the shuttle the whole time," Weathers said. "And you should go, too, for eighty shekels, only for being such a jerk." Users laughed.

"Maybe he should find another stayback to screw," tittered Sia, breastfeeding Weathers's newborn. Scott was rumored to have gone off the grid in the backcountry.

"Maybe if the possibilities in the Wad were any decent, I wouldn't have to," Scott whispered back at her pointedly. Sia responded with two thumbs, but he dismissed her; he was already basking in the light of becoming a viable breeder, with Rina's baby doing well enough and April 78-F showing signs of life.

"All right, then." Weathers regarded his to-do page with a frown. The station out there had just a purpose-built study cabin with two bunks. The rest of the inspection team normally slept in dome tents or in the shuttle, which was uncomfortable. "How many domes do you have, April?"

The clone smirked. "Two should be perfect," she said, shrugging. It didn't matter to her; she slept in the shack and had often said that she would be content to remain there forever, alone with her incubator. She did, however, love sex, which was challenging with fish. "Elon, it's whatever people want to bring. But I'd still appreciate it if Scott could sit in the station with me, "she said, absently rubbing her stomach. Scott bent once again to scowl triumphantly at Sia, and Racheal wondered how long they'd been fucking for.

"All right." Weathers paused before shrugging. "Scott is in the shack, and Erno is in a tent. Is it you, Sia? Which is better, a shuttle or a tent?"

"The tent. Using a hammock, "She shuddered at the prospect of staying in the shuttle.

"So I'll take the bus," Racheal said easily, her scheme falling into position neatly. She'd be damned if she slept in the shuttle, but no one needed to hear that just yet.

"Excellent. There's even a dome for the girls." Weathers already sounded bored. "Thirty domes plus rations, April."

The clone returned the commandant's stare as if the guy were mentally disabled. "Why are you telling me this, Elon? Enable a Domestic to tackle all of the nonsense." She shook her head and threw her dark hair back. "Sergey and Janicka's names are Sergey and Janicka, respectively. They are capable of doing so."

"No, they can't," Racheal said flatly. "They're not yet eighteen." She was delighted when that elicited a general chuckle and even a grin from April, but Racheal was careful not to display any sentiment.

She had a legacy to uphold.

* * * *

The challenge, of course, was making sure Erno was at the Plant when she wanted him to be. The guy was an agronomical engineer, but he was just in the Plant once a week or so, but she informed Juuk she'd stop by when she felt Erno might be there. The indent didn't inquire as to why not that Racheal noticed. After all, if she could reveal to everyone that she was carrying Erno's child, all of her deceptions would be for naught.

So, on a late Thursday afternoon, Racheal sat at an empty desk in the Prototype Room with JuukkoLerman and RinaSevenpee, her feet propped up on the desk as she rubbed her pointy chin and waited for Erno to enter the building through the large floor doors. Whether he did, that is. "So, you guys made this to Juuk's specs?" she wondered, looking up at Rina.

"Ok, Vivy did most of the construction job." Rina laughed. Juukko's project had piqued the attention of any woman at the Plant. The two construction engineers were Vivy and Rina. "I was mostly responsible for the materials research. There were about fifteen separate prototypes."

"Oh, no! Is it okay for me to see them?" Racheal made sure she was smirking as she peered through the windows at the Plant door; waiting for Rina to return with the other designs could take at least five minutes. "Of course, with their medical aspects," she winked.

"AaaaaaaaaaaaaaaaaaRina stood up while the three of them laughed. "Don't get yourself into some trouble when I'm out." She was already giggling when she walked forward, leaving Juukko to prop her a$$ up on the bench.

"Five weeks already," she mused, ironically sighing. "Which makes sense. I craft the ultimate dildo just when I'm allowed to get laid again."

"Mmhmm," Racheal said, nodding. "Nonetheless. 'Perfect dildo,' you're correct." She examined the object with both her palms and nothing about it indicated it was artificial, even to her medical eye. She'd have to stop herself from checking at the back to inspect for leaked blood; it was as though Juukko and Rina had cut it from a donor. "Can you tell me who the model is?"

"Well, that's when you come in," Juuk said, purring. "There is no such thing as a blueprint. It's intended to be modular. It is movable."

Racheal gave a smile. "But didn't you do the production work?" Juukko gave a smile. "That's incredible. That's some ability."

The indent grinned humbly. "Most of my patternmaking is experimental work by design engineers. This was a lot more enjoyable."

Racheal raised a quick eyebrow at Juukko. "Have you raped yourself?"

"The name of Jesus. Possibly twenty to thirty times." She smiled contentedly. "Research and development can be quite enjoyable at times." As Rina returned with a big briefcase, they were all laughing. "Oh, I see. The remaining prototypes."

"Outstanding." Racheal bent over with clinical curiosity, sweeping her foot off the desk to allow space for the designs. "Are they made of various things, or are they all different shapes?"

"It's both." Rina yanked on the locks. "Delight your mind."

With neatly fitted baize dividers, the case was a sea of cocks of every scale, color, and definition, all as lifelike as the one in her lap. "Holy shit," she exclaimed, her arms wide open.

"The balls are inflatable as well, for the right kind of dangle," Rina said.

"Adjustable scrota?" Racheal exclaimed. "Wow," I say.

"I was planning on consulting with you on a method that would deal with others and pheromones. So it smells and tastes like a clean, sweaty cock who's spent all day in the fields." Rina was unsure. "I get a kick out of that shit," she admitted.

"There are worse syndromes," Racheal politely responded. "Of course, I'd be delighted to contribute my medical experience insofar as it is."

"And maybe a remote control. To use the partner-assist function."

"Fuck you, girls." Racheal made a shaky motion of her head. "You took the balls and played for them." She sat there waiting for the giggles to end. "You know what I'm talking about, don't you? This is a legitimate export. This is what the colony will sell to other worlds." She cast an absentminded look back out the window: no Erno. "That is, only Captain Weathers approves."

"I'm certain I can reassure him." Rina seemed optimistic, which made sense that she was the Captain's vice-commandant and had a stellar reputation as a bedmate. "Favorable."

"Then make sure we're all included on the intergalactic patent," Juukko murmured. She'd never considered the commercial ramifications of this. "In a few weeks, I'll be a resident. It'd be cool to have a job as a dildo entrepreneur that I can only step into."

As Erno walked through the door on the factory floor, Racheal realized it was time to get to work. She had a few minutes until he passed by their doors, and she realized just what she needed him to see. Her tone became sterile and bland. "So there you have it. Aside from business opportunities, I'm here to ensure the device is medically secure." She looked over at the others and grinned. "I'd suggest there's just one way to find out." She lowered herself in the chair and grasped for the hem of her gown.

"There's no way!" Juukko's hand was already reaching for her lips, her eyes brightening. She cast a brief look over at Rina. "Do you like some anonymity, Ms.Fourbee?"

"Do I seem to be concerned?" Everyone in the world knew she and Brian were both strong in a crisis, but Chonn had a comfort to her while she wasn't saving lives, an amiability that made people want to be her mate. Racheal has never had the issue and had never felt the need to lie. Her coldness was an armour she wore now; she didn't think twice about propping her stretched legs on the prototyping desk and shoving a silicone dick into her twat, and if these women decided to watch?

What's the harm?

"Of course." Erno was approaching the print heads from the corner of her eye; it was time to make this possible. The dress slid up her naked thighs as she threw her legs up high. "Can you show me how to inflate the balls again?"

Rina, with slight distaste vs. grotesque curiosity on her lips, let the fascination prevail. She bent down and pointed to the sense controls on the dildo's base. "It all depends on the kind of event you choose to replicate. Whose scrotum are you seeking?" She laughed. "For example, Erno has large balls, whereas Mikka's are smaller and denser."

"Erno," Racheal yelled. It was a waste of time. Rina changed the gadget while Racheal jammed her panties down her left ankle, leaving them hanging, and there it was: he'd step by the window quickly, and presumably, he'd look, and what would he see? Racheal focused on a worn pair of teenage legs splayed wide open, the pussy in between being separated by a hyperrealistic silicone dick, her expression presumably clenched in red-cheeked desire... this couldn't have turned out easier for her purposes. The pure naughtiness was already juicing her up. And the best thing is... She'd have an orgasm as a result of the entire thing.

A second later, the tiny servopump inside the artificial scrotum buzzed. "We'll use a quiet motor until we're out of prototyping," Rina grumbled. "What do you mean, veininess? Is it better to go up or low? Oh, and what about curvature? The temperature"

"I don't care." Racheal could tell she was in a hurry from the tone of her speech. "All I want is the damn penis, Rina."

"She's dying here, Ms.Sevenpee," Juukko said, slapping the dildo into Racheal's open hand. Racheal could detect the phlegm in the indent's speech from a distance; sorry,Juuk. I'm as horny as hell, but I'm not allowed to take a dick. "Please help the poor kid."

"Please feel free to join in." Racheal nodded across to the open briefcase, hearing the clipped eagerness of her expression. "Choose the poison. I'm sure they're all clean." She was already distantly listening to Rina's nervous bark of laughter when she used her left hand to pull aside her labia minora, picturing it, the inflammation there, the glistening flesh ready; she felt her throat constriction and the snot in her nose and briefly considered pulling her neck ties so he could see the flush spreading across her chest. Still, a glance between her legs convinced her otherwise.

The head felt so real, nudging along her slit, beginning up high the way she wanted it: a fast, insistent pressure against the clit to bring the first jolt zapping along her nerves before she sunk the cock down, slipping it inside herself with that now-familiar soupy glopping tone. It came in smoothly, amazingly, and felt like heaven. "Fuck," she sighed to herself, and as she opened her eyes, she found the woman looking at her with big eyes. She swallowed hard. "I'm not sure. A medical examination is being conducted. "Rina's fragile laughter gives way to the looming figure of Erno and Lance approaching.

Why can you wait?

Racheal's body reacted by nearly drawing the cock into herself. She couldn't recall ever being so enthralled. The clinical portion of her brain, the part that never shut down, kept repeating itself: clitoral removal. Skene's gland is overly active. Muscular strain is rising, with the most pronouncing at the pubococcygeus and vaginal clamping.

Fuck you. He was right there, going through the doors.

She saw Erno's eyes widening to balance Rina's and Juuk's, her eyelids fluttering, and she thought briefly about her features. Her forearm flexed rhythmically, causing the dildo to go in, out, in, out.

Unwilled vocalizations Spasm of the pharynx. Muscular strain persists.
Her left hand gripped the side of the desk, next to her foot, firmly. There were squeaks somewhere, whether from her throat or the overworked chair; it didn't matter. Juukko's speech, low and calm: "No, no! Did you use the artificial sperm reservoir?"

"I'm not sure... I can't recall something." Rina sounded surprised, and Racheal started to yell at them: phony sperm? Who gives a fuck? Already, I'm feeling awe-inspiring! Her speech failed her, slipping into a string of soft grunts as the two men outside listened, blinked, and shuffled away, leaving her lost in a warm-water haze as she approached.

It's difficult.

Racheal lost her equilibrium, her knees spastic, pressing so forcefully into the prototyping desk, and the chair clattered to the tile floor. She didn't feel her head smacking the cement, but she didn't care; she stood where she was, reaming herself with her legs flailing, thinking vaguely how terrible the discoloration on the back of her head might be, and when she succumbed to oblivion a few seconds later, it wasn't the crash. It was the adrenaline rush from her marijuana.

"Umm," I say. A few minutes later, she was still sweating, staring up at Rina's worried frown, the plastic penis still wedged against her cervix. In a mucus-filled mouth, she choked. "Yeah, I guess. It is successful."

* * * *

"Hello there! Racheal, you're messing up again with the directional vanes!" Leonor was showing to be one of those people who experienced a loss of personal control during the third trimester of her pregnancy. When they'd been Domestics together, she'd always been quite even-keeled. "With hands like yours and a mind like yours? Then can't you get this?"

"I understand," Racheal confessed sadly. "It shouldn't be this difficult."

"Once again," Leonor emphasized, "never use clobbers beyond the Blue Point." This isn't difficult."

"Fuck off," I say. Racheal gnawed at her lower lip, struggling with the levers as the shuttle lurched forward. The thruster lights glared back at her accusingly. "So there you have it. Thrusters, correct?"

"Thrusters are a kind of thruster. That's right, "Leonor smirked, adjusting her weight in the pilot's seat once more. "I have to go pee. Will you do it? Or am I obligated to stay here and pee my pants?"

"Don't be such a jerk." Racheal squinted through the window through the fog. "I know pregnancy stinks, so live with it." She took a swallow. "Don't make me regret coming along to look after your pregnant a$$." Racheal steadied the shuttle as it wavered, the horizon ahead blurring for a moment. "Let's go. I had to pee. I'm not going to fail."

"Of course." Leonor rolled her eyes and shuffled back into the crew field. Racheal sighed as she watched her walk away, knowing what conception would do to her body if Dr. Brian couldn't get the mesmerize to act in the goddamn bisches. Leonor Raantta had been a beauty a few years before when she'd gotten her citizenship; Racheal recalled private exchanges between Chonn and Captain Weathers, conversations about which of the men should be encouraged to breed with her. Her genes were thought to be ideal in a variety of respects. Mikhail had earned the lottery even though she had never liked him. And what for now?

She was now huge and overweight, and she was losing control of her bladder. Racheal trembled. Sure, the gene studies all indicated that Leonor would recover well, with just a brief refractory time until she could tolerate a second pregnancy, but who could tell?

The alarm board chirped at her, and she sighed. It's best to stop collapsing. After that, she focused and zoned out as the world passed through the glass. It was possible to see how vulnerable the colony was now: it had been nearly six years, and it was still clear where the terraforming ended, and the natural environment began, even though Weathers and Sevenpee were pleased with how the infilling was progressing.

Around an hour later, Plastic Harbor loomed through the fog, Leonor chewing her lip and squinting back. "Racheal, you're a jerk. Take a look at how the reef is increasing." She blinked and removed the condensation off the windshield. "Do you remember when we were kids? It jutted out into the bay like a stub. Now what?"

"Now what? There is a real harbor." Despite herself, she grinned, recalling the flavor of the smoking purgeon on those rambunctious trips back then. "They did a good job planning the coral."

"Hello." Erno appeared from behind them, bending forward to peer through to the flight floor. "Do you mind flying a slow loop across the coral for me? It's the simplest way to keep track of its progress."

"All right." Leonor shook her head and reached behind her stomach to grab the buttons. "I have it, Racheal." The trainee surgeon gasped, her hands ached from their long hold on the control sticks, and raised her arms toward the sky. She laid her head against the seatback, her entire body arched and feline, and looked Erno upside down.

"Are you going to search from up here?" she inquired innocently. "I'm willing to relocate so you can have a better view."

"Oh, no." She was pleased when his gaze moved down over her extended body, toward her neckline, and she remained motionless to allow him to see. "No, thank you. On the rear viewport, I use a reticle symbol. I'll just need one widdershins circle. A kilometer in diameter."

"That's nice." Erno ducked out of sight, and the engines momentarily raised as Leonor increased their capacity. As she completed her stretch, she cast a look at Racheal. "The nipples are visible, Racheal."

"Take it easy." Racheal sniffed as she sat back down in her seat. "You were eighteen at the time and not pregnant. Sexual arousal may occur involuntarily at times, Leonor."

"Mmhmm," he says. With a knowing nod, Leonor directed them into the new path and banked so Erno could conduct his observations. "I'll tell you one thing," she confessed openly. "I'm not any less horny when I'm breastfeeding."

Racheal shook her head. "Sex is perfect as long as you can mentally handle it," she clarified airily. "That is if you can locate a man willing to screw you."

Leonor chuckled. "Don't be concerned." The shuttle rattling around them made them laugh.

* * * *

Janicka sat back on the makeshift couch under the shelter, eventually finished erecting the last of the shelters, and observed the tamed seas slurp at the shore thoughtfully. Plastic Harbor had once been a devastated beach with relentlessly crashing waves; the attempt to erect and anchor the hatchery booms had taken ten months on the ground. According to Erno's estimates, the strategically planted reef breakwater marched deeper into the bay for each passing week. The tight corner of the harbor was a comparatively gentle lagoon, the dim seas a shuddering mirror for the clouded moons. "Someday," she sighed, "this place will have a town."

"That's right." Racheal sent her a friendly smile. "They'll even need the services of a physician."

Erno grinned but cut himself off; he still looked uncomfortable when he chuckled so loudly. "Are you planning on settling here, Racheal?"

"Only if you want to." Racheal had no notoriety for flirting, but she loved it nonetheless. At the very least, now that the stakes were raised. She cast an enigmatic look over at Erno. "We would be able to, you know. Elon Weathers will be remembered as the Interim

Commandant, the father of whatever civilization this world becomes." She shook her head. "Why not Taconic and Fourbee as the city's pioneers at Plastic Harbor?"

"I mean, why not?" She managed to elicit a rare grin from him, and she lifted her beer. He reached for the clink. "However, we'd need to entice settlement."

"It's easy." Racheal takes another shot of her drink. "We'll make prostitution legal." The party chuckled, exhausted from their hard day, the air already crisp and clean after the storm.

"As though it counts." April let out a yawn. "Why does anybody want to pay for it? I'd suggest the Wad still has a thriving sexual community." Nods, as well as a sidelong look or two at the two Domestics. "That is what I mean. In either case, for men." Then everyone's gazes were drawn to Erno, and the pause that followed was agonizing. Racheal quietly waited for someone else to crack it. Scott, most likely.

"Well," Scott drawled (a fair guess), "the whole 'breaking out and beginning your own city' thing sounds pretty good." He shook his head. "That is something I might see myself doing. My village will be called New Wadlwengula."

"That's a waste of time." Racheal threw up her hands. "Take advantage of the situation, Scotty. Modify the word."

"Yeah," April concurred. "Wadlwengula is a jerk. I'm confident the Permanent Commandant will make that the first item he updates."

"I believe it's traditional to mark the first settlement after the Interim Commandant," Sergey speculated. He was lying down on the grass. "So, Mr. Weathers. What is the weather in Weathers City? What is the weather like in Weathersville?"

"Yes, indeed. No, it does not." April gave a firm shake of her head. "In a First Settlement, I was cloned. It also bore the name assigned to it by the terraformers three hundred years before? Four hundred people?" She grinned at the thought. "Unless, of course, the IC's name was S-h-i-t-p-i-l-e." She spelled it out for us.

Scott smiled, his gaze fixed on April's legs. "You're from the town of Shitpile?"

"Well, we can't just be from the Heart," she snapped, flipping her hair. Scott had been raised on one of Jupiter's asteroids. "They don't say it that way anymore. They pronounce it sh'PEE-lay." She shook her head. "Linguistic drift occurs. It's a pain in the backside. But at the very least, you won't have to pretend you're from Shitpile."

Leonor snorted, "Damn straight." "I'm curious what they'll name me in the history books on this world."

"Leonor Raantta," says the narrator. Scott ruminated about the terms. "I'm having trouble pronouncing that right now." She smacked him in the face. They'd spent their whole childhood together, barely a year apart. Racheal smirked, wondering if she'd fucked him yet. "I'm sure they'll start calling that 'fucking slut from hell.'"

"You'd know," she retorted, knocking him off her folding chair. Real. They'd fucked, Racheal concluded. And why shouldn't they? He'd fucked everybody else, including Racheal. But there was a distinction between once, twice, and daily. And he and Leonor seemed to be a normal couple.
She wondered if April had seen it.

Dinner consisted of more smoked purgeon than either of them should eat; it had been a long few months at the incubator, and the auto-processor was in full working order. "Purgeon Bay," she murmured, nudging Erno. "When we build our town. Purgeon Bay is a good name for it." She nodded into the still sea, with the breakwater's furious line behind. "And we can sit around all day in the smoker's exhaust heat."

"No," I say. He swirled the rest of his drink and considered his next step. "The name Purgeon Bay is overly literal. Anything more substantive would be preferable. And a bit of backstory."

She let out a light chuckle. "I think New Promise is out as well?" He sent her a brief smile, and she kept her gaze from falling onto his lap. He liked her. This had been an excellent idea, and she was also beginning to want to screw him, apart from the difficulty of obtaining his semen. She yawned, "What are you thinking?" "A little seaside town all to myself? Maybe a puppy. Any youngsters." She watched as his eyes momentarily closed, indeed. It was a sensitive area. "Or you can't."

"I don't care." Fuck, he was too hesitant! "In any case, it's a dream. I doubt the Permanents would want anything to do with us until they arrive. That's the point, isn't it? "He shook his head.

"All the more justification for us to take the better bits first," Racheal observed, but she wasn't necessarily complaining. She turned her drink over. "Right now. You are welcome to mine." He cracked a grin. "So there you have it. What is your given name? For your community?"

He cast a look around, but everyone was engaged in their conversation; he was used to people not paying attention to him. "It's ridiculous," he warned.

"I'm a trainee surgeon," she winked. "I'll hold your secrets to myself." She asked whether he was aware of how husky her voice was becoming. "You have a plan in sight."

He lowered his gaze and bowed to himself. "I've always thought that if I had to call anything like that, Tiamat would be a good option."

"It does," Racheal said, stepping next to him. "It's simple to tell. What exactly is it, Old Chinese? That's what it sounds like."

"I don't believe so," he said. "It's the name of a long-forgotten deity or goddess. Earth in its early stages." He made a shaky motion of his head. "But that's not the only reason I like it," he confessed, staring at her sideways, and she wished he was tasting her cunt now, remembering the scent on his hand after she'd smeared his doorway. It's just subconscious. She thought what the others would think if she bent forward right now and kissed geeky Erno harshly and eagerly.

"What's the real reason?" she inquired.

"It's stupid," he said emphatically. "It's even a player in an old computer game. It's a dragon. There are five to six heads."

"Is it a game?" She reached back and lightly smacked his forearm. "What's the point with that?"

He shrugged and laughed once more. "I'm not sure. I did some analysis on it. The game was neither cool nor historical." She remembered the chess knight on her desk. "It was just a stupid kid's game. It seems silly to call a city after anything like that."

"I'm not sure." Racheal bent over, reclaimed her malt, and took another drink. "As far as everyone knows, it's some kind of ancient historic goddess." She winked once more.

"That's all I'm doing. Erno, your secret is secure with me. And, by the way, I like the term." She leaned back, her tiredness palpable. "RachealFourbee, City of Tiamat Resident Surgeon." She let out a gentle chuckle. "This is what a woman might become accustomed to. Then what will you be? What do you mean, King? What do you mean, commandant? Emperor-in-waiting? Chief Agronomical Engineer?"

"Maybe an apprentice physician," he joked, and the pulse from Reille's vagina was surprising. It felt like a wet, surging jet of adrenaline was shooting up through her stomach. She realized she was going to love fucking him now. The need grew too strong to resist, and she bent in close to plant a wet kiss on his cheek while avoiding his glasses. But for a beaming April, no one seemed to care. "What was the point of that?"

"There is none." She sent him a kiss on the face. He'd become a little prickly against her mouth. "Does a just have to be given?" She was now whispering into his ear. "If it rains later and the dome floods, I'll have room in the shuttle." She looked back down once more. "I'd rather you didn't have pneumonia. Overall, prevention is the safest cure. But, what exactly did you tell me? You don't enjoy being fussed with, do you?"

He glanced down at her, astonishment flashing over his face before reapplying his mask. He paused; it was unusual for Racheal to be a stronger flirt than someone else, but it was happening now. "The old shuttle has a better chance of leaking than my bubble."

She brushed her fingers through her hair, which was now free of its ponytail. "All right, then." She slyly stared him up and down, making sure he didn't see. "Maybe I'll be the one to take refuge." Her instinct advised her to abandon it there, that the harpoon had sunk far into the ground and that there was little more she could do here under the pavilion. As a result, she grinned cheerfully and spread her arms wide. She sighed heavily, "Fucking early morning tomorrow." "I'm going to bed, fellow men," she announced. "Oh, no. Domestics, too." She looked down at Janicka and Sergey and nodded. "The Domestics are never forgotten."

"Fuck off, Ms.Fourbee," Sergey said with a grin. "In a few months, I'll be eighteen," he said emphatically. "Just for you."

"Pretty important few months, then," Racheal said with a smile. "Good night, everybody. Keep dry."

It was never easy to find a warm spot to sleep in the shuttles. There were a lot of rooms, but it was all stiff, cold, and angular. The sleep pads slipped around a lot, and the illumination seemed strange when the moons weren't whole. Tonight, one was a crescent and the other a fifth, so the crew bay was bathed in a strange bluish light. Racheal stood over the tiny chemical toilet, waiting for the ovular sensor to calibrate; after it beeped, she quietly took it out of her vagina and examined the readout. Fuck you. She was very hot.

The percentage chance of her being knocked up by some average guy in the next eight hours is 92.2. And, after she entered Erno Taconic's most recent motility figures, the chance increased to over 97 percent. The tingle ran through Racheal's body in a stiff heat surge, but it will be tonight.

She didn't want Erno to show up there, so that was the idea of not taking the fourth tent. She willed herself to forget the wet tingling in her pussy and scheduled her neural alarm for local two in the morning, swaddled herself in the air covers, and set herself up for alpha wave initiation to lull her into sleep. There was the normal short, pulsing sound as the wave generator synched itself to the wake-up moment. Then she felt her brain slipping, dragging, pulling her back into that treacherous half-state on her path to oblivion, just as the rain started lashing the shuttle's roof again.

* * * *

The machine operated as it always had, pacing down the delta waves about five minutes until two; a fast swoop back into REM, and the implant prodded her back into wakefulness on time. The bluish light was already there, lighter than ever because it hadn't moved; the Lower Moon here was perfectly antisynchronous, but the shadows didn't change through much of the local year.

She stood up, worried if she'd hit her head on the aft crew release; her pad had slipped into the deckwell, as predicted. The hatchery station slept all around her: the muffled roar of the waves against the breakwater, the nighttime sounds of the region's nameless bugs and vertebrates, the sting of raindrops on metal. Racheal kicked the air blanket off her bare body and raised her neck, her stomach churning with excitement. She didn't need to look at her dream journal to remember she'd had a sex dream.

The time: 02:01 flashed before her grey eyes, and she decided to get laid. Racheal groped for a water spigot on the bulkhead, marveling like she often did that humanity had tamed the stars and attained perfection in the cosmos, so it hadn't worked out how to eradicate the plague of the halitotic wakeup.

She rose to her feet with grace, pushing her finger through the hair above her vag, feeling the matted gumminess alongside her clit. Yes, really. A sex fantasy, and a good one. She could still feel a wet flutter behind her belly.

The rain wasn't too hard, and she questioned what to bring; Erno had, as predicted, declined her earlier invitation. She wouldn't require clothing in his tent, of course, but when the sun came up, she'd be doing a walk of shame, and even her brief knowledge had shown her that it was still better not to do that naked.

She was twisting in the dark, searching for a moisture gown, when the external hatch shook, a deliberate and heavy echo that had little to do with the night's gentle wind. Hesitantly, Racheal directed wide eyes at the entrance, curious who the heck was attempting to get in; she knew instantly that it had to be Scott, slipping out of the shack after April had gone to sleep for some nocturnal fun. There was a slim possibility it was one of the other kids, but it didn't seem like it. Racheal clenched her jaws.

A complication was the last thing she wanted. On any other night, she'd have turned around with her back to the hatch and bent down as soon as Scott opened the latch. But, dammit, he wasn't the cock she wanted to take tonight.

Nonetheless. If Scott passed up his pregnant wife for some carefree pussy on a station with three open vaginas, it made her only a little bit more buzzy to hear she was his pick. When the door slowly slid open, and the silhouette outside wasn't Scott's, her mind was already racing for an explanation to send him.

Racheal couldn't help but exhale. Her mind was still buzzing when she spoke, and she felt compressed, her speech sounding distant to herself. "I'm sorry. So, I'm assuming your tent is leaking after all?"

Erno's shrug appeared almost impolite in its lack of confidence. "I know, it's just... you made a bid."

"I did it." She was suddenly aware, really aware, of her nakedness; he'd seen it all before, just the other day in the factory window, so she straightened nonetheless, with an instinctive urge to place herself on show. She imagined her skin in the blue Illum, every lean muscle outlined in inky black, her hair concealing her features. That's great. He wouldn't have been willing to see her surprise. "I'm just getting up to pee. Erno, please make yourself at home. I typically use an air scarf, but if you choose, we can use fur. That's fine with me." Then she was going to the restroom, feeling the wind against her bare butt through the open hatch, and her mouth was bone-dry again.

As the sun crept up, the tiny analog mirror in the shuttle's chemical latrine revealed a pair of crazy eyes in a flushed face, and she considered herself for a few moments. Racheal was astounded Erno had found it in himself to come to her tonight, and she was excited to see what other depths he possessed. Her mind lingered on his expression as he'd pushed himself into the desperate climax in the sickhouse, the way his big balls had jumped so madly; distantly, she remembered she was slightly tachypneic, and as her hand slapped absently to stir the unused toilet, she got her breathing back under control.

She didn't need to look down to discover she was weeping all along her inner thighs, as aroused as she'd ever been for others. She bit her lower lip and recalled Erno's hard dick as he pushed himself into his climax in the sickhouse storeroom, and it was that sight that drew her back out of the restroom and into the crew bay.

He'd closed the hatch and was now half-visible in the moonlight through the flight deck windscreen. Racheal's heartbeat quickened as he fumbled for his waist brace, his bare, wiry abdomen catching the bluish glow in his sparse chest hair. Then she pulled herself into a steady, slipping glide, her bare feet pattering on the metal decking, and knelt next to her sleeping pad. "So there you have it. Erno, what's the poison? Which is better, air or wool?"

He paused before slipping his trousers down over his waist, where they fell with a damp whisper at his bottom. After a few seconds, he managed to say, "It's your home." In the dim light, she could see the shape of his cock, half-hard; nobody in the colony wore clothes to bed, but she was fascinated by the absence of underwear. She licked her lips without thinking.

"Aero." She entered the temperature code into the air blanket, taking into consideration the extra body. "It's just a one-person sleeping pad, but it'll suffice." Expectantly, she peered up at him from her feet, her back straight, despite the chill in the sea.

When he moved forward, she could hear him take a deep breath, the shadows flickering over his skin. "Those fucking domes," he thought. "It's too leaky."

"A lot of that goes around," Racheal muttered, referring to the wetness that was steadily seeping down her leg. His cock became firmer and jumped as he walked; she could almost see his interest building. She grinned to herself as he came to a halt within arm's reach of her, his heavy, masculine scent wafting toward her. Her body was reacting ferociously. She raised her jaw. "Are you going to bed?"

Racheal could hear him swallow. "That's why I'm here," he said softly. She chuckled a little too brightly.

"It's not because of the leaking tent?" She sighed, slipping from the pool deck to the wet pad on her feet. As the blanket drew itself up around her, the air around her became warm and comfortable. "I'm starting to believe you're here to take advantage of me, Erno," she teased, her voice burrowed.

He gave a nervous chuckle. "Not at all, Racheal," he murmured, and then his sweaty legs slipped under the air cover, down her bottom, and she couldn't resist the shudder as his body clung to hers. When she sensed coldness around her hip, she laughed. "Is there anything wrong?"

"Fuck you. Is that liquid?" She was perplexed by the experience when she realized it had been raining outside. "They're in your hands."

She could sense his chest vibrating against her skin as he chuckled. He was feeling healthy. Warm and sinewy, her trust expanding alongside the cock she felt nestling between her butt cheeks. She twisted her hips amusingly to show him how much she loved it. "I'm all clammy," he admitted, his mouth a few centimeters from her ear. His breath tickled the back of her throat. "If only we could figure out how to warm my palms up."

Racheal exhaled, watching the heat rise. She had him; there was no doubt about it; now she must rest and let him have her. She lifted her foot and placed the instep on his top ankle, then steadily shifted her foot up his thigh, opening herself while she bent at the knee, waiting for Erno to accept the invitation. She thought she was interpreting him correctly and wouldn't need to poke him that she'd synchronized him to her wishes as well as she'd hoped in the commandant's office.

She rolled her head back, feeling his chin push against her ear as his icy hand crept around her, along her hipbone, and she leaned back into him. Erno's lips met her throat at the same time his fingertips found her vagina as she lifted her hand to rest gently around his thumb.

Racheal sagged into his embrace, a contented sigh escaping her mouth. All of this: the excitement of the occasion, the surprise of her man's presence in the shuttle, the refreshing trust in his rain-cold side, the pure animal joy of being played with... She lost herself completely and quickly, much as she had on the first night with Roni: this wasn't about her anymore. It has anything to do with them. And Erno was demonstrating that he was aware of it as well.

He wasn't content with just shoving his fingertips through her snatch. He held them going, gently, in and out and about, gradually bringing her up to where he needed her before deciding to take her. That was perfect with Racheal; the hard dick rolling with growing urgency against her skin was even better, and she turned her shoulders around to grab Erno's lips with her own. She was taken aback by his grunt as their tongues collided, which was both urgent and arrogant.

Erno's handheld pace as Racheal rolled her body over to face him; his eyes were fixed low, gazing at the darkness where his fingertips melted inside her, totally captivated. She sat down on the pad and cupped his face between her palms. "I'm so goddamn hot," she mumbled, her body sleek and taut against his, and Erno smiled as they kissed. Rachealmoaned into his mouth as she began to melt because he felt amazing, and his fingertips were doing incredible stuff to her clit.

He broke the kiss and stared at her hard in the moonlight while her leg rose up and over his thigh, and when she reached between them to force his cock lower, down along her slit, he broke the kiss and stared at her hard. "Yes," he said plainly, his voice quiet and sure.

"I'm not asking," she said into his ear, her tongue chasing the terms, her whole sinewy body a steady caress. "I'll have it."

"Good," he whispered back against her skin, and Racheal took a slow breath as she rolled her soaked pussy back and forth against the hot flesh of his dick, teasing him. His lips had been fascinated with her throat, chewing and sucking intensely, and her whole body was vibrating. He was rolling his hips with her, and the two of them were breathing faster and deeper. "After that, carry."

Racheal sighed and pushed him down onto his back; he was halfway off the pad, but none of them noticed. The air cover ripped them off, exposing their bare flesh to the chilly night air inside the shuttle. Racheal, on the other hand, was drenched with sweat as she swung her leg up over him, her breath a dog-pant of desire, gluing her body to his thighs and reaching confidently down to grab his cock. In the hazy blue sky, their eyes glowed at each other, wild, both of them lost in each other as she grew up on rippling youthful thighs to place herself. Erno's gripping fingertips drew her closer, encouraging her, assisting her in impaling herself on the firm, strong cock she guided toward the mark, toward her wet, slick pussy.

There was no mystery or transcendence inherent in the moment his head wedged itself into her slit; it wasn't a heart-stopping moment, nor was it especially memorable. It was pure, sweet relief, like a cool shower after a desert hike; the enjoyment of quenching, of satisfying a desire more intense than any she might conceive, and the joy of that had her laughing breathlessly as she steadily lowered herself over every ridged inch of Erno's able penis. She could hear him sigh, even whisper, but she didn't pause before she noticed the tickle of his pubic hair on her skin; it wasn't until she opened her eyes that she knew she'd shut them.

"Jesus," Erno said in hushed tones, "the vagina."

"Do you like it?" she crooned, relaxing into the fullness. Any portion of her pussy was packed; she gasped as he flexed his cock, pulsing inside her.

"You sound fine," he exclaimed, lowering his head down into the cool metal of the deck. "Excellent."

"Thank you," Racheal said softly. She cinched her grip on him tighter, relishing his groan in response, the strength in her body. She'd gotten what she wanted; the rest was all icing on the cake because she'd gotten what she needed. "Now, if you don't mind, I'm going to fuck you dry," she said.

"I do," he said, sharply bucking his hips, and Racheal took the hint. She lifted and slammed her rear, bending in tight so she could scent his breath, taunting him with the shudders of her nipples as they thrust into each other. Her hips were youthful and limber, and she'd discovered in the last few months how to use them with lethal effectiveness: grinding hard into her man's crotch, experiencing the thick, firm root of his cock-squeezing her clitoris, and keeping it there until the spasm went through her before beginning again, growing, dipping, slipping, in an endless pattern that made them both insane.

Erno's motility tests, along with knowledge gleaned from him through the years, indicated a stagnation phase of nearly seven and a half minutes, and Racheal was determined to send him all she had. She went faster and faster, slamming hard into his hips, and he proved a rather astute lover: his fingertips skated gently up and down her thighs, from thigh to armpit, while he bucked rhythmically upward at just the right moment, enticing her, driving her deeper.

"Goddamn," she grumbled, her legs clenched, hoping she'd cum until he did. It was already around the corner, rushing uncontrollably into her mind. "Fuck you."

He was more than willing to comply, pushing his legs deep upward to turn her onto her back. The breeze filled her lungs and continued to do so as he climbed on top of her and dove deep into her selfish hole, leaving her hollowed-out and gasping as he thrust. She could hear herself sobbing, his hands grappling for hers on the insufficient sleeping pad, then desperately squeezing her fingertips as he fucked her.

"You sound too close," he grumbled into her face, stinging her with his saliva. "I'm trying to make this a routine."

Her mind was racing with a million sexy, funny, racy responses, but she couldn't stop herself from yelling, "Fuck yeah!" The dazzling, melting-chocolate sensation in her belly as his cock churned there, the pink aura in her head, overtook her, and she trembled as she approached. "Oh my God! Yes, indeed!"

He was surging now, their sweat-slicked bodies frictionless but for the pain in her pussy, which was now escaping in her shuddering core. Desperately, in reaction to some lizard-need in her hindbrain, a longing for the closeness of his flesh, she craned upward to capture his lips in a searing, moist embrace, needing the touch, wanting nothing more than to feel every aspect of him filled her at that moment.

She was vaguely aware of herself urging him on. Her heels crashing into his thighs, but Erno didn't need any urging at all: he was an animal, racing his libido, needing to get as far into her body as he could before he came; she had no doubt he knew, at some pre-mammalian level, that she was deeply in heat, that he was the man she'd chosen to fertilize her, and that But his form was crumbling, both of them trembling, and Racheal was already lost in her climax when Erno slipped off the cliff and had his own.

Brian had listed his ejaculation power, and Racheal could feel it now, dimly, the swelling of his shaft and the jagged blasting of the semen blitzing out of him, right into the base of her womb. It struck her as a pervasive warmth that grew and renewed in the seconds before he exploded another spurt through her. And yet another. How about five? How about seven? Neither of them was certain. Everything they knew was a beauty, the heightened enjoyment of two individuals doing what their bodies were designed to do well.

Her next embrace was soft, her legs wrapping around him, her body sloshing with his semen. Thank you. Thank you so much. And so was his.

* * * *

The bisch wasn't amused; they didn't like being confined, and this one was upset about seeing a human embryo developing inside it. Yet she seemed calm enough, chewing the cud inside the new corral, and ChonnBrian nodded.

"I figured out this morning that your paper has been approved for print," she winked. She took a look outside. "Of course, I'm on the byline as well."

"Of course," Racheal asked whether she could experience some emptiness, loss, or something else emotionally, recognizing that her child might be gestating within an animal. But other than a faint joy that the project was successful, she felt nothing. It was a big deal, sixth year, and already a good embryonic transplant! No other colony had ever accomplished such a feat; of course, they'd welcomed the document. Racheal was proud that it was her first publication, and she wasn't yet a doctor.

And consolation that Erno wouldn't be sent to the Fringe. Aron 471-G is also a modern resident.

"Ok, I think I'll be going then," Brian said after a brief delay. Remember, Vivy is due to give birth at three o'clock this afternoon. Mikka, on the other hand, needs a checkup until that."

"I understand." Racheal smiled as she looked down at her manager. "You know I'm conscious."

"Correct," Brian replied quickly. "I'll see you later." She smiled at Erno and walked back to the nearest sickhouse, leaving the two of them to ponder the animal in the mud.

When Erno spoke, he felt as nervous as ever. "Thank you, Racheal," he said quietly. "I get that you did that."

"There is no reason for gratitude." She was standing against the gate, his warm arm against hers, and she surprised herself by leaning over and resting her head on his back. "It's good to have you around. You've always been my favorite member of the group."

"Is there no shit?"

"There's no shit." She paused, then grinned. "On the way back, I recall you showing me how to play chess. Moments of peace happiness are few and far between." She grinned at him as she lifted her head. "At least we're even." Other than that, they'd been fucking now and then since they'd returned from Plastic Harbor, and she could tell he was planning to screw someone else. "So, assuming anything remains viable?" she continued. And why shouldn't it?" She turned to face him. "Can you think of a name for our daughter?"

He returned her nervous smile and cleared his throat. "You already remember." He tapped her on the arm. 'Tiamat.'

Racheal grinned, remembering that namesakes like biblical goddesses and fantasy-game monsters weren't the greatest. She sat back down to think about the beach and wondering what she might mention to him it was carrying babies.

Explicit Erotic Sex Stories

The Summer Melody

A free spirit meets his or her soulmate. Then they do it, like (Lesbian)

Pamela Vance

"I'm hot," Julia said, tilting her head up, somewhat counter-intuitively towards the heat.

She reflected on what she had written. She didn't mean that physically, but she realized there was some merit to that as well. She didn't believe there was a single way to look "nice." She dismissed the model. Even if she ever wondered if she suited the conventional definition of Hollywood-approved elegance, she'd recall being asked as a Sophomore by some sleazy photographer man if he might take nudes of her for some "Coeds of the Pac-12" special some men's magazine was running. She'd declined him. She didn't have any reservations about her nakedness, mind you. She just didn't like how those magazines objectified women and portrayed a limited image of attractiveness that she did fall into.

No, Julia was hot because it was hot - the sun was shining, it was summer because they were somewhere in the Desert. There are many reasons for someone to be too hot.

Julia considered this. All the coincidences that had to happen for her to be one of seven billion souls on this huge spinning planet are circling the big ball of fire up there, how its rays were both magnificent and terrifying, capable of both making and destroying life. How the weather, which seemed unpredictable, triggered massive ripples in people's lives, ripples she understood caused other ripples. She was curious about the ripples. She knew what might happen when it was too sunny today. Will anyone perish? Will anyone be born? She grinned as she reflected on the idea. Maybe two people would be working somewhere together and, since it was so hot, they'd be wearing a little less than usual, chat about the weather, remember they enjoyed each other, and then they'd make love. What kind of repercussions would it have?

Julia's mind seemed to drift while she was high.

She was also stoned. She could sense it, the joint she'd rolled at their previous stop. Her mouth was dry, her hands were as heavy as rocks, and her mind was racing all over the city. She hadn't wanted to smoke the whole joint; it was potent material, but Fin had taken her time eating it, then she'd strolled off and lit it up, and before she realized it, she'd burnt it down to the crudely crafted cardboard filter.

"It's insane how hot it is, isn't it?" Julia said, her gaze shifting away from the sun and back to the lane. Fin stood by the side of the track, staring sadly at the rusted, battered husk of a 1986 Pontiac Parisienne. Fin has little knowledge about automobiles. Julia, on the other hand, did not. She just recognized the type, shape, and year since they'd only purchased it a week before.

Julia's boyfriend's name was Fin. Fin, on the other hand, must have said that anyway. "Traveling Companion," Julia must have written. She'd have taken that both practically and metaphorically. Figuratively, it said that Fin was someone Julia had met during her senior year in college as a guy who sold pot and other soft substances and was a decent guy to know about when she needed it. They'd gotten along well and begun sleeping together. True, Julia realized that certain people would assume that they were boyfriend and girlfriend or something similar, but Julia preferred to ignore those labels. They were going along life's course together during this chapter in her life. Still, she didn't expect it would continue forever.

It said they'd agreed to go on a trip in any sense of the word. They'd already finished and wanted to spend the summer traveling around America. They could go anywhere they chose. True, Julia figured, Fin would mention going to big music festivals and gigs to get rid of any pot and molly he had before "joining the real world" when the summer was done, but that didn't worry her. She decided to travel to certain festivals because she realized Fin was already paying for most of the trip. She did dismiss the idea that the universe Fin wanted them to enter was any "more real" than the one she was in now, even if she realized it was only a change in personalities. Fin assumed they were all going through a stupid, drugged-up college process. It wasn't just the medications for Julia. And though she wasn't high, she didn't want to be either the suburban yuppie Fin was pulling her towards or the pretentious, hipstery things her other friends appeared to be destined towards. Looking for "authenticity" in a gentrified commercial neighborhood where you pay $12 for an artisanal peanut butter sandwich looked almost as phony to her.

Julia simply desired to forge her course and do her own thing. As a result, she was flying with Fin. For the time being.

"While I do sort of wants a peanut butter sandwich," Julia said to no one, her thinking process audible.

Fin leaned over palms on his shoulders, brushing moisture from his forehead in what Julia perceived as excessive irritation.

Julia started to make her way back to the vehicle, kind of. She rose on one foot and jumped to the other, her arms outstretched to balance herself. She just did so a couple of times until the leaping action became too much for her. She wishes she had bigger breasts at times. And if she'd been wearing a bra. She lowered her gaze to her chest. Her shirt, a light and flowy chemise with a pretty little neckline that she'd placed on that morning at the motel, was now sticking noticeably to the damp skin of her massive breasts.

"Do you ever think I had smaller breasts, Fin?"

"How big are you, Julia?" Fin inquired.

Julia took a brief break to run an internal diagnostic.

"Very big," Julia reported her results. "Is there something we should consume or drink?"

"You might have had plenty to eat when we started," Fin said, ducking his head under the car's roof.

"What they had was burgers," Julia said.

"You should have gotten fries," Fin pointed out.

Julia came to a halt. She wished she could claim that almost any fast-food restaurant fried their fries in cow fat, but she couldn't. She had lost all sense of her justified outrage at the fast-food industry's activities at that stage. Her munchies had taken over. She should have gotten fries because she craved them more than everything else in the universe at the time.

"Fuck, why didn't I buy fries?" she lamented.

Fin slammed the car's hood down.

"Dammit, Julia, I'm trying to repair the engine," he said.

"Did you do it?" Julia inquired, hoping for the best. She didn't like living in the Desert, with its amazing colors of browns and reds reaching as far as the eye could see in front of her. It was breathtaking scenery. She wishes she could color it. She wishes she could color.

"No," Fin replied, "I told you we should have gotten an Oldsmobile."

Julia smirked. Fin had planned to buy junk vehicles and drive them before they broke down. He'd also likened it to saving livestock from a sanctuary, recognizing it would make Julia's refusal unlikely. He described it as "finding old machines and offering them one last taste of the highway." Julia had hoped to simply purchase a respectable van and provide a consistent place to sleep at night.

"Fritz, on the other hand, listened to me," Julia said, patting the hood of the brown Pontiac she'd named for herself. "It had a vibe that convinced me it was going to lead me where I needed to go."

"Did you just want to be stuck on the edge of the road in the center of nowhere?" Fin inquired, evidently frustrated. Julia let out a breath. She didn't like Fin because they weren't in the same condition of sobriety. When things didn't go his way, he had the rich kid's propensity to whine. Julia, who a single mother had adopted and, at times, her grandmother, had built a laid-back demeanor that things didn't always go her way. It wasn't the end of the universe if your vehicle broke down.

Perhaps more exciting, Julia learned something exciting as Fin mentioned their location as "nowhere." She had no idea where she was. She had no idea where the closest town was in either way. She has no idea what condition they were in. Julia attempted to recall the traffic signs, but there had been too many in the past few days. 491? 191? 160? It was one of them.

"Something positive will come of this," Julia said before sitting back against the car and leaping ahead. Her buttocks were covering her buttocks, but the hot metal felt uncomfortable on the backs of her thighs.

When he stared at her, Fin shook his head.

"Nobody's even passed by for an hour," he said as he took his phone from his pocket. "Fortunately for you, one of us is responsible."

Suppose Julia had been sober and in the mood for a confrontation. In that case, she might have said that having your father buy you a 700 dollar mobile phone and compensate for the admittedly amazing coverage that got him a signal even where they were wasn't the most responsible thing in the universe. Still, Julia didn't have time for that. All protests against Fin's categorization of their different degrees of accountability were overshadowed by something much more urgent and important in her state.

The strange-looking insect on the field. Julia was captivated.

2.

It took a long time for the tow truck to appear, with the heat already high in the afternoon sky. Julia had spent most of the time in the back seat of the vehicle, feeling like a treasure hunter who had discovered hidden treasure. She'd forgotten about the tiny farmer's stand they'd passed the day before and the small bag of carrots she'd purchased. No, they weren't french fries, but they were indescribably delicious in her altered state. They were crunchy and crispy and yet young enough to quench most of her thirst. Julia figured they were the best carrots she had ever produced.

Fin, on the other hand, seemed to be irritated by the wait. He seemed to be paranoid and jumpy about any disturbance or passing vehicle. Julia had given Fin the other joint she had in her purse in an attempt to calm him down, but he had declined, citing concerns regarding law enforcement. Julia was aware that he was paranoid about the medications in his luggage. Julia was once again hoping Fin hadn't carried them. True, Fin had claimed that selling them would cover most of their expenses, but Julia really didn't think it was worth the stress.

Julia discovered an unsettling fact when she considered being convicted. Fin wasn't on her wavelength, but they were equalizing, just not in the way Julia had hoped.

As she descended from her peak, she began to express some of Fin's frustration with their circumstance. Julia was characterized as a "free spirit" by others, which may have been slang for space cadet or something much more derogatory, but she wasn't dumb or completely carefree. She was aware that staying the night in the car wasn't desirable, given that the Desert was home to coyotes and other items. So she was glad when she saw a vehicle approaching them and slowing down. And more so as she glanced out the windshield and saw that it was, indeed, a tow truck.

"I'm going to go say hello," Julia said as the truck pulled alongside them, unlocking the crooked back door after just two tries.

"Babe, don't," Fin said, immediately turning around from where he was seated in the front, already anxious.

"How come?" Julia inquired, her arm still resting on the threshold.

Fin stared at her as though she were a moron.

"When a seemingly sweet stranger meets a hot girl stuck on the side of the road? This is how a hundred separate horror films have begun." He said it as though it were the most natural thing in the universe.

"Don't be dumb," Julia said, laughing.

Julia stepped out of the car and stretched her exhausted frame, her palms over her head as if searching for the already unbearably hot heat. She basked in the warmth of its rays before turning her gaze to the gleaming frame of the vehicle that had pulled up in front of them.

The vehicle was the first thing that hit her. Julia had thought it would be ancient and worn out, like Fritz, and although it did seem aged, it was a very different definition of the term. It seemed to be a tow truck from the 1940s or 1950s that had been carefully repaired and preserved. One of the side doors has some writing on promoting "Lonely Valley Customs and Repairs," along with a phone number. Julia concluded that it seemed to be something cherished and cared about. Julia was suddenly taken with the vehicle.

The door then swung open.

Julia thought the driver was a guy. In her mind, she saw a happy, heavy-set guy full of laughs and smiles. Kind of a humanized version of the tow truck from that dumb animation video her younger brother had enjoyed too much.

She realized right away that it wasn't. It took her a second to remember it was a woman, but it was still a woman. She was tall and slender, with one side of her head shaved and the other hidden by a brushed-over bob of dark black hair. She used to be one of the famous girls in her high school. The cool ones, not the famous ones. They were the ones who smoked in class and rolled their eyes at all. Julia loved the ladies, even though they occasionally made fun of her for being a little spacey. She was big (at least a couple inches taller than Julia's 5'4 frame), with coppery eyes, sharp cheekbones, and thin, pale lips. Julia's one visible ear was pierced by at least five separate hoops, difficult to count from a distance. The judicious application of dark eyeliner emphasized her dark, almond eyes.

The mystery driver was also not dressed as intended. Instead of the greasy coveralls, Julia had assumed, her and Fin's rescuer was dressed in a casual, sleeveless black T-shirt that revealed muscular, strong-looking tattooed arms and equally loose cargo pants slung low on her slender hips. Julia felt she had a very interesting kind of gothy, punky, androgynous thing going on, and she just looked cool. Anything that put an end to any Fin-inspired horror movie fantasies she may have been getting.

"Wow, look at you," he says.

Julia takes a breather. Was it what she said or something she just thought? It took her a moment to know it wasn't one. It was said to her by the tow truck owner. In reality, their gazes were closed. Julia figured the driver had excellent vision.

"Hello," Julia said with a wide smile, "we need your support."

"Right, well, I spoke to some guy on the cell." Only staring into Julia's eyes, the driver said. Julia was well aware that others admired her eyes. They were a deep, rich blue. Fin had claimed they reminded him of the Caribbean sea's blue. Julia, who'd never been somewhere exciting like that before, had just smiled at the compliment.

"That's me," Fin replied, having climbed out of the car as well. "You said you would be able to repair the car?"

"Technically, I said I'd take a look," she explained, "and if it's anything minor, I'll get you on your way, but if it's a major issue, well...I'm not a mechanic." Dougie, my cousin, is the mechanic; I only drive the tractor. I'm handy enough, however, given that you've got a very ancient beast on your hands and-"

"Great," Fin said, throwing up his hands as he distracted her, "but I'd like to get on the lane, so if you could take that look..."

Julia gave Fin a shady look. She didn't like it when people were mean to them, particularly when trying to support them. Julia had worked as a server the previous summer and considered those who were mean to service sector workers to be the lowest of the poor. Fin wasn't usually this way.

Julia observed as the truck driver sent him a vacant look for a few seconds before returning his attention to her. Julia showed her what she hoped was an apology shrug. As Fin sat in the driver's seat, the driver grinned and moved around to the hood of the sedan. She bent over, propping it open, to study the old motor. Julia could tell that the driver was slim and toned, rather than skinny, as she moved her gaze to her well-inked muscles.

Julia squinted as she struggled to make them out from a few miles away. There were initials in stylized script "T.G.R." and a heart with the name "Mary" in the middle with a tribal pattern and what looked like the black wings of a raven on her shoulder, but Julia was guessing at the bird because the driver's shirt just showed the wing on her shoulder and Julia found herself wishing the driver's shirt was off and then Julia realized, the wom

"I simply..." Julia attempted and struggled to come up with an explanation for what she was doing. The driver immediately laughed and returned to his seat.

"All right," the driver said clearly, still smiling, "give it a try."

As Fin turned the knob, Julia heard the car engine sputter.

"Come on, you piece of ass," Fin said through the windshield. The driver, on the other hand, was deafeningly deafeningly deafeningly. It just groaned and sputtered. Julia was heartbroken when the item Fin mentioned as resembling an animal seemed to be gasping its last breath. Fin twisted the keys again, but this time there was just sputtering.

"OK, OK," the driver replied, "there's no need." It's over. The injection system is completely messed up, and the whole system would need to be replaced."

"Fuck," Fin yelled, banging his palms against the steering wheel. Julia, who knew little about automobiles, had no idea what that meant but thought it was horrible.

"Don't spaz out," she said as she wiped her hands on her jeans. "I'll hook you up, drive you into town, and Dougie can get you back on the track."

Fin grumbled but resolved himself to not being back on the road for a second.

"Of course, can I travel with you or..." he replied.

The driver turned to face Julia, then back to Fin.

"No, there's just space for the two of us in the car." "You keep there, and Blondie will come with me," she said.

Julia thought that sounded interesting. She loved the tow truck because, to be honest, sitting in it felt a lot cooler than getting in a vehicle that was being towed. She still wished to speak with their enigmatic savior. One of the reasons she decided to go on the trip was meeting people and learning their tales. She was spending the day with strangers and experiencing new things in general.

"I'm not sure," he said, rubbing his chin and shifting his gaze between the two ladies.

"What's the harm?" Julia said, "Look at that semi; I just want to ride in it. It's vintage, but it's gleaming."

"Riding off with strangers isn't very healthy, Gab," Fin said. Julia creased her forehead. She couldn't figure out why Fin was even more concerned that an easy trip could have allowed him. They'd done much riskier stuff together.

"Look, dude-" the driver began, but Julia cut her off.
"Fin's correct," she said, seeing the Truck Driver's face droop slightly. "My name is Julia, and as I previously said, this is Fin."

The driver grinned.

"My name is Jean," she said, obviously grasping the concept.

Julia returned her attention to Fin.

"Do you see what I mean? We are no longer outsiders, "Julia triumphantly proclaimed. Fin, on the other hand, simply rubbed his eyes and climbed back into the taxi.

"I don't care."

3.

It turned out that the closest town was around a twenty-five-minute drive away. Julia's high had worn off, and her chatty, goofy personality had begun to fade. She'd planned to spend the day chatting to Jean. I'm learning her background. Julia found herself shy inside the semi's cab, which was an amazing vehicle, which she rarely did. She hardly said a word for the whole drive, apart from a few looks and more Tattoo counting. However, now and then, she would throw a glance Jean's way and catch the driver staring back at her, prompting both of them to return their gaze to the lane quickly. It was a 25-minute silence that was both uncomfortable and wired, according to Julia.

Jean eventually brought the truck to a halt in the center of a tiny lot in front of the Lonely Valley car store, which was branded on the truck's door. The garage, like the vehicle, seemed to be an enticing mix of old and modern. There were a few vintage, junky-looking vehicles in the parking lot, including a black one that caught Julia's attention as cool.

"All right, here it is." Finally breaking the silence, Jean said. Julia nodded and exited the cab, closing the door behind her just as Fin exited the Fritz. Julia followed Jean out and walked back to stand on the same side as the two of them.

"So," Jean said, "I thought I'd leave the car here for the time being, and Dougie would look at it in the morning and let you know the deal."

"Fine," Fin replied, "but you should realize that I only invested about a thousand dollars on the car in the first place." If it's as bad as you say, I don't think it's worth paying to repair it."

Julia gave a smile. Even if the thought of Fritz dying filled her with sorrow, she realized it made sense.

Jean shook his head.

"That's fine with me. If that is your preference, there is a bus station in town." Jean said.

Julia turned to face Fin, trying to be reassuring. Wasn't this what they desired, after all? Are you up for an adventure? A vacation that didn't consist of only relaxing at a spa and staying away from something interesting? On the other hand, Fin was as irritated as he had been before the car began to sputter and die along the edge of the highway.

"Fine," he said, "but at the very least, tell me there's a motel in town."

Jean shook his head.

"That's the Valley Inn on Route 4."

"All right, great," Fin said, "will you push us?"

Jean made a shaky motion of her head.

"No, but I will send you the number of a cab that would." Looking over at Julia, Jean said. "However, I don't think she can accompany you."

"Please excuse me?" Julia inquired, wondering what she intended.

"Sorry, excuse me?" Fin said it again, this time a bit more confidently.

"Look, I know it's dumb," Jean shrugged, "but this is a fairly conservative country, and I know it sounds insane, but the owner there is this crazy Bible-y dude, and he doesn't rent rooms to unmarried couples."

"Wait, what?" Fin yelled.

"Seriously, is it 1958?" Julia inquired.

"Hey, don't look at me," Jean said, raising her hands in anger. "My first night in town, he took one look at me and wouldn't even send me a single."

"Fine," Fin replied, obviously too exhausted to argue the case. "We'll just be able to get two rooms."

"Do you have two rooms?" Julia said, returning Fin's gaze. She didn't have almost as much money saving for the travel as Fin did because she didn't want to waste it all on Motel rooms. Even sharing them with Fin was depleting her resources, and she despised the thought of having one herself.

"I'll pay for it, Julia," he promised.

"Fin, I don't want you to compensate for it," Julia objected, "it's as much my adventure as it is yours, and..."

"And even though it worked out financially," Jean interjected, "the guy's not dumb." He'd know what was up if you walked in and placed two rooms on your credit card."

"So, what are we going to do?" Julia inquired.

"We should call ourselves married," Fin suggested.

Julia sighed at the thought for a few reasons. She chose the more urgent of the two.

"You know I don't like lies, Fin," Julia said. She didn't do so. If the motel owner refused to rent her the room frankly, she would not humiliate herself by forcing the matter.

Jean returned Julia's gaze.

"Look, I'm going to propose, and it might not be a perfect scenario for lovebirds, but I think it'll fit." Jean asserted positively,

"You go call a taxi and get a motel room," she said, referring to Fin.

Fin nodded, his face doubtful.

"And you," Jean said, motioning to Julia, "come with me and sleep on my sofa for the night." In the morning, you all meet out here, and then the car is patched, and you can go on your way, or it isn't, and you can go to the bus station."

Julia cracked a smile. That sounded pretty sweet. She'd been staying in hotel rooms for days, and although she was used to roughing it, she liked the thought of sleeping in a real house where people slept. She was also glad that Jean seemed to be cool enough with her to allow the deal. The awkwardness of the drive-over had raised some questions regarding Jean's feelings for her, though Julia reasoned that it was still some of the hangovers from the joint.

"Oh my gosh, do you have a proper shower?" "Because I despise hotel baths," Julia said.

Julia started her point emphatically. She realized how much she despised motel baths. Her last two baths had both been in motels; each of them had been disrupted by a cockroach the size of her palm.

"Excellent water pressure and a large reservoir." "Put in the showerhead myself," Jean said, nodding.

"Oh my god, I love you," Julia exclaimed, already anticipating the tub. Her exclamation, on the other hand, made her feel a little ashamed.

"Bullshit," Fin chimed in. He wasn't pleased with the proposal, Julia reasoned.

"What's the point of this nonsense?" Jean inquired, his voice shocked.

Julia glanced over at Fin, who seemed perplexed as to whether it was, in his words, "bullshit." Eventually, he appeared to come to a decision.

"How come she can crash with you, and I can't?" he inquired, sounding like a disappointed child who wasn't invited to a birthday party.

"Bro," Jean said emphatically, "you've never been a woman before." Inviting strangers you've just met into your home is risky except under the best possible circumstances. I'm not sure; maybe you'll rough me up or something."

"And weird women are okay?" Fin went on, looking at Julia.

"Well, it's more my specialty," Jean said with a knowing smile before pointing her hand in Julia's direction, "besides, she's what? What are you talking about, a hundred and fifteen pounds? I believe I would be well."

Julia wasn't sure exactly, but she felt oddly offended about that. The thought that she couldn't do physical damage to people because of her height felt strangely demeaning. She felt compelled to defend herself in the face of imminent risk.

"You have no idea..." "I may be a Ninja," Julia asserted defiantly.

Jean burst out laughing. But it was a happy joke, not a sarcastic one. Julia cracked a smile.

"I'm going to take my chances, Shinobi."

On the other hand, Fin was less entertained and pointed his finger straight into Jean's chest. Everything that Jean appeared to find amusing.

"Look, if you believe I'm going to make her accompany you home..."

Julia was now the angry one.

"Will you let me?" "Fin, it's not your place to 'let' me do something, and, very honestly, I think maybe you spending the night alone will allow you time to think about where you got that crap," Julia said, feeling an odd feeling of frustration rising inside her.

Fin stared at Julia, and, obviously getting the message, his eyes changed, then he looked over at Jean and looked concerned once more. He then held up his hands in defeat.

"That's fine. We'll spend the night at her house and come back here at 10 a.m."

"It's eleven." "I like to sleep in," Jean admitted.

"All right, eleven." Fin said flatly that he was no longer able to struggle for something.

Fin called his cab after exchanging corresponding numbers with Jean, and the three waited, still standing by the truck. Julia eventually discovered something unusual and concerning. Fin hadn't taken his bag out of the back of their taxi, and there were a ton of drugs in it, Julia recalled. Julia had no idea how much Fin had with him, but she had a feeling it was a lot. He was normally just a small-time trader, selling quarters to college kids and the like, but he'd sold his car to spend heavily on a ton of merchandise for the tour. Julia had objected at first, citing the danger involved, but Fin had assured her that all would be perfect. On the other hand, Julia had felt vindicated by Fin's paranoia any time they passed a patrol vehicle.

Julia realized she needed to say something when she saw Fin walk away without his wallet. She didn't like the thought of Fin being afraid of being busted but putting the risk on anyone else.

"Don't you agree, Fin, that you can get your clothes from the back?" Julia said, thinking that by stressing the word clothing in such a way, it would be clear that she was referring to the medication.

Fin turned to face her, then back to the driver, then back to her.

"Will the car be secure here?" he asked, staring at Jean.

Jean pointed up at the eight-foot chain-link fence topped with razor wire that enclosed the repair shop lot. Finn grinned and agreed.

"Then Nah," Fin said, "I guess I'll wear these clothes tomorrow rather than risk dragging around all of those...clothes."

"Fin," Julia said firmly, "I truly believe that the good people here, who are doing us a huge favor, might not want to be held accountable if anyone finds your...clothes."

As Fin stared at Julia, her comments hang in the breeze. Fin believed that the danger of transporting the drugs outweighed the risk of putting them in possession of an unknown person.

"Hey, Alan Turing and the Bletchley Circle," Jean joked after a few seconds of silence, "kudos on the impenetrable code and all, but if you've got any marijuana or whatever in the vehicle, don't worry, it'll be secure."

"Really?" Julia asked, taken aback by Jean's eagerness to pursue what appeared to a crime.

"No," Fin said as he opened the trunk and lifted his suitcase out. "I guess I'll take my bag after all; I might use the fresh clothing."

Julia paused for a moment to consider this.

"Clothes don't mean drugs anymore, right?" she asked Fin quietly. Fin gave an irritated nod.

Before I could react, a four-door sedan pulled up outside the lot, and a young, dark-skinned Latino man appeared.

"Hey Luis," Jean called out from across the parking lot, "are you sober enough to carry this sweet gentleman to the motel?"

"I'm soberer than you've ever been, gringa," the guy replied. Julia, on the other hand, didn't speak Spanish, but it was wasted on her.

"Well, it's not much of a statement," Jean shrugged, "but it'll do."

"Well, call me if something goes wrong," Fin said, bending over to kiss Julia on the cheek before turning to look daggers at Jean. "Don't let something happen to her. We're leaving here in the morning. Together."

"Don't worry," Jean smiled, "she'll be in safe hands."

Fin shook his head.

"Also, remember to tell your cousin not to patch it if it'll cost something actual," he said.

"OK," Jean said, nodding.

"And, even though I have the...clothes, warn him not to do something else in the car, since Julia's stuff is already in there."

Julia gave a little smile in response. Julia figured there was some chivalry in thinking for her things after a day of fairly solidly behaving like an asshole. Julia wasn't carrying anything, just a couple of clothing changes, her small savings, and a few personal things, but she was carrying a gold locket her grandfather had given her that meant a lot to her. It was good to be reminded that Fin wasn't a complete jerk, Julia figured.

"Fine, I'll tell him now, Vamos. Luis doesn't have all night," Jean said, and the cab's horn honked as if prompted.

Fin grinned, and Julia followed him into the parking lot. She made a sweeping gesture as though to beckon him onward, irritated that he kept staring over his shoulder back at her. He eventually tossed his bag into the back seat of the cab before climbing inside.

"Your boyfriend is a jerk," Jean said as he saw the cab pull south.

"He's not my partner," Julia said emphatically.

"No?" Jean inquired, intrigued.

"Well, I mean, he is, and he isn't," Julia said, "I mean, we're together, so I don't like labels like that. I had a pretty nice metaphor for him and traveling earlier, but I can't recall it now."

Jean nodded, obviously unsure about what Julia said.

"Well, he's an a$$hole in any case."

Julia gave a smile.

"I know, well, I understand how you'd say that right now but...not normally," she said, feeling compelled to defend him even as she realized that, based on what Jean had seen of him, there was no need for the dark-haired girl to think otherwise.

"Sure," Jean said flatly, "want to grab your bag, and we'll break the bill?"

Julia made a shaky motion of her head.

"No, I'll leave it here if all is the same."

"You don't need clean clothing?" Jean inquired. "Remember, I don't have access to the Enigma computer, so I'm only talking about sheets."

Julia gave a smile. She didn't understand the allusion.

"No, my clothes are all filthy anyway," she said, "and I need to go to the laundromat before we break up tomorrow."

Jean slapped the tow truck and nodded.

"Would you want to split?" she asked.

Julia grinned, a little is excited at the prospect of having more time with the beautiful punk chick, vowing not to make the next trip as quiet.

"By the way, it's a wonderful vehicle," Julia said as she watched Jean unhook Fritz the Car from the tow.

"Yeah, it's fine. My cousin Doug designed it," Jean said, shrugging.

Julia wondered absentmindedly, "What's its name?"

"Name?" Jean inquired, perplexed.

"You don't name the cars?" Julia inquired as though that were the most normal thing in the universe.

Jean paused for a moment before answering the query. She was staring at Julia as if she were attempting to crack an invisible mystery printed on Julia's forehead. Julia shivered on the inside. She didn't want to come off like too much of a space cadet, particularly to someone as intelligent and cool as Jean.

"You're a little strange, aren't you?" Jean said, but with the wry, above-it-all tone she seemed to use with anything. Julia gave a smile.

"That's what people tell me," she said, hoping she could go back a couple of minutes in time. Jean, on the other hand, appeared to notice and laughed as she shook her head.

"No, it's okay," she reassured, "I like strange."

Julia couldn't help herself. She was beaming.

4.

Julia finds herself trapped in the cab of the tow truck with the enigmatic dark-haired kid for the second time that day. There was a charged spirit once more. Julia had reasoned that it might have been her imagination performing a joke on her. That the pot had instilled in her the kind of hyper-awareness that it sometimes did.

Julia was in the act of getting her seat belt on the second time she and Jean got into the truck when she noticed she couldn't see where it was attached.

"Oh yeah, it falls under the seat occasionally," Jean observed the problem. The punk-y girl had reached over and softly laid her hand on Julia's left thigh, niggling her away for a second. Julia, who wasn't stoned anymore, couldn't deny the charge she got as Jean's long fingertips rubbed across her thigh. Something was going on. Something Julia didn't want to worry about or describe too much in case it was, even if true, completely one-sided. Julia had done up her belt and started chatting after Jean had freed the missing piece of plastic. I'm whining. She couldn't help herself. She couldn't stand the quiet of the first trip any longer, so she filled it with fast, nervous chatter. Mostly about her worldview and how it had led her to that desert side path.

"...so, yeah, everybody I went to college with was the same; you'd think they'd relax a little bit and take some time to find themselves after they'd gotten into a good school, but everybody was just like, 'I have to get the right major and get great grades and be in the right sorority and the right grad school, or I could be poor when I graduate, and there's nothing worse than being poor."

With a lifted brow, Jean turned to face her. Julia noticed she'd been talking for about five minutes straight when she realized she'd been talking for about five minutes straight.

"I've seen college students before, so what I wanted to know was why you were on this trip in the first place."

Julia gave a smile. She'd seen the query and assumed she'd addressed it, only to find she'd only come to the preamble.

"I didn't want to fit into it, I guess. Everyone had it so planned out because they were too concerned about starting their careers right away, and I just wanted to go out there, you know? Take a step without knowing where I'd end up. I'd never traveled before, really, and I guess I just wanted to get a ton of experiences before I settled somewhere."

Jean burst out laughing. Julia was used to people laughing at her as she got moving, and she was worried that Jean assumed she was stupid or strange, but it wasn't a nasty chuckle. Julia figured it was a happy one. Julia enjoyed her chuckle a lot.

"OK, I asked," Jean said, "but it begs the issue, I mean your boyfriend-"

"He isn't my-"

"Right, right," Jean corrected herself, "your traveling partner doesn't seem to be on the same hippy spirit quest thing."

Julia gave a smile. Given what Jean had seen of Fin, she could see that the two of them were together. Julia reasoned that they shouldn't be married. But only together.

"Well, Fin, I mean Fin seemed different when I met him. He was so laid back and fun, and he's an amazing guitar player," Julia said, not sure whether she was defending Fin or her decision in that regard, "and we'd often just go into these woods around school with a picnic. He'd have his guitar, and we'd chill or make love or hang out. He didn't seem to be faking it just to get into my pants."
"And so what?" Jean inquired.

"I don't know," Julia admitted, "but I'm starting to believe that Fin, the Fin I always loved, was just someone who felt those stuff were distractions." That being cool like that, and even I, was just a fad. He realized he was going to be like everybody else ultimately, but he felt that since his Dad was still so wealthy, he might fool around before it was time to go get it offered to him."

Julia paused for a moment to let it sink home. If she was protecting Fin, she knew she wasn't doing a really good job.

"But, you see, he did accompany me." "And he even sold this incredible car his dad gave him so he could fund the trip, and he does want to take care of me, which is cool even though I can take care of myself," Julia said, redoubling her efforts.

Julia decided to change the topic. The reality was that the distinction between Good Fin and Bad Fin bothered her.

"And just so you know," Julia said, "I get that branding me a hippy is a simple shorthand for people, but I don't like it."

In Julia's opinion, Jean glanced down at Julia and was sincerely concerned that she had offended her.

"I'm sorry, I didn't intend it." I like what you're saying, you know, I've always been a bit of a wanderer myself, and I think your whole idea is pretty interesting."

"Sorry," Julia apologized, sounding as though she'd yelled at Jean too harshly about something she was, admittedly, sensitive to. "Only, you know, I guess when people call me that, it's like they're accusing me of, like, cosplaying what I think people did in the '60s, you know?" I feel like I'm attempting to fit into a scene from a movie I watched. As in, I went to the mall and bought a bunch of clothes to suit a certain picture. But, you know, I purchased this shirt for $5 at a thrift store because I wanted it."

Jean lowered his gaze to his sweater. Julia realized it was something Jean had done before. Julia looked down as well, realizing that, despite going bra-less and it still stuck to her due to the humidity, the thin cotton of her blouse didn't leave anything to the imagination.

"It's a cool shirt," Jean said, slyly smiling.

"Thank you," Julia replied, uncertain of her feelings. She always left herself vulnerable in this manner and was sometimes creeped out by how guys would look at her. Julia was surprised to discover that she enjoyed the looks Jean was showing her. Nonetheless, each second left her in the charged awkwardness, and she stepped on.

"Anyway," Julia said, "I'm not attempting to be anything. "I'm myself."

Jean grinned.

"Well, if it means something, and believe me, this isn't something I say very much," Jean said, "I guess I'm beginning to like you."

Julia cracked a smile. She was taken aback at how much the terms meant to her. She didn't want to think about what they said, why she was saying them, or how much it had to do with the way Jean had praised her...shirt, but she liked Jean. Julia felt she was charming and straightforward because she was witty, sarcastic, and pessimistic. exposing a genuine flaw behind the rugged exterior

And, once again, the exterior was stunning. Julia could get a clearer glimpse at her slim, sinewy arms and the exquisite artwork on them by sitting closer to her. Julia had never gotten a tattoo since she was scared of the needle. Still, after seeing Jean and the elegance and permanence of what she had inscribed on her skin, Julia started to reconsider her cowardice.

Julia's nerves overtook her once more, and her gaze shifted from Jean's body to the lane. She attempted to confuse herself with the moving landscape, the long stretches of brush and Desert, and the beautiful rocks in the distance, and she succeeded for a moment. It was a harsh but majestic landscape.

"So you're from the West Coast?"

Julia returned the smile.

"Well, sort of," Julia admitted, "I stayed with my mom in Reno on occasion, but more with my grandparents in California."

"Huh," Jean said with a smile, "and is that where you got all of this free spirit stuff?"

Julia laughed.

"Not at all. My mother, on the other hand, is a complete shambles. She'd just send me to the coast if she had a new boyfriend who didn't want to cope with seeing a kid around or simply got lonely because my grandmother is pretty stern about it. However, my grandfather..."

Julia took a brief break. It had been a year after her Grandfather died, and she hadn't spoken anything about it. Even with Fin, it's impossible. Nonetheless, she thought she could pull it off with Jean.

"My grandfather was a fantastic guy. He wasn't a hippy or something, he was an electrician, he'd been in the army, he was sort of pragmatic, but one thing he was always about was not having other people tell you what to do, you know? In a town full of people who were all into sports and shooting and stuff, he was super into farming and bird watching because that was something he did."

Julia reflected on those days, and a pleasant feeling washed through her.

"I remembered we'd go into the woods where he'd designed this blind, and we'd just stay there peacefully for hours, he got me my binoculars, and I'd have the little notice pad, and when he'd see something, he'd say 'Quick, Little Blue Jay,' and he'd tell me to look and then I'd write down what it was and..."

Julia came to a halt. She knew she'd weep if she mentioned something more about her grandfather. It had been a year, and she was still not over it. There was a certain kind of quiet in the vehicle now. One that Jean shattered.

"That's amusing," Jean said.

"What exactly is it?" Julia inquired, happy to have a change of topic but unsure what was amusing about her favorite experience.

"No, it's just that I have a similar story." My father is a jerk, and my mother died when I was eight, so I was sent to live with my grandfather in Washington."

"Oh," Julia said with a grin, "it was just a coincidence."

"Well," Jean said, her sarcasm returning, "I tell my Grandfather, but it was my Great Aunt." She was a lovely lady who welcomed both my cousin and me. But my Grandfather was there; he was a rugged older man, a full-blooded Chinook Indian. He didn't have much empathy with us, but he'd sometimes get pounded and tell us tales of ancient tales. My cousin and I were nicknamed "Little Bear and Little Crow Girl."

"How come?" Julia replied, unsure of what Jean was referring to,

"In the old myths, the animals have all these personalities and stuff." Doug, my cousin, was still tall and friendly, so he was Bear. I've always been a shit disturber, always causing problems for others, and evidently, Crow was the supreme trickster and prankster and such."

"Wow," Julia said, blinking when she realized what was going on. The Blue Jay and the Crow.

"Yeah, you see this," Jean said, taking one hand off the wheel and reaching back to her shirt collar and pulling, exposing some of the wings on her back. "I got this cause of that," Julia said, looking intently as the copper-skinned girl unveiled more of what she finally saw was a gorgeously lifelike representation of a Crow in flight.

"Oh, no." "So he's gone?" Julia said, her face sad once more.

"Can you tell me who my grandfather is?" "Fuck no," Jean said with a grin. He's still up there somewhere. If Death comes for him, Gramps would most likely knock the old spirit in the nuts and fuck Death's mom."

Julia chuckled as well. Jean returned a fleeting glance to her side before letting her shirt slip back and resuming control of the vehicle.

"No, but the night before Doug left for basic training, the two of us got crazy messed up, and I finished the Crow, and he finished the Bear."

Julia gave a smile. She was curious if any tattoo has a common backstory. She returned her gaze to Jean's sides, needing to inquire about each one. Particularly, and with an intriguing feeling that Julia could characterize as Jealousy if she didn't know any better, the heart that reads "Mary." Julia decided to go on a new path.

"Why did you end up here?" Julia said as Jean drove the truck away from the main lane. They were getting close to their destination.

"Well, I took off at 18 and spent a couple of years just, I don't know, getting into all sorts of shit before I get tracked down by this lawyer out of nowhere, right?" "Remember the worthless father I mentioned?" "Well, he had a mildly less pointless father," Jean said. "This is my other grandfather."

"And he stayed right here?" Julia said, still unsure of where "here" was.

"It appears." "I never met the man, and he was a jerk, but he did know about me, and when he died, I was his last living relative, so he left me the house he had and his little garage in town," Jean shrugged. Like I previously said, I'm not a mechanic, so I was going to sell the place for what I could offer, but then Doug got discharged and found me, and he's fucking nuts about vehicles, so I let him have the shop."

"Oh, then you stayed," Julia said.

"Well," Jean said, his voice conflicted, "I know it's not much and not where I expected to end up, but, as I said, I had a free house, and Doug's the only real family I've got, so I stuck around and did odd jobs for the store." Doug has even turned it into a legitimate company. We might have done some shady stuff in the beginning.

Julia turned to face her. She considered asking what "shady crap" meant for a split second, then decided against it.

"Now," Jean said, "it's just repairing SUVs for soccer moms and towing hot chicks' vehicles before bringing them back to my spot and seducing them."

Julia took a breather after that. For a split second, she figured she'd overheard something. That it may have been her mind playing tricks on her. Yet Julia glanced over at Jean, and Jean was staring at her, and there was no question in her mind that she'd understood right.

"'Excuse me?' Julia said, brushing some of her hair behind her ear as she considered herself seduced.

"You heard me," Jean said firmly as she turned into a narrower lane. Julia couldn't stop smiling. She couldn't quite begin to process the actual realities of what Jean had meant, but just hearing Jean agree that what Julia had been experiencing all day was, well, genuine, was undeniably exciting. On the other hand, Julia was unsure how she thought about being faced with the truth of it and decided to ignore it.

"Does that happen a lot?" Julia inquired, trying to seem coy when within a dozen tiny explosions of enthusiasm, anxiety, and nerves erupted. It was as though she had butterflies in her stomach, except the butterflies were on fire and jet-powered.

"No, you'll be the fifth," Jean said when the vehicle came to a halt. Julia hadn't even noticed they were there when she noticed they were parked in front of a garage connected to a tiny ranch-style home. Julia stood there, her black eyes practically sparkling back at her, as Jean turned off the car and got out. Julia stood in the car for a few seconds, thinking of how the last few minutes of their discussion had been dumped like atomic bombs. True, Julia remembered, but all they were was an acknowledgment of the anxiety Julia and Jean had been experiencing all day. And then, it was noteworthy that it was spoken aloud. And with such casualness.

Julia resented it for a split second. The informality behind it. Jean had thought she'd seduce her. What if she'd only brought Julia alone? They'd wind up in bed together. But Julia soon discovered that it wasn't a prediction at all. It was just that Jean was more mindful of what was going on than Julia. Julia realized it wasn't a matter of whether she was about to be seduced when she saw Jean's lithe, slim, inked body move around the front of the vehicle, seemingly as relaxed as Julia was nervous. Her step full of the same Don't Give a Fuck swagger she'd displayed all day.

She was already there.

"Are you coming?"

Julia was jolted out of her reverie by the beautiful dark-haired girl's accent, who was leaving her front door open and staring at her. Julia paused. She reflected on her nerves, Fin, and the reality that she wondered what would happen if she stayed the night at Jean's place and how it simultaneously scared and fascinated her more than she'd ever been. It was so powerful that she could sense it inside her. Her already hot body became much hotter when she felt a slickness between her legs that referred to how much her imagination had already run away with her.

"Ok, you did mention you needed new opportunities," Julia thought as she opened her passenger-side door.

5.

Jean was an excellent kisser. And a fast one.

Julia and Jean were in each other's arms just as soon as she reached the threshold into Jean's front room and saw Jean waiting for her. Jean had sent her a hungry embrace. Fierce, unyielding. Her light pink lips were tender to the touch, and her hands were heavy and tight on Julia's back. Julia, who always preferred the darker side of things in the bedroom, was taken aback at how much she enjoyed what was going on. When she was kissed rough, it was mainly handled badly. Too hard, and no regard for her feelings. Only anyone is jamming their tongue down her neck, oblivious to the buildup.

Jean, on the other hand, was a perfect blend between the sluggish and the hungry. Her tongue was playful, allowing Julia's tongue to react and caress her. Julia was shocked to find that she was quickly a very fair participant in the embrace, the day's stress leaking out of her in surprising ways. She bit Jean's lower lip and noticed her hands closely squeezing Jean's hard buttocks against her. Julia shocked herself by opening her legs somewhat, wrapping herself around Jean's hard forearm, and eventually satisfying an urgent need by rubbing herself against Jean's powerful thigh in reaction. She groaned when she felt some friction against her sex, even though it was just a leg and there were already two layers of clothes between them.

Jean's hand slid up her top and cupped at her breasts, and she only realized how hard her nipples were as Jean's hands brushed against them and clenched, eliciting a moan from Julia. Jean's hands were solid and hot to the touch, much like the rest of her face. Again, Jean seemed to be an amazing blend between the hard and the gentle. Many of Julia's lovers believed that since her breasts were big, they weren't delicate and could be kneaded like dough. Jean's grip, on the other hand, was gentle and professional though remaining strong. She was always displaying a yearning for more.

But it was Jean's hand on Julia's breast that made her hesitate—feeling self-conscious. Enough that, she shattered the kiss. Jean saw this as a positive indication and started kissing Julia's ear. Again, the sensation was incredible, but Julia's mind wandered when she felt Jean's hot breath and lips on her and how Jean seemed to want to kiss every aspect of Julia's body.

"Jean, should we slow down for a second?" Julia asked.

Jean came to a halt, but Julia could see there was some hesitancy there. The taller girl moved her face away from the blonde's neck and also took a step back, so they weren't so close together.

"'What's the matter?' Jean inquired, obviously taken aback. Nothing Julia had said, she knew, meant that she didn't want things to escalate. In reality, she desired things to progress further. Far, much more. She simply desired a break.

"Look, I know this is weird, but could we just stop this for a second?" Julia said, "When I mentioned the pool, I meant it. I haven't had a good one in days, and I'm feeling sweaty and dirty. I don't know, if I'm going to be with you, I'd like to be at my highest."

Jean let out a breath. According to Julia, it was one of annoyance, but unlike in the past where she'd told a man to calm down, it wasn't an upset or frustrated frustration. Jean had a strong desire for Julia. Julia had to confess she enjoyed it a lot.

"Yeah, I mean, just so you know, I would always bang you if you were a lot dirtier than you are right now," Jean said. "I mean, without a second glance, but I understand. And follow me."

Julia smiled and nodded. The action touched her. She pursued Jean around the building, remembering how lonely it was for someone who had lived there for years. The tiny TV in front of the couch was on top of a milk carton, and the video game console behind it was inside said milk carton. It used to be one of Julia's multiple off-campus rentals through the years.

"As you can tell, I never relaxed," Jean admitted. I'm not sure; I think I expected to be going on."

Julia gave a smile. But, more than just getting a response to her query, she loved the fact that Jean seemed to understand what she was saying. Any part of Julia's mind understood that Jean had no choice but to admit it to someone she took around, but Julia loved it when there appeared to be an unspoken bond between her and whom she was with. They seemed to be in the same thinking train.

Jean led Julia to a tiny bathroom close to what Julia mistook for the main bedroom. Julia was enthralled by the sight of the modern-looking shower inside.

"Would you want me to accompany you?" Jean said in a low, provocative voice as she wrapped her arms around Julia's neck, her lips nuzzling at Julia's face. Julia relaxed into Jean's embrace once more when she felt Jean's hands reach out towards her breasts and moaned at the feeling.

"I'll only be a minute," Julia said, trying hard not to listen to her instincts, which were urging her to do whatever Jean wanted. "And I've always considered shower sex to be more difficult than sexy."

"Yeah, I'm one of them," Jean said, sounding sincere despite another exhalation of irritation. She kissed Julia on the cheek before letting her go.

"You should see the towels," Jean said, "but I'll be out here if you need me."

Julia returned Jean's grin as the door closed. She quickly pulled her top over her head and down her shorts and underwear, relieved to be rid of them. She could sense herself becoming wetter with each move, and she realized she needed to take a short shower. Only enough to make her feel a bit less gross before returning to where she left off.

Julia was grateful for Jean's quick shower because she recalled from previous sleepovers and nights out how she despised trying to figure out a fresh one and often ending up burning or cold. Julia wanted to admire the water that flowed out of the new-looking shower head with a lovely coolness. The heat of the day had eventually caught up with her, and she felt instantly renewed. She let the water flow down her back, soaking her hair and flowing down her body. Within seconds, she felt ten degrees colder.
Still, she didn't take her time. She didn't want to be there for very long. She desired to spend time with Jean. She wished she could feel Jean's hands on her and her mouth, and she wished the shower would end. She was certain that she'd washed the last few days of travel from her system. Julia stepped outside and took one of the clean white towels that Jean had pointed out to her. Julia couldn't help but love her own body's curves as she dried. She wasn't very big, but her legs were long and well-shaped. Her hips had a generous swell that tapered to a slender waist and flat stomach before swelling again at her broad, jutting breasts. Two grapefruit-sized teardrops, the same softly tanned color as the rest of her, and tiny chocolate nipples that appeared much tougher now that the colder night breeze brushed across her moist neck.

Julia had no idea that she was judging herself so harshly. It was all her body to her. Everything she was familiar with and was unconcerned regarding. Still, she realized it was for the same cause she'd chosen the shower in the first place. Her bronze skin and expressive features, the curl of her powerful limbs, the silky black of her hair, and, well, all about Jean drew her in. Julia could not help but feel self-conscious. Julia discovered she was more drawn to Jean than she had realized. Julia simply needed Jean to find her equally attractive, which meant being at her peak. For a split second, she wished she was dressed in something frilly and lacy. The sort of item that girls in the film would wear after saying they needed to change into something more convenient. Julia, on the other hand, was wearing nothing but filthy shorts and a filthy top.

Julia took a deep breath and steeled her courage before opening the bathroom door and walking out nude. Not lingerie, she reasoned, but it will do in a pinch.
6.

"Hello,"

Julia had been at a loss for words. Julia recalled how the ladies in the movies in their lingerie still have the best come on. But when Julia came out of the bathroom and saw Jean seated on the corner of her bunk, her mind diverted by a magazine, she couldn't think of much else but how badly she wanted to kiss her again. "Yeah" will have to do.

"Fuck me," Jean exclaimed. Julia could tell Jean was pretending to be cool, but there was something in the way Jean's wide eyes stared at her that let Julia realize she'd made the right choice. Jean was fascinated by her body made Julia feel much more seductive. She enjoyed seeing the gritty punk chick speechless.

"I don't have clean clothing," Julia said, "and I thought you wouldn't mind."

"You go in there all scruffy hippy chick and come out a Playboy rabbit," Jean said, getting up from the bed and gently rubbing her palm across Julia's bare stomach.

"Do you think that's good?" Julia was uncertain how she thought about it. She'd seen a few Playboys in her day, but she didn't consider herself to be like the girls in there. She artificially posed for men's amusement.

"Maybe from the 1970s," Jean said, running her fingertips lower. "When they had incredible real boobs and looked like sexy little surfer girls," she said, pointing down her stomach to the light golden curls right above Julia's glistening sex.

Julia cracked a smile. It was a much better idea for her. Jean's hands traveled to Julia's hips and ran over them, but just with her fingers, creating a path of heat around Julia's body. Julia needed to feel those fingertips all over the place. Julia considered her toes, which were now gently running up Jean's sides, and realized she would soon be in new terrain.

"And so you know, you should be aware that..."

"What do you mean, straight?" Jean commented, entertained by the apparent contradiction.

Julia made a shaky motion of her head.

"I don't think about it that way," she said, "but it's like, I don't eat meat, right?" Although I don't consider myself to be a vegetarian. But if I'm hungry, I'm always motivated by my desire not to consume meat, so I don't, right? But often, I see a hamburger and say, wow, that looks amazing, and I want one, but then I realize I don't know how to eat hamburgers or how they'll make me feel or how I can eat it. So that the Hamburger is happy, you know?"

Julia realized she had rambled and made no sense after the sentences stuck in the air for a second.

"Do you mean to compare me to a slice of meat?" Jean said this with her eyes narrowing and a grin on her lips.

"No," Julia replied, feeling ashamed and looking for the words to reply, "I think of myself as fairly elastic, you know? For example, if I'm with a guy I like and want to be with, I'm not so much straight as I am straight around him. Is that what you mean?"

"Sure," Jean said, lowering her head and gently brushing her lips across Julia's shoulder. Kisses from her clavicle to her neck and then to her lips.

"So," Julia said, her heartbeat quickening and her breath shallowing, "I won't know what to do."

"Girl, I've wanted to fuck you since the first time I saw you," Jean said hungrily into her ear, "and I'm tired of waiting."

Julia felt Jean's hands grab her buttocks and spin her around, pushing her up against the tiny wooden dresser next to the wall. Julia paused just a second before winding her legs around Jean's slender body, her hands twisting in Jean's dark shirt and drawing her tighter.

Julia wasn't a big fan of the F word when it came to women. She enjoyed saying sex, making love, or doing something along those lines. Fuck still felt brutal to her, and aggression was the polar opposite of what Julia wished to do with somebody she loved. But there was something in the way Jean touched her, the ferocity of it, the way it responded to a longing Julia was aware of that made it seem right. Julia said, that's more than right, that's exciting. She desired to f*CK Jean. She wished Jean would fuck her.

Jean's mouth had not been on hers for long. It kissed Julia's neck again but continued lower, settling on the great slope of her breasts, Jean's lips, teeth, and tongue rotating between the two, kissing, sucking, and lightly biting at her nipples and hungrily sucking her flesh inside her lips, leaving it spit-drenched and ever so slightly soft. Julia enjoyed the feeling and wished Jean would stay at her breasts for as long as she wanted, but she soon realized Jean's interests were elsewhere.

Jean knelt on her knees, her lips brushing Julia's stomach down to her inner thighs. Julia moaned at the sensation, despite her apprehension.

Julia wasn't a huge fan of men going down on her in the past. Not because it didn't feel nice, because it did, but Julia still assumed it was something they were doing out of guilt or in the transactional expectation of getting a blowjob. Julia felt there was something phony in it, that when she was with somebody, she needed sincerity. She encouraged them to be doing something they enjoyed.

"Holy shit," Julia moaned as Jean's tongue ran down the length of her moist lips. Her long, gentle tongue caressed her folds and rolled across her clitoral region. Julia immediately knew there was no trickery going on. Jean's eyes lit up as her tongue slid inside her, obviously secure about what her tongue could do to the face of whoever she was with.

Julia sighed as Jean began kissing her deeply. Jean's seemingly prehensile tongue explored her fully, and I felt every contortion and twist. Julia was taken aback by Jean's long, slow licks as well as his fast flickers of a darting tongue, which left her breathless and her hands bunched in his fur, drawing her tighter. She needed to feel Jean's tongue as deeply as she could inside her.

Jean complied, her tongue locating and sensations inside Julia's pussy that caused her knees to bend with jolts of sheer ecstasy. Julia felt as though she were being devoured, and Jean's insistent mouth was reveling in the feeling of it as well. Touch, taste, scent, tone, and the sight of it, with her wide eyes, still fixed on her lover's smile.

Julia couldn't stop laughing. A happy voice. About the ferocity, Jean's treatment of her was lighthearted. A sly remark. Jean's tongue would strike a sensitive area, Julia would beg for more, and Jean would mercilessly use the knowledge against her. She was giving her a taste of everything she desired before removing and relocating it. Julia felt her legs stretch, needing to open them even further to allow Jean even more access to her, and then she felt her lover's strong hands raise one of her legs up and around her so that the back of Julia's knee was at the back of Jean's arm, her foot hanging in the air.

"Holy sh*t," Julia groaned, her freshly opened posture allowing Jean's tongue to enter her evermore. She felt the feeling making her tired and unbalanced with her knee in the air. Reaching behind her, she tried to tighten her grip on the dresser but only found her arms tossing everything over. Julia turned in time to see a medal dropping to the field, the little Karate dude posing on top snapping off before it reached the ground.

"Oh my gosh, I'm sorry I split..."

Jean didn't seem to note the devastation. She didn't stop chewing. Her nose is scraping into Julia's clit, bringing jolts of gratification through Julia's core, faster and faster, deeper and deeper.

Julia could feel a weight rising within her. One that she recognized as a sign that she was getting there. Every lick, every roll of the tongue from Jean contributed to it. Julia's insides felt like a dam, pushing back a current that just kept rising. She felt herself bite down on Jean's tongue, but tensing her inner walls just added to the suspense. As the river soared, it seemed that the dam had shrunk.
Finally, it became too many. Julia broke out laughing. Her inner walls tightened, and she gushed all over Jean's amazing tongue. Her fingertips gripped the dresser almost too closely for her good as she felt her legs wobble and her climax flow into every fiber in her body. She didn't say anything as she approached, just breathing deeply as the wave went over her. Little throbs from deep inside her pussy extend across her, flowing up the length of her legs and through her back, both cooling and heating her.

Jean continued to tongue her, apparently enjoying the flavor of the fluids that spilled out from Julia's depths. Julia went almost thirty seconds until she felt her tensing body relax, her breathing back to regular, and her mind quit swirling due to the intense pressure that seemed to extend the orgasm. Julia struggled to bring into words her admiration, appreciation, and relief when she finished when Jean finally withdrew her tongue and smiled up at her, her chin glistening with Julia's wetness. She didn't come across much.

"Wow, that was incredible."

"Mmm," Jean said, her teeth scraping Julia's inner thigh. Julia found something else when she watched Jean's hands travel down to her buttocks. The energy that had been flowing between them all day had shifted. It was always there, fewer and more than it had been. Happy but not satisfied. Recognized still not thoroughly explored

Julia was then pulled down into Jean's fluffy bed, and Jean almost pounced down on top of her.

"You Vegetarian girls taste fantastic." Jean smiled as she embraced Julia passionately. However, there was less ferocity—only a long, slow, languid embrace. Julia could taste herself on Jean's lips, and she had to confess that she had no disagreements, even though she couldn't speak to the comparable effect of her diet.

"So, what are you expecting me to do?" Julia wrote, still unaware of the lesbian sex dance moves. Jean just grinned. When she arose from Julia's frame, she drew the sleeveless top over her head and yanked off her thin bra, exposing her bronzed, inked torso. Julia couldn't help but be impressed. Wiry and strong, with well-defined abdominal muscles and taut arms, yet undeniably feminine. Her breasts were slim and pert, with large-ish brown nipples, and her body was smooth bronze skin with no dye. Julia desperately tried to impress her in the same way she'd been happy.

Jean, it seems, has other ideas. She was soon kissing her way down Julia's body. But it was now moving more slowly. Her tongue seemed to leave a trace of moisture that touched every inch of Julia's impassive face. She licked her areola, the undersides of her breasts, and her belly button, eliciting a quick giggle from the ticklish Blonde, before setting up shop between Julia's legs once more.

"But...I..."

Julia attempted to object. After all, it wasn't her turn. Julia despised being in bed with someone greedy, and the last thing she wanted to do was be that way with Jean. Still, Jean appeared adamant, and Julia was soon protesting for another cause.

Her climax had virtually buzzed her, but it wasn't until she noticed Jean's tongue on her clit that she knew how responsive she was down there. Jean's tongue brushing along her most delicate point sounded like nails on a chalkboard, if nails on a chalkboard could be both unbearable and wonderfully wonderful at the same time.

"Oh, no," Julia exclaimed when she remembered what Jean was up to. Her tongue was rubbing about on her clit, bringing it between her lips and sucking gently. Julia felt the tip track through it, writing notes, drawing pictures, or doing something that made her squirm uncontrollably. She wanted to combat it, but it was too much for her. She felt like she was about to yell or collapse, so she clamped her legs around Jean's head as though to shield herself from the unbearable, horrible, beautiful feeling. As she did so, she became aware of a strange and wonderful sensation. Jean's unusual hairstyle rubbed one leg against silky, thick fur, the other against a newly shaved scalp. Julia felt her hold on Jean's head relax as a result of the stark comparison.

Jean continued until he was freed from Julia's grasp on his thighs. Julia was tortured by her tongue's long, leisurely licks across the hood of her clit. Julia wished for her to slow down and hurry up, to cut it out and never come back. Julia felt her own hands on her breasts, the big orbs filling her soft hands, her fingertips pinching at her sensitive nipples as a second orgasm overtook her.

Julia whimpered as her body shuddered with ecstasy once more. She bowed out. She would do whatever Jean demanded. It didn't matter whether it was passive or aggressive. She was in her grip. Jean was her guide, and she would do what he said.

Jean kept going until she'd taken Julia to another orgasm, this time after slipping two fingers into her and thrusting her long, firm digits into Julia as her tongue started writing a novel on her clit. Finally, she was panting and felt as though she'd been drained of the last drop of gratification her body had to give. Jean eventually came to a halt, leaving Julia panting and in what she knew was a slightly wet area on the sheet.

Julia was engrossed in her ecstasy. Jean was back on top of her, their breasts close together and their mouths touching in long, easy kissing.

"You like," Jean said confidently, her voice as happy as Julia's.

Julia nodded, "Uh-huh." She couldn't think of a way to express how much she enjoyed it.

Julia recognized Jean's contentment in his expression, even though she didn't like it. As much as she loved her physical satisfaction, Julia's biggest excitement was taking the guy she was with off. Causing them to lose balance, Jean appeared to feel the same way, and Julia realized it was a well-earned satisfaction for the taller kid.

Julia had found the determination to no longer be the person who was getting something done to her because of the feeling of kindness. She turned onto her side while her leg snaked around Jean's back, knocking the other girl off her. Julia's hand started romantically touching another woman's body for the first time now that they were both on their sides. Her hand traced up Jean's broad forearms, along with her tattoos, to her solid biceps and along her rounded shoulders. Her hand moved down Jean's breasts and each abdominal until it came to rest between Jean's thighs.

Julia gently stroked Jean's moist mouth, much like she'd done with the rest of Jean's body, except unlike the rest of her, Julia let her fingertips stay there, going back and forth. Familiarize herself with its contours, how it varied just marginally from her own, experiencing a lovely little shudder from Jean when she found her clit. Julia started to understand the act of having a woman off a bit better as she went along. She wasn't an expert, she realized, but she'd had several orgasms through the years, and, after licking her fingers to make them wet, she discovered that Jean appeared to react to Julia's fingers in the same way Julia did.

"Mmm, that's sweet," Jean said, her lips catching and tugging on Julia's earlobe. Julia rubbed a little faster, tiny circular movements that replicated themselves with increasingly rising intensity, buoyed by the encouragement. Julia paused, her body stiffening as the tempo accelerated, and for the first time since they'd begun making out, hell, since the two had first seen each other, Julia thought she had an advantage over the dark-haired female.

"Fuck me, yeah," moaned Jean. Julia couldn't help but grin at Jean's expression, her face contorted with delight. For the first time, Jean didn't seem to have all the solutions or be the coolest guy in the room. Jean now seemed to be someone whose body responded to anyone else's contact and has the same desires.

Julia knelt, kissing and sucking one of Jean's nipples into her mouth, then the other. Her fingertips rubbed at a faster speed, the kind Julia used on herself while her self-exploration was messing with her punctuality, and she just wanted to get off quickly. She didn't want to hurry Jean, far from it, but she did want Jean to go. She was curious whether she should.

Julia was so focused on getting rid of the other girl that she almost didn't realize Jean's passivity was just a passing phase. Jean's limbs were large enough to stretch behind her thighs, and she appeared to try to mimic Julia's movements.

"It's not fair," Julia grumbled, chewing Jean's lips, "this is your turn."

"Shut up and fuck me," Jean said, laughing in a way Julia could only define as giggling. She would have bet her life on Jean's lips, never making the noise again. Julia had found it exhilarating to see the hip girl laugh with joy.

The two girls fucked each other in this manner, their hands frantically grinding across each other's legs. Julia felt her knees lock back on Jean's hand once more and knew it was because she was getting so tight. She bit her lower lip and attempted to ignore the pain. She was unable to cum again. She had first to make Jean cum. She was aware of another potent climax inside her, one she could sense coming but had to stop. Julia was not a softie. She'd either get Jean off or die trying.

"Fuck me, yeah, shit, shit, shit, shit, shit, shit, shit, shit, shit, shit, shit, shit, shit, shit, shit, shit, shit

Jean yelled and bucked her hips. Julia watched her leg convulse and her stomach contract before crashing down like a steel trap on Julia's hand. Julia couldn't take her eyes off the prize, and she couldn't stop laughing from ear to ear. She's resisted. Jean had been cum and cum hard as a result of her behavior. Jean rode her hand as she made little cooing sounds as her climax grew to a crest and then faded. Jean's lips curled into a shocked grin, almost as though she was scoffing in shock at what Julia had been able to do to her.

"Yay," Julia said quietly, her throat dry with all the joy she'd yelled. She nipped at Jean's collarbone, the taller girl's hands temporarily resting behind her thighs.

"Beginner's luck," Jean said, but the smile she offered Julia showed she was grateful.

"I'm a little ahead of you." Julia downplayed her feat.

"Ok, plan to get the smirk off your face swept clean," Jean said as she forced Julia onto her back and reclaimed her commanding spot on top of the busty blonde sharing her room.

Julia moaned, spreading her legs wide. She'd come so close to cumming herself, needing to bite her lip to hold and resist her orgasm, that she was relieved. She bit her lip once more, this time in hungry suspense, and braced herself for the sensation of Jean's fingertips on her clitter.

"Oh," Julia exclaimed, taken aback by Jean's confusion. Julia knows fingertips just lingered on her clit for a second before trailing lower down and seeking her close entry, rather than the circular rubbing motion she was anticipating. Julia moaned when two of Jean's fingertips slipped inside her, curving gently outward before slipping out to the knuckle.

Julia relished the feeling of being more familiar for the first time. Being invaded like this was a happy return to what Julia was used to. Anything she always enjoyed. As Jean pulled back inside, she rotated her hips, spreading her legs to meet Jean's palms. She

exclaimed when Jean's slightly crooked fingers find a place that made her quiver with every little twitch and pressure after a few seconds of looking.
"Oh, that's sweet," Julia moaned, "actually, really good."

"Nice," Jean said before enticingly kissing Julia.

Julia almost squealed in delight. This was ideal sex for her—the kind she was used to and had come to appreciate. On top of her, inside of her, a passionate lover interpreting her anatomy. They were completely in harmony, responding to each other's wishes and desires. The fact that it was a stunning, slim woman on top of her was novel, and the sensation of Jean's breasts against her own was accentuated by Jean's breasts against her own. Still, to Julia, it just added a wonderful aspect of uniqueness to something wonderfully familiar.

Inventiveness. Julia's mind raced over the phrase as she felt Jean's fingertips speed up in her. Julia was aware that it had two definitions. It could refer to something modern, a fad, or a craze—anything out of the ordinary only to be out of the ordinary. Julia quickly dismissed the second as the one she was referring to. Jean had unleashed something in her with her talent, gentleness, and playfulness that she realized couldn't be placed back in a container. Anything that refused to go away. Being with another woman was not something she was trying out for the first time. Julia knew that was a result of her sexuality. She was aware of who she was. Maybe it hadn't been completely understood, but it was a path she desperately desired to take.

And, when Julia exclaimed as Jean slipped a third finger inside her, she had to do that for Jean.

Despite Julia's wetness, she could sense the third finger stretching her beautifully. She noticed her inner muscles tighten around it reflexively, but this just heightened the sense of fullness. It was unfamiliar ground for Julia, but when Jean kissed her again, she knew she had no fear of the unknown. She had faith in Jean. I had confidence that all of Jean's sweetness and skill in taking her to orgasm will manifest itself again here.

"Do you like it?" Jean inquired.

Julia felt that confidence as she looked up into Jean's beautiful deep, dark brown eyes. Julia enjoyed it because she could tell Jean understood. Her moans and swaying hips betrayed whatever pride she might have felt. But she could see how relevant it was to Jean for her to admit she enjoyed it.

Julia agreed with a smile. Jean's hand sped up, her fingertips once again seeking the extraordinarily vulnerable place inside Julia's pussy and making sure she penetrated it with each thrust. Julia's hands grasped the back of Jean's neck and drew her in tighter, embracing her as passionately and gratefully as she could. Jean was right. The third finger had just intensified her feelings. Julia could sense another orgasm coming on, and she realized it would be a huge one. A strong internal strain engulfed her, and as stretched as she was, she imagined herself with nowhere for it to go. As if she'd explode if it entered her, it just grew and developed inside of her.

"Fuck, Jean, god yeah," Julia moaned as her hands traveled from Jean's neck to each arm, her nails digging in roughly as a spike of ecstasy coursed through her.

"Would you like to cum?" Jean inquired.

Julia could just smile and say, "Uh-huh." Julia succumbed to her selfishness for a split second. She desired the orgasm inside her. Despairingly. She was unconcerned with percentages or justice. She simply required the sweet release.

"You have to inquire first," Jean said, her hand almost slamming against Julia's clit, the bottom of her palm almost slamming into Julia's clit.

"Just let me cum," Julia begged, her voice pleading, "Fuck Jean! It's fantastic."

Julia let out a squeal. Jean had inserted a fourth finger. Julia had a feeling she was about to pop. She was stuffed, shocked that Jean had done anything at all. Yet Jean was fucking her almost as intensely with her whole hand inside her in an instant.

Jean hissed, "So cum for me slut, cum all over my goddamn hand."

Julia trembled. Normally, she'd never encouraged herself to be named that, but it sounded perfectly fitting coming from Jean's mouth. It didn't refer to a woman who was too assertive or mean. It represented a woman giving in to her most primal, primal impulses. Her dire situation. Julia felt herself squeeze down around Jean's hand again and move her hips, her muscles spasming and her body shaking as the massive orgasm stayed tantalizingly out of control.

"I said cum, slut," Jean said harshly again.

Julia broke out laughing. Her body was trembling, and her voice was a primal howl. Her back arched up against her boyfriend, and she felt her fluids gush out of her, filling Jean's hand with sperm. She tried rolling her hips, but she found herself doing it wildly and uncontrollably, bucking against Jean's hands when sparks flew inside her. Julia swears she saw the desert moon above her, stars twinkling in the cool blackness of the night until her eyes rolled within her brain. Every muscle in her body tightened, her fingertips digging into the small of Jean's back and her toes curling. The pleasure was intense, unlike anything she'd ever experienced before.

Julia had no idea how long it had continued. Everything she realized was that she'd be sweating, panting, laughing, weeping mess at the end of it. Her body was sore and electric, and she was fully fulfilled. She looked like she was on a higher level, one she'd wanted to be on but had never gotten to. Lying there, Jean had rolled off of her and was at her side; she felt compelled to articulate herself in any way. She had a new sense of contentment, enlightenment, and oneness.

"That was...fucking...awesome," she exclaimed.

7.

Julia drew a deep breath and noticed her body tremble. She couldn't accept how delicate her body was. She couldn't remember how long it had been before Jean's hand had lifted her off the ground. She was convinced the time had elapsed. Space was now pitch black, with just the soft moonlight lighting the bed and the two bodies on it. Julia had been vaguely conscious of the passing of time, but she had been preoccupied with the supercharged situation in which Jean's hand had abandoned her. She had the impression that every portion of her body was composed of pop rocks. She felt like she was going to whine, yell, or weep any time a cold wind brushed over her skin, or she twisted subtly so that the sleek cotton her nude body was tangled in dropped across her thighs.

"It was goddamn amazing," Julia heard herself say as her breath returned to her.

"You know you've said that about six times already," Jean said, sitting on her side with her head propped up on her knee. Julia's slight burn from the second joint she'd been saving in her pocket was burning softly between her fingertips in the dark chamber, joining with the moonlight to produce a haunting glow that, Julia realized, made her look like a sexy ghost.

"Wow," Julia said, surprised that she'd repeated herself too many times, "sorry."

Jean grinned.

"Please don't apologize; I like hearing it, but if you want to massage my ego, you should adjust it up a little. You might tell that was the best sex you've ever experienced, or you could claim no one has ever made you feel that way, or you could suggest, and I realize this is a little messed up, but it turns me on, I've ruined you for all guys."

Julia grinned as she rolled onto her back, letting the sheet slip off her bare chest and taking the joint from Jean's grasp.

"I'm not sure if we're there yet," Julia admitted after taking a deep breath, "so it was nice yet maybe not 'write off my whole sexual past' good."

"Your whole personal history?" Jean said, scratching her head. "You've never been with a girl?"

"Never," Julia said, reflecting on her life until a worried expression appeared on her forehead, "but I was OK, right?"

"It's why it's so hard to believe," Jean said, bending forward to kiss Julia on the forehead, another feeling that coursed through Julia even more than she anticipated. You've never desired or been drawn to girls or..."

"No, it's not that," Julia clarified. "I've always assumed women were, you know, sexy, and in high school, I had this major but sort of chaste crush on this Math instructor I had, and she was so stunning, but...it just never happened."

"Because you're straight?" Jean asked, returning the joint.

Julia paused for a moment, watching the joint's wave blend with her post-orgasmic haze to produce an extremely peaceful feeling. She turned to face Jean. She had everything she had to express but wasn't sure how it would be received. When she'd said something identical in the past, she'd normally been yelled at. Jean, who was clever, cynical, and sardonic, seemed to think so as well. Julia resented Jean's presence.

"I said that's not it," Julia scoffed, "it's not about brands, and it's not about ethnicity, it's..."

"What?" Jean said, shrugging.

Julia wanted to take the risk of being mocked.

Julia began, "Like, wavelengths, you know?" Jean's expression was perplexed, but Julia concluded that perplexed was preferable to dismissive.

"Like, when I've been with people in the past, it hasn't been about, you know, knowing they're sexy or whatever; it's mostly been about picking up on a kind of mutual vibe, and occasionally it gets sexual and then, you know, I have sex. I've never been like, oh, I'm getting this vibe from a girl, but I'm straight so I can't do it."

"That's what you were having difficulty saying?" Jean inhaled again.

Julia stood there motionless for a while.

"When I speak like that, a lot of people laugh at me."

"I mean, well, I wouldn't say it that way," Jean agreed, "but there was certainly a thing between us, and if you want to name it a wavelength or vibe or something, yeah. I've been sensing it since I saw you, and it's like for me too, okay, it's more than just, you know, the sexy blonde with big boobs thing that I'm pretty into."

Julia cracked a grin. She'd been named that before, but it didn't sound objectifying or anything in Jean's words. It is exactly right. And Jean hadn't mocked her. As a result, she was feeling quite an at ease. Then she went on.

"Because I've always been open to it, you know," Julia said. "Like Fin once asked if I wanted to have a threesome, and I was like, 'Yeah, I do.' But it was different. I was like, yeah, eventually, if we ever had the same vibe between us, but another girl or guy was sharing it, then I'd want to see if it played out with three people."

Now Jean was laughing. Julia mistook her for smiling at her, but Jean corrected her.

"That wasn't going to happen, Gab, even though I liked men."

Julia gave a smile.

"Well, no, I mean. It didn't turn out that way at all. I figured it would happen spontaneously like that when Fin proposed it at first, but he only suggested this girl he met who, as he put it, was 'down with whatever.' I don't think he wanted to create that type of mutual experience; he just wanted to see me making out with a girl."

"Well, I'm happy it didn't happen like that," Jean said, softly kissing Julia's upper arm, "I'm glad I got to be the first."

"Me too," Julia said, her grin uncontrollable. She was truly amazing.

Jean stubbed the joint out on an ashtray on her bedside table before leaning back into Julia, their curves curving into each other with ease.

"Anyway, I can't fault Fin too much; after all, I want to see you making out with a kid." Jean slyly whispered.

"Do you?" Julia inquired. She felt a bit uneasy for a split second. Julia considered being with two girls simultaneously, and while there was some attraction there, she found herself feeling somewhat...jealous? Julia was experiencing a different sensation and was uncertain how to deal with it.

"Absolutely," Jean said with a smile, "but just in the first person."

Julia burst out laughing.

They kissed again, this time with increasing fervor. Julia could sense herself heating up again, her skin already sticky and vulnerable to contact. Yet, the weed had triggered an overwhelming craving that, amazingly, Jean hadn't been able to satisfy. Jean's lips contributed significantly to this, kissing Julia's jaw to her ear and snaking her tongue inside while lightly tugging at her earlobe with her teeth.

"Fuck, I wish we had more than one night," Jean mumbled.

"Night isn't done," Julia said, her teeth digging into Jean's arm, just above the Crow's wing.

Jean grinned, and the two embraced passionately, their tongues dancing around each other once more. Julia turned onto her stomach, and Jean was back between her thighs, rubbing into her.

"I want..." Jean broke the embrace, "I mean, are you okay with me fucking you with a strap-on?"

Julia took a breather. She was at a loss for words. She'd never really played with toys before. She had to shake her head, telling Jean that they didn't need it. That Jean's fingers, lips, and tongue were more than enough for her and that she had no idea how anything else, anything beyond them, might affect things. But Julia could see in Jean's eyes that it was something Jean wished to do, and Julia, who felt like she hadn't done anything for Jean before, didn't want to turn down the lovely black-haired girl.

"Cool," Julia said, nodding.

And as she hopped up and searched for the little drawer on her nightstand, Jean smiled. She took out a sturdy-looking black harness with what Julia figured was a very long, very thick cock attached.

"Just..." Julia said, sitting up and hugging the sheet to her stomach, a strange explosion of modesty in her voice, "just, you know, remember I'm always studying."

Jean grinned as she cinched the belt around her stomach before softly placing her hand on Julia's chest and pushing her down onto her back. The two wound their arms around each other once more, kissing. Julia clutched Jean's back while Jean cupped the sensitive skin of Julia's breasts. Julia could feel the rough plastic pressing against her hip, but it didn't feel as strange as she'd anticipated. It was kind of familiar.

Jean reached down somewhere in their hug and properly balanced the cock's shaft, rubbing it against Julia's sex's outer lips. Jean teased Julia with its head back and forth, nudging at her clit before heading back down and beginning again. Jean will push a bit, then pull back and rub some more. Julia's anxiety soon turned to excitement and then to desperate desperation.

"Just come on," Julia said, arching her back towards Jean. Jean just grinned that knowing grin.

"Do you like it?" Jean inquired.

Julia gave a smile.

"Say it," Jean said emphatically.

"Give it to me," Julia said, feeling herself burn from how badly she wanted it.

Jean pushed inside, pressing on. Julia sighed in response to the interruption. It was larger than it was, and she could feel herself stretching across it.

"Oh fuck," Julia moaned, throwing her head back when she felt the cock slide into her. Jean tilted Julia's head back down and kissed her again, and then they were making out as before, slowly and passionately, yet Jean was thrusting inside her. Slow, steady thrusts that Julia thought would drive her insane because they felt so good.

Jean kept it slow, expertly rocking the big thing out of Julia, allowing her to get used to it and feeling the resistance give in when Julia became wetter and wetter, allowing her to glide the thing in and out of her. Soon she was pushing in the whole thing, still in slow, steady strokes that ended as there was simply no more inside to push.

"Oh god," moaned Julia, "it's so fucking sweet."

Jean smiled and started thrusting faster. She had patience, but she had limits. Soon she was thrusting steadily, each time at a new angle, with slightly more force. Julia could feel the thickness of it, the big head rubbing over her clitoral hood at every entry and then coming to rest further inside her than everyone or thing had ever been.

Jean increased her pace, finally lifting Julia's slender, tanned legs from around her waist to above her shoulders, then fucked down onto Julia, crushing her against the bed.

"Fuck, don't quit," Julia pleaded as she felt Jean's cock reach yet another depth, triggering yet another surge of sensations. Every angle, every place, they seemed to discover something different inside her.

Julia had never really seen the appeal of muscly types before. Still, now, after feeling the constant pounding and the incredible sensation it was giving her, she could see the outline of Jean's defined muscles, straining under the force of how hard she was fucking her.

"Fuck don't quit, don't stop, don't stop, don't stop," Julia pleaded.

"I'm not fucking going to quit," Jean joked.

Julia grinned when she felt Jean move again, this time to the location Julia realized was the correct one; she howled her delight, and Jean got the message crashing into her at that angle again and again.
"FUCK," Julia yelled again as she approached, her leg twitching and shaking as the giant cock made her insane. As the ecstasy enveloped her, she bucked into the thrusts, her hips

riding the huge dick to the surge of pleasure's regrettable end. As Julia regained consciousness, Jean was back on top of her, her breasts pressing against Julia's bigger ones, with both of them panting heavily.

"Did you do it?" Julia inquired.

"Wow," Jean panted as he bit Julia's shoulder.

"How, though?" Julia was perplexed.

"There's a nub and my clit on the inside of the brace and...yeah." "I'm fine with it," Jean grumbled.

Julia felt Jean's hands on her back, softly extracting the dick, and they lay entwined for a few seconds. Julia exclaimed when she noticed the cold air on her bare bits for the first time, feeling free and empty but still amazing.

"One more thing," Jean said, rubbing her hand against Julia's hips and turning her onto her side.

Julia wore a cynical expression. She didn't usually like being fucked from behind. Since she was such a lover of eye contact, it still seemed less personal than any other role, and that was before the reality that much of the time, it only appeared to pick up, and therefore hasten, the end of the sex.

"You'll appreciate it," Jean predicted, as though he could understand Julia's mind. Julia obliged, thinking of the wavelength once more. Overall, she'd enjoyed everything else Jean had accomplished, so she turned over onto her hands and knees and braced herself for Jean's arrival.

Jean, on the other hand, drew her back onto her knees and stood behind her. Julia's legs apart, she put the cock underneath her and drew Julia together, their bodies spooned together on their knees. Julia groaned again when she leaned downwards against Jean's body and felt the cockhead slip into her again.

Jean swayed along, slowly rocking the cock up and into Julia's pussy while both of her arms enveloped Julia's voluptuous body. Jean's left arm curled upward and wrapped under Julia's left arm, her forearm leaning on Julia's chest and her palm softly gripping around Julia's waist.

Her right arm slid down over Julia's shoulder and into the space between her thighs. Jean's deft fingertips started scratching at Julia's clitter once more.
Julia moaned, "Oh sh*t."

Jean nuzzled Julia's ear, licking a mark on it before lightly chewing it.

"Do you want it?" she demanded in hushed tones.

Julia moaned almost breathlessly, "Yes." The tension between the cock inside her and the digits on her clit was unlike everything else they'd done.

Jean rocked her harder, her fingertips quicker spinning Julia's clit. Julia's neck was clenched gently by her side, barely enough for her to sense pain.

Julia moaned with delight. She had always disliked rough sex, but this was new. It was different being bundled in Jean's embrace and feeling her warm skin and breasts on her back. She needed Jean to be more rugged. It was not threatening in any way. She sensed a burst of energy inside her and decided to give in to it. She decided to reveal everything she'd held secret. Any latent ambition she couldn't reconcile with her enjoyment of intimacy and sweetness.

She was itching to be fucked.

"Fuck me," Julia replied, surprised by the sound of her accent.

Jean grinned as he pulled Julia back onto all fours. Grasping Julia's hair tightly, she started thrusting her hips violently into her, shocked by how Julia's body rocked back, fucking back into Jean's cock just as forcefully as she was thrusting into her.

Julia groaned as the pressure from her hair being removed mingled with her enjoyment, heightening it. That's the kind of stuff she'd always ignored. Now she realized it was possible, that it was inside her, and that every thrust of Jean's cock was taking it out of her. She desired more of it.

"Spank me?" Julia inquired, her pussy tightening around the intruding penis. This was the highest angle yet. The huge cock rubbed her clit from the inside, a place she'd never realized she had.

Jean complied, her smooth palm slapping against Julia's pert butt cheek. Julia moaned in excitement when a loud crack filled the building.

"Again," Julia grumbled. Jean delivered once more. More difficult. Julia was much more enamored of it.

"Harder?" Julia inquired. Jean brought both hands down on Julia's butt before gripping her fingertips into it for traction while she continued to slam her dick into Julia's obedient body.

The tempo just quickened. Jean's hand randomly cracking through Julia's butt or twists her hair to send Julia the unforgettable jolt. Julia felt an ecstasy starting to course through her that felt immense and overwhelming, the sensation of the cock rising and building inside of her.

"Cum for me," Jean said, and the gritty commanding accent affected her as well.

Julia arrived, but it was different than the other orgasms Jean had brought her that day. Julia was saddened for a split second because it was bigger and moved faster around her. But then, when Jean continued to screw her, she got another. Another pulse, another tremor zipped through her core, contracting her pussy together with her fingertips and toes. And there was the next one. And yet another. And yet another.

Julia could sense the sweat pouring onto her back as the bed shook from Jean's thrusts. But she had no idea where she was. It felt like any other thrust was a different one. They were conflicting, mixing, integrating, and growing in size all the time.

"JEAN, JEAN, JEAN, JEAN, JEAN, JEAN, JEAN, I adore you!" Julia yelled when the huge one reached her—slamming through her, causing her to tremble. She couldn't push back because she was fully surrounded. She couldn't hold her head up and slumped into the bunk, bending down at the waist. Metaphors let her down. Julia realized it wasn't explosions or shooting stars or something of the like. It was simply the greatest goddamn orgasm of her existence, one that came from deep inside her and dwarfed any she'd ever had. She looked like she'd been fucked into oblivion.

She wasn't sure until it came to a halt. There were already tremors and aftershocks coursing through her body. She figured it was over when she felt Jean's body sag against hers, finally exhausted, but it seemed that any inch of her skin that Jean's warm body brushed pulled out the memory of what the orgasm had meant and brought it back in tiny tingles of reminder. It was amazing.

Jean was soon nuzzled against her neck once more. Julia didn't care if it was already too hot to be tucked up against each other. She didn't want to be even a few feet removed from the lover who had taken her to this stage. She wished she could curl up against Jean and sleep for a thousand years. They eventually found themselves back at the head of the bunk, Jean with her hands behind her head in a kind of triumphant stance, while Julia twisted her leg around Jean's and leaned her head against the taller woman's arm. They were both panting as they'd just finished a sprint.

Julia could sense sleep engulfing her. A deep, contented slumber that spoke of happiness she'd never experienced before. And the heat didn't appear to be able to save it. On the other hand, Julia fought it, and, to her dismay, a touch of neurosis arose.

"Do...you...want...to...do...more...stuff?" Julia continued to breathe raggedly.

Jean burst out laughing.

"Good lord lady, I know the dick never softens, but I'm always flesh and bone." "Aren't you done?" Jean inquired.

Julia made a shaky motion of her head.

"No, no, I'm cool," Julia explained. She couldn't imagine feeling much better. "I also feel like you did more to me than I did to you because I know how it can feel when you're dating someone who doesn't want to give as much consideration to you as you do to them, and I feel like so much of this has been between me and..."

Jean kissed her on the cheek.

"Second and foremost, you are adorable." "But you're still tired," Jean laughed, "and I had an awesome time, and I came several times, and you were great, and I just am just exhausted and want to sleep."

Julia gave a smile. She was fully drained. Yet, she was aware of a conflicting feeling. One she couldn't get rid of.

"I know...just...we it just has one night, and I don't want it to stop yet and..." Julia paused.

Jean kissed her once more.

"It doesn't have to be for one night only."

Julia reflected on the sentiment. Part of her was ecstatic for it, although the other half was strongly opposed to it. She was on a journey. She wished to travel throughout the world. Even if she had encountered the most amazing, awesome individual in the first place, she didn't want to travel a few miles and stay there. Julia felt obligated to her quest, even though it meant no more nights like this one.

Still, Julia reasoned as sleep crawled back upon her with an insistence she couldn't resist; she should dream about it all tomorrow.

8.

Julia was captivated by the sights and sounds of the car store. She'd never been in a position like that before, and the small group of mechanics and their whirring instruments reminded her of science fiction cartoons.

Julia was ecstatic. There were no other options. She was overjoyed. Although she was already a little sore from the night before and her voice was hoarse from the crying she'd done, she looked like a wholly different individual. Refreshed and motivated, she found herself looking ahead to the day's struggles following what had been one of the most eventful and incredible days of her life.
"So, 6'5 240, Marine Linebacker." "Doug, have you ever threatened me before?" Jean continued.

"Shit no," Doug exclaimed emphatically.

"What's the harm?" Jean inquired.

The large man came to a halt and seemed to think for a moment.

"Because I know you'd knock the hell out of me and bury me in a shallow goddamn grave in the desert."

For a split second, the words hung in the balance. Julia could see Fin's stresses at least partly dissipate. He took a step back from Jean.

"Does that explain what's going on?" Doug inquired, his gaze fixed on Julia.

"It was," Julia agreed.

"Damn, I was expecting them to kiss or something." Doug grinned before returning his attention to the other mechanics. "Do you like to see Jean kill someone? It's amazing."

"I'm through with this." "Is the car fixed?" Fin inquired.

"It just required a belt removed," Doug agreed. I'm not sure why Jean didn't just fix it herself out there, particularly because she had the element."

Julia sent Jean a stern stare.

"Well," Jean said, talking suspiciously like a prosecutor, "I realize you're going to claim that's the third lie, but legally, technically, if you think about it, it was the first lie." So, even though I claimed the last lie was the last lie, it was indeed theoretically the last lie."

"All right," Julia said, scratching her head, "but just realize that when I look back on yesterday, I'll remember it as a little less magical because of all the lies."

"Are you sure?" Jean inquired, his face pained. Julia paused for a moment and quickly remembered she'd talked too fast.

"No," she said, shaking her head.

"Look, enough of this crap," Fin interjected, appearing much crazier than before even though his violent impulses had disappeared. "Can you tell me where the car is?"

Jean pointed to the parking area. Fin had been insane enough to stroll on by it.

"It is completely free. We don't accept douchebag money, "She said as she tossed him the keys.

"Um, yeah, we do," Dougie interjected, "and they invest well."

"I'll get you back, Doug," Jean said as he punched the big man in the arm, "just let him go."

"Whatever," Fin said, "let's go, Julia."

Julia took a breather. She considered Fin, Jean, and the path before making a decision.

"No," she replied, an agitated voice rising inside her.

Fin turned to face her, his face shocked for a moment before softening somewhat. He'd deduced something significant from her speech.

"Look, I don't care what you did to her last night; all I want to do is run out of here," he said. "OK, then get in the goddamn taxi."

"No," I say. Julia said it again, this time with greater certainty.
"Julia?"

"No, take a peek at me." Julia said when Fin's eyes found hers, her rage still simmering inside her and seeking a strong pillar of motivation, "It has absolutely nothing to do with her. Is this what you're like? That is not the case for us. That is not my style. That's everything I don't want to be a member of. You don't scream at me because I'm not your possession. You're not my lover, and to be frank, I don't even consider you a friend right now. I'm not interested in going out with you."

Julia's words lingered in the breeze for a few seconds, the whole shop deafeningly quiet. Fin's eyes seemed to be experiencing various feelings—confusion, agony, and, ultimately, anger. Julia couldn't help but be sympathetic to him. She stuck by what she meant, but she didn't like upsetting others at the end of the day. Nonetheless, she realized it had to be said. The chapter she'd imagined the day before, with her and Fin? It was the last time she saw him.

The only thing that pierced the quiet was a yell from one of the shop's mechanics, who were paying close attention to what was going on.

"Oh no! You were told, son."

Jean, Fin, and Julia all turned their heads toward the direction of the voice.

"Shut up, Jimmy," Jean replied, though her admiring grin made it obvious she agreed. "But, Julia, seriously, yay."

"Fine," Fin finally said, "stay here, screw her, I don't give a shit." We also had an expiration date."

Julia shook her head. That was most likely right. She observed as Fin marched out towards the brown sedan, her back to her. Julia reflected on the year and a half she'd spent "with" him and realized that it was all fond memories, although there was some sorrow there.

"Memories," Julia reflected.

"Shit, Fin, hold on a second," Julia said as Fin opened the car door. Julia could see in his eyes a desire that she'd come and reverse what she'd done as he stopped and smiled at her. Julia instantly regretted calling out to him in that manner.

"Are you coming?" he inquired.

"No," Julia replied, shaking her head, "but my bag is still in the back, and I have the locket from my grandfather in there, as well as my money and things."

"I'll submit it to you via mail," Fin yelled loudly as he walked into the vehicle and slammed the door shut. Julia considered chasing after him, but the motor roared to life, and she stood powerless as the tires squealed and the rusty car flew out of the parking lot like a bat out of hell.

Julia grinned against herself. She had a crush on Fritz. She was relieved that he wasn't gone. Julia reflected as she returned her gaze to Jean, who smiled at her. She'd been correct about the vibe from him, after all. He was the ideal vehicle. He'd escorted her here.

9.

Julia has a strong desire to sprint back into the store from the parking lot. Wrap her arms around Jean and lick her. But there was time for that because Julia was worried about what had just happened. One of the only possessions she'd carried with her was the locket. It was one of the only items she had a strong commitment to.

"Hey, Julia," Jean said as she stepped back into the garage doors, "are you OK?"

"Well, it's really," Julia began, "I'm not sure, my purse."

"Didn't I think it just clothed?" Jean said as he took Julia's hand in his and squeezed it reassuringly.

"It contained some objects. My money and a locket provided to me by my grandfather on my last birthday before he died. Not much more than a million hundred dollars."

Jean threw her arms around the shorter blonde in an embrace.

"He did mention he'd mail it to you," Jean pointed out.

"I don't have a physical address somewhere," Julia said as a tear streamed down her face. She couldn't take her mind off her Grandfather and the dumb locket. She thought of him every day, and now she'd lost the one bit of him she had left.

"You should crash with me," Jean said, brushing a stray lock of Julia's hair away from her ears. Julia cracked a grin. Her fun was finished because she had little capital and no Fin. And though she had no clue what to do about herself next, having Jean was a wonderful backup plan.

"Thank you." "So I'm guessing if I ask him to mail things back to your house...it'll be on fire," Julia said.

"Well, in any case, I'm happy you're staying," Jean said.

"Wow, me too," Julia said softly, kissing Jean on the face.

"Hey, what was all the fuss about?"

Julia and Jean turned around to find Dougie staring down at them, his large hands rubbing oil off his trousers. He was perplexed with what he'd just seen.

"Oh, the bastard just drove away with her bag and all her belongings," Jean said

"Oh," Dougie thought for a moment, "was that as a large red suitcase from the 1970s?"

Julia grinned and smiled up at him, optimistic.

"That's in my office, by the way. Before we placed it on the shelf, we pulled the crap out of the back."

"Didn't Fin warn you not to tell them, though?" Julia inquired, recalling Fin's strong statement the night before.

"Shit yeah, he did," Jean said, recalling the moment vividly before nodding, "I think I just forgot."

Julia's heart skipped a beat. She decided to leap into the big man's arms and give him a big kiss. Even she wasn't going to do that until she was certain she got it back in her hands. She observed as he stepped back into the tiny office before emerging with what seemed to be her suitcase. Julia almost broke into tears as she recognized it in her hands. She placed it in front of her, unzipped the narrow front pocket, and reached inside to retrieve her locket.

"Dougie," Julia said, her eyes welling up with joyful tears, "I just want to kiss you."

Dougie grinned, clearly satisfied with his deeds, even though he didn't realize the importance of them.

"Yeah, but don't," he said confidently, "because my wife is super-jealous and pregnant and mad, and you're pretty hot...so, buy me a drink sometime, and we can call it even."

Julia smiled and nodded.

"To be completely truthful, it's just chance." "I could have even left it in the vehicle," Dougie said, "but it was a little bit; it seemed like it had things that could get hurt."

Julia gave a smile. She hadn't noticed since she was preoccupied with her locket, but her bag was noticeably large. It made little sense. She just had her clothes. She unzipped the key pouch and opened it while lying the suitcase flat on the bed.

When it was opened, Jean screamed, "Jesus, fuck." Julia couldn't help but agree. Fin had purchased many of the medicines in there, and Julia was correct: there were manyof them. Three thick, closely packaged blocks of marijuana weighing at least a few pounds each, a large bag containing hundreds of MDMA tablets, and, most interestingly, a substantial quantity of white powder in a triple Ziploc bag.

"I think he thought that if you were caught, Daddy would be able to help him out better if the narcotics were in your bag?" "What a goddamn penis!" Jean exclaimed before turning to face the lane.

Julia just stood there, shocked on the carpet. Not so much because of the quantity of it all, she realized Fin had sold his car to invest in the pills, but because some events from the previous two days that had perplexed her at the time began to make sense. Julia reasoned that he didn't want to carry the pills with him to the hotel because it would have meant bringing her bag and showing her he'd kept them there. Similarly, he'd sped away because he thought if he gave her the purse, he'd have to ask her to pull the pills out first. It clarified why he'd been so adamant that no one carries the bag out of the store and why he hadn't only wanted to get out of the car and...

"Holy fuck," Dougie exclaimed as he approached the bag, "Was that in the shop all night?" I'm trying to operate a company here, Jean. "I can't have this nonsense around."

"Doug, you saw those two," Jean said, putting her hands up to absolve herself, "I thought they had like an ounce of marijuana on them." I had no idea I was hanging out with Griselda Blanco's reincarnation."

"Hey, did you go to college?" "Do you get the references she makes?" Doug asked Julia, who nodded.

"No," Julia said, shaking her head, "I'm not sure who that is." I'm guessing she's a heroin dealer?"

Following it, there was a collective pause. Julia was aware that she could close the suitcase and remove it from the garage bay door, but she merely sat there. She didn't consider her find to be fortunate. She was worried. She wasn't a smuggler. She had no idea what to do about it all. A part of her wished Fin would return if only to kick him in the balls for hiding it in her bag in the first place and then making him take it.

Jean, on the other hand, had taken the powder bag and dipped a digit inside, taking a swipe before snorting it and rubbing it on her gums.

"Shit, that's coke," Jean exclaimed incredulously before adding, "Nice coke."

"He's never dealt hard drugs before," Julia said with a shrug. She didn't mind that much. She'd tried coke a few times. It was just not her thing.

Jean first stared at the medications, first at Julia, then at Dougie, and finally back at Julia. Her eyes shone brightly, and she grinned broadly. Julia reasoned that a light bulb must have been flickering over her head if it had been a cartoon.

"OK, hang on a second," she replied, "Dougie, are you interested in buying the house?"

"Are you sure?" Doug said, his cousin staring skeptically at him.

"All right, well, you already remember the jerk who races with those moron bikers, right?" she went on

"Yeah," he said, nodding, "Pueblo Eddy." In reality, I just saw him last week, and he told me that if I came across something that...oh, I see where you're going with this."

"Okay, so wait," Jean added, "there's got to be six pounds of marijuana in there, right?" And if my misguided youth is any guide, I can get fifteen hundred pounds for decent things, so that's..."

Julia replied easily, "nine thousand."

"OK, and that looked like at least three hundred Molly hits, right?" And we can have them for thirty-five cents each? So three hundred thirty-five times three hundred thirty-five times three hundred thirty-five times three hundred thirty-five times

"In the office, there's a calculator," Doug said.

"10,000 and five hundred," Julia spoke rapidly. ,

"Okay," Jean said, oddly staring at Julia for a second before returning to Doug, "then that's about twenty grand, and then there's got to be around a pound of coke here." And, I'm not sure how many grams are in a pound?"

Doug and Jean both stared at Julia this time.

"Four hundred fifty-three points..." Julia reflected, attempting to recall the last time she did anything that wasn't metric. "How about four-five two?"

"Okay," Jean said, obviously perplexed, "and last time I tested, you should get at least 115 per gram for good things, so that's..."

"Fifty-two thousand and...nine hundred and ninety-five?" "I didn't add the stuff after the decimal to make things smoother," Julia said.

"What's going on here, seriously?" "Like, is she some sexy blonde robot sent back in time to destroy us all?" Dougie wondered.

Julia sighed and shrugged her head. The truth was, this was a response to her that she was very used to. She loved it when they underestimated her in that way. She grinned and seemed to be unconcerned.

"Wow, people believe I studied rainbows and flowers in college because of my hair, tits, and clothing." It was mechanics, with a focus on aeronautic propulsion dynamics. Orbital Mechanics and all such nonsense. "Do you recall the math instructor I mentioned in high school?"

Jean searched her brain for a split second before going blank.

"I guess that's why she so took me." I've always been a natural mathematician. You know how people often think, "That's not rocket science," while they're suggesting anything, isn't that difficult? "Well, I know a little bit about space technology."

Doug and Jean exchanged a glance before Jean returned his attention to Julia.

"O....k," Jean said, continuing on but still obviously impressed by Julia's new dimension. "So, with more than seventy grand, you should be able to relocate to Eddy, right?"

"Wow," Doug agreed, "he carries weight like that."

"Then give me a house deal," Jean said

"What can we do now?" Doug inquired,

"Yeah," Jean agreed, "and tell me how much you think it's worth."

"I'm not sure, a hundred thirty thousand?" "About there?" Doug inquired.

"OK, so here's what we do," Jean said, nodding and sputtering, "you carry the medicines to Eddy, get what you can with them." Let's say 70,000. And you go to the bank and promise to give me a hundred and thirty dollars plus seventy dollars less, say, ten percent of each so..."

Julia sighed and rolled her eyes.

"You're not going to need me to do the math for you."

"One hundred eighty thousand," Dougie said.

"Right, so the bank offers me a hundred and eighty thousand dollars, and I write Blondie a check for seventy dollars for, claim, services provided..."

"And, much better, something else that doesn't feel like I'm the world's most luxurious prostitute." Julia stepped up to assist.

"And everybody is happy." "Right?" Jean replied, dismissing her. Is it you, Doug? What are your thoughts? "Am I correct?"

Doug took a long, hard look at his Cousin, who seemed to be brimming with eager fire.

"Ok, I guess you shouldn't do any more coke, to begin with," Doug said, "but I don't understand the plan; why not just offer her the drug money?"

Jean rolled her eyes and directed her finger at Julia.

"Do you want her carrying a suitcase full of drug money?" Or going to the bank and explaining how she earned it? You keep the drug money and make the huge offer; we all realize you can clean it up fairly easily because it doesn't seem suspicious."

"That's right," Doug agreed, "but what's in it for me?"

"Come on, Doug," Jean said, "you just want the home." You know, if I were to bring the screws in, I might get one fifty or one sixty for it on the street, but since you're my cousin and I love you, I'm taking your bid of one thirty and knocking ten percent off it for being the one who deals with Eddy, and you still get ten percent of the drug money to clean it. "I get a good lump of change for the building, and Blondie gets over $60,000 in clean money in a bank account."

Doug paused for a moment to consider it.

"Oh, well, well, I'm in." "Put the fuck in the office; I'll see Eddy tomorrow," he nodded.

Julia rose from the floor as Doug turned and returned to the store. Julia had to shake her head to process what she'd just seen. She'd somehow been a witness to a cocaine trade and money smuggling concocted by the kid she'd stayed with the night before in the space of five minutes. Dozens of thoughts popped into my head all at once, the most of which was on how and when Jean had built this feel for illegal conduct, but there was one more. One that won out when Jean reached over and drew her close.

"Are you selling your house?" Julia inquired.

Jean shook his head.

"Look, I'm not even a fan of the town. Doug, though, does. There is plenty of room for a growing family. You probably didn't notice, but there's a pretty yard out back."

"But where are you going?" Julia inquired,

"With you, dumb," Jean said as he kissed her on the cheek. "Ever since last night, when you were dreaming about the open road and fun, I knew I'd been trapped here for about five years and didn't even have something stopping me here." I'd like to join you on your trip. "Get on the path and go anywhere you want."

Julia gave a big smile.

"You know if you don't like seeing me," Jean said as he gazed deeply into Julia's eyes.

Julia kissed her on the lips. Angrily. None was more important to her. It was an experience along with Jean. It sounded fantastic. The two embraced deeply for a full minute before eventually breaking up.

"You should remember, though," Jean pointed out.

"Are you sure?" Julia spoke quietly.

"I understand your whole thing about labels and possessiveness and all, and I realize we just met, but I feel like I should be truthful with you and tell you that I am into labels." I dislike having to share. If we're going to be together, you know, it's going to be defined."

Julia gave a smile. She didn't mind the vibration because she was in Jean's embrace. She just didn't want to be with someone else. She couldn't conceive about that. If Jean just wanted to bend a bit further on that. Julia should put up with it.

"So, then," Jean explained, "you don't have to be my girlfriend because that is a loaded term, but I'll need to know that you'll at least be my person."

Julia laid her palms on Jean's sides, feeling them grip her closely. She couldn't deny the tinge of excitement she had at the prospect of being Jeans. To her belonging. In terms of Jean being hers. Jean's hands squeezed her butt through her cut-offs, and she screamed a bit. Julia acknowledged that it was a possessive shift, but she enjoyed it.
"Of course, I'm your girl." Julia said, trying to appear chic, "At least for the time being."

Conclusion

Julia couldn't believe her eyes. She'd never seen that much wealth before.

And if she had worried about it, she probably hadn't. It was nothing more than a bank account. But that was her checking statement, and although she'd had a bank account before, she'd never had one that said she had over $70,000 in it. They'd earned more money for the pills than they'd expected, even though Jean persuaded Julia to keep half a brick of marijuana.

"How are you, babe?" Jean inquired, holding a big brown box in her arms.

"I've never been this wealthy." "It's strange," Julia said.

"Are you sure?" Jean said as she put the package in a stack in what was once her garage.

"Well, when my scholarship came in every semester, I'd have four thousand dollars in it in about a second, but this..."

"Wow," Jean said, nodding, "I know, that's nearly twenty times that, right?"

Julia paused for a moment.

"Sixteen eight seven five times that, yes," she said.

Jean kept his gaze oddly still on her. Julia raised her head from her bank statement.

"Or seventeen if you like," Julia said, forgetting that not everyone valued numbers in the same way she did.

"I'm not sure why I should find that irritating, but I find it incredibly sexy," Jean said as he walked back into the building. Julia sat back in her seatbelt. A stunning new Cadillac convertible. It had cost her over 5,000 dollars. No, it wasn't a new car, and there were obvious indications of wear and tear, but it was hers. She'd purchased it and let Dougie repair it for her. Jean had wanted to propose something different, but Julia had refused. She'd also given it the name Delroy.

She received the same vibe from it. Not at all like Fritz. Delroy used to be able to sprint for a long time. It seems to be dependable. No, it wasn't easy, but it was functional, had a radio and a large enough back seat for her and Jean to pull over at times, and...

"Hey," Jean said as he exited the house with another package, "that's it. The last package. It's time to start packing."

"Isn't Doug supposed to be here to say goodbye?" Julia inquired, wanting to bid farewell to the big guy she'd grown to adore during the last few weeks.

"Nah," Jean replied, "I said my goodbyes at the store." It wasn't very comfortable. He sobbed like a little girl."

Julia sighed and rolled her eyes. She understood Jean well enough at this stage to realize that she, too, had cried, even though she'd never say it.

Julia, on the other hand, was also hesitant to enter the building. The truth was that she would have a difficult time saying goodbye to the home. True, she'd just been there a few weeks, but what a few weeks it had been—dedicated to the early days of her and Jean's friendship. It was full of talks and getting to know each other and movies, as well as one mild clash that resulted in incredible make-up sex and, well, a lot of other sex.

"Hey," Julia said, "I was wondering, what if we didn't pack anything?"

"Wait, what?" Jean said as she wiped her brow. Another hot day had arrived. Julia was sorry to leave the building, but she couldn't wait to go back to a beach or anywhere that wasn't too darn hot every day.

"We're all about the shirts on our backs. If we need new clothing, we buy them, and if we need food, we go out and buy it, you know? We're the only ones." Julia went on. She'd considered it before she'd set off with Fin and fallen in love with the romanticism of it, but it was unrealistic with just $500 and no address. They should do that now, with stuff like her locket in one of the boxes Doug had promised to let them store in his workshop and nearly a hundred and seventy-five thousand dollars between them.

"It's an idea," Jean said as she took Julia in her arms, "but that would imply you don't want me to carry the strap-on." Or maybe the handcuffs. And that would mean you couldn't wear those high heels and that little red teddy you got, which makes me want to fuck you every time I see you in it next week."

Julia remembered something similar happening a couple of nights before. She bit her lip to attempt to suppress an unwanted sigh as Jean, who seemed to be remembering the day as well, took a tight grip of her buttocks and kissed her cheek.

"Well, then one bag each is always pretty daring," Julia said.

"Yeah, one pack," Jean said, running her hands up to Julia's waist, causing her girlfriend to recoil in agony.

"Ow," Julia sighed.

"I'm sorry, babe, I assumed you were fine by now."

Julia nodded and shifted her weight to raise her shirt. A small Blue Jay, its wings extended in flight, flew just over her hip. It was her first piercing, and it had just been a few days. It always hurt, but positively, she reasoned. It was now a nice little permanent reminder of both her grandfather and Jean. She'd had the tattoo done right when Jean had first touched her in the vehicle.

"God, it's hot on you," Jean said as he kissed Julia once more, "let's fuck before we go."

Julia shook her head, despite the fact that the idea made her squirm.

"No, we have plenty of time for that," Julia replied. The sun was about to sink, and she decided to get at least a couple of hours of driving done.

Julia dashed into the house and rapidly gathered her belongings, recalling the red lingerie and shoes that Jean had requested. Julia had never been the girly kind, but there was a part of her that enjoyed being particularly girly around Jean. Not sorority girl girly, but just girly, Julia reasoned. Before leaving the now-empty house where her life had changed so much, she put everything into a tiny suitcase. She said a final sad farewell and closed the door behind her, only to be relieved when she saw her girlfriend, relaxed toward Delroy. She was just as calm and beautiful as she had been the first time she saw her in the noonday light.

"I'll take the wheel first," Jean said. Julia gave a smile. She desired some time in the passenger seat to relax. Keep an eye out for the yellow lines to vanish.

Julia climbed into the sedan, tossing her purse into the back seat. Delroy had comfortable leather seats that Jean had professionally detailed, and she sunk happily into them. Julia had the same rush of giddy expectation when Jean entered from the other hand, knowing she'd soon be going on her adventure. Here's another. A new one. For the correct partner.

"You know, there was a Blue Jay in those tales my Grandfather told me," Jean said.

"What do you mean?" "How was Blue Jay?" Julia inquired.

"He was helpful, friendly, a little of a goofball, and said a lot of nonsense." "Anyway, Blue Jay, where are you going?" Jean asked.

Julia considered it. They'd thought about where they'd go a lot. Julia was also determined to visit New Orleans. Jean had said that she would go somewhere. They discussed driving to the East Coast first, visiting anywhere they pleased, before returning west. Jean had said that when they returned west, they would take a cruise. Cross the Pacific, and you'll be able to see Tokyo, Australia, or India. Julia realized they'd have to rest somewhere; she knew the money wouldn't last forever, but she hoped they'd have plenty of time to find a spot they wanted.

"I'm not sure, Crow," Julia admitted as Delroy roared to life. "Let's see where the path leads us."

Lightning Source UK Ltd.
Milton Keynes UK
UKHW030631210521
384122UK00008B/497

9 781802 866261